HUNTED

THE BELLE MORTE SERIES

BELLE MORTE

REVELATIONS

HUNTED

CHANGES
coming soon

HUNTED

BELLE MORTE BOOK THREE

BELLA HIGGIN

wattpad books **w**

wattpad books **W**

An imprint of Wattpad WEBTOON Book Group

Content Warning: mentions of blood, mentions of violence, language

Published in Canada by Wattpad WEBTOON Book Group, a division of Wattpad WEBTOON Studios, Inc.

36 Wellington Street E., Suite 200, Toronto, ON M5E 1C7 Canada

www.wattpad.com

First Wattpad Books edition: April 2024

ISBN 978-1-99885-495-0 (Trade Paper original)
ISBN 978-1-99025-952-4 (eBook edition)

Names, characters, places, and incidents featured in this publication are either the product of the author's imagination or are used fictitiously. Any resemblance to actual persons (living or dead), events, institutions, or locales, without satiric intent, is coincidental.

Library and Archives Canada Cataloguing in Publication information is available upon request.

Printed and bound in Canada

1 3 5 7 9 10 8 6 4 2

Cover design by Ysabel Enverga
Interior illustration by Hannah Drennan
Typesetting by Delaney Anderson

For my cat, Sootica.
The last book I wrote with you by my side.
The first book published without you.
I miss you.

CHAPTER ONE

Roux

Standing in the doorway of the dining hall, Roux Hayes couldn't get over how quiet Belle Morte was now. Just a few days ago this room had been where the mansion's thirty blood donors had eaten meals and filled the huge space with the sound of talking and laughing. It felt like forever ago.

"Do you think it will ever get back to normal?" Renie asked from behind her, and Roux jumped.

Renie hadn't yet mastered the liquid, catlike grace of the older vampires, but she could move around a lot more quietly than when she'd been human. Roux was still getting used to it.

"Sorry," Renie said.

Roux took Renie's hand and gave it a little squeeze.

Barely a week had passed since Belle Morte had been reclaimed from Etienne and Jemima, the two vampires whose attempted power coup had nearly destroyed the system that allowed humans and vampires to peacefully coexist. But humans—security, staff, and donors—had died in the cross fire, and now none of the vampire survivors knew what future they had with the human world.

"Whatever happens, we'll get through it," Roux said.

Renie smiled wanly. "You don't have to be here."

Belle Morte's remaining donors had been sent home to their families, and though no donors in the Houses of Midnight, Lamia, Nox, or Fiaigh had been harmed, they'd been sent home too. No staff were left, and only a skeleton security detail still patrolled the mansion's hallways and grounds.

The vampires were surviving on bags of donated blood.

Roux affectionately rolled her eyes. "Like I'd abandon you."

Technically, Roux and Jason should have left with the other donors, but neither of them considered themselves donors anymore. They were a part of Belle Morte, and neither of them had any intention of leaving.

Edmond Dantès glided up to them, his dark hair spilling around his shoulders, his shirt open at the neck. Something soft and warm bloomed in Renie's eyes as she looked at the vampire she'd fallen in love with.

"Is no one else here yet?" he asked.

Renie shook her head. "Not even Ysanne."

"We're still a few minutes early," Roux said, checking her watch.

She strode into the dining hall and took a seat halfway down the trestle table. The silence and emptiness felt even more pronounced. Belle Morte was a ghost of its former self, and it made Roux's heart ache.

She wanted to believe that the mansion would recover, but there was a real chance that the donor system and vampires' place in the world had been damaged beyond repair. Roux didn't want to think about what that might mean for them all.

Renie and Edmond sat beside her, their hands clasped together.

Seconds later Jason entered the dining hall and threw himself into the chair on Roux's other side. His blond hair was mussed in a style that *looked* casual but that he'd have worked hard to create.

"Fashionably early, are we?" he said, then winced as his voice echoed around the huge room.

"Didn't have much else to do," Roux said.

More vampires trickled in, but no one spoke, and the silence grew heavier. Jason sat up a little straighter when Gideon Hartwright came in, but the blond vampire had his eyes fixed on the floor. Roux was sure she'd glimpsed some sparks between Jason and Gideon when they'd helped reclaim Belle Morte, but the vampire had retreated into himself since then.

The vampires took their seats; mingled with them were the remaining members of Belle Morte security. Seamus Kennedy, head of security at Fiaigh, sat near the top of the table. Ludovic de Vauban sat next to Edmond, and though his face was expressionless in the way that older vampires managed to pull off so well, Roux was surprised to glimpse a flicker of real nervousness in his eyes. She didn't know Ludovic well, but she'd seen him fight, and he was a force of nature when he wanted to be. Now he looked more vulnerable than she was used to.

Edmond leaned over and murmured something to his friend; Ludovic nodded, but his expression didn't change.

Ysanne Moreau swept into the room, her high heels clicking crisply across the floor. Her hair was a pale sheet down her back, not a strand out of place, and her sheath dress clung to her lean body. She looked beautiful and regal, a queen once again. But Roux had glimpsed the real person behind the icy mask, and she found it hard to be intimidated by Ysanne now.

A man Roux had never seen before followed Ysanne. Tall and square, his suit too tight across his shoulders, he surveyed the room with a scowl.

"Thank you all for coming," Ysanne said, and Roux blinked in surprise. Usually Ysanne issued orders and expected them to be obeyed. She didn't think to *thank* anyone.

"These have been difficult times for us all, and I'm afraid the storm is not over," Ysanne said.

She started to continue, then stopped, her eyes fixed on something at the end of the room. Roux looked over her shoulder.

Isabeau Aguillon stood in the entryway. Her gaze darted around the room, lingering on every face, before moving back to Ysanne. Roux saw the tiniest crack in Ysanne's marble facade, then it was gone.

"We're glad you could join us," Ysanne said.

Isabeau silently slipped into a chair at the end of the table.

"This is where things currently stand," Ysanne said. "Our prisoners are being held in the cells. I know many of you are unhappy about sharing a roof with traitors, but for now it's better to have them where we can keep an eye on them. The remaining traitors in the other Houses have been weeded out and imprisoned, and several European Houses are arranging to send support while we continue to pick up the pieces."

Ysanne waited a beat. "As you all know, two days ago Prime Minister McGellan issued a press release informing the public of exactly what happened here, except for one detail. During the final battle for Belle Morte, five of Etienne's newly turned vampires escaped the mansion, and are still at large in Winchester. The prime minister has decided the best course of action is to keep quiet about this."

"Why?" Renie asked.

"Damage control. The general public is reeling from what's happened, and the last thing we want is to cause further panic by telling them that potentially dangerous rogue vampires are roaming the city," Ysanne said.

Her voice was stiff, as if the words didn't feel right in her mouth, and Roux guessed McGellan had told her to say all this. Jenny McGellan, currently serving her second term as PM, had a reputation for getting exactly what she wanted, and taking orders from a higher authority must have grated on Ysanne.

Her word was still law inside Belle Morte, but maybe she no longer had similar clout in the outside world.

"Do you really think that's a good idea?" Renie asked.

"Truthfully, I'm not sure. Before I met with McGellan you told me we should be fully honest with the humans, and I agreed with you," Ysanne said. "But we must remember that the fallout of this catastrophe may affect Houses worldwide. People have glimpsed our dark side, and they won't quickly forget it. We don't want them to lose what shred of faith they might have left by admitting we don't have full control of the situation."

Ysanne paused again, looking around the room. "I shall be honest with you all. Our future is very uncertain. I don't yet know where we stand with the human world, or if there's even a place for us here anymore."

The wide-shouldered man standing a little behind Ysanne shifted his weight and made a noise low in his throat, as if he wanted to say something. But he didn't speak.

"McGellan won't entertain further discussion about our future until those five escaped vampires are caught," Ysanne said.

She beckoned to the man, and he shot her a dark look that she didn't see before he moved closer to her.

"This is Detective Chief Inspector Ray Walsh. Thanks to special permission granted by the chief constable of Hampshire Police, Walsh and his team are working with me to track down and capture our fugitives," Ysanne said.

Walsh's face darkened even more, but he still didn't say anything.

"Working with you how?" Roux asked. Something about the man made her uneasy.

At almost exactly the same time, Ludovic said, "*He* won't be capturing anyone."

"Oh really? Why's that?" Walsh said. His voice was raspy; maybe he was a smoker.

"Because you're human. This is a vampire mess and it'll take a vampire to sort it out," Ludovic replied.

Walsh smiled unpleasantly. "I wasn't planning on handcuffing them. If I had my way, I'd send an armed response unit after them."

"That wouldn't make a difference," said Ludovic quietly. "Any human who pursues these vampires will be at risk, guns or no guns. Vampires can heal from bullet wounds, and an injured vampire is a dangerous one. We're already dealing with angry, grieving humans wanting justice for their murdered friends and family—if we put any more lives at risk it will make us seem even more like monsters."

There was something desolate in the way Ludovic said the last word, and it tugged at Roux's heart. Was Ludovic afraid that the world now saw them as monsters? Or was he afraid they really *were* monsters?

"Ludovic is correct," Ysanne said. "Even uninjured these vampires will be scared and hungry, and that makes them a threat. The best person to deal with them is a much older, more seasoned vampire." Her frost-colored gaze flicked briefly to Isabeau. "That's why I'll be pursuing them myself."

A murmur ran through the room. Ysanne was more than capable of getting her hands dirty, but wading directly into the fray wasn't usually her style.

"You can't do that," Renie said.

Ysanne's eyes narrowed, but it was speculative rather than combative. "Why not?"

"You've worked so hard to maintain positive vampire/human relations, and now that Jemima and Etienne have royally fucked that up for everyone, your House needs you here. There are plenty of people at this table who can go after those rogue vampires, but only you can lead Belle Morte."

Ysanne's mouth tightened. Roux knew as well as anyone that the Lady of Belle Morte liked to be in control, so it couldn't be easy for her to take a step back, but Renie had a point.

Silence filled the room.

"I'll do it," Ludovic said.

Ysanne scrutinized him, her lips pursed. Walsh said nothing, but continued to scowl. Didn't the man have any other expressions?

"Are you sure that's wise?" Edmond asked, and Ludovic gave him a look that Roux couldn't interpret. He slowly nodded, but Edmond didn't relax.

"You realize these vampires are out in the human world, far beyond the reach of this house," Ysanne said.

"I do," Ludovic said.

"And you still think you're the best man for the job?"

Ludovic sat up a little straighter, lifting his chin. Light from the chandelier played over his blond ponytail. "I wouldn't have offered if I didn't think I could do it."

Maybe so, but Roux hadn't imagined the worry in Edmond's eyes. She didn't know much about Ludovic, but his strength and speed suggested he wasn't a young vampire, and Roux had always assumed he was about Edmond's age—somewhere around three or four hundred years old—which should have been plenty old enough to take care of himself. So why did Edmond look so worried?

It suddenly struck Roux that Ludovic, like most vampires, had spent the last ten years sealed in this mansion. Renie had mentioned to her that Ludovic avoided technology even more than most vampires, and despite how strong and fast and brave he was, he had little to no experience of the modern human world.

Despite being stronger than any of the escaped vampires, he'd be out of his element in a way that they wouldn't, and that could put him at risk.

"You need someone to go with you," Roux blurted.

Ysanne cocked an eyebrow. Ludovic's face was a blank mask.

"What are you talking about?" Jason said.

"Ludovic can't do this on his own," Roux said.

"He's a big boy, I'm sure he can handle it."

"I can," Ludovic confirmed.

Roux swiveled to face him. "How well do you know Winchester? What do you understand of the modern world and how it's changed since Belle Morte was built? Do you have any idea how to interact with people without them knowing you're a vampire?"

Ludovic said nothing.

"Do you even know how to use a cell phone?" Roux continued.

A couple of other vampires exchanged uneasy glances.

"See, this is the problem with you all locking yourselves away in these houses: everything changes around you but you stay exactly the same." Roux stared at Ludovic, though he seemed reluctant to meet her eyes. "If you jump straight into the deep end, you'll drown. Unless you have a lifeline."

"A lifeline," Ysanne repeated, testing the word.

"Yes. Someone who knows the world outside, who can make sure Ludovic doesn't run into trouble."

"You mean a human," said Ludovic flatly.

Roux nodded.

"And who do you suggest?" Ysanne asked, but the wry note in her voice suggested she already knew.

Roux licked her lips, bolstering her courage. "Me."

CHAPTER TWO

Roux

Renie and Jason spoke at the same time.

"Oh, hell no."

"No way."

"I'll go," Edmond cut in.

"Not without me, you won't," Renie said.

Roux held up both hands.

"Neither of you are going. Renie, some of this might have to be done by day so that rules you out. And you"—she pointed at Edmond—"are not charging off on some mission and leaving Renie. You've more than done your bit; you can take a step back now."

"Isn't that for us to decide?" said Edmond.

"You don't always have to be the hero. It's okay to let someone else handle this one," Roux said.

"Ludovic already has a human to help him," Jason said. He gestured to Walsh. "This guy."

"I'm not a fucking babysitter," Walsh growled. "I'm here to track down the vampires that you all let loose into the city, and the only reason I'm working with any of you is because I'm not stupid enough to try to bring down a vampire by myself."

"You can't even help Ludovic when he needs to be outside the mansion?" Jason said.

"Not when he'll need to be outside for as long as it takes to catch these bastards."

Jason frowned. "Why would he need to do that?"

"Perhaps I didn't make this clear earlier, but whoever goes after our fugitives will have to leave Belle Morte for the foreseeable future," Ysanne said. "In order to keep all this under wraps, we need to draw as little attention to ourselves as possible. Between the protestors at the gates and the intense media scrutiny that we're under, we can't afford the questions that will arise if Ludovic, or anyone else, is seen frequently coming and going from Belle Morte."

"So what was your plan?" Roux asked.

"I intended to stay at a hotel."

"Then Ludovic and I can still do that."

"Or I can do that by myself," Ludovic said.

Roux gave him an exasperated look but he still wouldn't meet her eyes.

"What will you do when you get hungry? You can't go chomping on strangers' necks," she said.

"I'm perfectly capable of hunting animals," Ludovic said, and a shadow that Roux couldn't interpret flashed across his face.

"Sure, because *that* wouldn't draw attention to you," she muttered.

Ludovic shot her a cool look. "I have hundreds of years' experience with hunting in the shadows."

"But cell phones didn't exist then. All it would take now is one shrieking fangirl with a camera, and you're screwed."

"She has a point," said Renie.

"You can't be Ludovic's only donor, especially when you have no idea how long you'll be away," Jason objected.

"I don't have to feed him every day. We can take bagged blood with us, but that's not the point. I'm not just going as a donor." Roux looked around the table. "This is a situation unlike anything we've faced before, both vampires and police, and I'm guessing that the normal rules won't always apply?" Her eyes landed on Walsh. He tipped his head slightly, which Roux took as confirmation. "Ludovic and I aren't just going to sit around in a hotel room and wait to be called for help, are we? You're going to need us to be more involved, right?"

Walsh nodded, a short, sharp movement.

"If we want to stay under the radar, then we need to be able to blend in, and trust me, I'm very good at that."

"But this is dangerous," Jason said, frustration coloring his voice.

"I'll stay away from any of the violent bits. I'll be there to feed Ludovic when he needs it, help steer him through the modern world, cooperate with DCI Walsh's team whenever they need it, and stay in touch with the mansion so you always know what's going on. I'm guessing we can't rely on Walsh for that," Roux said.

"You guessed right," Walsh snapped.

Roux's gaze moved to Ysanne, whose porcelain face was as unreadable as ever. "I can do this," she said.

For a heartbeat or two no one said a thing. Ysanne stared at Roux, her eyes like drills, and Roux stared unflinchingly back. She needed to do this. She and Jason had both joined the fight for Belle Morte a few days ago, but their contributions had made little difference against angry vampires. This time Roux felt she could be a key player.

"Roux, Ludovic, would you come to my office?" Ysanne said at last. "I'd like to speak with you privately."

Roux sat in Ysanne's office, looking around at the surprisingly modern decor: the leather and chrome furniture, and the white carpet that looked even brighter beneath the black desk. The room didn't fit the rest of the mansion.

Ludovic occupied the chair next to her, straight-backed and stiff, refusing to look at her. His hands were tightly folded in his lap. Ysanne sat behind her desk, one hand resting on a slim folder, while Walsh, who'd refused to be left out, hovered nearby, arms folded, eyebrows still twisted in a scowl.

The small room felt thick with tension.

Ysanne took several glossy photos from the folder and slid them across her desktop.

Roux and Ludovic leaned forward.

"These are the five vampires who escaped Belle Morte after that final fight," Ysanne said. "Stephen Johnson, Delia Sanders, Neal Morris, Jeffrey Smith, and Kashvi Patel." With each name, she tapped one of the photos. "It appears that Stephen and Delia were in a relationship before they were turned."

Roux couldn't help noticing that Ysanne's nails were unpolished and slightly ragged around the edges. It was a silly little thing, but Ysanne was the epitome of elegance, never appearing in public without being primped to within an inch of her undead life. Something like this spoke volumes about the pressure she was under.

"Walsh's team has been working on this almost since that night, and he's confident that none of our fugitives have left Winchester," Ysanne said.

She pulled four more photos from her folder and spread them out. "These are the four vampires who never even made it *to* that final fight."

Roux frowned. "I don't understand."

A quick glance at Ludovic's expression told her he didn't either.

"Neither do I," Ysanne admitted. "Susan Harcourt was responsible for helping Etienne gain access to people who'd do anything if he turned them, and she's since provided us with the names of every vampire that Etienne turned. These four were among them. But over this last week, Caoimhe and I have been working out which vampires were killed in the attack, which ones are currently held in the cells, and which ones escaped." Ysanne tapped the photos again. "These four aren't among any of them."

"Wait, so Etienne turned them and then they just disappeared?" Roux said.

Ysanne didn't answer.

"Could they have escaped him after he turned them?" Walsh asked. For once, he didn't sound confrontational.

Ysanne turned in her seat to face him. "All these people agreed to do Etienne's dirty work on the proviso that he would grant their greatest wish—to become vampires. I find it hard to believe that they'd have fled as soon as he'd given them that."

"Even if they wanted to, it wouldn't have been hard for Etienne to catch them. Newly turned vampires aren't as strong or as fast as older vampires," Ludovic added.

Walsh's face darkened again. "Then what the hell did that bastard do with them?"

"That's the question," Ysanne said.

Roux didn't like where this was going. Etienne and Jemima were dead and couldn't hurt anyone else, but that didn't undo the damage they'd caused—the damage that Roux was starting to suspect ran deeper than anyone had initially understood.

"There's more to Etienne's plan than we realized, isn't there?" she said.

"It's possible," Ysanne said.

"So even if we catch the Five, this isn't over."

"The Five?" Ysanne said.

"It's easier to give them a collective name."

"Finding these five fugitives is our top priority. The fact that they were willing to attack Belle Morte means that we must consider them to be the biggest threat."

Walsh looked like he really wanted to say something to that, but he kept his mouth firmly closed.

"Once we have the Five safely in custody, we can turn our attention to these other missing vampires," Ysanne said.

"Why am I only just hearing about them?" Walsh demanded.

This time Ysanne didn't look at him. "Because I've only just learned about them myself. Etienne turned several dozen vampires, and it wasn't until we'd traced each name to a death, a prisoner, or an escapee that we realized anyone else was missing."

"Does the prime minister know?"

"I shall inform her this afternoon," said Ysanne stiffly.

"Just so I understand this, Walsh's job is to track down the Five, and Ludovic's job is to capture them, but once that's over they have to start again with these four?" Roux said.

Ysanne nodded.

"No pressure, then."

Ludovic glanced at her, surprise in his eyes. Maybe she was being too flippant with the Lady of the House, but Roux Hayes wasn't about to change who she was.

Not again.

"Do we have any leads?" Roux asked.

"Yeah," Walsh said before Ysanne could answer. "That's why I'm here. This morning I got a call from Stephen Johnson's mum. Apparently, she has some info that could help us, but she's not prepared to discuss it over the phone."

"Why not?"

"The fuck should I know?"

Roux rolled her eyes.

"Walsh is going to visit the family at their home later today, and I intended to go with him. Ludovic, if you're serious about taking this on, then you will go in my stead," Ysanne said.

"I really don't need backup for an interview," Walsh said.

"What if Stephen's at his home and he wants to turn himself in?" Roux said.

"Then he won't be a threat to me, will he?"

"Unless he changes his mind and makes a run for it."

Walsh's expression cleared. "Right, because vampires are untrustworthy."

"That's not what I meant," Roux said, shooting him a hard look that he ignored.

"Vampires are better at discerning lies than humans are. If the Johnsons aren't being truthful, I'll be able to hear it." Ludovic spoke up.

"Hear it?" Walsh repeated.

"In their heartbeats."

Walsh's lip curled.

"There's another aspect of this we haven't discussed," Roux said. "Ludovic's a famous vampire, and even I'm pretty recognizable these days, thanks to everything that's happened. I get that we're going to a hotel to draw attention away from Belle Morte and vampires in general, but it won't take long for some squealing Vladdict to spot Ludovic. What happens then?"

"We'll have to be careful," Ysanne replied.

Roux shook her head. "I'm sorry, but that's not good enough."

Ysanne's eyes narrowed.

"Look, I don't know how many more times I can tell you this, but you guys are not prepared for the modern world and how intrusive it can be. Way too many people are obsessed with celebrities, especially the undead variety, and one sniff of a famous vampire wandering the streets, and every cell phone in England will be trying to capture photos and videos."

"Then what do you propose?" Ysanne said.

Roux studied Ludovic's face, appraising how a little shading and contouring could alter the shape of his eyes, his nose. "We need disguises," she said.

Walsh made an irritated noise. "We don't have time for this."

"Make time," Roux said. "This isn't just about keeping things under wraps. A lot of people are pretty pissed at vampires right now. Did you ever consider that it might not be safe for Ludovic if he's recognized?"

The look that Walsh gave her suggested he couldn't care less. Roux was really starting to dislike the man.

"Roux is correct," Ysanne said. "Compile a list of everything you need and I'll make sure you get it today."

Walsh started to bluster, and Ysanne's expression turned to ice. "Do not ask me to put one of my people in danger, Chief Inspector."

"No one would be in danger if you fanged freaks hadn't let this happen in the first place," Walsh snarled.

Ysanne's hands tightened on her desktop, and Roux held her breath. An agonizingly long pause ticked by.

"Roux, how quickly can you prepare a list?" Ysanne asked.

"Ten minutes?" Roux said.

Ludovic looked distinctly uneasy. "What sort of disguise do you have in mind?"

Roux grinned.

"Are you sure you know what you're doing?" Ludovic said, warily eyeing the makeup laid out on Roux's dressing table.

"Do you doubt me?"

He didn't answer—a wise move.

"I promise I won't mess up your pretty face. I'll just make you less recognizable," Roux said.

She guided him into a chair then placed a finger under his chin, turning his head this way and that. The tiniest flicker of heat stirred in her stomach.

She'd been attracted to him as soon as she arrived at Belle Morte—and who could blame her? Ludovic was six feet of hard muscle, blond hair, and chiseled jaw. His eyes were as deep and as blue as the ocean, and more than once he'd come to her rescue during

Etienne and Jemima's coup. A bit of old-fashioned gallantry was enough to turn any girl's head.

But this was no time for a crush.

"Can vampires grow beards?" Roux asked, studying the edge of Ludovic's jaw.

"We can, but it takes a very long time."

"I never imagined vampires shaving."

"We only have to very rarely. Why do you ask?"

"Just curious. Facial hair would change the shape of your face, but we wouldn't have the time even if you were human." She tapped her chin, thinking. "I can't give you a beard, but I can pencil on some convincing stubble. Is that okay?"

Ludovic nodded.

"Great," Roux said.

Ludovic's ivory-pale skin was the first thing to change. If they'd had more time she'd push him into a tanning booth but, like the beard, it wasn't an option, so makeup was the answer. Did tanning booths even work on vampires?

Roux applied foundation to Ludovic's face and neck, blunting the lines of his cheekbones and jaw, used subtle eye shadow to alter the shape of his eyes, then carefully penciled on some stubble. It wasn't perfect, but it would fool anyone who didn't look too closely.

Seamus had procured everything on Roux's list with impressive speed, including a pair of Clark Kent–style glasses, which Roux slid onto Ludovic's face.

"Almost there," she said.

Reaching one hand around his neck, she released Ludovic's hair from its usual low ponytail. He stiffened.

"I won't cut it, if that's what you're worried about," Roux said.

Ludovic said nothing as Roux set to work with wax and hairspray, coaxing his normally straight hair into loose waves, giving him a geeky surfer look. Then she took the beanie that Seamus had picked up with Ludovic's clothes and put it on the vampire's head. He still sort of looked like himself, but more like a human who vaguely resembled a famous vampire.

"You look adorable," she said, and Ludovic scowled.

He turned in his chair, seeing his reflection for the first time since Roux had started working on him, and gripped the edge of the dressing table.

Roux's voice softened. "I know it's weird, but it's only temporary."

"I look human," Ludovic said, and there was a wealth of emotion in those three words—surprise, disbelief, even regret.

"Are you okay?" Roux said, and he nodded.

Tearing his eyes from the mirror, he turned to her. "Why are you helping me? This isn't your fight."

Roux leaned a hip against the table. "I'm part of this, too, you know."

Even through the thick-framed glasses, Ludovic's gaze was intense. "But why do you care?"

"Because no one in Belle Morte deserves whatever shit might be coming thanks to Jemima and Etienne. Besides, you've saved my life before. Let me return the favor."

"Thank you for caring," Ludovic said quietly, looking away.

"You sound surprised that I do."

"Vampires are facing the possibility that our time in the spotlight is over. Not everyone would care how we feel about that."

"Don't jump to the worst conclusion yet. We don't know what'll happen."

Despite her words, Roux couldn't ignore the tight knot of anxiety in her stomach. There was a chance that Etienne and Jemima had damaged vampires' reputation beyond repair, and Roux had no idea how the vampire world could survive that.

CHAPTER THREE

Roux

Roux had told Seamus to get them clothes in dark, solid colors; nothing with noticeable patterns, mostly cheap jeans and long-sleeved shirts—very different from the tailored cuts and luxury fabrics that occupied the wardrobes of Belle Morte. They needed to blend in, not stand out.

But as she picked up the long brown wig on top of the pile, she felt a sharp surge of self-doubt. Her reflection stared back at her from the mirror on the wall, and the memory of mocking laughter flitted through her head. Even now, it made her flinch.

Roux knew she was beautiful.

She also knew she hadn't always been.

The kids at school had known it, too, and they'd never let her forget.

It hadn't been that long since she'd shed her ugly duckling skin and emerged as a graceful, gorgeous swan, and suddenly Roux felt like she was covering up the person she'd become.

She didn't want to go back to who she'd been.

Swallowing hard, Roux pulled on the wig and arranged the thick fringe across her forehead.

"Hmm," she murmured, examining her reflection. It was a very different style from her pixie cut, but she looked damn good with long hair too. She decided to ditch her makeup altogether rather than focusing on a new look—as soon as Ludovic was out of the bathroom, she'd clean her face. She and Renie knew each other well enough to waltz into the bathroom when one of them was buck naked, but Ludovic probably wouldn't take it so well.

It was a shame really, because Roux wouldn't mind seeing him without his clothes.

Jason poked his head around the door, and his eyes widened. "Oh wow."

"Good wow or bad wow?" Roux touched her wig. She'd thought it looked okay, but she *was* biased.

"Roux, my darling, you could shave your head and men would still fall at your feet."

Roux couldn't stop a smile.

"Where's Ludovic?" Jason asked.

"Getting changed in the bathroom."

"Can we talk to you for a moment?"

"We?"

Renie's head popped around the door, just below Jason's.

"Let's take this into the hall," Roux said. She ushered her friends back, then stepped out of the room and closed the door. "Everything okay?"

Jason smiled, but it was tight around the edges. "We're worried about you."

"Have you thought this through?" Renie said.

Roux suspected they'd rehearsed this. "Guys, I know what I'm doing," she said.

"Do you, though?" Jason pressed her.

"Yes. I'm not stupid."

"But this is dangerous. Those vampires won't go down without a fight," Renie said.

"That's for Ludovic to handle. I'll be okay, I promise."

"You can't promise that when you have no idea what's going to happen," Renie said.

"Then I promise to be exceptionally, extraordinarily careful with everything I do from the second I leave the mansion."

Renie's mouth pulled down in an unhappy shape. "This isn't a joke."

"I'm serious." Roux hugged her. "Everything will be fine," she whispered into Renie's hair. "It'll be over before you know it."

She let Renie go, and then found herself in Jason's arms, mashed tightly against his chest. "Make sure Ludovic takes care of you," he said.

Roux laughed. "Outside the mansion is *my* world, not his. If anything, I'll be taking care of him."

"Taking care of a hot vampire." Jason's voice turned wistful. "Sounds like my ideal job."

Roux swatted his chest.

Less than a month ago she hadn't even known Renie and Jason, but they'd got under her skin and into her heart, and now she couldn't imagine life without them.

"No matter what happens, I'll come back to you both," she said.

Ludovic

Roux was gone when Ludovic came out of the bathroom, but he could hear her voice on the other side of the door, talking to Renie and Jason, and when Ludovic heard his name, he paused, listening.

Bringing down the Five could—and probably would—get bloody,

and Ludovic could handle that, but he didn't blame Roux's friends for being worried.

He opened the door. Roux and her friends stared back at him, blatant surprise registering on Renie's and Jason's faces. Self-consciously, Ludovic touched his knitted hat and tousled hair. Even when he was human he hadn't looked like this; he felt like a stranger in his own skin.

"Is Edmond in your room?" he asked Renie.

She nodded.

Ludovic felt their gazes on him as he walked down the hallway, but he didn't look back.

Edmond's door was open when Ludovic reached the north wing, but he hesitated at the threshold, suddenly unsure. At any other time in the ten years he and Edmond had lived here he'd have walked in without a second thought. But now this room was Renie's too.

Ludovic knocked on the doorframe.

Edmond, straightening out the bedcovers, looked up, and a flicker of confusion passed across his face. "Are you all right?" he asked, looking Ludovic up and down.

He'd only known Ludovic as a vampire—this human facade was as new to Edmond as it was to Ludovic himself.

Ludovic wasn't sure how to answer. Soon he'd leave the place that had been his home and haven and go back out into the world. Traveling to Ireland a few days ago hadn't counted; then, he and the others had been running for their lives. These next few days—or maybe weeks—would be very different.

"Ludovic?"

"Am I doing the right thing, letting Roux come with me?"

"You say it like you have a choice," said Edmond wryly.

Ludovic walked into the room as Edmond sat on the bed, watching his friend. Ludovic couldn't sit down. He felt agitated, full of nervous energy.

"I could refuse," he said.

"You could, but you can't force her to stay. Besides, she raised some valid points."

"You think I need her."

"I think any of us would."

"But I'll be responsible for her."

"Roux isn't made of china. She won't break."

"I'm not used to being responsible for anyone," Ludovic muttered.

Edmond was his dearest friend in the whole world, his brother in every way but blood, but if one of them was responsible for the other, it was Edmond who was responsible for Ludovic.

"Are you worried about Roux depending on you, or are you worried about depending on her?" Edmond asked.

That made Ludovic pause. "What do you mean?"

"You don't like depending on people, especially not a human you barely know."

Ludovic sat on the edge of the bed.

"I can still go with you, if you want," Edmond said.

"Renie needs you here."

"Maybe this'll be good for you," Edmond said.

"Maybe."

And maybe that was exactly why he'd volunteered in the first place.

Edmond's lips twitched. "Even if Roux has made you look so . . . different."

Ludovic looked at his hands. "She's made me look human."

"It is impressive."

What Ludovic didn't say—but that Edmond had probably guessed—was that he was afraid that looking human would remind him how it felt to *be* human. He didn't want that. In the safe cocoon of Belle Morte he didn't have to think about everything he'd seen and done, all the things that haunted him.

"No matter what happens, I'll be here when you get back," Edmond said.

Ludovic pulled off his prop glasses. For most of his life as a vampire he'd been alone, but when he'd met Edmond, in the blasted trenches of the First World War, they'd become friends, inseparable.

No matter how bad things got, Edmond was the anchor that always saw Ludovic through the storm, and now Ludovic had to leave that anchor behind and strike out in the world with a girl he barely knew.

Ludovic slid his glasses back on and got to his feet. "We're leaving soon."

"I know this is hard for you, but don't make it hard for Roux," Edmond cautioned. "She's trying to help."

"I know."

Before the doorway, Ludovic paused. "I love you, Edmond. You do know that, don't you?"

"Of course I do," Edmond said.

Ludovic heard the rustle of clothing as Edmond stood up, and he turned around to hug his friend.

"I hope this is all over quickly so you can go back to normal," Edmond said, holding him at arm's length. "You look unbelievably strange."

Roux

While Ludovic was with Edmond, Roux packed their bags and Renie helped her carry them to the vestibule, where Ysanne waited. There was no sign of Walsh, and Roux was glad. It was easier to breathe when he wasn't looming like a thundercloud in the background.

Ysanne appraised Roux's new look, then looked past Roux to the main staircase, her eyes visibly widening.

Roux and Renie both turned.

Ludovic and Edmond walked down the stairs, and Ludovic's newly human appearance was even more incongruous next to Edmond's ebony-and-ivory vampire beauty. Plus, he looked awkward as hell.

Roux made a mental note to teach him how to walk and talk a bit more casually. His physical appearance was human but he still moved with the fluid grace of a vampire.

"I see that Roux is already proving her worth. I hardly recognized you," Ysanne said.

Ludovic tugged on his beanie, avoiding anyone's eyes.

"There's a car waiting outside for you." Ysanne's lips thinned. "I'd hoped that you could travel with Walsh to the Johnsons' house, but he insisted on meeting you there. You're staying at the Old Royal on Romsey Road. Seamus assures me that the car is equipped with the necessary technology to find the hotel without need of a map. The trunk is stocked with enough bagged blood for two weeks, and there's an envelope of money in the glove compartment. I trust you'll use it wisely."

She looked hard at Roux, then Ludovic, and a hint of red crept into her eyes.

"Ludovic, you are to take these vampires alive if possible, but your life comes first. You must kill them if you have no other choice," she said.

"Understood," he said.

Roux peeked under her new fringe at Ludovic, trying to gauge how he felt about this, but his face was a blank mask.

"I took the liberty of adding a supply of silver handcuffs to your things. You're not to take any chances," Ysanne said.

"The silver will burn Ludovic too," Roux objected.

"I included gloves."

Roux peeked at Ludovic again, but his face still gave away nothing.

"There's one more thing," Ysanne said, and held up a slim black cell phone, dangling it gingerly between her thumb and forefinger. "This is for you. I trust you know how to use it?"

Roux suppressed a smile. "I think I can work it out."

"Seamus has also provided one of these devices for the mansion, and programmed the number into yours. You must call regularly with progress updates."

Roux glanced at Ludovic, who was eyeing the phone with a kind of horrified fascination. He wouldn't be making any progress reports, then.

"Not to sound patronizing, but do *you* know how to use it?" Roux said to Ysanne.

Ysanne lifted her chin, proud as ever, but she didn't pretend that she understood the modern technology.

"Renie shall help with this aspect of the mission. In fact, I shall need her to help the entire House enter the modern world." Ysanne sounded as if Renie was going to teach the older vampires how to swim in sewage.

Roux slid the phone into her pocket. "I guess that's it, then," she said, her nerves suddenly twisting in her stomach.

Renie gave her a final hug. "Stay out of trouble," she whispered.

"I'll do my best."

Parked close to the front door was a sleek black car—one of the Belle Morte vehicles usually housed in the garage around the right side of the mansion. The keys dangled from the lock of the driver's door.

Tucked away inside Belle Morte, Roux had almost been able to forget about the protestors gathered outside the gates, but out here, the sound of their anger was horribly loud. Roux had faced a lot of scary shit since coming to Belle Morte, but so many voices shouting and raging made her flinch.

"Are you all right?" Ludovic said.

The midday sun was high in the sky, and Roux wondered how long Ludovic could be out in it. A vampire's tolerance for the daylight depended on how old they were.

"I'm fine," she muttered. "You?"

"Why wouldn't I be?" His voice was flat and inflectionless.

"Don't pretend you can't hear them."

"I never claimed not to."

Roux looked curiously at him, scanning his face for any hint of expression. If this was hard for her, then it was a damn sight harder for him—he was the one these people were protesting against.

"So this is the car?" Ludovic said, eyeing it with ill-disguised apprehension.

"Looks like it."

Ludovic looked at her, his silence expectant, and after a moment or two, something clicked in her head.

"You can't drive, can you?" Roux said.

"Technically, yes, but I last drove a car in 1905. I suspect the process has changed somewhat since then."

Roux's lips twitched. "Maybe a little. Cars have proper roofs and windows now."

Roux unlocked the door, slung her bag into the back seat, and gestured for Ludovic to do the same. There was something monumentally weird about all this. She'd arrived at Belle Morte in a limousine, with a glass of champagne in hand, surrounded by flashing cameras; now she wondered if donors would ever again arrive like that.

Ludovic climbed into the passenger seat, sitting stiffly and uncomfortably.

Roux paused before getting into the car, gazing at the mansion. When she'd first filled out a donor form she'd never imagined that Belle Morte would be anything like home to her. So much had happened here, bad and good, and Roux had become part of the house in a way donors weren't meant to.

"Are you coming?" Ludovic called.

"Yeah."

Turning her back on Belle Morte, Roux climbed into the car.

CHAPTER FOUR

Roux

The Old Royal was a modest hotel wedged between two taller buildings. The redbrick facade blended in with the rest of the street, and the sign above the black front door was so small Roux almost missed it.

"Try to relax a bit," Roux advised as Ludovic got out of the car.

"Excuse me?"

Roux walked around to him. "Like this." She put both hands on Ludovic's shoulders and pushed down, but it was like trying to shift concrete. She rolled her eyes. "Work with me here."

He relaxed his shoulders a fraction. "What's the point of this?"

"I'm making you look more human. Trust me."

A tiny frown appeared between Ludovic's eyebrows, and suddenly Roux realized how close they were standing. She was tall, even in flat shoes, but the top of her head only reached Ludovic's chin, and the way she held his shoulders was almost as if she was reaching up for a kiss.

Clearing her throat, she stepped back. "We should get inside," she said.

It took a couple of minutes to check in, then Roux led the way to their room, Ludovic trailing behind. He seemed steadily more uncomfortable as they climbed the stairs to the second floor, and she wondered if this was the first time in a decade that he'd stayed somewhere that wasn't a Vampire House.

Their room was small; three walls were painted cream and one was exposed brick, featuring a large painting of the Winchester cityscape. There was only one window, and the curtains were dark and thick, just how Ludovic needed them. The wall opposite was interrupted by a door that Roux hoped led to a bathroom.

There was only one bed.

When Ludovic saw it, he froze, the more casual posture that Roux had coaxed him into snapping back into rigidly straight shoulders and back.

"What's this?" he said.

"Looks like a bed."

He gave her a hard look. "Why is there only one?"

"Because Ysanne originally arranged this room for herself, and she didn't need two beds."

"This is no good." Ludovic actually backed away.

"It's just a bed, Ludovic. It won't bite." Roux grinned mischievously. "I promise I won't bite either."

He gave that little frown again.

Roux slung her bag onto the right side of the bed. Usually she preferred to sleep on the left, but even with those curtains, she figured it was better for Ludovic to be as far away from the window as possible. Vampires were very coy about how much sunlight they could withstand, and Roux didn't want to find out the hard way.

Ludovic still stood near the door, staring at the bed like it was the worst kind of hell.

Roux sighed. "I know this isn't ideal, but it won't kill you. I'm sure you've shared beds with girls before."

"That's not the point." His tone was clipped.

"Okay, here's how I see it. We have one bed and I'm not giving it up, so you can share with me or you can sleep on the floor. Your choice." She climbed onto the bed and gave a little bounce, testing its softness. "The bed is much better, I promise."

Still Ludovic said nothing, but the gears in his head were probably turning so hard that steam was about to come out of his ears.

Roux felt a prick of pity. Maybe she'd underestimated how old-fashioned he was, and how confusing this might be for him.

"Fine, *I'll* sleep on the floor if it's such a big deal," she said.

"No," he said at once.

Roux waited.

"I'd never expect you to do that," Ludovic muttered, looking anywhere but at her.

"That's nice to know, but will *you* sleep on the floor?"

He thought a little longer, then shook his head.

"Good. Let's unpack."

Ludovic

When Roux had volunteered for this, he'd seen her as a liability. Oh, he knew how brave she was—he'd seen her kill a vampire with a curtain rod to protect Renie—but she was still human, still vulnerable, and he didn't want to compromise the mission to take care of her. And, if he was being completely honest with himself, the last person he wanted to work with was *this* girl. He'd held Roux in his arms when they'd jumped out of a window to escape Etienne's flunkies, and he could still feel the slender curve of her body pressed against his, still smell the citrus sweetness of her hair, still hear her quickened breaths. Since that day, she sometimes crept into Ludovic's head, unbidden and unwanted, and he didn't like that.

But he couldn't have disguised himself without her help and, though he'd never admit it, he was glad that he didn't have to do this on his own.

He studied Roux as she unpacked. She looked so different in plain clothes, her short hair hidden under that wig. The tiny ruby she usually wore in her nose was gone, and there wasn't a scrap of makeup on her face, but she didn't seem remotely uncomfortable in her disguise.

Ludovic envied that.

He hadn't been comfortable with who he was for a long time.

Roux straightened, and Ludovic quickly averted his eyes.

"Are you going to unpack?" she asked.

Ludovic silently approached the bed. His chest felt like he'd swallowed a rock. It wasn't just from sharing a bed with someone for the first time in a very long time; it was how domestic this suddenly felt. It made his world seem off-kilter somehow, like he no longer had control over what was happening, and the thought of ever losing control again was terrifying.

"When do you think Walsh will call?" Roux asked.

"I don't know," Ludovic said.

"It's kind of bullshit that we have to hang around waiting for him. If he'd given us the address we could be on our way to the Johnsons' now."

Ludovic glanced up and found Roux watching him, her expression expectant. Was he supposed to respond? He looked away again and said nothing.

Roux climbed onto the bed and pulled out the flat black phone that Ysanne had given them. The sight of it baffled Ludovic. It had no buttons, just a glass screen, which Roux tapped away at, her nails making small clicking sounds.

"Just calling the mansion to let them know we've arrived," she explained.

Ludovic took the portable freezer box filled with donated blood and plugged it into the wall—even he knew that much. Then he busied himself with unpacking, and hoped that Walsh wouldn't take too long, because he had no idea what to say to this girl.

By the time Walsh called an hour later, the sun was going down, and when Roux drew back the curtains, the wintry sunset looked like blood spilling between the clouds.

"Oh, that's not ominous at all," she muttered. She turned to Ludovic and looked pointedly at his shoulders. "Remember to relax a little. Most humans don't care that much about perfect posture."

"*You* don't slouch," Ludovic said.

Roux tweaked her wig and smiled. "Yes, well, I'm one of the humans who *does* care."

The Johnson family lived a few miles away on a quiet street of terraced houses with small squares of front lawn. A couple of the neighbors had For Sale signs outside; one of them was about to fall over. It could have been any street in any city in the UK.

After she parked, Roux opened Stephen's file and leaned over so Ludovic could see it. "Okay, Stephen Johnson, twenty-three years old, lived with his mum and younger brother, Iain. He looks so normal, doesn't he? But I guess that's the point—everyone Etienne turned was just a normal person who wanted something they weren't supposed to have."

"Do you think it's normal to want to be a vampire?" Ludovic asked.

Roux gave him an odd look.

Ludovic climbed out of the car before she could say anything.

A door slammed farther down the street, and Ludovic turned to see Walsh striding toward them. Even his walk was angry.

"Hi," Roux said, closing her own door.

Walsh ignored her, and it made Ludovic's hackles rise. He might be uncomfortable around Roux, but she *was* trying to help, and the least Walsh could do was respect that.

"Let's get this over with," Walsh said.

He marched up the path to the Johnsons' house. Roux and Ludovic exchanged a look, and Roux's lips twitched.

"He's such a charmer," she whispered.

Following Walsh up the path, Ludovic expected the man to knock as if he was trying to beat the door down, but Walsh surprised him by knocking quietly. The door opened immediately and a middle-aged woman with tired eyes looked out. She gave Walsh a strained smile, which faded when she looked past him to Roux and Ludovic.

"Who are they?" she asked.

"The representatives from Belle Morte that I told you about," Walsh said.

Roux stepped around Walsh and offered the woman her hand. "You must be Mrs. Johnson," she said.

"They're here to help," Walsh said, and he almost sounded as if he believed it.

Mrs. Johnson didn't shake Roux's hand, but she nodded and opened the door wider. Walsh went in first, then Roux, but Ludovic paused on the threshold, staring down a short hallway. It was just a house, not so different from places he'd called home in the past, but that was before Belle Morte. Sometimes he forgot he'd only lived in the mansion for ten years—it should have been no time at all to a centuries-old vampire, and yet it felt like so much longer.

"Hey," Roux said softly. "You okay?"

Ludovic nodded.

Roux reached out as if she was going to take his hand, and Ludovic sidestepped her and continued down the hall.

He entered a small living room, where Mrs. Johnson was already slumped in an armchair. A man and a woman a few years younger sat on a matching sofa opposite, while Walsh stood by a bookcase in the corner, his arms crossed.

"You can call me Linda. This is Mark and Caroline, Delia's parents," Mrs Johnson said. "You know that Stephen and Delia were a couple, right?" She gave herself a little shake. "Sorry, *are* a couple."

Caroline Sanders leaned forward, her eyes keenly focused on Ludovic. "That's why we're here. We want to know what you're going to do about this."

"What do you mean?" Ludovic said.

"We want to know about a cure," Mark said.

"A cure?" Roux's voice faltered.

"Mr. and Mrs. Sanders, there is no cure," Ludovic said. "Vampirism is not a disease."

"But there must be some way of reversing it," Mark insisted.

Anger sparked in Ludovic's chest. If there was a cure for vampirism, didn't this man think vampires would have found it already? Did he think they'd have lived such long, painful, and bloody lives if there was a way back?

"To become a vampire a person has to die. There's no coming back from that," he said shortly.

Walsh cleared his throat. "Mrs. Johnson, you asked us here because you said you had information that could help."

"First, I want to know what'll happen to my daughter," Caroline said, pinning Ludovic with another intense stare.

He hesitated.

Vampire justice was swift and brutal. Edmond had been whipped with silver for punching another vampire. Jemima's treachery had led to her heart being ripped out of her chest. Anyone who'd worked for Jemima and Etienne had been rounded up and imprisoned. If Ysanne had her way then the Five, and everyone like them, would meet similar punishments, but she answered to a higher authority now. Ludovic genuinely didn't know what would happen.

"She'll be arrested and taken to Belle Morte where they're equipped to hold vampire prisoners," said Roux.

"And then?" Caroline demanded.

"We're only representatives of Belle Morte, assisting DCI Walsh. I'm afraid we're not privy to anything more than that," Roux said. The lies fell smoothly from her mouth—she even managed to sound apologetic.

"You expect us to help you when you can't even tell us what will happen to our kids?"

"We expect you to understand that Stephen and Delia have blood on their hands and they have to answer for that," Ludovic said.

Caroline glared at him, but tears gleamed in her eyes.

Tension was thick in the room.

"This is Stephen's fault," Caroline burst out, and Linda flinched. "He's the one who got her into all this vampire crap."

"That's not true," Linda said.

"Yes, it is," Mark said. He looked at Ludovic. "He's one of those Vladdicts, and you know how those people are."

Ludovic did.

Idolizing vampires was one thing—people had idolized celebrities and godlike figures for pretty much all of human existence—but it was a problem when people became obsessed with it, and far too many people did. They got sucked into the idea of a decadent world where beautiful vampires lived mysterious, exotic lives, and they sank so far into the fantasy that they couldn't see that that was all it was ever meant to be: a fantasy.

The vampire lifestyle wasn't one people should aspire to.

"Stephen Johnson sucked my daughter into this mess, and now she's the one paying for it," Caroline snapped. "'A romantic getaway,' he said. He has a sick idea of romance."

"Sorry?" Roux said, frowning.

"We didn't even know Delia was missing until *he* told us she'd been turned into a vampire," Mark said, gesturing at Walsh. "Delia told us that Stephen had planned a holiday for them. I thought it was a bit odd that he could afford it when he didn't have a job, but figured maybe he had savings. That's where we thought she was."

"Do you think that Stephen made Delia do this?" Roux asked.

"Yes," said Caroline.

"No," said Linda.

The two women glared at each other.

"I didn't bring you here for this," Linda said.

"I don't *care*." Caroline clenched her fists. "Look me in the eye, Linda, and tell me that Stephen didn't have an unhealthy obsession."

A few tears slipped down Linda's face, but she didn't deny it.

Walsh raised both hands. "How about we all dial down the accusations? It's not helping." His voice softened. "Mrs. Johnson, why *did* you bring us here?"

The woman looked down at her hands. "I've been trying to contact Stephen ever since . . ." She swallowed. "You know. But he never responds."

There was no change in her pulse or heartbeat, nothing to indicate that she was lying.

"Then, yesterday, he finally called," she continued. "He said that he and Delia were planning to leave the city soon."

"To go where?" Ludovic asked.

"I don't know."

That sounded like the truth too.

"He told me that he'd call again when he and Delia had settled somewhere, but for now, he needed to say good-bye," Linda said.

"That's it?" Walsh demanded.

"I thought that could be important."

"It could be," Roux reassured her, aiming a subtle glare at Walsh.

"What happens now? You'll try to stop them leaving?" Caroline said.

"Yes," Walsh replied. "Vampires aren't above the law."

He didn't look at Ludovic as he said it, but there was still something pointed in his voice.

"If Stephen coerced Delia into this, that will be taken into account, won't it?" Caroline asked.

"He *didn't*," Linda cried.

"Oh please. Delia told me all about Stephen's vampire shrine." Caroline's gaze swung to Ludovic, then to Roux. "Go and look at his bedroom—you'll see."

Roux caught Ludovic's eye and lifted an eyebrow. He nodded.

"It might be helpful to take a quick look, if it's okay with you, Mrs. Johnson," Roux said.

Linda made a distracted flapping motion with her hand, which Ludovic interpreted as permission. He and Roux left the room while the two mothers started arguing again.

As they climbed the stairs, it occurred to Ludovic that they didn't know which room was Stephen's, but after opening a couple of doors, it quickly became clear.

"Holy shit," Roux said.

Ludovic couldn't find words.

Every wall was plastered with pictures, hundreds of them, layered over each other as they jostled for space. The faces of vampires— both UK and worldwide—stared back at him, little fragments of lives frozen in time and collected in this room. He did a double take when he spotted a photograph of him and Edmond, both tuxedo-clad and standing at the edge of Belle Morte's ballroom, and quickly looked away before he could pinpoint when the picture had been taken. There was something very unnerving about seeing his face, and the faces of people he knew, pinned to the walls of a total stranger.

He fought the urge to tear it all down.

Vampires were weighed down with hundreds of years' worth of memories. They'd live forever but they'd see the people they loved turn to dust around them.

Almost everything bad that had ever happened to Ludovic was because he was a vampire.

Almost every bad thing that he'd ever done was because he was a vampire.

"Stephen really was obsessed. He'd have been an easy target for Etienne," Roux said, turning in a slow circle as she examined the room.

"That doesn't excuse anything," Ludovic said.

"I know." She bent to look at a framed photo of Stephen and Delia on the windowsill. "God, they probably thought that getting turned together was some great act of romance."

"There is *nothing* romantic about it," Ludovic said. It came out more harshly than he'd intended, and Roux looked taken aback.

"I never said *I* thought there was," she said, and Ludovic expected her to sound annoyed, but her voice was soft, almost soothing.

He was saved from having to respond by the sound of shouting from downstairs—a male voice that he didn't recognize.

"What the hell?" Roux said.

Warning prickled Ludovic's skin. The unfamiliar voice was angry, and it was an ugly, violent anger—the kind that promised blood.

"We'd better see what's going on," he said.

CHAPTER FIVE

Roux

A guy a year or two older than her stood in the middle of the living room, his fists clenched at his sides, and even with the scowl twisting his face, his resemblance to Stephen was striking. This was the younger brother then.

"He's a vampire. He's *dead*, Mum. Don't you get that?" Iain snapped.

"But he's not. He's still walking around, isn't he?" Linda said.

Iain's scowl twisted even more, morphing into a mask so full of naked rage that Roux went cold all over.

"That thing you think is Stephen? It's not. Vampires aren't fucking *people*," Iain snarled.

Out of the corner of her eye, Roux saw Ludovic stiffen.

She looked at Walsh, still standing over by the bookcase, and wondered if he'd intervene, but he stayed silent. Maybe he agreed with Iain.

Iain suddenly wheeled around, forcing Roux to fall back a step. Her back met Ludovic's chest. She expected him to move, but he didn't.

Iain was tall, though not as tall as Ludovic, and compactly built—not muscular exactly, but not scrawny either.

"You're the ones from that Vampire House?" he said.

Roux fought the urge to flinch. "We're representatives of Belle Morte, yes."

"What the fuck are you going to do to Stephen when you find him?"

"Stephen will be arrested and taken to Belle Morte." Walsh spoke up.

"You should just fucking kill him."

"Iain!" Linda cried, tears spilling down her cheeks. "He's still your brother!"

Iain swung back to his mum, and for a horrible moment, Roux thought he would hit her. From the way Ludovic tensed again, he probably thought the same thing.

"That thing is not my brother. It's a fucking monster wearing Stephen's skin."

On the sofa, Caroline Sanders let out a soft cry.

Iain turned again, the veins standing out like cords on either side of his neck. "You need to find him before any more kids get killed."

"Kids?" Roux was thrown.

Iain whipped around and stormed upstairs, his footsteps so loud and heavy that the framed pictures rattled on the walls. Roux looked at Linda, but she seemed as confused as anyone else.

Iain thundered back down the stairs and threw a fistful of crumpled papers at Roux. She crouched to gather them up.

"I don't understand," Roux said, flipping through pages of printouts.

"All these kids are missing. I saw the press release that French bitch and the prime minister put out, so I know all about the fuckup at Belle Morte. I know that bastard Etienne was sneaking out of the house to kill people," Iain said.

"Etienne was building an army. He did not go after children," Ludovic said.

"Bullshit. He did this. They're dead somewhere, and it's because of him."

Roux glanced at Walsh. His eyebrows were pulled low, his jaw clenched, but she didn't dare ask him if he'd known about this—not in front of Iain. His barely leashed rage made her jittery and on edge.

She tried to hand the papers back to Iain, but he sneered and batted her hands away.

"Keep them," he said, his stare raking over her. "You can look at the faces of those dead kids and remember what those pieces of shit you work for have done."

Linda touched her son's arm, but he shook her off. "Vampires are a fucking disease," he said, and turned a disgusted glare on Mark and Caroline. "Including your bitch of a daughter."

"How dare you?" Caroline shouted, jumping to her feet. Her husband followed a split second later, and the living room exploded into hurled insults and pointing fingers. Linda collapsed onto the sofa, sobbing.

Roux looked helplessly at Ludovic, but his face was like stone.

Walsh sidestepped the argument and joined them. "Might be a good idea to get out of here."

Roux felt a twinge of guilt at leaving like this, but mediating family disputes wasn't part of their mission. Reluctantly, she followed Walsh out of the house, Ludovic in her wake.

"What do you think?" Roux asked as soon they were outside the house. Iain's papers were wadded up in her pocket.

Walsh pulled a pack of cigarettes from his pocket, put one in his mouth, and lit it. "It's hardly a concrete fucking lead."

"Better than nothing, though, right?"

"Yeah." Walsh blew out a plume of smoke. His forehead furrowed in thought. "Okay, if they're leaving the city soon, they'll get a train. Stephen didn't have a job and Delia only worked part-time at a local pub, so neither of them were exactly rolling in cash."

"And trains are faster than cars. Stephen and Delia have been vampires for only a few days; they're incredibly vulnerable to sunlight still," Roux said. "They'll need to take the quickest route out of the city."

"Good point."

"It also means they can't have left yet." Roux looked up at the sky. "The sun's only just set."

"Winchester station has only two platforms. If we beat them there, there's no way they can catch a train without us seeing." His frown deepened. "Unless they're in disguise, like you two."

"I'd still be able to tell that they were vampire, not human," said Ludovic.

Walsh's expression flattened, and he made a disgusted noise. The hostility had faded from his voice while he was talking to Roux—they'd almost had a conversation. She should have known that wouldn't last.

The tip of Walsh's cigarette flared orange as he took a final drag, then he flicked the butt away. "We'd better get to that station, then."

"Wait." Roux pulled out Iain's papers and held them up so Walsh could see them. "Do you know anything about this?"

Walsh clenched his jaw. "It's got nothing to do with this."

"But you do know about it?"

His expression turned withering. "It's my job to know about crimes in this city."

"Then—"

"I'm not discussing an unconnected, ongoing investigation with you," Walsh interrupted. "What's happened to those kids is fucking tragic, but it's not your business."

He strode off, already pulling out another cigarette.

Sighing, Roux stuffed the papers back into her pocket and turned to their own car, then turned back when she realized Ludovic wasn't following her. He was staring at the Johnson house, his shoulders a stiff, straight line. The sound of shouting still drifted out.

"Ludovic?" she said.

His face was expressionless, but his eyes, now downcast, churned with emotions, and none of them were good. Something in Roux's chest squeezed.

"Hey," she said softly.

Finally he looked at her.

"What's wrong?" Roux said. "Is it what Iain said? Because you can't take that to heart."

Vampires could keep their voices as impassive as their faces, but when Ludovic spoke his voice was low and raw. "That's easy for you to say."

Roux moved a little closer. "Do you want to talk about it?"

He was a tightly closed book, so she expected a refusal, but Ludovic surprised her by saying, "Is this how it'll be from now on?" He sounded suddenly young, even lost. "I know we'll never live in a world where everyone likes vampires, but we've had ten years of peace and safety, where we didn't have to hide behind false identities or constantly uproot ourselves so no one noticed that we're not normal."

Ludovic shook his head and took off his glasses. "Now all that's changing. I know things can't go back to how they were before Jemima and Etienne started all this, but I never thought we'd see a world in which people truly turned on us. It was different in the past because most of them didn't know we even existed, but now? Where will we run to? Where will we hide? Where—"

"Ludovic," Roux cut him off gently but firmly. "I won't pretend I know how it feels to realize that the people who adored you a few days ago might now be out for your blood, but you don't know how the rest of the world feels, and you don't know what will happen yet. Don't assume the worst."

"Again, that's easy for you to say."

"That doesn't mean it's not true." Roux paused for a beat, giving Ludovic a chance to absorb her words. "Now, we can either stand out here and listen to people arguing, or we can follow Walsh to the station and try to stop two rogue vampires before they hurt anyone else."

She unlocked the car, climbed inside, and waited for Ludovic to join her.

After a moment or two, he did.

Ludovic

Outside the windows of the car, Winchester flashed past, stone-flagged streets running alongside ones of brick and concrete; Tudor-fronted buildings rubbed shoulders with newer architecture.

Ludovic felt like one more old thing trying to find a place in the modern world.

Sitting in the passenger seat next to Roux was a very different experience from being chauffeured around in a limousine or a Belle Morte vehicle, and he wasn't sure he liked it. It was too small, and the windows weren't tinted, so he could clearly see the world rushing by, familiar and unfamiliar at the same time.

Mounted on the dashboard was some sort of control panel, and Ludovic didn't have a clue what any of the buttons or dials did. Part of him was curious. Another part didn't want Roux to know just *how* ignorant he was when it came to things that had always been part of her everyday life.

Ludovic still remembered life before cars. He remembered the swaying gait of a horse beneath him, remembered his feet blistered raw when he'd had to walk for miles and miles on end.

He didn't want Roux to understand his past, because even he didn't like to look at the shadows lurking in the corners of his mind. But could he ever understand her world?

If the donor system collapsed, he might not have a choice.

He stole a glance at Roux. She looked straight ahead, focusing on the road, her hands in a relaxed position on the wheel. He wasn't used to donors like her. Usually they came to the mansion with stars in their eyes, trembling with excitement to be there, and maybe Roux had been like that at the start, but she certainly wasn't now.

Ludovic had to admit it was refreshing.

"You mind if I turn the radio on?" Roux said, snapping him out of his reverie.

He shook his head, and watched as she touched a button on the control panel. So that was the radio. Music blared out, and Roux winced, grabbing a dial and turning it. The volume decreased. Ludovic quietly memorized what she'd done. It wouldn't make much difference when he didn't know how to actually drive the car, but maybe it was a stepping stone to something bigger.

"You want to listen to anything in particular?" Roux asked.

She pressed another button and the music changed to some bizarre mess of synthesized noises, then from that to something soft and lilting. Ludovic recognized none of it.

"Choose whatever you like," he said.

Roux pressed the button a few more times, changing the music again and again, until she settled on something that even Ludovic knew.

She grinned at him. "Can't go wrong with classic Beatles," she said, as the notes of "Hey Jude" softly filled the car.

They drove in silence for about a minute, and then Roux said, "Did you ever see them live?"

"The Beatles?"

"Yeah."

"No," Ludovic said.

Roux shot him an incredulous look. "Seriously? You were around for the Summer of Love, and you never went to see one of the most famous bands of all time?"

"The Summer of Love was in America," he said. "And the Beatles had stopped performing live by then."

A mischievous grin played around the corners of Roux's mouth. "Just testing you."

"I doubt there was a single person in England who didn't know those things at the time. The Beatles were—and probably still are—the biggest band in the world, and the country had plenty of gatherings similar to the Summer of Love."

"But you never went to any of them?"

Despite himself, the smallest smile touched Ludovic's own lips. "I'm not sure even hippies would have been too happy to realize that a vampire walked among them."

Taking a hand off the wheel, Roux made a dismissive gesture. "Nonsense. They'd have braided flowers into your hair and painted rainbows on your cheeks."

"I'm not sure I would have liked that."

"Don't knock it till you've tried it."

She was quiet for another span of time, until the song changed, flowing into something Ludovic didn't recognize.

"How come you didn't get involved with the whole flower-power sixties vibe?" Roux asked. "Just not your thing?"

Ludovic pressed his lips together. Many vampires had greatly enjoyed the '60s, when people were taking so many drugs that they either didn't notice or didn't care if they spotted someone with fangs or red eyes, but Ludovic had lived as a relative hermit during that time, as far removed from the changing world as possible.

Roux was waiting for an answer, but he didn't know what to tell her.

Memories flashed in front of his eyes: the gasping breaths of an injured soldier, splattered with reeking mud from the trenches; the fury and disbelief in Maurice's eyes before the life faded out of them; the choking cry of a nameless monk; the love in Elise's eyes twisting into terrible violence.

There was blood on his hands and too many ghosts in his past. He couldn't begin to explain to Roux why he'd sequestered himself from the world for so long, and had only been coaxed out of his shell by Edmond's loyal, steadfast friendship.

"I . . ." A tiny flutter of panic lodged in his chest.

"You don't have to tell me anything you don't want to," Roux said.

She'd once asked him to dance, during a Belle Morte party, and she hadn't given him a chance to say no. Ludovic had thought she'd charge into other areas of life with the same brashness, but rather than pushing him, she was giving him space. Rather than getting angry when he was short with her, she showed only empathy.

He wanted to tell her that she wasn't what he'd expected, but he couldn't find the words.

So he stayed quiet.

CHAPTER SIX

Roux

It didn't take them long to reach the station. Walsh was already there, finishing a cigarette.

"I've checked at the ticket office. No one's seen either of them," he said as Roux and Ludovic approached.

"I thought it was too early," Roux said.

Walsh looked around the station. "I know we need to catch these bastards, but I really don't want to do it here. There're too many people about."

"There's no guarantee it *will* be here. Stephen didn't say they were leaving tonight," Roux said.

"You think the station will be less busy tomorrow?"

"I guess not."

Ludovic moved away from them, eyeing the information scrolling across the announcements board.

Roux realized that modern trains were probably as alien to him as modern cars, and her chest squeezed again. Ludovic was hundreds of years old, and she couldn't imagine everything he'd seen and done, but none of that experience helped him fit into this world.

She wanted to reassure him that she wouldn't let him drown, but maybe he wouldn't appreciate her drawing attention to his confusion.

"Is this the only way in or out?" Ludovic asked, glancing back at the entrance behind them.

"No, there's one on the other platform," Walsh said, pointing across the tracks.

"Do you know which one is more frequently used?"

"No idea."

Ludovic studied the station again, his eyes flitting back and forth behind his Clark Kent glasses. "I'll go to the other side. You two stay here," he said.

Roux protested, but Ludovic was already walking away.

Walsh relaxed a fraction once he'd gone. "How did you get caught up in all this, anyway?" he asked.

"I was Renie Mayfield's roommate. When I learned that her sister was missing, I decided to help her work out what was going on."

"All the other donors got sent home. Why not you?"

Roux hid a wince, remembering the most recent call she'd had with her parents. Unsurprisingly, they wanted her to come home. She was their only kid and she'd got herself tangled in a bloody and brutal vampire war—she was lucky they hadn't come to the mansion and dragged her out.

But Roux couldn't go home yet.

The old rules of Vampire Houses banned donors from returning once they'd left, and Roux didn't know if that still stood—or, if it did, whether those rules still applied to her. She *was* more than just a donor, after all.

But if Ysanne and Caoimhe—as the only two surviving members of the Council—*did* decide to seal up the Houses again, like it had been before, then Roux could lose Renie, one of the only two real friends she had. The thought of that terrified her.

Walsh watched her, waiting for an answer.

"They still need me," she said.

"You're not uncomfortable still being in that house?" Walsh said, his expression disbelieving.

"Aside from my family, the people I care about most in the world live there."

"What about him?" Walsh nodded to the other side of the station where Ludovic stood. "Can you really trust him?"

Memories spun through Roux's head—Ludovic saving her by slicing down an enemy vampire in the Belle Morte ballroom; Ludovic lifting her into his arms as he jumped out of a window when they fled the mansion.

"Absolutely," she said.

She might not really know Ludovic, but she did trust him.

Walsh just grunted.

They stayed at the station for hours, until the last train had been and gone. Stephen and Delia hadn't shown up.

Roux was tired, cold, hungry, on edge from being around Walsh so much, and deeply disappointed that tonight looked to be a total bust. Ludovic rejoined them as they left the station and headed back to their cars.

"We'll have to try again tomorrow night. You're absolutely sure Mrs. Johnson wasn't lying?" Walsh said to Ludovic.

"Some humans can lie adeptly enough that a vampire can't hear it. She is not one of them," Ludovic replied.

"Too bad Stephen didn't let slip to her where he and Delia are staying."

"Stupid question, but I'm guessing you've already checked that none of their friends are hiding them?" Roux said.

Walsh scowled. "Of course I have. I know how to do my job."

Roux sighed, making her wig flutter. "They could be anywhere in the city, then."

Ludovic took off his glasses, his eyes thoughtful. "Or maybe not," he said. He turned to Roux. "If Stephen didn't have a job and Delia only worked part-time, I'm assuming they couldn't afford to rent somewhere to stay during the day. But what if there was somewhere else they could go?"

Roux stared back at him, baffled.

"The same place that Etienne kept them after he turned them. That army camp," Ludovic said.

Understanding dawned. "Bushfield," Roux said. "It's only a couple of miles outside the city, isn't it? We could go there."

"My team combed that place as soon as Ysanne told me about it," Walsh said. "We found nothing."

"Vampires can find things that humans can't," Ludovic told him.

Walsh narrowed his eyes, as if Ludovic's statement was a personal insult.

"Do you know where the camp is?" Ludovic asked Roux.

"I can find it," she said, tapping the pocket that held her phone.

Ludovic gave her a puzzled look. "I'm unclear how a telephone will help."

"Oh, honey."

Roux googled the camp's location while Ludovic watched, still wearing that puzzled look. It was kind of adorable, really.

"I'll teach you how to do this at some point," she said.

"I'm not sure you will."

"Excuse me," said Walsh loudly. "It's almost midnight. We're not driving out of the city to an abandoned army camp now."

"You might not be. We are," said Ludovic.

He got a scowl in return.

"Got it," Roux declared, zooming in on the camp's location. Then she paused, a niggle of anxiety sliding through her. "Is it safe to go tonight? Should we wait until tomorrow?"

"New vampires need to feed more often than older ones, so either Stephen and Delia are hunting in the city, or they're feeding from wildlife, like they did when Etienne first turned them. If they have any sense, they'll feed as much as possible before they attempt to flee the city."

"Okay, you're not making me feel any more reassured."

"I'm not necessarily intending to find them at Bushfield. What I'm hoping to find is evidence to indicate whether or not they're staying there—or if any of the Five are."

"Why can't you do that during the day?" Walsh said.

"My instructions were to bring them in alive, wherever possible. For vampires as new as them, that would be very hard to do during the day."

Walsh's dark look suggested he didn't give a damn if Stephen and Delia went up in flames, but at least he didn't say it.

"What if they are at the camp?" Roux said.

Ludovic met her eyes. "I won't let anything happen to you."

There was something in his expression that she couldn't interpret, but her throat felt suddenly dry, and her heart was beating a little too fast. She hoped he couldn't hear it.

Walsh muttered something and pulled out another cigarette. "Let's just do this. We're wasting time."

Roux hurried back to the car, and Ludovic slid into the passenger seat.

"Good thing I came prepared," she said, popping open the glove compartment and fishing out the flashlight she'd stashed there when they left the hotel earlier in the evening. She switched it on.

"Is that really necessary?" Ludovic asked, looking away from the bright beam.

"You might have Superman vision, but us mere mortals can't see in the dark," Roux said, switching off the flashlight. "Unless you think I should stay in the car."

"No," said Ludovic at once. "I'm not leaving you on your own."

"I'd lock the doors."

He gave her a faintly exasperated look. "Do you think a locked door means much to a vampire?"

"Again, you really know how to reassure a girl," said Roux, swallowing.

"Roux," Ludovic said, and she looked up at him.

There was little light in the car, only what trickled through from the streetlamps outside, but even in the shadows Ludovic's eyes gleamed like sapphires. "If any of the Five are there, they'll have to get through me to reach you, and that's not going to happen."

His voice was low and intense, and Roux felt something shift inside her. Ludovic was a stranger to her in so many ways, but at the same time he wasn't.

"Okay, then," she said, tearing her eyes from his. "Let's go explore an army base."

Within a few minutes they were out of the city and almost at Bushfield, driving down a narrow, bumpy road surrounded by clumps of overgrown vegetation. The countryside was absolutely black around them, the car's headlights slicing through that darkness like twin blades.

A battered stop sign materialized out of the shadows. Roux ignored it.

When the camp was in sight, she angled the car off the road and killed the engine.

Walsh had already parked. The only sign that he was there was the tiny glow of his cigarette.

"What are you doing?" Ludovic asked as Roux opened the glove compartment again and pulled out two pairs of the silver cuffs that she'd stashed with the flashlight.

She slid a pair onto each wrist and raised her hands. "I know you can snap the Five like tiny matchsticks, but it doesn't hurt to be prepared. If any vampire grabs me while I'm wearing these, they're in for a nasty shock."

Admiration flickered in Ludovic's eyes. "You're rather resourceful, aren't you?"

"I have my moments."

Roux climbed out of the car.

A chill wind knifed through the air, but the shudder that rolled through Roux was due more to her surroundings. Winter-stripped trees loomed over her, their branches clattering together, and through the tangle of wilderness ahead, she could just about make out the blocky shapes of buildings. Once upon a time this place would have been a hive of military activity. Now it was silent and empty and dead.

She switched on her flashlight and the thin beam carved a path through the shadows. A rat scurried into a patch of brambles, its tail whipping across the ground, but nothing else stirred.

"How long has this place been abandoned?" Ludovic asked.

"No idea."

They advanced into the derelict camp, Ludovic leading the way. He'd completely shed any attempt at being human now, moving with the lithe grace of a vampire. There was something predatory about him, making Roux think of a wild animal stalking its prey.

Walsh crunched along behind them, and though Roux couldn't see his face, she'd bet he was glaring at them.

"Watch out for the steps," Ludovic said, and Roux shone her flashlight on the ground.

Just ahead was a set of stone steps, almost completely hidden beneath moss and leaf mold. Whatever they'd once led to was long gone, and the countryside had grown up in its place.

Ludovic paused, scanning the area. "We'll have to check every building," he said.

Roux shone the flashlight around, the beam dancing off walls and empty window frames. There were at least three buildings immediately in her eyeline, but she didn't know how big this place was or how many buildings were still standing.

Ludovic approached the nearest one, a small brick shape almost obscured beneath foliage. A tree sprouting inside had spilled out to smother the building, leaving only a glimpse of a doorway between the sagging branches.

"That looks creepy as hell," Roux whispered.

"I'll go in first. Wait out here until I say so," Ludovic told her.

He was tall enough that he had to crouch, practically on his hands and knees, to get through the overgrown doorway, and the knot in Roux's stomach tightened as she watched him disappear inside. It was like the darkness had swallowed him, leaving her alone with Walsh in the middle of nowhere.

Get a grip, she silently told herself.

A moment or two later Ludovic emerged, brushing dead leaves from his beanie. "It's empty," he said.

"What exactly are you looking for?" Walsh said.

"Any sign that anyone has been here recently."

"They have, though—my team."

Ludovic shook his head, his eyes roving over the ground. "A human's tread is different from a vampire's. You move more heavily. None of you will have left any blood or other evidence of feeding."

"Wait, are you telling me that vampires can tell the difference between a human footprint and a vampire one?" Walsh said.

"Not all vampires. But I can."

"Is it something you learned in the army?" Roux asked, intrigued.

All she knew of Ludovic's past was that he'd served alongside Edmond during World War I.

Ludovic tensed, just a little. "No," he said.

"You're military?" Walsh said. Was that respect in his voice? It was grudging, but it was there.

Ludovic's gaze was still fixed on the ground, but Roux wasn't sure he was studying it as much as he was trying not to look at them. "Once. A long time ago," he said, his words coming out clipped and terse.

"You ever see combat?"

Ludovic actually flinched. Walsh couldn't see it from his angle, but Roux could, and her throat tightened. What if Ludovic's habit of avoiding the world was about more than being a vampire?

"How does that work, anyway? You could only fight at night?" Walsh continued.

Ludovic's posture was rigid, his jaw clenched tight.

Roux stared at Walsh until he noticed, and then she made a slicing motion across her throat, wordlessly telling him to stop. She half expected him not to—he wasn't exactly sensitive—but Walsh fell quiet.

Slowly, methodically, they searched the camp. Some buildings had been graffitied, huge colored letters looking shockingly bright against the faded brickwork. Most were missing their roofs, and not a single one had windows left, only crumbling concrete frames. Other buildings were reduced to nothing but shattered foundations, slowly disappearing into the undergrowth.

They encountered clusters of concrete blocks and fallen girders that probably marked where walls had once stood, as well as some long, low brick stacks whose purpose Roux couldn't even guess at.

"Either Etienne had his people scattered wherever they could find shelter, or he kept them all in there," Ludovic said, at last, directing Roux's gaze to a much larger brick structure.

It was the biggest building they'd found so far, and the only one with an intact roof. Ludovic's logic was solid.

Roux swallowed and gripped her flashlight with both hands, her mind catapulting back to the first time Etienne had unleashed his puppets on Belle Morte. She tried not to think about it too much, but sometimes she woke up at night, shaking with the memory of smashing open a vampire's head with a curtain rod.

They approached the building. Ludovic paused outside, his head tilted, listening. He shook his head, and the tension winding through Roux's muscles deflated. They were almost out of places to look.

Ludovic entered first, and Roux and Walsh followed a moment later. Strands of moonlight fell through the rusted ceiling ventilation, highlighting motes of dust and playing along the tangled threads of hundreds of cobwebs.

Light fittings with trailing wires were still attached to the ceiling, and the walls were daubed with more graffiti. Here and there Roux spotted defunct light switches, as well as a huge rusted pipe that projected out of one wall and dead-ended above the floor.

Ludovic crouched, examining the floor.

"Did you find something?" Roux asked, swinging the flashlight around the space.

"Footprints," he replied.

Roux aimed her flashlight at the floor, but all she could see were dust and dead leaves.

"From vampires?"

"I think so."

"Are they recent?" she asked, glossing over the fact that she couldn't even see them.

"A few days old at least, I'd say." Ludovic straightened, his face set in pensive lines. "Let's keep looking."

As they progressed through the building, he pointed out more footprints, countless pairs crossing over each other throughout the space, and several times he crouched to look at dried spots of blood, but he shook his head each time. They were too old to be from Stephen or Delia.

At the far end, a large metal cage was set against a wall, and Roux's stomach turned over.

Animal corpses were heaped inside, piles of little bones and carpets of feathers, tufts of fur and leathery tails. The bodies looked like they'd been picked clean, probably by scavengers, but Roux couldn't shake the image of newly turned vampires crammed into this building, feasting on stray animals and wildlife.

"Jesus," Walsh muttered.

"Not exactly the glamorous vampire life they'd imagined, is it?" Roux said. "How was spending weeks here not a wake-up call that Etienne was just using them?"

"Weeks?" Walsh echoed, a strange edge to his voice.

"Yeah." Roux glanced at him. "Why?"

Walsh didn't answer, but his lowered eyebrows and clenched jaw made Roux's stomach tighten. Something was wrong, even if he wasn't going to tell her what.

Ludovic advanced into the cage, small bones crunching under his feet.

Roux had to look away.

It shouldn't have unnerved her as much as it did. When Renie had believed her sister was buried in the grounds of Belle Morte, Roux had helped her dig up the grave. Instead, they'd found the remains of the animals that June had been surviving on. This was so similar, and yet at the same time, so different.

Ysanne had fed June because she'd been trying to save her.

Etienne had used his vampires as meat for the grinder, and that was what all these little bodies represented. So many lives thrown away because of lies and greed and selfishness and arrogance.

Ludovic crunched out of the cage. "There's no fresh blood or bodies," he reported. "I don't think Stephen or Delia have been back here. But there are other buildings still to search. This isn't over yet."

But they found nothing.

When they'd exhausted that place, they ventured farther into the camp, exploring the concrete expanse of the parade ground, the buildings reduced to nothing but metal framework, husks of brick and concrete peering out amid knots of foliage, bits of metal fencing barely distinguishable from the trees around them, weather-stained lampposts still standing tall and proud, and a lot of steps that led to nowhere.

There was no sign of any vampires, except the one striding ahead of Roux, his blond hair looking like spun gold under the beam of her flashlight.

When Roux realized they were back to where they had started, not far from the car, she kicked a nearby tussock of grass. Something shot up with a harsh cry, and Roux yelped, stumbling back. She crashed against Ludovic's chest and his arms caught her, holding her steady.

"What is it? What happened?" Walsh yelled, spinning wildly around.

"What was *that*?" Roux cried, only now realizing that she wasn't under attack.

"A pheasant, I believe." There was a distinct note of amusement in Ludovic's voice, and Roux twisted around to scowl up at him.

"It's not funny."

"Of course not."

Roux ran a trembling hand through her hair and almost knocked her wig off. "Stupid bird."

"I believe this is the first time I've seen you flustered," Ludovic commented.

"And all it took was a pheasant flying at my face. Who knew?"

Roux briefly saw the funny side, but then she looked around the desolate army camp, and her mood evaporated.

"We didn't find anything," she said, resisting the urge to kick another tuft of grass.

"No."

"Crap."

"That about sums it up."

"You got any other bright ideas?" Walsh asked Ludovic. "If Stephen or Delia are looking for blood, is there anything you can tell us about that? Do vampires have hunting patterns? Anything?"

Roux started to say that she didn't think it worked like that, then stopped when she saw the thoughtful frown settling on Ludovic's face. Maybe she still had a lot to learn about vampires.

"Delia worked in a pub," he said.

"So?" said Walsh.

"Before we had the donor system, we had to be very careful about feeding from humans. We couldn't risk them knowing what we were, so we often gravitated to places like pubs."

"The more drunk a person was, the less likely they were to realize what was happening," Roux guessed.

Ludovic nodded. His eyes were shadowed again.

"You think Stephen and Delia are doing that again now?" Roux said.

"If they don't want to draw attention to themselves, then it's very possible."

"Okay. There are a lot of pubs in Winchester, but maybe we already have a lead. Delia could be hunting in the pub she worked in."

"It's more likely that they'd go where they wouldn't be recognized," Walsh said. "They probably want to be nearer the station, too, so they could catch a train as soon as they've fed."

Roux checked her watch. "It's too late to visit any pubs now, but we could do it tomorrow."

"By tomorrow night I'll make sure I have a list of every potential hunting spot," said Walsh.

"Can't we work that all out tonight?" Roux asked.

"No," Ludovic said.

"It's just—"

"No," Ludovic repeated, fixing her with a stern look. "It's late and you're exhausted."

"I'm fi—" A yawn cut her off, midword.

"We've done enough for tonight and we both need rest." Ludovic's tone of voice brooked no argument.

"Whatever you say, Mr. Bossypants."

CHAPTER SEVEN

Ludovic

The moment they were back in their hotel room, Roux kicked off her shoes and let out a long sigh. "The meeting with those families was harder than I thought it would be."

"What were you expecting?" Ludovic asked, genuinely curious.

"To me, the Five are villains, but they've still got families, and I didn't think enough about the fact that all those people are grieving." Roux sat on the bed and stretched her legs. "At least Delia's parents still love her. I can't imagine that Stephen will ever be able to go home, not as long as his brother lives there."

"In some ways it's worse that Delia's parents still think she can come home." Ludovic surprised himself by saying that. He didn't usually strike up conversations with people he barely knew, especially not regarding sensitive subjects.

"How is it worse?" Roux asked.

"Because Delia *won't* come home."

Roux lowered her gaze. "Right. Even if she wasn't a wanted fugitive, normal houses aren't vampire proofed."

Ludovic pulled off his cheap knitted hat and tossed it onto the foot of the bed.

"I wonder if Stephen and Delia will think it was all worth it when they're chained up in the Belle Morte cells," he said, his voice bitter.

Roux keenly regarded him from under her fringe. "Why do I get the feeling you'd think it wasn't worth it even if they weren't fugitives?"

Ludovic flexed his fingers, remembering them stiff and sticky with drying blood. It was a feeling he knew far too well.

"Humans don't understand what eternal life really means. You have to watch everyone you love grow old and die while you yourself never age, and that's not always as wonderful as people think. Imagine never changing. Imagine looking in the mirror every day for hundreds of years and seeing the exact same face staring back at you. There's something truly exhausting about being stuck in time like that," he said.

Roux listened, her eyes soft.

"Stephen and Delia will never have children. Their parents will never have grandchildren," Ludovic said.

A memory flashed into his head—Régine pottering about the house, one hand resting on her rounded belly, her face glowing with love and life. He shoved the memory away.

"Not everyone wants kids," Roux pointed out.

"Maybe not, but Stephen and Delia don't even have that option. Believe me, sometimes you don't know how much you want something until you can't have it."

Roux's eyebrows lifted and Ludovic abruptly stopped talking. He hadn't meant to say that last part, but Roux's quiet patience had made the words spill from his mouth and now it was too late to take them back.

In those few moments, he'd felt almost comfortable with her, in a way he was very unused to.

He waited for her to probe deeper, but Roux pulled off her wig and raked her fingers through her short hair, coaxing it into spiky tufts. The movement caused her shirt to ride up, exposing a narrow line of tanned stomach, and Ludovic's eyes dropped before he could stop himself.

Even without makeup Roux was beautiful, but she wasn't what Ludovic would ever call his type. She was lean rather than curvy, and he'd never been attracted to women with short hair, though he had to admit it suited her angular, striking features.

"You don't see only the negative sides of being a vampire, do you?" Roux asked, draping her wig across the chair in the corner.

Her words were curious rather than accusatory, but Ludovic felt her question like a slap.

Was that what his ghosts had done to him?

In the safe confines of Belle Morte he hadn't had to think about that. Life never changed there, as if time itself stopped within those walls, and if time stopped, then so did Ludovic. He didn't have to think about the things he'd seen, the things he'd done, the reasons he'd shut himself away from the world in the first place.

But now that he was outside the safe little bubble of the mansion, time had started again. *He* had started again. And now he had to remember what sort of man he was—the good and the bad.

He smoothed a hand over his hair. The tousled waves felt strange beneath his fingers.

"You know I was teasing, right?" Roux said, concern threading her words.

"Perhaps you're right, but I can't pretend that being a vampire is as wonderful and glamorous as people seem to think."

Roux smiled and clambered onto the bed, shuffling up until her back rested against the headboard. "You sound like Renie."

Ludovic blinked, taken aback. "I do?"

"She never bought into the whole Vladdict thing, even before she found out what happened to June. It used to piss her off that people blindly worshipped vampires and never once considered that their lives weren't all sunshine and roses."

Ludovic almost smiled. "Edmond did mention that she saw our world very differently than most people. I think that's what drew him to her in the first place; the fact that she marched into Belle Morte, all fire and temper, and she wasn't in awe of him, she didn't treat him like a celebrity. I'm not sure any other donor has acted like that toward him, toward any of us, really."

Even Roux, despite how much she'd surprised him with her boldness, had come to Belle Morte because she was as enamored of vampires as everyone else. She didn't look up to vampires anymore because she'd fought with them, suffered with them. They'd become her friends, and she'd become their equal—she'd probably never look at any vampire with that doe-eyed awe again.

Ludovic rather liked it.

"Can vampires get married?" Roux asked, cocking her head to one side.

Elise's face flashed through his head, and Ludovic's heart gave a painful wrench. "If we want to. There are married couples in other Houses."

"But they've all been married for a long time, haven't they? I'm talking about getting married *now*. You've all spent ten years in each other's company, and some of you have known each other way longer than that, so how come no one's properly paired up in the last decade?"

"That's a difficult question to answer."

Roux waited, her face expectant.

"I suppose a prominent reason is that time doesn't have much meaning inside a Vampire House. The world turns on and on but we stay the same, and perhaps on some subconscious level that prevents us from forming proper relationships."

Roux leaned forward, pulling her knees up to her chest and propping her chin on them. "I'm not sure I understand." But she sounded like she genuinely wanted to.

Ludovic couldn't remember the last time he'd talked to anyone like this—anyone who wasn't Edmond, at least—but now that he'd got started, he couldn't seem to stop. It was like Roux had shaken something loose inside him, and he didn't know how to tighten it again. He didn't even know if he wanted to.

"Relationships develop over time. But can they develop if time itself has stopped?"

Roux scrunched up her face, thinking. "I don't know, but that's not exactly what's happened, is it? Time hasn't actually *stopped*."

"It feels like it has. Every day is the same. We dress ourselves in expensive clothes and surround ourselves with architectural beauty. We study the artwork in our hallways and read the books in our library. We drink from our donors but we never get attached to them because, sooner or later, they're always replaced."

Ludovic took a step closer to the bed.

"We have balls and parties and photo shoots, and we're so busy lapping up the attention that we don't think to look for anything more meaningful. Ysanne said she'd lost Belle Morte to Etienne and Jemima because she'd become complacent and there is some truth in that. I think we've *all* become complacent. We've become spoiled."

He almost didn't recognize the words coming out of his own mouth, but they were true. He just hadn't realized it until now.

"Maybe that will change now. People have always loved a good celebrity wedding, and a vampire wedding would be the event of the year," Roux said.

She seemed blissfully optimistic that enough people would still like vampires enough to care whether or not they got married, but Ludovic swallowed those words. He didn't want to strip away her optimism.

"I can't help thinking this is really about Edmond and Renie," he said.

Roux waggled her arched eyebrows at him. It was startling to see her full face now, when so much of it had been hidden under that thick fringe throughout the day. "You got me." She put a hand on her chest. "I'm a shameless romantic at heart, and Renie's my best friend. I want her to be happy."

"She's already happy," Ludovic pointed out. "A wedding ceremony won't change that."

"No, but who doesn't love a wedding? You get to buy a new outfit, and eat delicious food that someone else has paid for, drinks are either free or really cheap, and there's cake!" Roux's expression softened. "Above all, you get to see people you love making a special commitment to each other. Maybe getting married doesn't make much difference to people in the long run, but I like weddings and I hope Renie and Edmond get married one day. Don't you?"

The question took Ludovic completely by surprise. He'd warned Edmond not to become attached to Renie, and yet he'd known that Edmond had loved her even before his friend had told him. When June had driven a knife into Renie's chest and Edmond had found her bleeding to death in the snow, Ludovic could have sworn he'd heard his best friend's heart break.

It was why he'd told Edmond to risk everything and turn Renie.

Of course he wanted Edmond to be happy. It was all he'd ever wanted for one of the few people who hadn't hurt him, hadn't abandoned him. But he honestly hadn't given any thought to weddings.

"I haven't had much time to think about things like that lately," he said.

Roux grinned at him. Her teeth were white and even. "Plenty of time now."

A shadow slunk through Ludovic's mind, dark and cold. Roux's easy manner, the way he'd started to feel oddly comfortable with her, had brightened everything around him, but the memories crept back, just like they always did.

He didn't want to think about weddings because then he'd think about the one wedding that he really didn't want to: his own.

He'd have to remember how that ended.

"If they did get married, would you go to the wedding?" Roux asked. She sounded as if she'd chosen her words carefully, but the mere suggestion that Ludovic wouldn't go to his best friend's wedding stung.

"Of course I would," he said, a snap in his voice.

"Even if it wasn't at Belle Morte?" Her gentle tone never changed, and Ludovic's anger deflated.

"Why wouldn't it be?"

"Why *would* it be? Belle Morte isn't a wedding venue. And you don't seem to be very comfortable outside the house."

"I could put aside whatever discomfort I felt for their sake," Ludovic said stiffly.

Roux swung her legs off the bed. "I should probably check in with the mansion, let them know how tonight went."

Ludovic sat on the edge of the bed and watched as Roux pulled the phone from her pocket. Her fingertips skated over the screen, too fast for him to follow.

"Huh," she muttered. "Seamus put Jason's number in here. Since when is Jason allowed a phone?"

Over a hundred years had passed since the invention of the phone, and Ludovic could still recall his sense of total wonder the first time he saw one. The thought that he could talk to a person just by picking up a receiver was both awe-inspiring and baffling—and his opinion of them hadn't changed much. Decades ago he'd learned how to use an old-fashioned landline, but these modern cell phones were a totally different beast.

Ludovic hated feeling stupid—another reason that Belle Morte was such a haven for him. Modern contraptions weren't welcome there, so he'd never had to face his fears.

"So that's the situation," Roux said, as Ludovic tuned back into her side of the conversation. She smiled as Renie said something, and it occurred to Ludovic that he'd never heard Roux mention friends other than Renie or Jason. He knew nothing of her life before Belle Morte.

One thing about this mission that he'd never expected was that he'd find himself wanting to know more about the ex–donor girl who'd volunteered to help him.

In the space of less than a day she'd made him comfortable in a way that he'd almost forgotten, made him question himself, and challenged the things he thought he knew.

When she was talking, she kept the ghosts of his past at bay.

Roux ended the call and tossed the phone onto the bed. "That's that sorted," she said. She caught him eyeing the phone. "Do you want me to show you how to use it?"

"No," he said. It would be better for them both if she did, but he didn't want to feel like an idiot in front of her.

"Okay, then." Once again, she didn't push, didn't take offense at his short tone. She stretched, arching her back, and her shirt rode up her stomach again.

Something very unexpected flickered in Ludovic's chest.

"I'm going to have a shower," Roux announced.

She crossed the room to the television set—some huge, flat monstrosity—and picked up the remote control. Ludovic didn't see which button she pressed. The television flickered to life and Roux tossed him the remote. He caught it one-handed.

"Pick whatever you want. I won't be long," she said, and disappeared into the bathroom.

Ludovic stared down at the remote.

He had no idea how to work it.

Roux

She leaned against the bathroom door, a strange knot forming in her head. What had just happened? Ludovic had always seemed closed off from people, and she'd expected him to treat her the same way, especially when he hadn't wanted her to come in the first place.

Instead they'd had an actual conversation, and for a few moments, Ludovic had become a different man than the stiff and awkward vampire she'd arrived at the hotel with a few hours earlier.

Then she'd offered to teach him how to use the phone and the shutters had slammed over his eyes. She didn't expect him to spill his guts to her, but she got the sense that he was actually *fighting* to hold something back. Every now and then she caught a glimpse of something shadowed in his eyes, the flicker of deep-rooted sadness that she couldn't begin to comprehend.

What was in his past?

Roux sighed and tried to push it from her mind. She wasn't here to make friends with the man.

She turned on the shower and gave the water a minute to heat up, then undressed and stepped into the porcelain tray. She tipped her head back, letting hot water stream over her face.

Canned laughter filtered through the door from the bedroom, and she hoped that Ludovic had found something he liked.

Usually she liked long, luxurious showers, but tonight she found herself trying to get through it as quickly as possible so she could get back to Ludovic—

Roux froze halfway through washing her hair. She'd always found Ludovic attractive, but finding someone attractive didn't mean acting on it. And she *couldn't* act on it. They were here in a professional capacity.

But she couldn't forget the sudden vulnerability in his eyes when Iain Johnson had called vampires a disease and the helpless expression he'd given her when she'd offered to teach him how to use a phone.

"You are not going there," she firmly told herself, and carried on washing her hair.

She and Ludovic were working together. That was it.

She'd seen Renie go through the ups and downs of falling for a vampire, and that was not a situation she wanted to get into. Especially not when any romance with Ludovic couldn't end the way Renie and Edmond's had.

Roux turned off the shower and stepped out of the tray. She'd brought her pajamas in with her earlier so she didn't have to change in front of Ludovic, and she dried off and dressed as quickly as she could. A quick rub with the towel made the ends of her hair stand up like an angry hedgehog, but she quite liked it that way.

When she went back into the bedroom Ludovic was sitting exactly where she'd left him, staring blankly at the TV, the remote still in his hand.

Oh, crap.

If Ludovic didn't know how to drive a modern car or use a modern phone, he sure as hell didn't know how to handle a modern TV. She'd tossed the remote at him and sashayed off for a shower without even thinking.

"Do you feel like watching a film?" she suggested.

He looked at her, and she caught another glimpse of the helplessness he must be feeling surrounded by so many things he didn't understand.

She wondered when he'd last seen a film. Maybe he'd *never* seen one.

Finally, he nodded.

"First things first," she said. "We need to get that makeup off you."

Ludovic blinked and raised a hand to his face, as if he'd forgotten he was wearing any. Emotions warred in his eyes, and when he spoke, his voice was quiet. "How?" he asked.

Roux fetched a packet of wet wipes from her bag. "Taking it off is a lot quicker and easier than putting it on."

Ludovic suspiciously eyed the wipes.

Roux pulled one out. "You use it like a cloth, all over your face, until there's no makeup left."

Ludovic said nothing, but continued to eye the wipes.

"Or I could do it for you," Roux suggested, grinning mischievously.

Ludovic promptly held out his hand.

At first he was uncertain, dabbing at his face with small, twitchy movements, but his confidence grew as he saw the makeup coming off. Before long, the disguise was gone, and the real Ludovic was staring back at her. The only thing that hadn't gone back to normal was his hair, still casually mussed.

Roux blinked at him. He was still gorgeous as a human, but seeing the vampire emerge from his human disguise was seeing that gorgeousness in crystal clear clarity.

Suddenly, sharing a bed with him tonight didn't seem quite so casual.

Swallowing, she approached the bed and patted his knee. "Shuffle up," she said.

When he didn't move, Roux climbed onto her side of the bed and settled into a comfy position, propping herself up with a pillow.

Still Ludovic didn't move, sitting straight-backed at the foot of the bed, staring at the TV. Rolling her eyes, Roux launched forward and snagged the back of his collar. He was much stronger than her but he didn't resist as she dragged him up the bed and maneuvered him into position beside her.

"Now, we can try to work out which sort of films you like, or you can trust me to choose," she said.

"You choose," Ludovic said.

Roux flipped through channels, trying to decide what he'd like— which wasn't easy when she knew almost nothing about him. She wanted to find something that he'd really enjoy. She wanted him to have fun.

"Wait," Ludovic said, staring at the screen.

The film that had caught his eye was a straight-to-TV vampire horror flick, complete with cheap effects, cheaper acting, and plastic fangs.

Ludovic's eyes narrowed as he read the blurb, then read it again.

Roux hadn't expected him to choose a vampire film. "There are plenty more like this," she said.

"No. I'd like to watch this one. Please."

"Whatever you want."

An hour and a half later, Roux sorely regretted the choice. The vampire was the villain of the piece, and when the film ended with the survivors brutally staking him through the heart, Roux winced.

"It wasn't quite the image that we project to the public, was it?" Ludovic said as the credits rolled up the screen.

It hadn't been, but now? With all the death and destruction that

Jemima and Etienne had caused, maybe films like this were about to get a lot more popular. Not that there was a chance in hell that she'd say that to Ludovic.

"It's just a film," she said. "It doesn't mean anything."

"Doesn't it?"

Roux switched off the TV. "Ludovic," she said. "Ten years ago the human race didn't know that vampires existed. We thought you were fictional, like werewolves and fairies, and fiction manifests in many forms. Some people saw vampires as the villains, as brutal, immortal monsters that needed to be wiped out. Some people saw them as tragic, romantic figures. Some people saw them as something in between. All types of vampires found a fan base in films and books."

"And you?" Ludovic said. His eyes burned with intensity. "How do you see us?"

"As people," she said, looking steadily back at him. "You have strengths and weaknesses; you've made mistakes, but that doesn't mean you can't learn from them. Some of you are cruel, some of you are kind, some of you are selfish, and some of you are noble. Vampires, as a race, are not one thing, any more than humans are."

"After what Jemima and Etienne have done, I fear the world may be turning more toward the brutal monster viewpoint."

Ludovic wasn't looking at her anymore; his eyes were downcast and there was defeat in the slump of his shoulders. She should have just turned the stupid film off.

Putting a finger under Ludovic's chin, Roux firmly lifted his head so he was looking at her. She couldn't have moved one inch of him if he didn't want her to, but again, he didn't resist.

"Even if the whole world saw you that way, I won't," Roux said.

Something dark shifted in Ludovic's eyes. "Maybe you should. There's a lot about me that you don't know."

Roux moved closer, almost challenging him. "I know that I'll never see you as a monster."

They stared at each other for a long, tense moment.

Ludovic blinked first. "You may be the only one."

"Nah, Jason will never stop loving vampires," Roux said, trying to lighten the mood.

Ludovic leaned back a little. "Jason means a lot to you, doesn't he?"

"Of course he does." Together with Renie, Jason and Roux had clicked in a way that made it hard for her to imagine her life before them both.

"And he doesn't mind that you're here with me, like this?" Ludovic gestured to the small space between them.

Roux frowned. "Why would he—oh!" Realization clicked into place, and she couldn't stop a snort of laughter. "You think Jason and I are a *couple*?"

Ludovic pulled away from her, his expression shuttering. "You spend a lot of time together, and you shared a room with him in both Belle Morte and Fiaigh. You'll forgive me for thinking that you shared a bed too."

"Oh, we did, just not in *that* way," Roux assured him. "Jason's gay."

"I see."

A smile spread across Roux's face. "Did you think he'd have been jealous?"

"Perhaps."

"Well, rest assured that no one will care if I share a bed with you."

Except Ludovic himself, who stiffened at the reminder. Despite not enjoying the film, he'd managed to relax, but now he was on edge again, and she couldn't put her finger on exactly why.

When she looked at Ludovic, one word sprang to mind—*guarded*. There were walls around him, and he probably didn't allow many people besides Edmond to see over them.

But earlier, when they'd been talking, Roux felt that she'd got a glimpse over those walls, at the real man hiding behind them.

She was intrigued by what she'd seen.

She wanted to see more.

Her eyes flickered over him, traveling along the line of his jaw, now free of the false stubble, down his throat to the straight, strong width of his shoulders. His muscled frame took up most of the bed, even when he was clearly trying to keep some distance between them.

Roux didn't just want to get another look over Ludovic's walls. She wanted to get a look under his clothes too. Attraction surged in her blood, and she shifted position, trying to suppress it.

This isn't what we're here for, this isn't what we're here for, she mentally chanted.

"Do you, um . . . do you need to feed?" she asked.

Ludovic's eyes briefly moved to Roux's throat, exposed without her long wig, then he shook his head.

"Not tonight," he mumbled.

Roux felt a small stab of disappointment.

She'd come to Belle Morte because she loved vampires, and just remembering the sweet bliss of a vampire's bite made her toes curl, but she couldn't help wondering if it would feel even better coming from a vampire she was actually attracted to.

She told herself that it wasn't important, but she couldn't shake the thoughts from her head, and she couldn't unsee the glimpses of a more vulnerable Ludovic.

She couldn't ignore the urge to get another look over his walls.

CHAPTER EIGHT

Ludovic

When Roux went to brush her teeth in the bathroom, he considered taking a pillow and sleeping on the floor. But that felt like running away.

Ludovic de Vauban had run from many things in his life, but platonically sharing a bed with the most intriguing girl he'd met in a long time could not be a challenge he was too afraid to face.

He climbed off the bed and rummaged through his bag.

Their new clothes were cheap, but the loose-fitting trousers and T-shirt that Roux wore for bed looked surprisingly good on her, the fabric clinging to the lean angles of her body, the midnight blue color complementing her skin.

Ludovic went very still.

Why on earth was he thinking about Roux's pajamas? It didn't matter what she wore, and it didn't matter how good they looked.

He changed quickly, tugging on gray flannel trousers and a plain white shirt, then he lifted the lid of the freezer box and checked on the blood. Neat piles of red bags stared back at him, and his fangs reacted, pushing out of his gums. But he wouldn't feed tonight. The supply was limited, and drinking from Roux suddenly didn't seem like an option.

He returned to the bed as Roux came out of the bathroom. She paused, toothbrush in hand, staring at him. Maybe she'd expected him to retreat to the floor too.

Tossing her toothbrush back into her bag, Roux walked around the bed and pulled the covers back from her side.

"Is it okay if I turn out the light?" she asked, reaching for the switch just above her head.

Ludovic nodded.

Roux wriggled under the covers, stretching out her long legs, and switched the light off, plunging the room into darkness.

Ludovic's vampire vision immediately adjusted, cutting through the shadows and focusing on the lean, feminine shape lying beside him.

Something had sparked in his chest when Roux had told him she and Jason weren't a couple, and he'd only just realized what it was: relief. He was *relieved* that the handsome blond-haired boy wasn't Roux's lover, and that startled him almost more than anything else had that day.

"Good night, Ludovic," Roux mumbled.

"Good night, Roux," he whispered, but the rhythm of her breathing told him that she was already asleep.

For a few minutes Ludovic sat there, listening.

Cars trundled past on the road outside, but their headlights couldn't penetrate the thick curtains. In the next room, he heard the muted sounds of people having sex. Someone laughed on the street.

It had been a very long time since Ludovic had shared a bed with anyone, but now that he was here, it wasn't as intimidating as he'd expected. Moving as carefully as possible, Ludovic slid under the covers. He didn't want to wake Roux up.

Roux

She cracked open an eye. Her whole body felt sluggish, like it was draped in cement, and when her eyes adjusted enough to read her watch she stifled a groan. Six o'clock.

Nope.

Roux shut her eyes, rolled over, and tried to go back to sleep. When that didn't work, she rolled over again, trying to find a cool spot on the pillow, but it was no good. She was wide awake now.

She stifled a groan of frustration.

Ludovic was old enough to have built up a resistance to the sun, but it was dangerous for any vampire to be out for too long, so most of their work still needed to be done by night. Roux had no idea what to do with the long day ahead of them.

She rolled over once more. Something soft and warm curled in her stomach.

Ludovic lay with his back to her, his blond hair spread across the pillow like spun gold. He didn't move but she could tell he was awake—he held himself with just a little too much tension.

Before this mission, Roux had only ever seen him dressed impeccably, like he was always ready for a photo shoot. It made him look gorgeous, like most vampires, but also, on some level, unapproachable. Not that that had stopped *her* from approaching him.

When he'd donned his human disguise yesterday—jeans and a plain cotton shirt—he'd suddenly become more real to her, an actual man rather than a fantasy. That had continued when they'd got ready for bed. Ludovic's pajamas were as simple as his daytime disguise, but the white tee strained around his biceps and pulled tight across his chest, and the fact that he was wearing that tight T-shirt *and* lying next to her in bed made him a lethal combination of real man and blissful fantasy. Up until now, Roux hadn't realized that such a combination existed.

She pulled her gaze away.

She could lie here and think deliciously naughty things about the vampire lying next to her, or she could track down some coffee.

Coffee won.

As Roux dragged herself out of bed, rubbing her sleep-gritty eyes, Ludovic turned over. His gaze was sharp and alert, almost as if he hadn't been asleep at all.

"Where are you going?" he said, and she thought she detected a faint note of something in his voice—not panic, not suspicion, but something in between.

"Just to get some coffee."

Roux grabbed her clothes and disappeared into the bathroom. When she emerged, Ludovic was sitting up, the covers bunched around his waist. Roux stopped, and stared. She couldn't help it.

Why did this suddenly feel so intimate?

"Aren't you forgetting something?" Ludovic asked, looking pointedly at Roux's hair.

Self-consciously she touched it. She hadn't bothered to look in the mirror, and she probably had some serious bedhead going on.

Then Ludovic looked past her to where her wig was still draped over the chair, and understanding rushed in. She didn't need a disguise as long as she was in this room, but the second she stepped outside it was imperative that no one recognize her.

It wasn't like her to forget something as important as that; she blamed Ludovic and his tight T-shirt and his muscles.

She put the wig on. "Better?" she asked, striking a pose.

Ludovic stared at her, his face unreadable. The man she'd talked with yesterday was gone and the awkward vampire was back. Roux swallowed a sigh.

"I won't be long," she said.

The city was bathed in the sharp, bright light of an English winter morning. Thin films of ice had formed on the puddles, and Roux's breath plumed white on the frigid air.

She shivered and pulled up her collar.

None of the cafés or coffee shops were open yet, but it didn't take her long to spot the familiar golden arches of McDonald's, rising like a beacon among the historic architecture.

The staff were ridiculously perky considering the god-awful hour, and Roux was struck by the urge to get a bag of greasy, salty fries. Food like that was banned in Belle Morte, and it felt like a lifetime since she'd eaten good old-fashioned junk. But it was too early for fries, even for the junk-food deprived. Roux stuck with her coffee.

The icy February air hit her like a slap as she stepped outside, and she caught her breath. It felt bizarre to be back in the real world like this, almost as if the last few weeks had never happened.

No one on the street recognized her, or even gave her a second glance, but that would change if she took off her wig. Almost all donors enjoyed some level of minor fame, and Roux had thought she wanted that—it was one of the reasons she'd gone to Belle Morte in the first place.

Now she was no longer sure she did, but it was too late to undo it.

It had been years since Roux had cast off her ugly duckling self, but her old anxieties were still there, lurking beneath her skin, wrapped around her bones, and now they rushed to the surface, making her heart race and her lungs empty.

Suddenly she felt very alone out here. She wanted to hear a voice she cared about, but she couldn't call her parents—they'd only beg her to come home. Renie and Edmond would be asleep, safe and sound from the sun.

That left only one person.

Jason answered on the fourth ring.

"Good morning, gorgeous," he said, his voice hoarse with sleep.

Roux winced. "Shit, did I wake you?" She'd forgotten how early it was.

"I'll always wake up for you."

The sound of his voice brought a smile to her lips. How had she gone years without someone like him at her side? How had she coped all that time without someone to talk to, someone to turn to?

"Since when do you have a phone?" she said.

She couldn't see him but she could imagine the wicked grin spreading across his face.

"Since I begged Seamus to get me one. Did you really think I'd let you out into the big bad world without a line of contact?"

"Does Ysanne know?"

"Um . . . pass. Renie knows, but no one mentioned Ysanne."

That meant she probably didn't know. "Jason Grant, you shameless rebel," Roux said.

"Guilty," he said, chuckling.

The sound of his laughter was as warm as a hug.

"Seriously, though," said Jason, sobering. "Are you okay?"

"I think so. I just needed to hear a friendly voice."

"How's it going?" he said.

Roux told him what they'd learned yesterday, and about watching a film with Ludovic, and when she got to the part where they'd shared a bed, Jason made a noise of pure excitement.

"Please tell me he sleeps naked," he said.

"Sorry to disappoint, but he kept his clothes on."

"Bummer."

"He thought we were a couple," she told Jason.

"You and me? That's cute."

"I thought so too. I'm not sure he grasped the idea of guys and girls sharing beds platonically."

"Ha! I bet he gets it now."

"After a night with me, sure."

Roux heard the faint sound of the bed creaking as Jason shifted position.

"So you're following up a lead on Stephen and Delia tonight?" he said.

"It's not much of a lead, but yeah."

"It could be worse. What if the Five were leaving a trail of bodies across the city? It would make it easier to find them, but it'd be a fucking depressing lead," Jason said.

Roux swallowed a gulp of coffee, but it felt like ice in her stomach. Something was shifting in her head, a tendril of fear that had been planted last night and was now taking root.

"What if they *had* left a trail of bodies, though? Or at least a trail of disappearances?" she said.

"What are you talking about?"

"According to Stephen Johnson's brother, kids have been going missing throughout Winchester. He thinks the Five have something to do with it."

"Okay," said Jason cautiously. "Do you think he's right?"

"I don't know. On the one hand, this guy really hates vampires, so he could be jumping to pin anything on them. On the other hand, kids *are* going missing. Maybe it's coincidence that it's happening at the same time but"—Roux's stomach twisted—"I don't think I believe in that kind of coincidence."

"Have you asked Walsh?"

"He insisted it wasn't connected. But what if he's wrong?"

"Why would the Five go after kids?"

"Maybe they're easier to hunt down and feed from?" Roux said, and the words tasted bitter in her mouth.

"But if the kids are missing, it suggests one or more of the Five have killed them and hidden their bodies, and I don't get why they'd do that. Vampires only need to take about a vial of blood a day from a donor—that doesn't kill anyone."

"How much control do new vampires have—both during and after the turn?" Roux said. "Remember when Renie turned? It took three days, and we were banned from seeing her."

"I thought that was just because donors aren't allowed in the north wing," Jason said.

"Okay, but remember how much Renie struggled with drinking blood at first? How did that turn out for her?"

A pause.

"She lost control and attacked Dexter," Jason said, his voice heavy.

Once again, Ludovic had been there to keep anyone from getting hurt, and Roux swallowed again, thinking of the desolate look in his eyes last night, after Iain had called vampires a disease. Despite Ludovic's warning that there was a lot about him she didn't know, Roux couldn't believe he was the monster that Iain thought all vampires were.

Did Ludovic even realize how many times he'd saved either Roux or the people she cared about?

Her stomach fluttered, and she tried to ignore it.

"Etienne fed his vampires on animal blood while they were hidden at Bushfield, and that's not as good for them as human blood. Some of those vampires then lost control once they were unleashed on Belle Morte and had access to fresh human blood, so what if the same thing happened again once the Five fled the mansion? Do we know that none of them were injured?"

"No," Jason admitted.

Another pause. Roux didn't know what to say. Her head was a mess.

"Let's think about this logically," Jason said. "We know that Stephen and Delia are still a couple and are planning on leaving Winchester together, yes?"

"Yeah."

"Has anyone given you any indication that they're with the rest of the Five?"

"No."

"So either they split from the others once they fled or the whole group separated and are now scattered across the city."

"Okay."

"In either situation, the Five only escaped a week ago. Did these kids go missing in that time frame?"

Roux frowned. "I don't know. Iain didn't say."

"Then do some research and see if you can find out how many kids he's talking about and when they went missing. Maybe Walsh is right and this isn't connected at all."

"Yeah, but like I said, I don't think I believe in coincidences like that."

"And I don't think you should panic until you know more."

"But what happens if it is connected?" she asked.

"We'll cross that bridge when we come to it."

Roux let out a long breath. Jason was probably right.

She and Ludovic were here to clear up the mess that Etienne and Jemima had created, and if it turned out that there was any link between the Five and these missing kids, then they'd do what they could to clear that up too.

Somehow.

"Are you still there?" Jason asked.

"Yeah, just thinking."

"I thought I could hear the cogs in your brain turning. They sound a bit rusty."

"Screw you," said Roux, laughing.

"Thanks for the offer, but you're not my type."

Roux could hear the grin in his voice, and a rush of affection swept through her. Jason wasn't just a link to the mansion and her new life there; he was a warm, solid reminder that, no matter what happened, she'd never go back to being friendless and alone.

"I should go," she said, thinking of Ludovic. He might panic if she stayed out too long.

"You know you can call whenever you need me?"

"I know. Thank you."

"Anytime."

Roux ended the call and slipped her phone back into her pocket. She drained the last of her coffee and tossed the paper cup into a nearby trash can, and a crumpled newspaper inside caught her eye. She took a corner and tugged, straightening the paper out.

VAMPIRE MENACE the headline declared, splashed across the paper above a photo of a stern, handsome face with dark coiffed hair, a square jawline, and broad shoulders clad in a tailored navy suit.

Roux vaguely recognized him—Karl Kendrick, a low-tier politician who'd always been critical of vampires and how they fit into human society, and in this front-page article that criticism had blossomed into outright hostility.

Alongside his article was a column about *Bite Me*, one of the UK's biggest vampire magazines, which had allegedly suspended production for the foreseeable future, putting over a hundred jobs at risk.

Roux's heart sank.

Last night she'd reassured Ludovic that humans wouldn't completely turn on vampires, but what if she'd been wrong? She worried about what would happen if Ysanne and Caoimhe decided to seal up the houses again, but if the donor system collapsed, could the vampires even *keep* their houses?

Roux crumpled the paper and shoved it deeper into the trash.

She wanted to do everything she could to help her vampire friends, and any other innocent vampires affected by this, but she couldn't fight every battle.

She had a job to do, and that had to come first.

CHAPTER NINE

Roux

Ludovic was still in bed when Roux got back, and she was hit again by the domesticity of it. She was the one who'd insisted that sharing a bed was no big deal, so why did it now feel so couple-y?

Trying to ignore the hot vampire watching her, Roux retrieved the handful of crumpled papers that Iain had thrown at her yesterday and slumped into the chair.

"What are you doing?" Ludovic asked, as Roux straightened the papers.

"I can't stop thinking about these kids. I need to know if there's even a chance that Iain's right," Roux said.

Ludovic stiffened and sat up, his eyes guarded. "How do we find out if he is?"

"I'll start by looking into when the kids disappeared."

Ludovic pushed back the covers and climbed out of bed. His casual clothes and slightly mussed hair made him look more human than normal, but there was nothing human in the way he moved. He prowled toward Roux's chair and stood beside her, tilting his head to read the papers.

"How do you do that?" he asked.

Roux waggled her phone at him. "Through the power of Google."

She got a tiny frown in response.

Vampires were so adorable when they were confused.

"Okay, let's start with Curtis Bell," she said, focusing on the first printout.

She entered his name into the search engine and waited for the screen to load. Ludovic still stood beside her, and he wasn't breathing down her neck because vampires *didn't* breathe, but Roux was acutely aware of him in a way she'd never been before.

"That's him, isn't it?" Ludovic asked, bending so that he could point at the screen.

Did he even notice how close he was to her?

"Yeah," she said, and clicked on the link in question. She scanned the article, and slumped in her seat. "I don't know whether to feel relieved or not. Apparently, Curtis Bell ran away from home nine months ago, and though several sightings of him have been reported to the police, no one's actually managed to find him. This can't be connected to the Five, then, can it? Not nine months ago."

"I suppose there is some measure of relief in that," Ludovic said.

"But it's sad, too, because this poor kid's still out there somewhere. He's only fifteen."

Ludovic shifted beside her, but he said nothing.

"I'll still check the others, to be sure," Roux said.

She entered the next name into the bar, but this time, as the results filled the screen, her heart plunged.

"Preston Howard was reported missing eight days ago, and his disappearance is being treated as suspicious," she said. "He's fifteen too."

"The Five hadn't escaped then," Ludovic said.

"But what if one of them did it *before* they escaped? Couldn't they have sneaked out of Bushfield one night? Etienne wasn't there all the time."

"Search for another name," Ludovic said, his voice unreadable.

Roux did.

"Lewis Oakley vanished from his back garden twelve days ago. Another fifteen-year-old."

Ludovic was silent, but the atmosphere in the room felt like it was changing somehow, like a chill was sweeping in. Roux's skin prickled.

"Lindsey Miller, also fifteen, disappeared while she was walking home from school five days ago. Aisha Taylor disappeared on the way back from a friend's house almost two weeks ago. She was younger, only fourteen," Roux said. "Molly Bolan, another fourteen-year-old, has been missing for two and a half weeks." Roux scrunched up her forehead. "Why do I know that name?"

"I have no idea. What about him?" Ludovic said, pointing to the final printout clutched in Roux's hand.

She searched the name. "Leonard Mitchell, another reported runaway almost six months ago." She swallowed the sudden knot in her throat. "His family are apparently still hoping he'll come home in time for his fourteenth birthday next month."

Roux let the phone drop into her lap, her mind churning. "So Iain was wrong to pin all these disappearances on vampires, but five kids *have* vanished under suspicious circumstances recently, and Iain isn't necessarily wrong to assume that one of the Five is responsible."

"He's not necessarily right either," Ludovic cautioned her.

Roux clenched her fist, crushing the papers even more. "But what if he is? How the hell do we fix this?"

Ludovic was silent again.

"And why is that name, Molly Bolan, so familiar?"

"Do you recognize the girl?" Ludovic asked.

Roux glanced at the printout. Molly stared back, her face slightly sullen and surrounded by a bushy mass of blond hair.

"Nope. I know the name, but I'm sure I've never seen her before," she said. "I'll search her name again." She scrolled down the results. "Oh no," she muttered.

"What is it?" Ludovic asked, bending lower again.

"I remember this now. Molly is Jessica Bolan's sister."

There wasn't a flicker of recognition in Ludovic's eyes, but Roux didn't expect there to be. Cooped up in Belle Morte, he didn't have a clue what was happening on the human news.

"Jessica Bolan was kidnapped five years ago, when she was seven. I was only thirteen at the time so I didn't pay much attention to it, but it was a major news story for months. She was eventually found locked in a bedroom in an abandoned house."

"Alive?" Ludovic asked, and the room seemed to get even chillier.

Roux tipped back her head to look up at him.

Ludovic had braced one hand on the back of the chair, and his jaw was tight, his blue eyes dark with clashing emotions. He looked like he had on the night that Belle Morte was first invaded—like he was ready to rip someone apart.

"She was dehydrated and underfed, but she didn't appear to have been hurt," Roux said.

"Did they catch whoever did it?" Ludovic's voice had dropped lower, almost a growl.

"No."

Ludovic's eyes darkened even more.

"You're looking a little scary there," Roux said. "You okay?"

"I don't like people who hurt children," Ludovic said, a flash of red creeping into his eyes.

Roux touched his hand and he tensed even more, his eyes flitting down to her.

"Is there any chance that Jessica's kidnapping is connected to Molly's?" he asked.

"How could it be?"

"You said they never caught the person who did it."

"Yeah, but that was five years ago. What are the chances of someone coming back after all this time to attack the same family?"

"What are the chances of two different kidnappers targeting the same family?" Ludovic said.

Roux bit her lip. "I don't know. Maybe I should call Walsh."

"Do you think he'll listen?"

"Probably not, but it's worth a try."

Walsh didn't even answer the phone, and after three attempts, Roux gave up.

"This sucks," she grumbled, tossing the phone onto the bed.

She'd been pacing the floor while she'd tried to get a hold of Walsh, but Ludovic hadn't moved from his position by the chair. At least the red had faded from his eyes. Now he watched her, his head tilted, his face an expressionless mask again.

"May I ask you something?" he said.

"Go ahead."

"Why do you care so much about people you've never met?"

Roux cocked her own head, mirroring Ludovic. "That's a weird question."

"I don't mean that you shouldn't, but a lot of people aren't concerned with much beyond themselves and their own problems. You seem to care about everyone."

"Do you think that's so unusual?"

He considered it. "I'm not sure."

That was telling. Roux didn't like to think that caring for other people—whether they were people she knew and loved or people she'd never met—was unusual. She wanted to think there was always more good than bad in the world, but, judging by the bleak look in Ludovic's eyes, he didn't feel the same way.

What had he been through that made him see the world in such a harsh light?

What had happened to make him actually surprised to find someone who gave a shit about strangers?

"I care because we're people. We *should* care about each other—both humans and vampires. As far as I'm concerned it's as simple as that," she said.

Ludovic slowly nodded, his eyes thoughtful.

He looked at the printouts that Roux had left on the chair. "Perhaps we should also consider the possibility that the mystery four are responsible for this in some way," Ludovic said.

Roux clicked her fingers. "Oh, that's a good point."

She didn't want to admit it, but she'd almost forgotten about them since leaving Belle Morte.

"If they are, did Etienne know anything about these missing kids?" Roux said, pouncing on new theories. She started to pace again, her wig whipping around her shoulders. "What would Etienne want with a bunch of kids?"

"If he did, Susan Harcourt didn't know anything about it, or she'd have told Ysanne."

Another good point. Susan Harcourt, one of Belle Morte's longest-serving security guards, had defected to Etienne's side after he'd promised her immortality. She was the one who'd helped him procure people to turn, and once Etienne and Jemima's power coup had failed, she'd confessed everything.

"Clearly she didn't know anything about those missing four vampires either. Etienne didn't trust her as much as she thought he did," Ludovic said.

Roux rubbed her arms. The Five were loose threads that Etienne had left dangling, and she'd hoped that once she and Ludovic cut those threads, the horror that Etienne had wrought would finally be laid to rest. But maybe there were more threads than they'd realized.

"Is there any chance that he wasn't planning on doing anything with them?" she asked, clinging to a shred of hope.

"He wouldn't have wasted his time turning them if he didn't intend to use them," Ludovic said.

Roux's hope deflated.

"Maybe they refused to fight for him," she suggested.

"Do you think that would have stopped him?"

Roux sighed. "No."

"Etienne was prepared to sacrifice anyone to achieve his vision. If those four had refused to fight, he'd have found a way to make them," Ludovic said.

"Yeah, I know," Roux mumbled, playing with the ends of her wig. "Maybe we need to focus on one problem at a time."

A cold gleam crept into Ludovic's eyes. "Or maybe not. What if Stephen and Delia know something about this?"

"The missing kids or the mystery vampires?"

"Both."

Roux shrugged. "I can't see why they'd know about the mystery four—not if Susan herself didn't. And what would *they* want with a bunch of kids?"

"I don't know yet, but they may be our only link to anything. It would be foolish to return them to Belle Morte without questioning them first," Ludovic said.

Roux nodded, trying to ignore the unpleasant twisting in her stomach. There was still a chance that none of this was connected, and it was pure coincidence that it was all happening at the same time, but gut instinct told her that everything was tangled up in the mess that Jemima and Etienne had created.

She folded the printouts and slid them into her bag. Things were confusing and frustrating right now, but she had to believe it wasn't more than they could handle.

Than *she* could handle.

As she straightened, she realized Ludovic was looking at her—or, more specifically, at her neck.

"Would you like to feed?" she said. Her throat felt suddenly dry and she licked her lips a couple of times. Ludovic was the one who needed blood, so why did she feel like *she'd* gone days without something?

Ludovic nodded, not taking his eyes off her neck.

Roux perched on the bed, her heart drumming against her ribs. The sudden attack of nerves took her by surprise. When she'd first arrived at Belle Morte, it had briefly occurred to her that being bitten might hurt—vampire fangs were long and sharp, after all—but her first bite had put those fears to rest.

She'd fed vampires plenty of times since then, but this was different. This was Ludovic.

That *shouldn't* make a difference, but it did.

Ludovic slid onto the bed next to her, as fluid as a cat. Roux had forgotten about her long wig and she almost jumped when Ludovic swept the hair out of the way, exposing her neck. He placed two fingers under her jaw and gently tilted her head to one side. Her throat felt dry as cotton and her blood thundered in her veins.

Ludovic leaned in, the solidity of his body crowding her, and her eyelids fluttered shut, anticipation twisting and coiling, making her feel as strung tight as a piano wire.

His teeth grazed her neck, the sharp points gentle enough that all she felt was a little shiver of pleasure.

Ludovic bit down.

Roux's whole body jolted, a tiny gasp escaping her lips. For a split second she felt the sting of his fangs, and then a wave of pleasure washed over her, making everything seem fuzzy around the edges. She felt herself sagging on the bed, felt her shoulder hit the hardness of Ludovic's chest. He laid one hand on her back, holding her in place while he drank.

Every pull of his mouth was like sweet fire skittering to her nerve endings, making her squirm. A moan built in her throat but she forced it down. Deep inside her a different ache sparked to life, one that wouldn't be satisfied with a mere bite. She curled her fingers into the bedcovers, trying to remind herself that this was part of the job.

Ludovic pulled back from her neck, and despite herself Roux whimpered. He ran his tongue over the puncture marks, healing them, and even that was enough to make her press her legs tightly together, trying to suppress another ripple of pleasure.

"Are you all right?" Ludovic said. He was still so close to her, their bodies pressed together, his mouth hovering over her neck.

Roux managed a nod.

Ludovic slid off the bed, and Roux, still boneless and blissed out after his bite, almost toppled backward. She quickly righted herself, then swept her wig back into place, covering the place that Ludovic had bitten. The marks were gone, but it didn't stop her from running her fingertips over the spot that his fangs had sunk in, the spot that still sweetly tingled from the imprint of his mouth.

"I'm going to have a shower," Ludovic mumbled.

When Roux glanced at him, his eyes were fixed on the floor, as if he was trying not to look at her.

Mortification flooded her cheeks. He must have heard her whimper when he withdrew his fangs, and maybe she'd made other noises while he was drinking. Or maybe he could sense her reaction on a more primal level.

"I didn't think vampires needed to shower," she said, for the sake of something to say.

His mouth tipped up at the corners. "Generally speaking we don't, but we still enjoy it."

Roux swallowed. She still felt tingly all over, and thinking about Ludovic in the shower, hot water streaming over his naked body, *really* didn't help.

"Okay . . . have fun," she said, and cringed.

Have fun? Really?

Ludovic disappeared into the bathroom, and Roux silently groaned, burying her head in her hands.

"Think professional thoughts," she sternly told herself.

Easier said than done.

Stephen and Delia couldn't flee the city during the day, which meant Roux and Ludovic had to wait until the sun went down before they could meet up with Walsh and investigate pubs close to the station.

What to do for the rest of the day?

There was no point in Roux pretending that she wasn't really, *really* attracted to the blond vampire, and his incredible bite had just pushed her feelings from cute-guy-I-can-resist into ridiculously-hot-guy-I-want-to-strip-naked-and-ravish.

But acting on that attraction was not an option.

All Roux could do was stuff those feelings deep down and try to handle Ludovic's next bite with a little more stoicism—even though just thinking about it sent shivers through her.

She pointed at her reflection in the TV screen. "You can do this, Roux Hayes. Resist the sexy vampire."

Daytime TV sucked: old soap operas, endless shows about antiques or property development, and repeats of ancient game shows in which everyone had '80s perms and shoulder pads.

The only upside was Ludovic.

Some of the shows they watched were decades old, but he'd never seen any of them and his curiosity was infectious. Roux explained everything to him, flipping between different channels so that he always had something new to look at, and though she wasn't convinced he was truly *enjoying* any of them, he was fascinated by the experience.

And while they sat on the bed together, alternating between channel-hopping and researching the people and places they had to investigate, Ludovic forgot to be stiff or distant. Maybe he wasn't fully *relaxed* yet, but he was as close to it as Roux had seen him.

For a few hours Roux could almost forget that Ludovic was a vampire and she was a human and they were here on a serious mission. She could almost imagine that they were just a guy and a girl, getting to know each other and enjoying each other's company.

It was over too soon.

Midafternoon, Walsh texted to tell her that they were starting their search at the Golden Oak, a pub barely five minutes' walk from the train station, and as the sun started to set, Roux reluctantly tore herself away from the vampire stretched out on the bed next to her.

"Are you ready to put on your human face?" she asked.

It had been easy to transform him yesterday—already it seemed much longer ago than that—but it felt different today. She was so much more aware of Ludovic—as a man rather than just a vampire.

She applied his foundation with crisp, even strokes of the brush, bringing a more human tint to his pale skin, and carefully penciled on the stubble, trying to ignore how close it brought her to his lips.

When she moved farther up his face, applying shade here and there to subtly alter the shape, she found herself looking into his eyes.

Roux didn't really have a type when it came to men, but she did like blue eyes, and now that she was looking into Ludovic's, she noticed details she hadn't before: the brightness of his irises, the way they were streaked with light and dark shades of blue, and ringed with an even darker blue. They were like the sea on a summer's day, the most beautiful eyes she'd ever seen.

Abruptly she pulled back. Maybe she should teach Ludovic how to apply his own makeup. It would save the intimacy of having to get so close to him, even though there was nothing remotely sexual about what she was doing. Then again, Ludovic already had so much to learn about the world, and trying to master makeup techniques overnight was a burden he didn't need.

"I just need to do your hair," Roux mumbled.

That should have been less intimate since she wasn't right in front of his face, but as she teased his hair into the tousled style from the day before, all she could think was how soft it felt and how she wanted to see it spread out on the pillow while she—

Stop it, Roux.

Hastily, she finished up. "That's everything, I guess," she said. "We're meeting Walsh at the pub, so we'd better get going."

"You're sure you know where it is?" Ludovic asked, adjusting his knitted beanie.

Roux waggled the phone at him. "I looked it up earlier."

Even though she'd been using the phone in front of him all day, she got a blank look in return.

"Just trust me," she said.

Ludovic nodded, and it sent a flush of warmth through Roux that she tried very hard to ignore.

The Golden Oak was a traditional-looking pub: redbrick walls and a moss-patched roof interrupted here and there by chimneys and gabled windows. A dark board, bearing the pub's name and a tree painted gold, dangled from a cast-iron bar that projected out from the wall, just above the door.

A couple of people stood outside, huddled over their cigarettes.

Roux parked the car as close as she could. She couldn't imagine they'd need to make a quick getaway from this place, but she wanted to err on the side of caution.

"This is weird," she said, killing the engine and peering at the pub through the windshield.

"What is?" Ludovic said.

"You, me, going to a pub." Roux gestured to the small space between them. "It almost feels like a date."

For a moment she wondered if Ludovic even really knew what that meant, or if he was still entrenched in the style of courting that had been around when he was alive. But then he stiffened slightly and she realized he knew exactly what she meant.

"Obviously it's not," she hurried on. "But it's still weird."

Weird didn't begin to cover it. Roux had been attracted to all six feet of Ludovic's blond gorgeousness from the moment she'd arrived at Belle Morte, but she'd never imagined that she'd go on anything even resembling a date with him. It didn't matter that it wasn't real.

Ludovic didn't respond; Roux had probably made him feel awkward again. Usually she had an easy confidence around guys, but Ludovic wasn't just any guy. He made her feel hesitant, unsure of herself, but not in any way that she'd felt before.

In her younger years, when she'd been the ugly duckling, Roux had been permanently unsure of herself. Kids at school had made it their daily mission to tear her down, to rip apart any shred of self-worth she might have, and she hadn't dared tell anyone about her crushes because that was one more thing she'd be mocked for. She'd rather have died than ask a boy out.

But when she finally reinvented herself, she'd built her confidence into a shield that no one could shatter. Or so she'd thought.

Ludovic didn't make her feel like that lonely, bullied kid anymore, but he also didn't make her feel like her usual, bold self. It wasn't his fault, but Roux didn't quite know how to act around him.

"Is this what you'd normally do on a date?" Ludovic asked.

"Me personally or people in general?" she asked.

He looked at her with those blue, blue eyes. "You."

"I guess it depends who I was going on a date with. I've been to pubs with guys, yeah, but it's not necessarily something I'd do every single time."

"Do you go on a lot of dates?" There was a hint of gruffness in Ludovic's voice.

"A few, yes." Roux couldn't help a smile. "In fact, I've gone on more in the last couple of years than the whole rest of my life."

"Why?"

Roux hesitated; she hadn't meant to say that last part. She cleared her throat and squared her shoulders. The past was the past, and it would not bring her down.

"I wasn't a popular kid, and I definitely wasn't an attractive one, so no one wanted to date me. Things changed when I turned sixteen, and suddenly lots of people *did* want to." She winked at Ludovic. "I probably said yes more than I needed to, but I had a lot of catching up to do."

There was a strange look on Ludovic's face, and Roux didn't know what to make of it. Was it disapproval? Curiosity?

"I'm guessing vampires don't go on a lot of dates," Roux said.

He shook his head.

"What about before the donor system?" Roux asked.

Nothing.

Ludovic wasn't even looking at her anymore; his walls were going back up. If Roux wanted to see over them again, she needed to tread softly.

She climbed out, and Ludovic silently followed her.

Walsh was waiting outside, smoking, and maybe it was Roux's imagination, but she thought his expression darkened as they approached.

"You took your time," he said.

Roux rolled her eyes. "Well, we're here now."

"Yeah." Walsh didn't sound happy about it.

"Problem?" Roux asked.

Walsh sucked hard on his cigarette. "You have no idea how completely we've been going against normal police procedure, do you?"

"No, but I thought that the normal rules didn't apply because no one's ever dealt with a situation like this."

"Maybe I'm not comfortable with completely tossing the rule book out the window. If we can do that for vampires, then what's to stop us from doing it in other circumstances?"

"Ideally, we'll never have another circumstance like this," Roux said.

"If the rules are bent once, they can be bent again, and I don't like that. It could open some doors we really want to keep closed."

"Are you saying you don't want to work with us anymore?" Ludovic said.

"Nope, just thinking about all the ways that this sets a bad precedent." Walsh flicked his cigarette into a nearby metal bucket. He missed, and the embers flared on the ground before winking out. "You two go in first. It'll look less obvious if we don't all sit together."

"You okay with that?" Roux said, glancing at Ludovic.

He nodded.

Together, they walked into the pub.

CHAPTER TEN

Ludovic

He understood the basic concept of modern dating, though it wasn't something he'd ever practiced, and he was genuinely surprised by Roux's admission that, up until recently, she'd struggled to get dates.

She might not be his type, but anyone with eyes could see how beautiful she was.

But more importantly, she was kind and compassionate and generous, and Ludovic couldn't believe that had blossomed only when her looks did. She knew when to push and when not to. She saw light when he saw darkness, and sometimes that meant he could see the light too.

Maybe she hadn't always been as physically beautiful as she was now, but Ludovic still reckoned that the human boys who'd overlooked her all those years had seriously missed out.

Abruptly, he caught himself. Missed out? That train of thought veered far too close to liking Roux in more than a professional capacity, and he did *not* think of her like that.

Sidling through the smokers outside, Roux led the way into the Golden Oak. In the doorway, Ludovic stopped dead.

The space inside was large enough—all wooden floor and paneled walls—but it was filled with so many people, and he knew none of them. He'd been in unfamiliar territory since leaving Belle Morte, but this was on a different level.

His instincts told him to flee back to the safety and security of the mansion, where the past didn't matter so much and he didn't have to face everything he'd hidden away from for so long.

"You're okay," Roux whispered, brushing his hand with her fingers.

It was the lightest touch but it felt like a lifeline in a stormy sea. He fought the urge to grab her hand and hold it tight. It was bad enough that just being around people made him feel so lost and out of place; he didn't need Roux to know how pathetic he was too.

Roux led the way to the bar and Ludovic followed her, his eyes flicking over the throngs of people laughing and joking and drinking and flirting.

They were all so . . . normal.

After what he'd seen and done in World War I, Ludovic had isolated himself from the world. There were too many ghosts clawing at his head and he couldn't rid himself of any of them. Separating himself from everything and everyone meant that *he* could never be hurt again. More importantly, it meant that he could never hurt anyone again.

As time passed he'd started to think of the world as something strange and alien, something that existed only in his past. He'd remembered only the bad parts, and in the process he'd forgotten that it hadn't *all* been bad.

He'd forgotten that, for the most part, the world was a normal place filled with normal people.

The young man behind the bar appreciatively eyed Roux as she approached. Ludovic glared at him.

"What can I get you?" the man asked.

"A couple of halves of cider would be great, thanks," Roux said.

Was she even aware that the barman's eyes were bugging out of his head? Ludovic suspected she wasn't.

Roux paid for the drinks and Ludovic picked them up. He was out of his depth here, hopelessly so, and he hated feeling useless. Carrying the drinks was the least he could do.

Roux deftly wended her way through the crowd, passing a couple of empty tables before picking one at the far end of the room.

As they sat down, Ludovic allowed a small smile. Their table was tucked away in the corner, more or less out of sight of people coming into the pub but still managing to offer a decent view of the room and everyone in it. Roux had chosen well.

Roux took a long sip of her drink. "Aaah," she said, smacking her lips. "That's better."

Cautiously, Ludovic sniffed his own drink. The type of cider that he was familiar with was amber colored, giving off the distinct aroma of apples. The things that Roux had bought were pinkish red and smelled sickly sweet, more like chemicals than fruit.

"You realize I can't actually drink this, don't you?" he said, though he wasn't sure he would have even if he could.

Roux grinned at him over the rim of her glass. "But I can. It would have looked odd if you were sitting here in a pub without a drink."

Of course she'd thought of that.

He'd been so reluctant at first to accept her help, and not only because he didn't know her. The thought of relying on someone so much younger and more inexperienced had been galling, to say the least.

Now, sitting here with her, he felt ashamed of his own pride. In some ways Roux's experience was decades ahead of his. It didn't matter that she was young; it mattered that she knew what she was doing. He did need her, and even if he didn't, he realized he was glad to have her there.

That was something he hadn't expected, and he wasn't sure what to do with those feelings.

Roux

He was doing his best to hide it, but Ludovic was obviously horribly uncomfortable with their surroundings. Roux watched the way his eyes flicked around the room, lingering on people, studying the way they laughed and talked with each other, as if he'd never seen it before.

Roux leaned forward. "Relax," she whispered. "You're not supposed to look so uncomfortable on a date."

Ludovic stiffened.

"Fake date," Roux amended. "I'm not going to strip you naked and ravish you on this table, but you could at least pretend you're enjoying being with me. It'll make us blend in better."

When Ludovic spoke, it was so soft Roux almost didn't hear it. "I *am* enjoying being with you."

Roux took another long sip of her drink, trying to hide her surprise. "Don't answer if you don't want to, but have you ever done this before?"

Ludovic looked around again, his eyes still wary. "Not in the modern sense."

Roux waited for him to elaborate, but he didn't. His gaze was now fixed on the cider that he couldn't drink.

Out of the corner of her eye, she saw Walsh enter the pub and head for the bar.

"Can I ask you about Etienne?" she said.

"What would you like to know?"

"No one's talking about him at the mansion. It's almost like people don't even want to say his name."

"Does that surprise you?"

"Yes, actually. When someone does what he did, people tend to talk about it."

Ludovic rubbed his thumb over the whorls of wood on the table-top. "Etienne betrayed us in the worst possible way. Talking about him is almost like giving him more power."

"But you can't forget what happened," Roux objected.

"We were all betrayed by Etienne, but it's far worse for the people who were his friends. Perhaps they're simply not ready to talk about it yet."

"Was he your friend?"

"I lived with him for ten years," Ludovic said.

"That's not what I asked."

"No," Ludovic said quietly. "I wasn't friends with him."

"Why not?"

Etienne had fooled everyone in Belle Morte. He'd operated under Ysanne's nose, playing on her trust. He'd befriended Renie, pretended to help her, and the whole time he'd been orchestrating her death. The people he'd been close to, the people who'd trusted him, had been the most hurt by his treachery. Ludovic wasn't one of them.

"I suppose it's because I never really let myself get close to anyone other than Edmond," he said.

Roux frowned, her mind riffling through memories of her time in Belle Morte, as well as the thousands of photos and fan videos of the UK vampires that dominated the online world. Many of them were staged—photos of vampires posing for magazines or carefully selected stills from televised events. It wasn't uncommon for fans to ship various vampires together, even without any basis for the imagined romance, but she'd always assumed that the vampires in each House were all friends with each other.

But now she realized that although she'd seen Edmond and Ludovic together at various events, she couldn't recall seeing Ludovic with other vampires, not properly anyway.

"He can't be your only friend," she said.

Ludovic's lips tightened. "He's the only person I truly trust."

"What about everyone else who fought to get Belle Morte back? What about Ysanne and Caoimhe and Isabeau?"

Ludovic said nothing.

Frustration gnawed at Roux. In the short amount of time she'd spent with Ludovic, she'd got to know him better than she'd ever thought she would. But there was still so much she *didn't* know.

Ludovic owed her nothing. They hadn't come on this mission to become friends, which meant they didn't have to tell each other anything personal. But sometimes Ludovic did, and that was what frustrated her. Sometimes he offered information she didn't expect him to, and other times he completely clammed up and left her hanging.

Like now.

Still, she didn't push.

Sometimes Ludovic made her feel like she was dealing with a wild animal, one that was starting to show signs of trusting her but wasn't sure yet. If she pushed too hard, she might scare him away altogether.

Physically, Ludovic was near superhuman, but beyond the strength and the immortality, there was something vulnerable, something that could be hurt, broken. Roux caught only a glimpse of it from time to time, and she didn't think Ludovic showed it to many people.

But it intrigued her.

She wanted to know why he remained secluded.

She wanted to know why he didn't go on dates and why he didn't have friends.

She wanted to know what made him tick, what sort of man he really was behind the walls that he put up.

And the fact that she wanted to know worried her. It was one thing to be attracted to someone; it was another to want to dig into the core of that person's being.

A flurry of motion distracted her. Three guys, loaded with instruments, had pushed their way through the crowd and into a small area a few feet to the left of Roux and Ludovic's table.

"What's going on?" Ludovic asked, instantly alert.

"It's a band," Roux said. "The pub's having live music tonight."

"I see."

It didn't take the band long to set up and launch into a sound check.

The sudden noise made Ludovic tense. They were close enough to the stage area that they probably wouldn't be able to hear themselves talk—at least, Roux wouldn't—but maybe that was for the best. Sitting here with Ludovic, longing to know more about him, was making this whole thing feel more like a real date.

It wasn't, and Roux needed to remember that.

Ludovic

He hadn't anticipated the band.

When he looked around the room, he saw people were smiling and nodding in time to the beat, some even singing along—although in Ludovic's opinion, it would be kinder on everyone's ears if they stopped.

His initial instinct was to leave.

This was part of the human world, something he'd avoided for so long. At Belle Morte, balls and similar events were accompanied by uniformed orchestras playing classical pieces—a far cry from the three young men standing in the stage area, with ragged holes in the knees of their jeans and hair that flopped over their eyes, making a cacophony of noise with electric guitars.

Before Belle Morte, Ludovic would have stayed away from this sort of scene. Now he couldn't leave, and when his gaze settled back on Roux, he wasn't sure he wanted to.

Roux bobbed her head along with the music, her lips silently shaping the words. Obviously it was a song she knew well—and one she liked, judging by the sparkle in her eyes.

Ludovic hadn't listened to much music just for the sake of it in the last few decades, and he hadn't thought he was missing much.

He still wasn't convinced by the vocal skills and technical ability of this particular band, but everyone else was enjoying it. It made them smile, made them laugh, brought them together under a common interest. Several people even jumped up to dance. Wasn't that enough?

The song came to an end, followed by a round of applause. Roux clapped, too, her face lit up.

Ludovic stared down at his own hands. Slowly, hesitantly, he clapped.

Roux looked at him from under her fringe, surprise flickering in her eyes. Her smile widened and softened at the same time.

The next song started up, and Roux let out a squeak of excitement.

"I love this song," she exclaimed, and jumped out of her seat.

Ludovic froze, his hands still pressed together, as Roux grabbed his arm.

"What are you doing?" he said.

"We're dancing."

"You can't be serious."

"Why not?" Roux swayed her hips, strands of the brown wig trailing around her shoulders. Something stirred in Ludovic, something he hadn't felt for a long time.

Ludovic fumbled for an excuse, but the words wouldn't come. He'd danced with Roux once before, but she hadn't given him much choice. Then, she'd grabbed his hands and pulled him onto the dance floor before he could protest. He'd spent the whole time wishing he could get away.

This time, he wanted to dance with her.

He shouldn't do this.

Dancing wasn't part of the job. And they were supposed to remain incognito, not dance in front of an audience.

But as he looked up at Roux, her eyes gleaming, her hips gently swaying, any objections fled his mind. He wanted this, and he didn't know why.

Roux leaned forward. "Dance with me," she said.

"All right," Ludovic whispered.

CHAPTER ELEVEN

Roux

She really hadn't expected him to say yes. She shouldn't even have asked him, but she hadn't been able to stop herself.

And then he'd agreed.

She blinked and leaned back, trying to process what had just happened.

Ludovic stared up at her, and for a moment she could see past his walls. She wanted to wriggle through that gap, to widen it until he trusted her enough to let down all his defenses.

He climbed to his feet, his eyes still fixed on her face, and she wasn't about to show how taken aback she was. Taking his hand, she tugged him onto the small area of floor in front of the band.

The lead singer smiled indulgently at her.

As the beat of the drums moved through her body, Roux moved, too, coiling her hips in a sensual figure eight.

Ludovic stared at her. "That's not dancing," he said.

"Of course it is."

His gaze lingered on her hips, tracking the sway and shimmy. "It's not what I'd call dancing," he muttered.

Roux grinned. "Bet you still like it, though."

He didn't deny it, and something surged deep inside her, like a wave breaking loose.

She looped her arms around Ludovic's neck and let the music fill her up, let the beat and sway take over her body. A long moment passed when she thought Ludovic would stand like a mannequin in the middle of the floor. Then his arms tentatively slid around her waist, his hands resting on the curve of her spine.

His posture was still stiff, and panic flickered in his eyes, but this time Roux didn't tell him to relax. The fact that he'd got up to dance at all was incredible, and she wouldn't spoil it by implying he wasn't doing it right.

She nudged Ludovic's hip with hers, and his arms tightened around her, just a fraction, but enough for her to notice. His expression didn't change and she wasn't sure he was even aware he'd done it. But she was aware.

Very, very, *very* aware.

The hard length of his body was a hairsbreadth from her own, and the masculine power radiating from him seemed to sizzle through every single one of her nerve endings. That power had nothing to do with him as a vampire and everything to do with him as a man.

She tried to distract herself by focusing on the music. There was another urge growing inside her, altogether different from how she felt about Ludovic. She wanted to sing. The words climbed up her throat, begging for release, but she held them back.

There were many things that Roux would do in front of people, but singing wasn't one of them.

"Don't you ever get embarrassed by things like this?" Ludovic asked, glancing around. The music was loud enough that he had to lean down, his mouth almost by her ear. It made her tremble.

"Why would I? Do you?" Roux asked.

She danced when she felt like it because when she was younger, she wouldn't have dared. It would only have given her bullies more ammunition. For years those people had held a lot of power over her, and she would not let that happen again. She would not give a damn what people thought of her.

Ludovic took a moment to reply. His head was still bent over hers, and a few loose strands of blond hair tickled her face.

"No," he said.

"You sure about that?" Roux teased.

And then he smiled at her, and it was a proper smile, bright and full-blown, making his whole face glow. Roux's breath caught in her throat. Ludovic was always gorgeous, but he could be distant too. His beauty reminded her of a sculpture, something carved into marble, wonderful to look at but cold to the touch. But when he smiled it was like watching that marble sculpture come to life—like, for a brief, shining moment, Roux could truly see the man he was.

All too soon his walls would go back up, but for now Roux wanted to cling to the moment. She wanted to bask in his smile, because she didn't know when she'd see it again.

Ludovic

This should have been everything he hated.

He didn't like being the center of attention—it made him feel exposed, as if the people around him could see right past his defenses and into the most rotten corners of his soul.

Standing in the middle of a room filled with strangers, his arms around a girl he barely knew, should have been his idea of hell.

And yet, oddly, it wasn't.

Because of who that girl was.

Roux's long, lean body sensuously writhed in time with the music, her hips moving in a way that hypnotized Ludovic. Her arms were looped around his neck, her fingers slightly tangled with his hair, and his arms were around her waist, feeling every movement of her body.

Dancing had changed a lot since he'd been human. Even someone like him, practically living under a rock for decades, couldn't completely miss the many ways that social change manifested. He knew that some people danced like they were having sex with the air itself, shaking and grinding and thrusting. The way Roux danced was suggestive, but less blatantly so, tantalizing rather than brazen, and far more intriguing because of it.

He couldn't look away from the motion of her pelvis. His hands itched to move farther down, to touch her in a way he hadn't touched a woman in a very long time.

But he couldn't.

With an effort he tore his eyes away, fixing them to a point firmly above Roux's head. If he didn't look at her, maybe she wouldn't affect him like that.

It didn't work.

Even when he wasn't looking at her, Ludovic was aware of her. He could hear the beat of her heart and the rush of blood in her veins, the sound of her breath as she whispered the words to the song.

Despite himself, his gaze drifted down to her lips. Her features were as sharp and angular as cut glass, but her lips were soft and full, and he found himself fascinated by them as they shaped each whispered word.

While he was with her, everything else seemed to melt away. He could almost forget that they were only here because they had a job to do. He could almost forget how painfully uncertain his future was. He could almost forget that dozens of pairs of eyes were watching him.

For a few brief minutes, none of that seemed to matter.

The song came to an end and Roux spun out of Ludovic's arms, turning to face the band and loudly clapping. Applause echoed throughout the rest of the room, and Ludovic realized that some of it was for him and Roux—at least he assumed so, based on the way people were looking at them and smiling.

Roux must have come to the same conclusion; she executed a curtsy and waved, lapping up the attention.

Walsh, sitting in the opposite corner, had his mouth pulled into a tight line, but Ludovic couldn't tell if the man was holding back a smile or a frown.

The glow of dancing with Roux was wearing off, and suddenly Ludovic was painfully aware of all those eyes on him. He turned away, trying not to look at anyone, and Roux caught his hand.

"Let's go back to our table," she said.

Had she noticed his discomfort or was she just tired of dancing? He looked at her, at the compassion and understanding in her eyes, the way she held on to his hand so he wouldn't drift away in the tide of his own fears. She knew.

That realization stunned him.

She didn't know the root of his fears, but she recognized when he was sinking and she threw him a line, without question or judgment.

But how long would that last? How long before she started asking questions?

Besides Edmond, few people knew about his history, and if Roux ever learned about the stains on his soul, she'd turn away from him in disgust.

"I'm going to order some food," Roux announced as Ludovic sat down. "Wait here."

The young barman's face lit up as Roux drew nearer, and even though she still didn't seem to notice, Ludovic couldn't quell a strange spark of irritation.

Roux came back, and Ludovic quickly rearranged his expression into neutral lines. Sitting down, she poured half of Ludovic's untouched cider into her near-empty glass.

For a short while they sat in silence and watched the band, Roux tapping her foot in time with the drumbeat. The atmosphere in the pub felt bright and alive, buoyed by laughter, and Ludovic felt that brightness nudging at his defenses.

Then the barman emerged through the crowd, carrying a huge plate of fish and chips. He placed it in front of Roux, leaning farther over her than was necessary.

"Can I get you anything else?" he asked.

"I'm good, thanks," Roux said, smiling up at him.

His own grin widened in response.

Someone showing an interest in Roux shouldn't have affected

Ludovic at all, but it had. Under the table, his hands curled into fists.

"If you need anything, you know where I am," the man said.

He headed back to the bar, and Roux eagerly attacked her dinner.

"Oh my god," she mumbled around a mouthful of chips. "These are amazing."

Ludovic eyed her food. The fish was almost as long as Roux's forearm, thickly coated in gleaming, crispy batter, and lying on a mountain of golden chips. A smaller mountain of peas sat on the side of the plate.

"Do you miss food?" Roux asked, liberally squirting ketchup onto her chips.

"When I was human, food wasn't particularly pleasant." Ludovic watched Roux drop a chip in her mouth. A drop of oil glistened on her lower lip. "And it's been so long since I've eaten anything that I barely remember it."

Roux paused, staring down at her meal. "I can't imagine not being able to eat."

Ludovic wondered if she was thinking about Renie, who'd never eat human food again.

"Do you ever wish you could try it?" Roux asked.

"I haven't thought about it in hundreds of years. It's not something I can do, so I don't waste time on what-ifs."

"I guess that makes sense." Roux popped another chip into her mouth and dabbed the oil off her lip.

"I take it you enjoy food," Ludovic said.

Roux nodded. "Normally I'm pretty healthy, but after everything that's happened, I've earned a treat." She speared a piece of fish with her fork. "Don't worry, though, I won't spend our whole mission stuffing myself with junk. I know I'll be feeding you again, so I've got to keep myself in good shape."

She was referring to her blood, but the moment the words were out of her mouth, followed by the movement of her lips as they slid along her fork, Ludovic's brain was blasted with an image of her naked and panting beneath him. It wasn't real, but it was so sudden, storming into his head in vivid detail, that he jumped.

Roux looked at him curiously.

Ludovic swallowed hard. Where had that come from? When he'd shut himself off from the world so many decades ago, he'd reduced himself to the most basic form of survival. Sex wasn't necessary for survival. The only thing he'd focused on was getting enough blood to stay alive. When Edmond had found him again, in the '80s, Ludovic had slowly emerged back into the world, but some things had stayed firmly switched off.

His sex drive was one of them.

While the vampires of Belle Morte—of every House—happily indulged their sexual appetites with each other, Ludovic hadn't even thought about sex for a very long time. It hadn't seemed important.

Now, in the blink of an eye, Roux had flipped a switch. He tried to think about something—*anything*—else but the thought of her naked and gasping his name was firmly etched into his brain.

He shifted uncomfortably.

Roux reached for her cider and froze, her eyes fixed on something behind Ludovic. Her face had gone very still and serious, and when he twisted in his seat, he realized why.

Delia Sanders had just walked into the pub.

Roux

Covertly she studied the vampire.

Delia was pale and drawn, her eyes flicking around the room, resting briefly on Ludovic, then Roux, but there was no glimmer of recognition in her gaze. They were safe behind their disguises.

Physically, Delia was unhurt, but there was something twitchy about her body language that made Roux think of a wounded animal. There were so many little changes that a person had to adjust to once they became a vampire, things that they'd probably never even thought about. Vladdicts saw the immortality and the beauty, and thought that it was worth giving up everything else.

Looking at Delia now, Roux wondered if she regretted her choice.

The band announced they were taking a twenty-minute break, and Ludovic leaned across the table. "Where do you think Stephen is?" he said.

"Maybe the pressure got too much for them, and they split up," Roux suggested.

Delia approached a man sitting alone at the end of the bar. His face was weathered and his eyes slightly bloodshot, his body hunched over his pint like he was afraid someone would snatch it away. Roux had seen his type before: heavy drinkers who propped up the bar for as long as it was open.

Leaning over, Delia said something to the man, but they were too far away for Roux to eavesdrop. She glanced at Ludovic; his head was tilted, listening, but there was a little frown on his face. Even with the band on a break, it was noisy enough that even he might be struggling to hear.

At the bar, the man's eyebrows shot up in surprise, and through the dull haze of alcohol in his eyes, Roux spotted a gleam of interest. Whatever Delia had said to him, he liked it.

Delia leaned one hip against the bar and smiled at him. It was a slow smile, a secret one that promised bare skin and gasping breaths in the dark. She leaned forward, whispered something else, her lips brushing his earlobe. His throat bobbed as he swallowed.

Delia turned and walked away, her hips deliberately swaying. The man stared after her, his mouth slightly agape. His pint, previously guarded with both hands and a glare, was forgotten.

Roux saw what he didn't—that the second Delia turned around, the smile vanished from her face. She walked out of the bar without looking back, and after a moment or two, the man followed her.

Ludovic got to his feet, his face grim. "Stay here," he said.

"Not yet."

"Roux—"

"I know, I know, I'm supposed to stay away from the fighting and I'm not dumb enough to throw myself into the middle of a scrap. But we still don't know if Stephen and Delia are running away together or if they're with the rest of the Five. If anything goes wrong, I need to be nearby so I can be the getaway driver."

Ludovic wasn't happy with this—that was stamped across his features—but they didn't have time to argue.

Walsh was already shoving through the crowd, heading for the door.

Roux and Ludovic followed him.

A sharp gust of wind sliced through the air as they stepped outside, and Roux impatiently shoved strands of her wig out of the way.

"Which way did they go?" she said.

Already there was no sign of Delia or her victim.

Ludovic looked one way, then the other, his nostrils flaring. "This way," he said.

"How do you know?"

"I can smell the alcohol on him."

Walsh shot Ludovic a narrow-eyed look that Ludovic either didn't notice or chose to ignore.

Ludovic started down the street and Roux scurried behind him, Walsh bringing up the rear. He turned left and then right, cutting through tightly packed historic buildings, and then stopped.

"There," he whispered, pointing across the road.

Roux's eyes took longer to adjust. The man from the Golden Oak stood in a small concrete parking lot. Only two spaces were occupied, the cars tucked in a corner against a brick wall. Shadows wrapped around the space; the streetlight that reared up from the pavement was broken.

Delia stood in front of her victim, her body pressed against his as she murmured into his ear. He was still upright, still talking; it didn't look as though she'd bitten him yet.

Delia had picked her spot well. The buildings around them were mostly small businesses, all closed now. There was nothing residential, no windows that people would be looking out of at this time of night, and no one else was around.

Something moved in the darkest corners of the parking lot, taking a vaguely human shape, and Roux's heart skipped a beat.

"It's Stephen," Ludovic said.

"What's going on?" the man from the pub said, finally noticing Stephen as the vampire stepped out of the shadows.

Shafts of moonlight fell across Stephen's face, highlighting the dark splotches of exhaustion under his eyes. His lips were clamped tightly together, probably to hide his fangs.

Delia murmured something, tilting her head and batting her eyelashes, drawing the man's attention back to her. There was no denying she was a pretty girl, and barflies like her victim didn't get approached by girls often, let alone good-looking ones.

So Roux was completely unprepared when the man whipped a knife from under his denim jacket and plunged it into Delia's chest.

CHAPTER TWELVE

Roux

Delia let out a hoarse cry and stumbled back, the knife hilt sticking out of her chest. Her would-be victim lunged after her. Grabbing the knife, he pulled it free and blood sprayed through the air, glittering under the strands of moonlight.

With an animal snarl, Stephen rushed at the man—

—and the streets came alive.

Figures in black charged out of the shadows around the lot, their feet thudding on the pavement as they launched themselves at Stephen. Moonlight flashed off another naked blade.

"Stay here," Ludovic told Roux.

She'd known this was coming—fighting was Ludovic's job, not hers—but the thought of him wading into a battle when he didn't know how outnumbered he was made her heart clench.

Her mind flashed back to the time that he'd saved her from an enemy vampire during the first attack on Belle Morte, when he'd appeared just in time to cut off the vampire's head with his sword. That night it had seemed as if no one could touch him; he'd been a force of primal fury, wreaking bloody havoc on the people who'd invaded his home.

He could handle this.

Ludovic and Walsh ran toward the fight, while Roux hung back, hugging herself and wishing there was something she could do. A tight knot of fear and anxiety formed in her chest like a fist.

He's a vampire, she reminded herself. Ludovic had strength and speed on his side, and he'd already proved he could more than hold his own in a fight. But he was still outnumbered and his enemies were armed.

Ludovic reached the parking lot just as Stephen flung off his knot of attackers with a roar. They circled him, so focused on their target that they didn't notice Ludovic was behind them. Ludovic grabbed the nearest attacker and almost casually yanked him off his feet, tossing him out of the way.

Roux felt a spurt of satisfaction as the guy skidded along the pavement.

Who the hell were these people, anyway?

Had they only just realized they were dealing with vampires or had they always known?

Her stomach went cold as options raced through her mind. There was no reason for the man from the bar to have stabbed Delia—unless he knew what she was. But how could he? Even if he'd glimpsed her eyes turning red or got a look at her fangs, why did he have a knife in the first place?

Roux didn't buy that he was the kind of guy who just *happened* to carry weapons around. He'd known he had backup out here. He'd known exactly what was going to happen.

Delia had tried to lure him into a trap, but she'd walked into a much worse one.

Ludovic punched another guy to the ground, but he must have been pulling those punches, or his opponents wouldn't be getting back up. Did he realize that these people knew they were dealing with vampires?

Fear slid down Roux's spine.

What if those knives were silver?

Another man surged at Ludovic, his face twisted with rage, and though Ludovic could easily have dodged, he let the guy deck him in the jaw.

Roux winced.

A flicker of movement outside the fight caught her eye, and she gasped.

Delia lay where she'd fallen, blood darkening the ground beneath her. Roux had thought her dead, but she was moving, one hand help-lessly pawing at the wound in her chest.

A figure broke away from the others and approached the prone woman. Delia tried to climb to her feet, but the figure placed a foot on her chest and shoved her back down. He cocked his head, watch-ing her, and Roux's blood turned to ice as she saw his face.

Iain Johnson smiled, and even from across the road, Roux could see there was nothing but malice in that smile. Iain knew it was Stephen and Delia he was attacking—he knew and he didn't care.

In one hand he held a hammer, and he slapped the head across his palm as he looked down at Delia, still smiling.

Horror churned inside Roux.

Even vampire healing had its limits. If Iain smashed Delia's skull, she wouldn't recover. Iain was going to murder her. Roux couldn't let that happen, even if it meant breaking her promise to stay away from the fighting.

She pulled two pairs of the silver cuffs from her pocket, and slid the bracelets over her knuckles. She'd never thrown a punch in her life, but she'd throw a few now if it would save a life.

Taking a bolstering breath, Roux charged across the street and threw herself in front of Delia.

Iain paused, his eyebrows twisting in confusion.

"Stop this," Roux said, her voice shaky with fear. The handcuffs were cold against her skin, and she clenched her fists until the metal ridges bit into her palms. Iain scared the crap out of her but she wouldn't back down in front of him.

His face darkened, something cold and ugly sliding through his eyes. "You," he said. "I should have known you'd defend the fucking monsters."

"I'm trying to stop you from murdering someone," Roux said.

"It's not murder if they're not human."

"Yes, it is," Roux said, even as her eyes slid to the hammer in Iain's hand.

"I'm warning you," Iain said, his voice low and deadly. "Get the fuck out of my way."

Roux wasn't a fighter, and she didn't fool herself into thinking that luck hadn't been massively on her side that time she'd taken down a vampire. She couldn't rely on luck again now. Iain was bigger and stronger than her, and fueled by irrational rage—there was no way she could win a fight against him, knuckle dusters or not.

The thought of Iain murdering Delia made Roux feel physically sick, but she wouldn't die for Delia either. She opened her mouth—to call for help, to beg Iain for compassion, she didn't even *know*—and the loud wail of a siren split the night.

"You hear that?" Roux said, trying to keep her voice steady. "The police are coming. What do you think will happen if they find you trying to smash a woman's head in with a hammer?"

The look in Iain's eyes was murderous. "You fang-loving bitch," he snarled. "This isn't over." He slid the hammer into his waistband, arranging the hem of his shirt over it so it couldn't be seen. "Lads," he yelled, "let's get out of here."

His eyes met Roux's once more, and there was nothing remotely human in them. His gang scrambled away from Ludovic, and like cockroaches they scattered, disappearing among the streets and alleys of the city.

Roux's legs shook with relief. If those sirens hadn't sounded, things would have gone from bad to seriously fucked-up. Maybe she could still rely on a little luck after all.

Someone had knocked off Ludovic's beanie during the fight, and he bent to grab it. A shallow slice ran across his collarbone, turning his shirt collar red.

Walsh was breathing hard, and there was blood on his knuckles, but it didn't look like his own. His face wrinkled as he looked Ludovic over.

"I thought vampires were meant to have superhuman speed. How the fuck did you let one of them get that close?" he said.

Ludovic's voice was cool as he replied. "It was deliberate. I couldn't risk them realizing I wasn't human."

Walsh made a noncommittal noise, but his scowl lessened.

Ludovic turned to Roux, and she braced herself for him to berate her about getting involved, but a loud groan distracted them both. Stephen lay in a miserable heap on the ground. Even a new vampire should have been able to hold his own against humans, but maybe the ferocity of the attack had taken him too much by surprise.

Or maybe he hadn't been able to cope with the fact that those particular humans—his own *brother*—had tried to kill him.

Ludovic grabbed Stephen's arm and hauled him upright. The other vampire swayed on his feet, his eyes glazed with terror and disbelief.

"Can you walk?" Ludovic said.

Stephen stuttered something, and Ludovic shook him.

"Can you walk?" he snapped, and clarity came back into Stephen's eyes.

"I think so," Stephen mumbled.

Ludovic immediately let him go and turned to Roux.

"I'm okay," she said before he could say anything.

"I'm okay, too, if anyone gives a shit," Walsh mumbled, examining his knuckles.

The sirens were getting closer. "What happens now?" Roux asked.

Walsh sighed and pulled out a cigarette. "I'll handle this if you two can handle the vampires."

"You don't need to actually arrest them?"

Walsh shrugged, his expression troubled. "If they were human, yeah, but apparently those rules don't apply to vampires."

Ludovic scooped Delia into his arms. She moaned, her eyelids fluttering as she drifted in and out of consciousness.

Stephen made a choked sound and reached for her, and Ludovic gave him a lethal glare that stopped the younger vampire in his tracks.

"There are two ways we can do this. Either you come quietly and help make sure that Delia is all right, or I beat you down and cuff you with silver. Which would you prefer?" Ludovic said.

A hint of fang showed as he spoke.

Stephen looked from Delia to Roux, then back to Ludovic, whose expression could have been carved from ice. His face crumpled. "I'll come quietly."

"Excellent choice."

Walsh blew a coil of smoke into the air. "Let me know when you've got them back to Belle Morte."

"We will," Roux said.

Ludovic was already striding out of the parking lot, Delia limp in his arms. Stephen scuttled after him.

Roux's stomach pitched. Whatever else Stephen and Delia were, they were still in love, and Stephen would go wherever Delia went. That should have been beautiful. Instead, each of them had followed the other into a place they were never meant to go, and now the rest of their lives was a giant question mark.

She sighed and hurried after Ludovic.

Two down. Three to go.

When they reached the car, Ludovic ordered Stephen to sit in the back, behind the passenger seat, then he slid into the car next to the younger vampire, still holding Delia.

Roux didn't miss the deliberateness of the seating arrangements.

Ludovic had made sure he was sitting behind Roux—if Stephen tried anything, he'd have to go through an older, stronger vampire. Roux didn't think he was stupid enough to do that, but she appreciated the precaution.

"Take us back to the hotel," Ludovic said.

Roux met his eyes in the rearview mirror.

Their job was to return their prisoners to Belle Morte, but neither of them had forgotten their conversation from earlier. Ludovic still planned to question Stephen and Delia about the kids, and obviously he didn't intend to do it at the mansion.

Roux swallowed past the sudden tightness in her throat.

How much *questioning* did Ludovic have in mind, and what kind?

Delia moaned again, shifting in Ludovic's arms. Her blood had soaked his clothes.

"Is she going to die?" Stephen whispered.

"No, but she needs blood," Ludovic said.

Roux gripped the steering wheel with both hands. "I could feed her." She *really* didn't want to, but it was a small price to pay if it would help them get the info they needed.

"Absolutely not," Ludovic said, and Roux was surprised by the sharpness in his voice. "There's plenty of bagged blood at the hotel. She can have that."

Roux's eyes slid to his in the mirror and she held his gaze for a moment, before looking away. She started the car and pulled away from the curb, heading in the direction of the Old Royal hotel.

When they arrived, Roux thanked their lucky stars that they were in a room with a fire escape. They'd never have smuggled a blood-stained, unconscious vampire past the desk clerk.

On second thought, Ysanne had probably arranged this room for just such a situation.

Ludovic jogged up the steps, Stephen trailing him, and Roux brought up the rear a couple of moments later, making sure there was still space between her and the vampires.

Delia was helpless, and there didn't seem to be any fight left in Stephen, but Roux wasn't taking any chances.

The second they were inside the room Stephen slumped against the wall and dropped his head into his hands. "This wasn't supposed to happen," he whispered. "Who the hell are you people, anyway?"

Ignoring him, Ludovic laid Delia on the floor, while Roux hurried to the freezer box. She handed a bag of blood to Ludovic and he used his teeth to rip it open. Sliding one arm under Delia's neck, he lifted her head.

Her eyes flickered open, hazy with pain.

"Drink this," Ludovic told her, and put the bag to her lips.

He had to tip the blood down her throat at first, but as the bag drained, the hazy look faded from her eyes, replaced by a hungry red glow. Roux grabbed another bag without being asked, and Ludovic promptly ripped into that too. Droplets of blood splashed his chin, and as he held the bag to Delia's mouth, Roux silently reached between them and wiped the blood from Ludovic's face.

He shot her a grateful look.

By the time the second bag was drained, Delia was strong enough to sit up on her own. The knives wielded by Iain's gang hadn't been silver, after all. "More," she whispered.

"No," Ludovic said.

Delia started to protest, but Ludovic shot her a deadly look and she fell quiet. Neither she nor Stephen recognized Ludovic, but on some level they must still understand that he was the superior predator.

"We're from Belle Morte," Roux said.

Stephen's eyes widened, darting from Delia to the door. He couldn't have telegraphed his intentions any more obviously.

Ludovic was a blond blur as he flashed across the room and positioned himself in front of the door. "If you try to run, I'll bring you
back, and this time I won't be gentle," he warned, and the soft threat
in his voice raised goose bumps on Roux's skin.

Stephen crossed his arms, trying to pretend that he hadn't, in fact,
been thinking about making a run for it. "What do you want?" he
said, almost sulkily.

Roux's temper rose. "How about a little justice for what you've
done?" she said.

Stephen glared at her before turning his attention back to Ludovic.
He screwed up his eyes, looking Ludovic over. "I don't get it. You're a
vampire, right? Why don't I recognize you?"

"He's disguised," said Roux, unable to ignore a twinge of pride in
the job she'd done.

Ludovic stared the smaller man down. "I'm Ludovic de Vauban,
sent by the Lady of Belle Morte to bring you back."

Stephen closed his eyes. "Great," he muttered, his shoulders
sagging.

Roux couldn't help herself. "Exactly what did you *think* would
happen? That you could invade the most famous Vampire House in
England, help the traitors who killed vampires, security guards, staff,
and donors, and then just get *away* with it?"

Anger thundered in her veins. She didn't know what she'd expected
from Stephen, but the guy was acting like a petulant teenager. No
gratitude to Ludovic for saving Delia, and apparently no chance of
him taking responsibility for his own actions.

Stephen said nothing.

"People are dead, you do realize that," Roux said.

"I didn't know this was going to happen," Stephen said.

"What did you think *would*?"

"We were going to be vampires, and then . . ." He trailed off.

"And then you thought you'd live happily ever after? Welcome to the real world."

"Why did you join Etienne?" Ludovic asked.

Stephen shuffled his feet. "Because he said he'd turn us. He said we could be together forever and live in Belle Morte and have everything we've ever wanted."

"Once you'd scrubbed away all the bloodstains of the people who died there," Roux snapped.

Delia looked away.

A powerful wave of disgust threatened to choke Roux. "You wanted to be vampires, and you didn't care who you trampled in the process."

"*We* didn't kill anyone," Delia protested, picking at the blood on her clothes.

"You think that makes you any better? You knew what Etienne was planning, you knew people would get hurt, and you helped him anyway. It doesn't matter if you killed anyone or not. There's still blood on your hands."

A thick knot was working its way up her throat, and she didn't know whether to scream or cry. She hadn't said it to Ludovic, but part of her had hoped there might be more to Stephen and Delia's story than this, that they weren't just two people who'd been blinded by greed and selfishness. But no. That's exactly what it was.

Stephen's face twisted with anger, and he took a step toward her. "Screw you," he said.

"Stay back," Ludovic warned, and tension crackled around the room like lightning.

Stephen took another step, testing the waters.

In a flash, Ludovic had him by the throat, shoving him against the wall. "I said, *stay back*," he growled.

The anger fled Stephen's face, replaced by terror. If he didn't already know how strong older vampires were, he'd be able to feel the iron strength in Ludovic's fingers as they wrapped around his neck.

With an effort, Roux reined in her fury. Getting mad at Stephen and Delia wouldn't change what had happened, and it wouldn't help anyone now.

"We need to ask you both something, and you'd better be honest," she said. "Five kids have gone missing from Winchester over the last couple of weeks. Do you know anything about it?"

"What?" Stephen gaped at her.

Ludovic tightened his grip, pushing Stephen harder against the wall. "Did you kill them?" His voice had dropped to a near whisper, yet he sounded more menacing now than he ever had.

"We don't know anything about any kids," Delia cried.

Vampires didn't have heartbeats and they didn't need to breathe, so Ludovic couldn't hear lies from them the way he could from a human. But as scary as he looked right now, Roux didn't think the younger vampires would lie to him.

"What about Neal Morris, Jeffrey Smith, and Kashvi Patel? What do you know about them?" she asked.

"Nothing. They stayed at Bushfield with us, but we never got to know any of them," Delia said.

"You didn't plan to flee the mansion together?"

"No," Stephen said, still pinned against the wall. "When we realized everything had gone to shit, Del and I took our chance and ran. We knew Kashvi and Neal ran, too, but we didn't know about Jeffrey."

"Have you seen them or been in contact with them since that night?" Ludovic asked.

Stephen managed to shake his head; Ludovic must have relaxed his grip at last.

"Were they friends? Would they have stayed together or separated once they left the mansion?" Roux pressed him.

"I don't *know*." Stephen sounded like he was about to cry.

"You don't know anywhere they might have gone to?" Roux continued.

Delia slumped onto the edge of the bed, and Roux felt a powerful urge to kick her off. This was her little space with Ludovic, and having two enemies here made her feel sharp and prickly.

"I swear, we don't know anything. All we've done since leaving Belle Morte is try to stay alive and plan what to do next," Delia said.

"One more thing," Roux said. She fetched the files that Ysanne had given her and pulled out the photos of the mystery four vampires. She showed them to Delia, and then to Stephen. "Do you recognize any of these people?"

Stephen looked blankly at her.

Delia shook her head.

"They weren't with you at Bushfield? Are you sure?" Roux said.

"I've never seen them in my life," Stephen said.

Roux caught Ludovic's eye. He gave away nothing, but he had

to be as confused as she was. If those four vampires hadn't been at Bushfield, then Etienne hadn't turned them to use as soldiers.

So what the hell had he wanted them for?

Roux drove to Belle Morte in silence, Ludovic sitting in the back with Stephen and Delia. The atmosphere in the car felt tense and jagged, like it was full of broken glass, and Roux thought that would ease off once they delivered their prisoners, but it didn't.

She had to park around the side of the mansion so the protestors still gathered at the gates couldn't see what was going on. Edmond and Isabeau were already waiting for them, as pale and still as sculptures under moonlight. Roux stayed in the car while Ludovic handed Stephen and Delia over, and once they'd disappeared through the grounds, heading for the back door, she started the engine.

Ludovic climbed into the seat beside her, and they drove back through the gates and away from Belle Morte.

Within two days, they'd caught two of the Five—Roux should have felt elated. Instead she just felt sad.

Ludovic was quiet, too, gazing out the window.

The prickly silence pressed down on Roux, and suddenly her throat was knotted and her eyes stung, and even though they weren't far from the hotel, she pulled down a side street and killed the engine.

"I feel like such an idiot," she muttered, wrapping her arms around herself.

"Why?" Ludovic asked.

"Because part of me hoped that maybe Stephen and Delia had

misunderstood what they were getting into, or maybe they'd been coerced into it, or maybe one of them had turned the other."

"It's very hard for a new vampire to turn anyone," Ludovic said.

"Really?"

"To turn a person, a vampire has to drain them to the point of death but not actually kill them." Ludovic's eyes darkened. "New vampires don't have the control that older ones do, so it's much harder for them to reach that perfect point."

"Anyway, the point is, I stupidly hoped that Stephen and Delia hadn't done this out of pure selfishness. But they did. They weren't tricked, they weren't bullied, they just didn't care who they hurt. And they're all like that, aren't they? Everyone Etienne turned." Roux clenched her fists, her face hot. "I don't know why I considered anything different, especially not after those bastards who kidnapped Renie."

It had only happened a few days ago, and the memory of it was seared into Roux's brain. After they'd fled Belle Morte when it fell into Etienne's hands, Etienne had deployed two of his human minions to trap Renie so they could torture her for information. Renie had escaped, but Roux would never forget the battered, bloody state of her best friend when Edmond pulled her from the river she'd jumped into.

Roux exhaled, and tried to let go of her anger. "But I can't make it personal, can I?"

"No. This is about punishment, not revenge," Ludovic said. Then his voice dropped an octave. "But I do know how you feel."

Roux sucked in a breath.

Ludovic's face had gone dark again, cold fury sparking in his eyes.

"I was the one who took Edmond to his room after he was whipped with silver for punching Adrian, and then I had to stand by and let him be chained with silver and imprisoned in the cells. I know as well as anyone what it feels like to see someone you love suffering, and believe me, I wanted to break Phillip's jaw for whipping Edmond."

The side of Roux's mouth tipped up in a smile. "Gideon took care of that for you."

Ludovic didn't smile back, but his expression softened, and that was close enough.

"While we were at Fiaigh, Edmond mentioned that you broke his nose once. I can't imagine him pissing you off that much—what did he do?" Roux asked.

Ludovic's face slammed shut and the air in the car felt colder than it had a minute ago.

"He didn't do anything. It was an accident," Ludovic muttered.

Roux suspected there was more to it than that, but it clearly wasn't something Ludovic was comfortable talking about.

She wished she hadn't said anything.

They sat in silence for a few moments, then Ludovic rubbed the back of his neck and said, "I like that you thought about giving Stephen and Delia the benefit of the doubt."

Roux couldn't help a short laugh. "Even though I was wrong."

"They didn't deserve your care, but you were right to give it to them. Don't change that about yourself—it's what makes you special."

Startled, Roux looked up. Ludovic was leaning closer than she'd realized, his blue eyes intently fixed on her, glittering like polished sapphires. Her heartbeat quickened and she abruptly turned away, hoping he wouldn't hear it and know he was the cause.

"How do you think Iain and his friends knew that Stephen and Delia would be at the Golden Oak?" she said.

"If he knew they planned to flee the city, I can only assume he came to the same conclusion that we did," Ludovic said.

"I guess."

Roux slumped back in her seat. She should have been celebrating a job well done or contemplating where they'd start with the rest of the Five; instead, all she could think about was what Ludovic had said.

It's what makes you special.

Ludovic thought she was special?

Where had that come from?

And why did it make her feel all fuzzy and warm inside?

"I hope Walsh has a lead on the other three, because I have no idea where to start," she said, trying to distract herself.

Ludovic pulled off his beanie and ran his fingers through his hair. "It might be worth looking into reports of missing pets in the area, see if we can uncover a pattern," he said.

Roux pulled a face. "I know it's better than snacking on innocent people, but I kind of hoped the Five would be feeding from wildlife rather than pets."

"Pets are easier to catch."

"Funnily enough, that doesn't make me feel better."

"Feeding from animals isn't ideal, but sometimes we have no choice."

The odd note in Ludovic's voice caught Roux's attention. He stared through the windshield at the darkened street ahead, a faraway look on his face, like he was watching a memory play out.

"Have you had to do that?" Roux asked.

He looked sharply at her, and there was a flash of something raw and awful in his eyes, the glimpse of an old wound, perhaps one that had never fully healed.

"Yes," he said, his voice barely a whisper. "Edmond and I were forced to feed on rats when we were in the trenches."

A hard lump formed in Roux's throat.

"Did you—"

"I don't want to talk about it." Ludovic abruptly cut her off again. He looked away, his whole body tense.

Roux gazed at the back of his head. What had Ludovic seen during that war? Vampires could heal from so many injuries but that didn't mean their psyches weren't at risk. Many men had physically survived the war but had been left with shattered minds, and vampires weren't immune to that.

There was so much Roux didn't know, and didn't think she could tackle. But there was so much she *wanted* to know, and she wasn't quite sure what to do about that.

CHAPTER THIRTEEN

Roux

Roux didn't sleep well that night.

Since the war had been brought up, she could feel Ludovic retreating into himself, slowly but surely distancing himself from her. The air in their room felt as tense and sharp-edged as it had in the car, and when they went to bed, Ludovic slept as far away from her as he could.

She couldn't get her mind to stop churning.

Tackling Stephen and Delia had taken an unexpected turn, thanks to Iain, but capturing them had been relatively smooth, all things considered. Roux wasn't naive enough to think that the rest of the Five would go down so easily. Even if they did, there was still the matter of the four mystery vampires to consider.

And all those missing kids.

They had so many pieces to fit together, but every piece seemed to be from a different puzzle.

Roux wished she could discuss it with Ludovic, but he'd been so quiet, so distant, that she wasn't sure how to reach him.

She was lying awake, staring at the ceiling, when Walsh called her early the next morning.

"Hello?" she said, trying to ignore the fist clenching in her chest.

Walsh wasn't interested in making conversation with them—if he was calling, something was wrong.

Ludovic didn't move, but Roux sensed him come awake next to her.

"Are you busy?" Walsh said, his voice as brusque as ever.

Roux checked her watch. "It's not even seven. I'm in bed."

"Get up. I need to talk to you."

Roux shoved back the covers. That fist was squeezing tighter. "What's wrong?"

"Not over the phone. Can you meet me at the Coffee Bean Café, around the corner from the train station? Don't bring the vampire."

Roux bristled. "Excuse me?"

"You heard."

The mattress shifted slightly as Ludovic turned over. "Do it," he said, his blue eyes inscrutable.

"But—" Roux started.

"Just do it. It could be important."

"I'll be there in ten minutes," Roux told Walsh.

He promptly hung up, and Roux glared at the phone.

"You'll be okay here on your own?" she said to Ludovic.

He gave a short nod.

"I'll try not to be long," Roux said.

She threw on some clothes and her wig, and hurried out of the room.

The Coffee Bean Café was a tired-looking little place with a brown-painted facade and dead flowers hanging limply from a basket by the front door. Inside, Walsh was hunched over a steaming mug. His clothes were rumpled and there were dark rings under his eyes.

Roux took the seat opposite him. "What's going on?" she said.

"You want a drink?" Walsh said.

"Why couldn't I bring Ludovic?"

"He's a vampire," Walsh said, gripping his mug a little tighter.

"So?"

"So I don't trust him. I don't trust any of them."

Anger sparked in Roux's chest. "That's not fair."

"Do I look like I give a shit?"

They glared at each other across the table, then Walsh sighed and sat back in his chair. "I didn't ask you here to discuss what's *fair*. I want to talk to you about those missing kids."

That spark of anger winked out as cold fingers of fear slid through Roux's chest. "What about them?"

"There's been another one. Chloe Hegerty, thirteen years old, lives a mile from here, reported missing this morning. Apparently, she was staying with a friend last night, but they had a fight so she decided to walk home. She never made it."

"We questioned Stephen and Delia about this, but they swore they didn't know anything," Roux explained.

Walsh leaned forward, bracing his elbows on the table. "I need to know if there's anything you two haven't told me, or if there's anything that Ysanne's holding back."

"More than anyone, Ysanne knows how important this is, and she wouldn't jeopardize it by keeping secrets," Roux said.

"Have you ever heard her or anyone else at Belle Morte mention the name Roger Schofield?" Walsh said. His eyes bored into her.

"No."

Walsh huffed out a sigh.

"Who's Roger Schofield?" Roux asked.

Walsh lowered his eyes to his mug, his jaw working.

"I'm guessing he's got something to do with the kids," Roux said. "A suspect?"

"Do you remember the Jessica Bolan kidnapping five years ago?" Walsh said.

Beneath her wig, the hairs prickled on the back of Roux's neck. "Yeah."

"You followed the case?"

"Not really. I remember seeing it on the news, but I was only thirteen, so I honestly didn't pay it much attention."

"You know that Jessica Bolan wasn't the only victim though, right?"

Roux shook her head, her stomach twisting.

"There were two others, kidnapped shortly after Jessica was rescued, and both were found alive in similar conditions. All of them identified Roger Schofield as the man who'd kidnapped them, and a full-scale manhunt was organized, but no one ever caught the bastard. Eventually the trail went cold. The last confirmed sighting of him was a year ago in Cornwall."

"And you think he's behind these missing kids too," Roux said.

"He was already the lead suspect, and now the route that Chloe Hegerty took when she vanished includes the street where Schofield used to live with his mum."

"What does this have to do with me?" Roux glanced around the café. "Why am I here?"

"The MCT have been investigating this since the first kid vanished—"

"MCT?" Roux interrupted.

"Major Crime Team," said Walsh impatiently.

"Right, sorry."

"The kids from five years ago ID'd Schofield as their kidnapper, but none of them knew *why* he'd taken them. That means we don't know what his long-term plan for them was."

"You mean if he eventually planned to kill them?" Roux said.

Walsh nodded. "When the kidnappings started again, Schofield was the immediate suspect, but not a shred of evidence has been found at any crime scene. The MCT have fuck all to work with."

"I still don't get what this has to do with me."

Walsh clenched his mug. "I'm guessing vampires don't leave evidence the way a human might. If Schofield had returned to Winchester, is there any chance that Etienne turned him, and Ysanne is covering it up?"

"She wouldn't do that," Roux said.

"Why not? She covered up June Mayfield's murder."

"That was different. She was trying to *help* June."

"When I first learned about these rogue vampires, I dismissed any possibility that they were connected, because the kidnappings had started before those vampires escaped Belle Morte. But I hadn't realized how long they'd been at Bushfield prior to the Belle Morte attacks. Was Etienne with them the whole time, or did he leave them alone?"

Roux's throat felt dry. "He left them alone most of the time. He couldn't let anyone in Belle Morte notice that he was missing."

"So any of those vampires could have sneaked off and started kid-napping kids, and Etienne himself might not even have known."

"I guess it's possible," Roux said, the words heavy as stones on her tongue. "But Ysanne has identified all of Etienne's vampires, and Roger Schofield isn't among them."

"You trust her?" Walsh asked.

"Absolutely."

Walsh made a disgruntled noise.

"You don't *know* that Schofield is behind this, though, do you?" Roux said.

"No," Walsh admitted, and it sounded like it pained him to say it. "There are some discrepancies between these kidnappings and the previous ones."

"Like what?"

Walsh scrutinized her with narrowed eyes, probably weighing up how much to tell her. "There were several weeks between each of the original Schofield kidnappings, but there have only been a few days between each one this time. The ages of the victims are different too—the kids that Schofield took were between seven and nine. These current missing kids are between thirteen and fifteen. So far that seems to be the only link between them."

"If it's not Schofield, do you think it could be one of the Five?"

"I think that vampires are ruthless, dangerous bastards," Walsh said.

"That doesn't mean a vampire's responsible for this. You can't *make* them the villain just because you don't like them."

"Considering the fucking carnage they've caused lately, I'd say I've got a pretty good reason for not liking them, wouldn't you?" Walsh snapped.

"No."

"Listen—"

"No, *you* listen." Roux matched Walsh's cold tone. "We're supposed to be working together to stop a potential threat, but if you can't be objective about this you're not the man for the job."

She expected a nasty retort, but Walsh thoughtfully appraised her.

"Maybe one of the Five *is* behind this, but Ludovic and the other vampires at Belle Morte aren't, so please stop treating them all like the bad guy," Roux went on.

Walsh rubbed the back of his neck. "Missing kid cases always rile me up more than the others, even when I'm not working them." He'd been a dick to Ludovic before they'd found out about the kids, but Roux decided not to point that out.

"Do you have kids of your own?" Roux asked.

Walsh shook his head. "You?"

"No, but I am only eighteen."

Walsh did a small double take. "Seriously?"

"Seriously."

He appraised her again. "You've always come across as older."

Roux shrugged.

"I don't have the patience for kids myself, but I've got nieces and nephews, and the thought of anyone hurting them—" Walsh clenched his fist. "It takes a special kind of evil to go after kids," he concluded.

"It's possible that whoever's behind this has nothing to do with the Five *or* Schofield though, right?" Roux said.

"Yeah, maybe the Bolans have just been dealt a really shitty hand and it's a complete coincidence that both their kids have been abducted a few years apart."

"I honestly can't tell if that's sarcasm or not," Roux said.

Walsh drained the last of his coffee. "It's not. Stranger things do happen. But I'll believe it a lot more once we've caught these vampire bastards and can rule them out as suspects."

"Is there any chance that the kids are still alive?" Roux asked, staring at the ring-marked tabletop.

Walsh paused.

"There's always a chance," he said.

"But?"

"Statistically, the longer that someone is missing, the less chance there is of finding them alive. Schofield didn't kill any of his victims, but that may have only been because all of them were rescued before he could do anything worse."

"Why would anyone do this?" Roux asked.

"I've asked myself that many times during my career, and sometimes you never get the answers," Walsh said.

"What do we do now?" Roux asked.

"We?" Walsh stood up and slung on his jacket. "My team is following up some possible leads on Patel, Morris, and Smith, but until I know if they come to anything, you go back to the hotel and wait for me to call."

"We can help."

"Yeah? How?"

"Do you know which way Chloe was walking home?"

"Yeah. She took the same route regularly."

"Have you found any evidence? Anything to indicate a struggle?"

Walsh pulled out his pack of cigarettes. "No."

"Why not let Ludovic take a look?"

"Because of that tracking shit he was doing at Bushfield?"

"Because vampires have sharper senses than humans. They can see things we can't. They can smell blood, too, even a drop that's small enough not to be noticed."

Walsh's lip curled.

"Yeah, yeah, it's freaky, I know, but it could help," Roux said. "Just let him try."

"You reckon a vampire has sharper senses than a dog?"

"Huh?"

"Search dogs went over the area before any actual people were allowed to compromise it with their size tens, and they didn't find anything. You think your vampire can do better?"

"I think it's worth trying."

Walsh tapped his cigarettes against his palm, his eyebrows pulled together.

"Worst-case scenario, he doesn't find anything, and no one's worse off than before," Roux said.

Walsh closed his eyes and groaned. "Okay, fine. Go get your bloodhound."

Roux stood up, fumbling in her pocket for the car keys. Her skin felt too tight and her stomach was sour. The Five. Roger Schofield. Six missing kids. Four mystery vampires.

There *had* to be a connection.

Her eyes strayed to the window on her right, and a soft gasp escaped her lips.

Ludovic stood on the pavement opposite the café, and even with his human disguise muting his vampire beauty, he looked like a ray of sunshine breaking through the clouds. Their eyes met and something close to a smile touched his lips.

Roux's whole heart lifted.

She hurried out of the café and crossed the road, without looking back to see if Walsh was following. Ludovic waited for her to reach him.

"What are you doing here?" Roux said.

"I didn't trust him not to bully you," Ludovic said.

"You came to have my back?"

There was that almost smile again. "Something like that."

"How did you find me?"

"I heard Walsh say the name of the café, and I asked at the reception desk if anyone knew the address."

"You walked here?" Roux said.

"I used a taxi."

"You arranged that by yourself?" A grin spread across Roux's face. "I'm very impressed."

"The young woman at reception may have helped," Ludovic admitted, adjusting his beanie.

"And you did your own disguise."

Ludovic lowered his gaze, almost sheepishly. "I attempted it."

"You did a great job." Roux couldn't stop herself from touching his shoulder. "We'll make a modern vampire of you yet."

A rare, real smile touched Ludovic's lips, and it made his whole face soften. "I wouldn't go that far. I had no idea how much to pay the taxi driver so I just threw a handful of money at him."

Roux snorted with laughter.

Ludovic's own smile widened, and the laughter caught in Roux's throat. Looking like that, his face bright and open, and his golden hair lit by the winter sun, he was the most gorgeous thing she had ever seen.

She wasn't supposed to think like this, or feel anything for him but friendship, but he kept creeping under her skin, little by little, and she had no idea how to stop him.

"Are you okay to be out during the day?" Walsh asked, joining them.

Roux looked at the sky. The sun was still climbing over the horizon, turning the morning sky into a blaze of fire, and it did little to chase away the winter chill, but it was the light that put vampires in danger, not the heat.

"I'll be fine," Ludovic said.

"I thought sunlight made you guys burst into flames," Walsh muttered, and Roux heard the *snick* of his lighter opening.

"That's because you don't know anything about us," said Ludovic, his voice cool.

"Yeah, okay, are you going to help or not?"

Ludovic's eyes settled on Roux again. "Help with what?"

She told him what she and Walsh had discussed, and her plan to visit the route that Chloe Hegerty had been walking when she disappeared.

"I can try, but I can't make any promises," Ludovic said.

"Anything you can do would help," Roux said.

She glanced at Walsh, and he nodded.

"Let's get on with it," he said.

Walsh led them to the house that Chloe had been walking back from when she disappeared. Her own home was only a seven-minute walk away—she must have thought she wasn't in any danger in that short space of time.

Sadness and anger clashed in Roux's head as she watched Ludovic prowl around the cordoned-off area, every movement sleek and predatory and so utterly inhuman that she couldn't help peeking at Walsh to gauge his reaction.

He was scowling, as usual, but it was a worried scowl rather than a hostile one. Maybe Roux's earlier words had had an effect. Or maybe Walsh really was more concerned with the missing kids than however he felt about vampires.

Ludovic moved farther down the street, his head down, and Roux and Walsh followed him at a short distance. While they walked, Roux googled a picture of Roger Schofield. She didn't know why, just that she needed to put a face to the name. A normal-looking guy in his late thirties stared back at her, and somehow his complete ordinariness chilled Roux even more.

Monsters should look like monsters.

But Etienne and Jemima hadn't.

"This is Chloe's street," Walsh said after a few minutes.

Roux looked up from her phone.

Ludovic had stopped, his whole body statue still, just a few strands of blond hair swaying in the wind.

"Have you found something?" Walsh said.

"I can smell blood," Ludovic said, his voice low and hard-edged.

Roux's throat knotted.

A loud ringing made her jump and spin around.

"Sorry," Walsh said, holding up his phone. "I need to take this. By the way, the search dogs already picked up that blood. You haven't told me anything I don't already know."

He moved away from them while he answered.

Ludovic turned to his right, heading off the pavement and onto a grassy space between houses. "Here," he said, abruptly crouching.

"I can't see anything," Roux said.

"It's only a couple of drops, but it's fairly fresh." Ludovic raised his eyes to Roux's, and the barely banked anger there made her want to take a step back. "It's definitely human."

The knot in Roux's throat thickened. "That doesn't mean it's Chloe's though, right?"

"No," Ludovic said, but his eyes slid away from her.

"Can I help you?" said an unfamiliar voice, and Roux and Ludovic both looked up.

A middle-aged woman in a gray cardigan stood on one side of the fence that boxed in the little patches of lawn in front of each house. Her arms were wrapped around herself, warding off the February chill, and her expression was hard with suspicion.

Roux pasted on her most winning smile. "Do you live here?"

"That's why I'm standing in the front garden," the woman said. "Who are you?"

"We're with the police."

The woman's sharp gaze switched to Ludovic, and her expression didn't soften. The geeky surfer look that Roux had given him had seemed like a good idea at the time, but now she wished she'd gone with something more professional.

Roux looked over her shoulder, hoping Walsh would come to the rescue, but he was still on his call, his back to her.

"We're helping the investigation into Chloe Hegerty's disappearance," she said.

A storm gathered on the woman's face. "That Schofield bastard took her, and we all know it."

"Roger Schofield?"

"As soon as I heard that Molly Bolan had gone missing, I knew it was him. He got away with kidnapping her sister, and now he's *back* for her."

Ludovic straightened. "Why do you think that?"

"Because he's back. She says he isn't, but I've seen the creepy fucker."

"Hold on." Roux raised her hand. "*Who* says he isn't?"

"His mum," the woman said.

"You know her?"

The woman pointed past them to a house tucked away at the end of the street. "That's where she lives. Her piece-of-shit son came to stay with her during his trial, then he disappeared, but I've seen him sneaking in and out at night."

"What trial?" Roux asked.

"For killing those kids."

The knot in Roux's throat moved down to her stomach, making her feel like she'd swallowed a rock.

"I thought he didn't kill anyone," Ludovic said, his voice winter-cold.

"Walsh said he didn't," Roux whispered. "Are you sure it's him?" she asked the woman.

"Who else would it be?"

That wasn't a yes, then, but there was no smoke without fire. The sick feeling in Roux's stomach was getting worse.

"What do we know about the Five?" she said to Ludovic.

"What do you mean?" he said.

"Their history, their background, how long they've lived in Winchester, what do we *know*?"

Ludovic frowned. "Why does that matter?"

A picture was taking shape in Roux's head, and she didn't want it to, because it was too fucking awful.

On unsteady legs she started toward the house that the woman had pointed out. Ludovic said her name, then Walsh called after her, but she broke into a run, charging along the street and down the front path to where the mother of a monster lived, then she pounded on the door with her fist.

"Go away," came a thin female voice from inside.

Roux banged again, harder, louder.

"The hell are you doing?" Walsh barked.

Roux ignored him. Her tongue felt like it was swollen and her head was foggy, like she was underwater.

Finally the door cracked open and a face peered out, creased with age, spectacles perched on the end of her nose.

"What do you want?" she said.

"Are you Roger Schofield's mum?" Roux demanded.

The woman tried to shut the door, and Roux set her shoulder against it and shoved. The woman gave a startled squawk and fell back.

Walsh grabbed Roux's arm but she shook him off and stormed into the house.

Mrs. Schofield scuttled away from Roux, moving farther into her living room. Tears shone in her eyes.

Roux didn't blame people for what their relatives had done, and in any other situation, she might have felt bad about scaring the woman like this. But she needed answers.

Her gaze flitted around the room, taking note of the empty shelves and surfaces, and the patches of darker paintwork on the walls that indicated where pictures must once have hung.

Pictures of Schofield?

With trembling fingers, Roux pulled up the photo of Roger Schofield that she'd looked at earlier. Then she scrolled through the pictures she'd taken of the Belle Morte files.

On Jeffrey Smith, she paused.

The man in the photo had blond hair, not brown, and he wore it long, ill-kempt, and straggling around his face, most of which was obscured by a beard. Roux would never have made the connection before, but now that she knew what to look for, she could see a similarity in the shape of the eyes and the cheeks, the tilt of the nose. If he shaved off his thick beard, would that sharp chin be underneath?

Roux thrust the phone in Mrs. Schofield's face. "Is this your son?"

Mrs. Schofield's whole face changed as she looked at the screen, fear becoming confusion becoming shock becoming horror. That was all the answer Roux needed.

The room seemed to sway around her.

She'd found the connection she was looking for: Jeffrey Smith, newly turned vampire and minion to Etienne, was really Roger Schofield, a known kidnapper—and, if what the woman outside had said was true, a murderer.

Six kids were missing.

Roux thought she was going to throw up.

CHAPTER FOURTEEN

Roux

This couldn't be happening. Roux stared down at her phone, at the face filling the screen, and her hand started to shake.

"Roux?" Ludovic said. He touched her back. "What's going on?"

Unable to speak, she held up her phone, showing him the picture. Ludovic frowned as he looked at it. "I don't understand—"

"Jeffrey Smith and Roger Schofield are the same person," Roux said. "Schofield got away with what he did to those kids, and he must have gone to ground and assumed a new identity. All this time we thought we were looking for this Jeffrey Smith guy, but he doesn't exist. His name is Roger Schofield and he's a fucking monster."

Finally Ludovic got it. He swore, his voice so low and harsh that Roux flinched.

"Those kids are missing because he's done something to them," she said.

Kidnapped them, killed them—she didn't know. Fresh nausea swamped her, and she swallowed hard. Ludovic placed his hand on her back again—awkward, but soothing in his own way.

She straightened, ignoring her pitching stomach. "Has Roger been back here?" she asked Mrs. Schofield.

"No," the other woman said.

Ludovic's head snapped up, his eyes narrowing. "That's a lie."

Mrs. Schofield's mouth dropped open. "Excuse me?"

Ludovic advanced a step, his tall frame seeming to fill the room. "I said, that's a lie. Your heartbeat is going haywire."

"*What?*"

Walsh made a warning noise in his throat, and Roux remembered that Ludovic was supposed to be human.

"When did he come back? Have you been helping him?" Ludovic asked, taking another step forward.

Mrs. Schofield sank onto the sofa. Her hands were loose in her lap, her face pinched and gray with exhaustion. "What are you talking about?"

"You know that five kids are already missing? Another one disappeared last night—Chloe Hegerty. Maybe you know her," Roux said, her voice shaking.

"You're just like all the others," Mrs. Schofield burst out. "Something bad happens and you want to blame my boy. But I already talked to the police. He has nothing to do with this."

"Six. Kids." Roux reiterated. "Molly Bolan is one of them, so what happened? Jessica got too old for Roger so he went after her sister?"

"What are you implying?"

"You know *exactly* what I'm implying. Is that why Roger's kidnapped these kids? Same as his victims five years ago?"

"He never *touched* those kids," Mrs. Schofield shouted.

"No, he just starved them and locked them in a room for weeks," Walsh remarked, his voice heavy with disgust.

"If he'd done that he'd be in prison, wouldn't he?" Mrs. Schofield said.

Walsh leveled a dark look at her. "Don't give me that crap. The justice system isn't perfect, and sometimes monsters walk free."

"I haven't seen my boy in years. Do you have any idea how that feels?" Mrs. Schofield half rose off the sofa, her hands balled into trembling fists.

"Do you have any idea how it feels to be the parents of those missing kids? If you're asking me to feel sorry for you because your son did something evil, then you can forget it," Roux snapped.

Ludovic caught her wrist. His eyes burned with rage but his face was a marble mask. "Perhaps we all need to calm down," he said.

Roux didn't want to. She wanted to scream and cry and shake the truth out of the woman in front of her. She wanted to go back to a place where she didn't know any of this was happening.

But Ludovic was right.

She needed answers, but the angrier she got with Mrs. Schofield, the less likely she was to cooperate.

Roux took several deep breaths, trying to calm herself. It didn't work.

Mrs. Schofield sank back onto the sofa. "I want you out of my house," she said. Her voice shook, though with fear or rage, Roux couldn't tell.

But her eyes, the guilt and fear and despair written so plainly there, spoke volumes. She *had* seen Schofield. She'd seen him and she'd kept quiet. Roux didn't need Ludovic to tell her that.

"Tell us what you know," Roux said.

"I don't know *anything*." The older woman launched herself off the sofa, forcing Roux to take a step back. "But if you don't get out of my house right now, I'm calling the police."

"I *am* the police," said Walsh.

Mrs. Schofield rounded on him. "Do you have a warrant? Do you have any legal grounds to be here?"

Walsh's jaw worked but, Roux realized, he couldn't answer because they *didn't* have any grounds to be here. She'd shoved her way into this woman's house but they had no evidence beyond the word of a neighbor and Ludovic's claim of an overactive heartbeat. Clearly there was a limit to how far the rules could be bent for the sake of a vampire.

"Get out of my house," Mrs. Schofield said, her voice catching in her throat.

"Six missing kids. Look me in the eye and tell me you don't think your son is responsible," Roux said.

Mrs. Schofield met Roux's eyes, her own blazing with grief and anger. "You have five seconds to get out or I'm calling the police."

"All right, we're going," Walsh growled.

Ludovic didn't move. He stared at Mrs. Schofield with eyes like chips of ice, and when he spoke, his voice was as sharp and cold as a blade. "There's a very special place in hell for people who hurt children." He leaned forward. "And the people who *help* them hurt children."

Mrs. Schofield flinched.

Walsh grabbed Roux's elbow. "Can you get him out of here before he makes this worse?" he whispered.

Saying Ludovic's name out loud would reveal their true identities, so Roux placed her palm on his back, like he'd done to her. His muscles were rigid, his fists tight, like he was physically holding something back, then he blinked and looked down at her. Red sparked in his eyes, and when he opened his mouth, Roux caught a glimpse of fang.

"We need to go," she said.

Ludovic gave Mrs. Schofield one last, lethal stare, then he let Roux lead him out of the house.

Walsh lit a cigarette as soon as they were outside. "Fuck," he said. "*Fuck.*"

"You told me he didn't kill any kids," Roux said.

Walsh blinked at her. "I meant the ones he kidnapped."

Ludovic advanced on him, and there was something so animal-like about the way he moved that Walsh stumbled back and almost dropped his cigarette.

"Tell us everything you know about Roger Schofield," he said.

Walsh looked at Roux over Ludovic's shoulder, but if he was expecting her to step in, he was out of luck. She had no idea what to say. Her mind was still reeling from what they'd just learned.

"Nine years ago, Roger Schofield was a happily married man, living on the outskirts of the city with his wife and two kids, and working as a teacher at a local school. But he got fired for turning up to work drunk, and it turned out he had a pretty serious drinking problem. In the months that followed, his marriage deteriorated. His wife tried to help him dry out and find a new job, but he was more interested in spending their savings on booze. His addiction finally took a fatal turn one night. He was picking his kids up from after-school clubs, and he was so drunk that he lost control of the car and crashed headlong into another vehicle, killing two of the three kids inside and leaving their mother with life-altering injuries. His own kids suffered only minor injuries, and Schofield himself walked away without a scratch."

"Jesus," Roux muttered.

"In the aftermath, his home was targeted by friends and family members of the dead kids. His wife took their kids to stay with her parents, and then a few weeks later she took them on holiday. She left no forwarding details, and she never came back. Schofield got bail, which he obviously fucking shouldn't have, because he disappeared before his court date. He went completely off radar for years, until he resurfaced to kidnap Jessica Bolan."

"What did he do with her?" Ludovic's voice dropped even lower.

Walsh flicked his cigarette away, even though he hadn't finished it. "He didn't sexually abuse her, if that's what you're asking. According to Jessica, he never touched her with any kind of aggressive intent, except to restrain her when she tried to run. She was malnourished and dehydrated when she was found, though she said that he some-times fed her, and she hadn't had access to a shower or a toilet in a week. The two other victims were found in similar conditions and had similar accounts of their experiences."

"Why was he kidnapping them?" Ludovic growled.

"To this day, no one has any idea."

"He's been in that house recently. I know it," Ludovic said.

"How do you know?" Walsh asked.

"There was a faint trace of cologne in the air. Somehow I don't think Mrs. Schofield's the type to have gentleman callers."

"That's not exactly proof," Walsh said.

"Do we have anything better?" Roux asked.

"He didn't stop at five children, and there's no reason to think he'll stop at six. As long as he's out there, children are in danger," Ludovic said.

"What do you want to do?" Roux asked.

Ludovic looked back at the Schofield house. "We come back here tonight," he said, "and see what we can catch."

Ludovic

As soon as they were back at the hotel, Roux called Belle Morte to let Ysanne know what had happened, and what their next step would be. Then she dropped the phone onto the bed and sank down next to it, burying her face in her hands. She wasn't crying, but hopelessness was an almost tangible cloud around her.

She needed comfort, and Ludovic had no idea how to give it to her.

Elise had preferred to be left alone when she cried. When Lucille or Régine was upset, they'd wanted to be held and soothed. He didn't know which approach Roux would prefer, but he couldn't stand here and do nothing.

Trying to push down the black cloud of rage that had swelled inside him since finding out who Jeffrey Smith really was, Ludovic sat next to Roux and put a tentative arm around her shoulders. She stiffened and he was about to pull away, convinced he'd done the wrong thing, when she sighed and relaxed against him.

"Ysanne said that finding the kids must be prioritized over everything else. Things are bad enough now, but"—Roux hesitated and looked up at him, her eyes big and sad—"murdered kids will make it so much worse."

Ludovic's fangs slid out, and he clenched his jaw. "Do you think Schofield killed them?"

Roux was quiet for a moment, leaning against him. "I don't know," she said quietly.

"What is the alternative? He can't keep them locked up forever."

"The longest kidnapping I've heard of was eighteen years, so maybe that's exactly what he has in mind."

"His victims can't live that long if he's not feeding them," Ludovic said.

"But Walsh said that for some of the time he was. And Jessica was denied bathroom access for a week, which is totally fucked-up, but it means she *was* allowed bathroom access for the rest of the months that Schofield held her."

"Then why did he suddenly stop?"

Roux sat up. "If he knew the police were on his trail, maybe he felt he had no choice but to abandon Jessica to save himself?"

That cloud of rage surged again. "That doesn't make it any better."

"I never said it did. I'm trying to understand why Schofield might have done this, because there's a very good chance that those kids are still alive somewhere."

"Unless Iain Johnson's right, and Schofield has killed them," said Ludovic flatly.

"But why would he? Besides the drunk driving accident, his history is *kidnapping* kids, not killing them. There's a big difference."

"But he wasn't a vampire before. Now he is," Ludovic said. The words tasted bitter in his mouth.

Roux pulled away from him. "That doesn't mean he suddenly became more evil."

"No, but it does mean he might not have the same control he had when he was human. Vampires don't always know their own strength, especially not when they're newly turned," Ludovic said.

His hand crept to his left side. Over two hundred years had passed since the night he'd been accosted by a gang of thieves, and he couldn't recall a single one of their faces, but he'd never forgotten the burning pain of the knife as it'd sliced across his ribs, or the animal fury that had overtaken him. He'd never forgotten the crunch of breaking bones, or how *easy* it had been to break them. He could still remember the warm wetness of blood splashing across his face, soaking into his clothes, and when he closed his eyes, he could almost still feel that urge to lick his bloody hands clean.

"How do they learn to control it?" Roux asked, still looking up at him.

She couldn't see it, could she? The monster that lurked inside him.

"Ideally, an older vampire would teach them. An unspoken rule among vampires is that if you turn someone, that person becomes your responsibility. Most vampires enjoy a close relationship with the one who turned them," Ludovic said.

"But not all of them?"

Ludovic rubbed his palm along his thigh. "No. Not every vampire feels that sense of responsibility." He tried to keep his voice neutral, tried to keep the memories of the night he was turned locked away in the dark corners of his mind.

"That's how Phillip and Catherine were turned, isn't it? Ysanne said that a vampire was turning people and abandoning them, and the first time she and Jemima met, they had to team up to take that vampire down," Roux said.

Ludovic nodded.

"That's fucked-up," Roux mumbled. She leaned against Ludovic again, and he instinctively tensed. But he didn't pull away. "Who turned you?" Roux asked.

Blood.

Screaming.

Wild red eyes.

The memories slipped out, and Ludovic shut his eyes, trying to fortify himself.

"Ludovic?" He sensed rather than saw Roux looking up at him again.

"I never even knew his name," Ludovic said, his eyes still closed. He didn't want to see her reaction. He didn't even know why he'd told her. He hadn't talked about the night he was turned in a very long time.

"Why not?"

Ludovic didn't reply.

The soft warmth of Roux's palm settled on the back of his hand, and Ludovic's eyes flew open.

The way she gazed at him, her face so gentle and sympathetic, the way she touched him so easily, made something in Ludovic's chest lurch.

She couldn't see the blood on his hands. She had no idea how stained they were. She'd never touch him like this if she did.

Ludovic stared at her, but suddenly it wasn't her face he saw, but the monk's, his kind expression twisting into a rictus of horror, his blood pouring onto the grass.

Ludovic's chest lurched again, but with self-loathing this time. He snatched his hand away.

"Why do you think Schofield has targeted older kids this time?" Roux asked, leaning back on the bed, acting as if Ludovic hadn't just treated the touch of her hand like it was red-hot.

"I don't know."

"Do you think Etienne knew who Schofield really was?"

Ludovic had nothing but contempt for Etienne, and he was glad the treacherous bastard was dead, but he wouldn't let that blind his objectivity.

"No," he said. "Etienne was many things, but I don't believe he'd have turned Schofield if he'd known it would put this many children in danger."

"I didn't think he had any moral compass," Roux muttered.

"I'm not necessarily saying he did. But I don't believe he was stupid enough to turn someone he knew could jeopardize his vision in any way."

"Then he and Susan should have vetted the people they were turning more carefully," Roux said.

"There are reasons why the Council issued laws to prevent spontaneous turning of humans. We have to be very careful who we grant immortality to," Ludovic said.

Roux gnawed on her thumbnail, her movements jerky, agitated. "But did Schofield believe in Etienne's vision? Did he really want to be a vampire, or did he see an opportunity to make it easier for him to snatch kids?"

Ludovic's fangs slid out, just a little. "When we catch him, maybe we can ask him."

"Only after we find out whether those kids are alive and where he's put them," Roux said. "Nothing matters more than that."

Ludovic stared through the windshield at the Schofield house. They'd been here for two hours already and though they could see that the living room light was on, shining faintly through the curtains, there'd been no sign of movement. Walsh had insisted on doing everything by the book this time, which meant that officers had set up daytime surveillance from a nearby empty house, despite Ludovic reiterating that Schofield was very unlikely to risk exposing himself to the sun. Now a fresh surveillance team was ensconced in that house for the night shift, while an arrest team was on standby nearby, out of sight and sound of the Schofield house. Walsh himself was parked farther down the street.

"How do we know he's not there already?" Roux asked, nibbling a peanut from the open bag in her lap.

"He wasn't there when you forced your way in earlier," Ludovic said.

Roux lifted her chin. "I had to. She wouldn't have let us in otherwise."

"I know. I found it rather impressive."

Roux shot him a quick, pleased look, then turned back to her peanuts. "How do you know he wasn't there?"

"Mrs. Schofield lied earlier when she said she hadn't heard from her son, but I'd have expected her to panic more if he'd been in the house at the same time. I'd have expected to see telltale signs in her eyes," Ludovic said.

"But that doesn't mean he's not living there."

"No," Ludovic agreed.

"Do you think he is?"

"I didn't see any evidence of it, but it would make sense for him to flee there after escaping Belle Morte. His mother either doesn't believe the allegations against him, or she doesn't care."

Roux crunched a peanut and narrowed her eyes. "How the hell can she not care?"

A smile, bright as sunshine, flashed through Ludovic's head, and something sharp and painful lodged in his throat. There were so many bad memories hanging like a chain around his neck, but some weighed more than others. Some wounds never truly healed.

"He's her son," Ludovic said. "Parents can't stop loving their children."

"I don't have kids, so I guess I wouldn't know."

Ludovic studied her out of the corner of his eye.

Roux was slumped low in her seat, her long wig spilling around her shoulders. She'd kicked off her shoes to put her feet on the dashboard, and Ludovic's gaze drifted over her long legs, down to her striped socks.

He felt again that tug deep inside, the urges that he'd thought long dead, but this time it sent a ripple of unease down his back.

He and Roux were worlds apart, separated by hundreds of years of suffering and grief, and even if Roux could understand that, he could never expect her to understand all the terrible things he'd done in his life.

"Tell me about this tracking stuff you do. How did you learn it?" Roux asked.

"I taught myself."

"Why?"

"I had no choice. For a while I swore off human blood, which meant I had to feed from animals. They're a lot harder to catch than you might imagine, even for a vampire."

Roux's lips twitched. "Now I'm imagining you chasing after bunnies."

"They were a staple food source," Ludovic said, the ghost of a smile touching his own mouth. "Over the years I taught myself how to track them so I wouldn't always have to chase them."

"Why did you stop drinking human blood?" Roux asked.

Ludovic's smile vanished. "It doesn't matter," he said.

"Hey," Roux said, suddenly sitting up. A few peanuts rolled out of her bag and onto the floor. "Is that him?"

Ludovic twisted in his seat.

A figure was heading down the street in their direction—a man, judging by his gait, though Ludovic couldn't see his face beneath his hat. The man looked around, peering into each front garden that he passed.

The predator inside Ludovic stirred, and his fangs slid out.

Was Schofield already hunting for a new victim?

Earlier it had seemed unlikely that he was killing his victims because he had no history of it, but he had no history of snatching multiple children at the same time either.

What if Schofield was kidnapping each child to replace one that he'd killed?

Anger formed a hard fist in Ludovic's stomach.

His own hands would never be clean, but it took a very special kind of evil to hurt children.

The man reached their car, and Ludovic tensed, ready to leap out and tackle him. Roux reached for the radio Walsh had given them.

Movement blurred farther down the street. The man crouched and whistled, and a small furry shape wriggled through the fence around someone's garden and charged toward the man.

The tension bled out of Ludovic's muscles, and Roux gave a nervous giggle and let go of the radio.

Not Roger Schofield. Just a man looking for his dog.

They watched him walk back the way he'd come, the dog now on a leash.

"What happens if Schofield doesn't come back?" Roux asked.

"Then we find another way of tracking him down."

"How?"

Ludovic didn't have an answer for that yet, but as his gaze returned to the Schofield house, his fangs reemerged. No matter what it took, he'd make sure that Roger Schofield didn't get away with this.

CHAPTER FIFTEEN

Roux

A hand gently shook her shoulder and she jerked awake. Her eyes were gritty; she had to rub them with both hands before Ludovic's face swam into focus.

"What time is it?" she mumbled.

"Just coming up to seven," Ludovic said.

"In the morning?" Roux pushed her feet off the dashboard and sat up.

Pale fingers of winter-dawn light were slinking through the windshield, and the street outside was misty.

Schofield hadn't come.

Her heart gave a dull thud of disappointment.

"I meant to stay up," she said, brushing crumbs off her clothes.

"You needed the sleep," Ludovic said.

Of course he looked as alert and fresh as he had last night, whereas Roux's wig had slipped halfway off her head and her mouth tasted like stale peanuts.

She yawned and stretched, dislodging a few more crumbs.

"What happens now?" she asked.

"We go back to the hotel," Ludovic said.

"We'll come back here tonight?"

Ludovic nodded.

"Right," Roux said, rubbing her eyes again. "You probably need some sleep too."

Ludovic made a quiet noise that could have been agreement.

They drove to the hotel in silence, and as soon as they were back in their room, Ludovic pulled off his knitted hat and ran his fingers through his hair.

Roux's heart stuttered.

It was such a small thing, but a few days ago he'd never have done something so casual in front of her.

For the first time she wondered what would happen once this was over and they went back to Belle Morte. Would the bond that they were building survive, or would Ludovic retreat into himself again? Roux couldn't imagine them going back to how they'd been before—virtual strangers—but a lot of things had happened recently that she couldn't have imagined.

"I should probably call the mansion and let them know that last night was a bust," she said.

Ludovic looked like he was about to say something, then he stopped, his gaze on the floor.

"You okay?" Roux asked.

A muscle flexed in Ludovic's jaw. "Will you—" He abruptly broke off.

Roux waited.

"Will you show me how to use the phone?" Ludovic said.

He said the words as if they tasted bad, and his whole posture was rigid—Roux wanted to giggle or hug him, but that would only make him more awkward.

"Can I ask why now?" she said.

Ludovic gave a stiff shrug. "I have to learn at some point, don't I?"

"I think it would be better for you, yes."

"We don't know how long we'll be away from the mansion, or what other problems we might run into, and as you've made clear to me, I'm completely out of my depth here," Ludovic said. Each word sounded as if it was being forced out. "The Five have that one advantage over me—they understand this world."

"Then we need to take that advantage away," Roux said. She patted the bed. "Come."

Teaching a centuries-old vampire to use a cell phone turned out to be harder than Roux had anticipated. Even people who weren't up-to-date with ever-changing modern technology had a basic understanding of how things worked.

Ludovic didn't have a clue.

It was probably embarrassing for someone of his age and experience to have to have everything explained to him like this, but he swallowed his pride and accepted her lessons, though she wasn't sure how much of it was actually sinking in.

"Do you want to call the mansion?" she asked, after a while.

"All right," Ludovic said, sounding far from enthused.

He brought up the number, then hit Call with a quick prod of his finger, as if he thought the phone might bite him. Roux hid a smile. His absolute cluelessness was the cutest thing she'd ever seen.

Ludovic looked vaguely startled at the sound of the ringing, which quickly cut off when someone answered.

"Hello?" Ludovic said, glancing at Roux.

She gave him a nod and a reassuring smile.

"Ludovic?" Ysanne sounded as unsure as Ludovic did—a novelty in itself.

Roux smothered a laugh, wishing she was filming this. There was probably a fortune to be made from videos of vampires struggling to come to grips with phones and TVs, and anything else like that.

"It's me," Ludovic said, eyeing the phone with no small degree of suspicion.

Ysanne quickly covered any further surprise she might have felt. "I see Miss Hayes has been quick to impart her knowledge."

Roux resisted the urge to ask if Ysanne was making as much progress in her lessons with Renie.

Ludovic relayed last night's events—or lack thereof—to Ysanne, and assured her that they'd return to the Schofield house tonight. Then he looked helplessly at Roux and held out the phone like it was radioactive.

"Are you asking me to take over or do you want to end the call?" she said.

"I want to end the call."

Roux showed him how. They'd gone through it a couple of times already but it took time to sink in, especially when Ludovic was still so wary around technology.

"You did it," she said, pumping her fists like she was waving invisible pom-poms.

Ludovic gave her one of those wonderful, rare smiles.

"Anything you want to teach me in return?" Roux said.

She was as fascinated by vampires as the next girl, but it wasn't just their beauty, grace, and mysteriousness. It was the history that they'd seen and lived. Most vampires rarely talked about it, and Roux had always found that frustrating. How could they not want to share those stories?

Ludovic's smile faded as he studied her face, and Roux wondered if she'd said something wrong. He was so hard to read.

"There is something," he said, and climbed off the bed. "Self-defense."

"Wait, seriously?" Roux gaped at him.

Ludovic nodded.

"You want to teach me self-defense?"

"Yes."

"I don't understand," she said. "I thought I was supposed to stay away from any fighting."

"You are. But you've already waded into one fight since we left Belle Morte."

Roux squirmed under Ludovic's hard stare. "I didn't have a choice. Iain was going to kill Delia."

"I'm not blaming you for intervening, but I am worried that you'll do it again, especially as this mission has become a lot more complicated. We have no idea what else we could be dealing with. I don't want anything to happen to you, Roux," Ludovic said.

Was it her imagination or had his voice softened?

"Vampires have superhuman strength. I'm not sure a few self-defense lessons will do much against that," she pointed out.

"Iain and his friends were human, and that's the fight you got involved with," Ludovic countered.

Roux sighed and blew her fringe out of her eyes. "Okay, show me."

"Do you know how to make a fist?" Ludovic asked.

"Yes."

"Show me."

Roux did.

"Good. Do you know how to throw a punch?"

"Um . . . I don't think so."

Ludovic grasped Roux's wrist with one hand, and lifted her fist until it was at eye level. "This is your middle knuckle," he said, tapping it with one finger. "When you throw a punch, this is what you want to strike with." His finger moved along the smaller knuckles on her pinkie and ring fingers. "These ones aren't as big or thick as your middle knuckle and they're a lot easier to break. The point of a good punch is to hurt the other person, not for you to break your own hand."

"Middle knuckle, got it," Roux said.

Ludovic's fingertips felt like velvet, gliding over her hand, and suddenly she was keenly aware of how close he was. He crowded her with his presence, making her breath hitch in her lungs and her heart thump against her ribs. He could probably hear that, sense the desire that was starting to throb in her veins, but she couldn't stop the way her body was reacting to him.

"Bend your knees slightly," Ludovic instructed, "and keep your left foot forward. Most of your weight should be on the ball of your other foot, but not so much that you'll overbalance."

Obediently, Roux shifted her feet into position. Ludovic still hadn't let go of her wrist.

"Don't tense up. Keep your shoulders relaxed." Gently, he pushed on them, the same way Roux had done to him when she was trying to get him to alter his posture. The role reversal made her smile.

Ludovic let go of Roux's hand and came to stand behind her. "Pivot your hips when you throw the punch," he said, and his hands rested on her hips, guiding her body through the motion. "And keep your wrist down. That will stop you from straining your elbow."

"You know a lot about this," Roux said, trying to ignore the feel of him touching her hips. There was so much power in those hands but they were so gentle with her.

"I've been around a long time. I may not fully understand the modern world, but boxing existed before I was born. I keep up with the basics."

"Did someone teach you?"

Ludovic went still behind her, and though he didn't move, she could feel him backing off, huddling behind his walls again. He had every right not to talk to her about this stuff, but she couldn't help a surge of frustration that he wouldn't open up about *anything*.

"Okay, so . . . punching," she said brightly, trying to bring Ludovic back.

She stepped away from him and demonstrated a few jabs.

"You're taking a deep breath before each punch," Ludovic noted. "Don't."

"I can't help it."

Roux had very little upper body strength, and taking that breath helped her feel like she was channeling everything she had into the punch.

"It gives you away," Ludovic explained. "If you're going to hit someone, it's better that they don't know you're going to do it. When you take that deep breath, you're telling any potential opponents exactly what you're about to do."

"Which means they can counter or block me, right?"

A small smile touched Ludovic's lips. "Right. Let me demonstrate." He positioned himself in front of her. "Hit me."

"What?"

He raised both hands, beckoning her on. "You heard me."

"I can't *hit* you."

"Probably not," he agreed, amusement gleaming in his eyes. "I'm only asking you to try."

"If you're trying to provoke my ego by implying I can't do this, it won't work," Roux told him.

Ludovic just smiled.

"Okay, then," she said, and shifted back into the stance Ludovic had taught her.

"Wait a few seconds and see if I can guess when you're going to punch," Ludovic said.

Maintaining her position, Roux waited, counting off the seconds in her head.

She let the punch fly.

Fast as lightning, Ludovic batted her hand aside. She tried to catch him off guard by throwing another punch but he grabbed her wrist and spun her around, crushing her back against his chest. One arm went around her waist, and the other, still holding her wrist, rested against her chest, holding her in place.

"Now what?" Ludovic asked.

Roux couldn't breathe—and not because Ludovic was holding her too tightly. His chest was a solid slab of muscle against her back and his arms were like bands of steel. He was completely calm, completely unruffled, while she was painfully aware that his biceps were pressed against her breasts, and his hard, tall body was flush against hers. Her skin prickled and her mouth went dry.

Roux knew lust. She knew how it felt to desperately want someone, but the fire that Ludovic was igniting inside her was stronger and more powerful than anything she'd ever experienced.

"Now what?" Ludovic said again.

"I don't know." There was no way she could break free from his grip; it was like trying to shift solid stone.

Her other arm was pinned at her side, but her hand had a little wiggle room. In a flash, Roux knew what she would do, but when it came to putting it into practice she hesitated.

"What are you thinking?" Ludovic said, and his voice sounded low and deep, rumbling straight to her core.

"That if I was in this situation for real, I'd get my hand behind me and twist your balls until you let me go. Obviously I don't actually want to demonstrate that," Roux said.

Behind her, Ludovic went very still again.

Maybe that wasn't the response he'd been looking for, but it would have worked. Vampire or human, a good ball twisting would hurt.

Ludovic laughed, a real, deep laugh that vibrated against Roux's back. It was the first time she'd ever heard him properly laugh, and it was a beautiful sound. She wanted to wrap herself up inside it.

"That's a good choice," he said.

"I thought so."

He finally let her go and she stumbled slightly. She hadn't realized she'd been leaning against him.

"You know, you don't have to be involved with this," Ludovic said, all humor gone from his voice.

Roux's cheeks felt hot, her whole body still tingling from where it had been pressed against his, but his words made her turn to face him.

"What are you talking about?" she said.

"This whole thing feels like it's spinning out of control, and it's not what you volunteered for."

"It's not what you volunteered for either," Roux pointed out.

"I'm not so proud that I won't admit I couldn't have got this far without your help, but everything seems to be getting worse and worse, and I don't want you to feel that you're obligated to stay," Ludovic said. "If you want to go back to the mansion, I'll understand."

Roux's gaze drifted along the perfect line of his jaw, the tousled blond hair that she ached to run her fingers through, the sapphire blue of his eyes. Something had shifted between them, and she wasn't sure what it was or when it had happened. The space between them was charged, crackling with tension, but Roux couldn't do a damn thing about it. She had to stay professional. She *had* to.

"Do you want me to go?" she said.

She had no intention of going anywhere, but suddenly she needed to know if he wanted her to stay—for *her*, not for what she could offer the mission.

"It's not about what I want—"

"Please," Roux cut him off. "Just be honest."

Ludovic stared at her for the longest moment, something raw and real creeping into his eyes.

"No," he said. "I don't want you to go."

Ludovic

He hadn't realized he was going to say it until it was too late. He didn't like admitting vulnerability, or that he needed help—especially to someone who wasn't Edmond.

But he didn't just want Roux to stay because he needed her help; he wanted her to stay because he liked having her around.

That was almost as confusing as the world she was helping him navigate.

Roux grinned. "Was that so hard?"

Actually, yes, it was, but he didn't want to tell her that. It turned out he didn't need to. Roux's smile faded as she looked more closely at him, and he didn't want to turn away when he didn't know what was going through her mind.

She clambered onto the bed, still looking at him. "You don't like to need people, do you?"

He stiffened, and she held out both hands.

"No criticism, just an observation."

An accurate one too.

He could have ignored the question or changed the subject, but he felt pinned in place by the look in her eyes—probing but compassionate, intrigued yet respectful of his privacy.

Something inside him felt like it was cracking, some intangible defense slowly coming down.

"You're right. I don't," he said, and it was actually a relief to say it. "But I do need you here. I can't do this on my own. I don't *want* to do it on my own."

Over the days they'd spent together, Roux had become a rock for him, a steady presence that he'd come to depend on. Maybe things would change when the mission was over and they went back to Belle Morte, but whatever this was between them, he didn't want to give it up yet.

"I need a friend I can trust," he said.

Something that looked like disappointment flashed through her eyes.

"Do you trust me, though? Really?" she asked.

It should have been an easy question to answer, but Ludovic hesitated. Trust wasn't something he gave easily—he was almost *afraid* to give it.

"I trust Renie," he said carefully.

"Renie," Roux repeated.

Ludovic nodded. "I trust her, and she trusts you. By extension, I trust you too."

"Wow." Roux shook her head, staring down at the bedcovers. When she looked back up, her face was set with determination. "Okay, I'm going to pretend I'm not monumentally offended that, after everything we've already been through, you only trust me because I'm best friends with *your* best friend's girlfriend. But I am going to ask whether you actually trust Renie."

"What do you mean? Of course I do."

"See, I don't think you do, not in the way you *think* you do, anyway," Roux said. "I think you trust her because Edmond does, and rather than forming your own opinions of people, your own bonds and your own levels of trust, you're piggybacking on Edmond's."

"That's not . . . I don't . . ." His gut reaction was to deny it, but when Roux looked at him like she could see right inside him, his words failed.

His defenses crumbled under the weight of her stare. He wanted to let her in, he realized, in a way that he hadn't let anyone in for a long time. Edmond didn't count—he'd been Ludovic's platonic other half for so long that he was practically part of Ludovic's orbit of existence.

But Roux was different. She was new and challenging, and she'd burst into his cloistered life and made him question everything he thought he knew.

"Am I right?" Roux's voice was gentle.

Ludovic couldn't find words. It sounded so pathetic when Roux said it out loud, but she was right. Ludovic was a fully grown man and he'd been around for hundreds of years, but he couldn't even trust people Edmond didn't trust first.

"It's nothing to be ashamed of," Roux said, and Ludovic surprised himself by letting out a harsh laugh.

"Really?"

"No," she said.

Ludovic didn't know what to say. Roux was poking holes in the bubble he'd surrounded himself with, tipping the whole axis of his existence off balance. In some ways it was terrifying—in others, exhilarating.

"You can talk to me about this stuff. I'll listen to anything you want or need to say, and I won't judge," Roux said.

"It's difficult," he said, suddenly awkward. This wasn't where he'd foreseen the day going.

"Why?"

Even when she asked questions like this, he didn't feel like she was pushing him. Nudging him, maybe, coaxing him. But never pushing.

"Because Edmond's the one I talk to."

"The only one?"

"More or less."

He had confided in Ysanne about certain things, but it wasn't the same. He had told her some of the darker parts of his past because she was the Lady of Belle Morte and it hadn't felt right to hide who he was from her. But he wouldn't go to her if he had a problem. He'd go to Edmond, always Edmond.

There'd been a time when he'd given his trust more freely, when he'd trusted himself—to keep his siblings safe, to be a good husband, to protect the people he loved, to do the right thing, to rein in the power he'd been given as a vampire. But that trust had been worn down over several hundreds of years, until he was afraid to give it again—to himself or anyone else.

Edmond was the only real exception. He knew Ludovic's mistakes, his failures, the dark spots on his soul. He knew the people Ludovic hadn't been able to save, and he knew the lives that Ludovic had taken.

Edmond understood because he'd experienced so much of it himself. How could Roux ever understand? If he ever showed her all of who he was, how could she not turn away in disgust?

He'd already come to depend on her steady, solid friendship in a way he hadn't expected, and though he accepted that that friendship might not last, he couldn't bear to be the thing that drove her away.

Roux spread her arms, indicating their room. "Well, Edmond's not here now, so you might have to make do with me."

"He might not be around so much even when we get back to the mansion," Ludovic muttered, before he could think better of it.

Roux put her head on one side. "Why do you say that?"

This wasn't a road he'd intended to go down, but he'd started now. And this might be the one thing he *couldn't* talk to Edmond about. He could keep his fears bottled up inside until they poisoned him, or, for the first time in a long time, he could put a little faith in someone else. And who better than Roux?

"Because Edmond has Renie now," he said.

"You don't think Edmond will drop you as a friend because he's with Renie, do you?" Roux sounded taken aback. "He wouldn't do that any more than Renie would drop me now that she's with him."

"I know I won't lose him as a friend, but the whole balance between us will shift now that Renie has become the most important thing in his life. Things won't be the same."

"But things aren't meant to always stay the same. Relationships change, including friendships. Besides, maybe it's not healthy for you to rely on Edmond so much."

Before he'd left the mansion with this girl, Ludovic would have rejected that notion outright. So often in his life he'd been let down, tossed aside, discarded, but never by Edmond. He hadn't considered that it was unhealthy to be so dependent on one person.

But yet again, Roux was right.

He couldn't cling to Edmond forever. It wasn't healthy for either of them.

"Do you resent Renie?" Roux asked.

"No," he said. "I love Edmond and I want him to be happy. Renie makes him happy. I could never resent her for that."

Roux smiled softly. "I know it must feel weird to open up to me, but I really can be your friend, if you want me to be."

Was that what he wanted? Was it *all* he wanted?

No.

When Ludovic looked at her now, sitting on the bed opposite him, as open and caring and compassionate as anyone could be, he wanted to press his lips to the delicate pulse point in her neck. He wanted to taste her skin, wanted to swallow her gasps and moans of pleasure. He wanted to hear her shouting his name.

The urge was so strong that he had to clench his fists to restrain himself.

"Tell me about *your* friends. Outside Belle Morte, I mean," he said, trying to distract himself.

Roux's smile faltered and she looked away.

Ludovic inwardly cursed himself. He always managed to say the wrong thing. He'd never been as silver-tongued as Edmond, but he never used to be this awkward either. Maybe he was rusty after so many years alone. Or maybe it was that Roux was something special, the likes of which he hadn't seen in a long time.

"Roux, I'm sorry, we don't have to talk about this."

"No, it's okay." Forcing a determined smile, she met his eyes. "There's no point in me insisting that you can talk to me if I can't do the same with you. So here's the truth: I don't really have any other friends."

That couldn't be right. Roux always seemed so easy around other people. She was smart and funny and caring and beautiful. Why would anyone *not* want to be friends with her? Then he remembered her telling him that, up until a couple of years ago, no one had wanted to go on a date with her. Had she been a different person back then, or had people simply not seen what had been right in front of them?

"I don't understand," Ludovic said.

Roux exhaled deeply and closed her eyes. "I wasn't always the sex kitten you see in front of you," she said, and there was a self-deprecating edge to her voice. "At school I was pretty much considered the ugly kid."

"I can't believe that," Ludovic said.

She shot him a startled look from under her lashes, but she didn't question him. He was glad; he didn't have a clue what else he'd have said.

"It's true. I was short and kind of dumpy, and I didn't know how to dress nicely, and I had no idea how to use makeup. I always had the wrong shoes, the wrong haircut, the wrong bloody pencil case. Kids didn't like me because I was smart, because I read books, because I was different—anything they could pick on. So I kept trying to change myself, kept trying to fit in, trying to make myself into the person I thought they wanted me to be. But it was never enough."

"Some things never change," Ludovic murmured.

Roux smiled sadly. "Anyway, I quickly made a name for myself as the kid everyone liked to pick on. If I didn't give them any ammunition, they'd just make something up. I didn't have friends to back me up because everyone was too afraid of being associated with me."

"How long did it go on for?"

"Years. I always hoped that, as we got older, my bullies would mature and realize how awful they were being." She gave a bitter little laugh. "Sadly, that didn't happen. Things changed when I did. For years I'd tried and failed to transform myself, and in the end, nature did it for me." She ran her hands down the sides of her body, and Ludovic followed the movement with his eyes. Roux wasn't curvy, not like he usually liked women, but in that moment he'd never wanted to touch a woman more.

"Basically, I got hot," Roux said.

Modern terminology often confused Ludovic, but thanks to the donors who'd been coming to Belle Morte for ten years, he was familiar with that particular bit of slang, though he still couldn't fathom what body temperature had to do with beauty.

"I had a growth spurt, shed the puppy fat, and cut my hair off. Suddenly I wasn't the short, dumpy kid anymore."

"Did people leave you alone after that?" Ludovic realized he was still clenching his fists. This had happened years ago, and most of the kids who'd tormented Roux had grown up and hopefully become better people, but all he could focus on was that she'd spent all that time sad and lonely, and he wanted to punish the people who'd made her feel like that.

"Kind of. The boys who used to laugh at me suddenly realized they fancied me instead. They started asking me out." Roux's lip curled. "Can you believe that? They actually thought that I'd date them, after everything they'd done."

Ludovic hoped she'd laughed in their faces, humiliated them in front of everyone, the way they'd humiliated her.

"I started getting more confident too. I was a whole other person, and the new Roux didn't keep her mouth shut when people picked on her." She made a wry shape with her mouth. "If only I'd stood up for myself earlier, maybe they'd have left me alone from the start."

"You shouldn't have had to stand up for yourself. No one had any right to treat you like that," said Ludovic angrily.

"No, they didn't, but I can't change the past. During the last year of school, almost all my old bullies had given up. It wasn't worth it now that I'd learned to fight back. But even then I struggled to make friends. I had to get out of school, shed that whole part of my life, and start again. But when I did get out, I didn't really know who I was. I knew I was someone who wouldn't take shit from ignorant idiots again, but besides that?" Roux shrugged. "I'd spent most of my teenage years keeping my head down; shaking that off wasn't easy. And it wasn't easy finding myself when I'd spent so long hiding."

"But that was years ago. How can you still not have friends outside Belle Morte?" Ludovic asked. The more she told him, the more he wanted to know.

Roux sighed. "Truthfully? Even after I left school, it was a long time before I let anyone get close to me. I'd stopped taking crap from anyone but I still expected them to give it, you know? I still expected people to laugh at the way I walked, talked, dressed, existed. So I still struggled to make friends. I started going on lots of dates because suddenly lots of people wanted to date me, but that wasn't the same as friendship. For the most part it was just sex."

She yawned, arching her back, and Ludovic's eyes were drawn to the long line of her throat. His fangs ached, longing to break through her skin and taste the delicious blood that pulsed beneath the surface.

"That's it, really," Roux said. "I was scared to make friends because, on some level, I was waiting for rejection. Then I came to Belle Morte, met Renie and Jason, and everything fell into place."

"Besides your family there's no one waiting for you when you go home?" Ludovic said.

It shouldn't matter because, sooner or later, Roux would leave this life and go back to the one she'd had before Belle Morte. Ludovic couldn't be a part of that life, but he still couldn't stop himself from asking.

"Just a trail of hearts that I've broken," said Roux, giving him a wicked smile.

"Do Renie and Jason know all this?"

Her smile faded. "No," she admitted. "Inside Belle Morte I felt like I finally knew who I was, who I'd always wanted to be. I didn't want to dredge up the past when we were meant to be having fun. Then we got mixed up in Jemima and Etienne's mess, and we haven't had time to think about much else."

Warmth flickered in Ludovic's chest. Renie and Jason were Roux's best friends, but Roux hadn't told them this. She'd told him, but not them. Maybe that was more due to circumstance than anything else, but it made him feel strangely special.

Roux yawned again. "I think I need coffee." She placed both hands on the bed, about to push herself to her feet.

"I'll get it for you," Ludovic said.

Roux blinked at him. "But that means going outside. In the city. On your own."

"I know," he said.

"You're supposed to be getting some sleep," Roux said.

"I have all day to sleep."

"How about we go together?"

"I'd rather go alone."

She looked hurt, so he hastily clarified: "I need to stop relying on other people so much, so why not start here? I'd really like to do this for you, Roux."

It was only coffee. It was something that millions of people in the country bought every day without even thinking about it, but heading into the city on his own was a big step on Ludovic's part—and one he felt he needed to take.

"Are you sure?" Roux said, her eyes searching his face.

"Yes."

He needed to put some distance between them because he wanted to kiss her so badly he could feel it like a burning ache beneath his skin. But he couldn't. Crossing that line would change everything. He couldn't let that happen. He was *afraid* to.

Besides, he *did* want to do this for her. He wanted to see her smile and to know it was because of him. And he hadn't lied when he'd said it would help him—he couldn't rely on Roux forever, and when he went back to Belle Morte, he couldn't always rely on Edmond either.

There was a big world out there, beyond the hotel, beyond the mansion, and it was time he got to know it.

As Ludovic left the Old Royal, the sounds and smells of Winchester washed over him. Pausing for a moment, he absorbed it, letting it flow through him rather than trying to block it out. The modern world was still a strange, intimidating place, and maybe he'd never fully understand it, but for the first time he didn't want to hide away. He felt he could face it.

But as he headed through the streets, his optimism dwindled. Where did someone get coffee these days?

Surreptitiously he studied the people around him. Several of them carried steaming paper cups, and Ludovic edged closer to one woman, trying to read the logo on her cup.

Starbucks.

The word was vaguely familiar, and though he wasn't sure what it *meant*, it was a place where a confused vampire could buy coffee. Now he just had to find it.

Finally, after a span of fruitlessly wandering the streets, he was rewarded by a familiar green sign spread across a shop front: STARBUCKS COFFEE. Despite the chill in the air, people sat in the chairs outside the shop, gloved hands wrapped around drinks.

Steeling himself, Ludovic strode inside.

The clatter of cups on saucers, the soft murmur of voices, the rich smells of coffee and chocolate hit him as the door swung shut. A couple of people glanced up, but to them he was just another human man walking in from the streets, not an uneasy vampire silently telling himself that he was not out of his depth.

He approached the wood-paneled counter, eyeing the display of pastries and cakes. Should he get Roux one of those? It was tempting, but he didn't have a clue what she liked. It struck him how little he knew about her. She'd shared things with him, and he was starting to understand how life had shaped her into the woman she was today, but there was so much that he still *didn't* know—her favorite foods, her hobbies, her hopes and dreams for the future.

Maybe he should stick to coffee for now.

"What can I get you?" said the perky girl behind the counter, flashing a smile that seemed to show off every single one of her teeth.

Ludovic looked at the board above her head, displaying the range of available coffees.

And promptly panicked.

He knew what coffee was. He vaguely knew what cappuccinos and lattes were. He did not know what a skinny caramel macchiato or a toffee nut latte with whip was.

Roux had said coffee, but did she normally have a standard cup or would she prefer one of these bizarre-sounding concoctions?

The girl behind the counter continued to wait, her perky smile never fading.

"I don't know what she wants. She just said coffee," Ludovic mumbled.

"I'm sure your girlfriend will forgive you if you don't get it quite right," the girl told him.

It would have been easy to correct her. But the words didn't come. He said nothing.

"Has she tried our molten chocolate Frappuccino? It's one of our limited editions," the girl said.

"I don't think so." Ludovic had no idea what it even was.

"It's coffee with mocha sauce and melted chocolate chips, blended with milk and ice, topped with espresso-infused whipped cream and an espresso mocha drizzle."

Ludovic blinked. He still didn't understand what the damn drink was.

"It's *very* popular. Your girlfriend will love it."

Once again he had the opportunity to correct the girl. Once again he didn't.

"Would you like to try it?" she said, turning on the smile again.

"All right."

Ludovic hurried back to the hotel, coffee in hand, still not sure what he'd bought.

If Roux didn't like this, at least it was one more thing he knew about her, one more little detail that he wanted to keep. She'd opened up to him today, and maybe he really could do the same with her. Maybe he could trust her—for her own merits, and not for any roundabout connection to Edmond.

But was he ready for that? He'd spent so long trying to shut out the ghosts of his past, and he was afraid of what would happen if he let them in.

His fingers tightened around the coffee cup and he had to stop himself from squeezing too hard, or it would burst in his hand. Blue eyes and an angel's smile danced through his head . . . he slammed the memory shut.

A woman skirted around him, giving him an odd look, and he realized that he'd stopped dead in the middle of the pavement.

His head felt like there was a storm inside, raging against his skull.

What was the point of opening up to Roux?

What exactly did he think he could tell her that wouldn't shatter the fragile bond they were building?

Why did this bond even matter to him?

Roux was little more than a stranger to him, and even if they were on this mission long enough for that to change, what then?

They'd become friends?

No.

They were working together out of necessity, but that was all it was.

It didn't matter that Roux had awakened the flames that Ludovic had thought he'd stamped out long ago, and it didn't matter that she was the first person, besides Edmond, to make him feel something other than fear and regret.

He heard the shower running before he opened the hotel room door, and then something else, something that made him stop in his tracks, halfway into the room.

Roux was singing.

And it was beautiful.

Wisps of steam curled under the bathroom door, and Roux's voice escaped with them, filling the bedroom.

For the first time since leaving Belle Morte, Ludovic forgot everything—their mission, Walsh, the uncertain future that vampires faced, the past that still haunted him.

Coffee in hand, he sat on the bed, facing the door, and listened. He didn't know the song, but it didn't matter—the rich, smoky sound of Roux's voice filled him up like light, chasing away the shadows. Closing his eyes, he lost himself to her song, and for the first time in what felt like forever, he felt nothing but peace.

The shower turned off but, in the lingering bliss of Roux's voice, Ludovic barely registered that. He was still sitting there, rapt, when Roux pushed open the bathroom door and emerged, wearing nothing but a towel.

She squeaked with surprise. "Jesus! Ludovic, what are you doing?"

"Listening," he replied. Honesty was the best policy.

"To me showering?"

"To you singing."

Color crawled along her cheeks. "You heard that?"

"Yes. It was beautiful."

Roux pulled her towel tighter around herself. "I didn't know you were here."

Ludovic got the impression he'd done something wrong, but he wasn't sure what. "I got back a couple of minutes ago," he said, holding up her coffee.

"Thanks." Roux took it, but she wouldn't meet his eyes.

Ludovic was confused. Roux seemed embarrassed rather than annoyed, but what did she have to be embarrassed about? If her lack of clothing was the problem, she could go back into the bathroom, but she just stood there, looking anywhere but at him. Her sudden self-consciousness was so different from the Roux he'd become familiar with, and he had no idea how to fix his mistake.

"I've never heard you sing before," he said tentatively.

Roux tensed.

"What's wrong?" he asked.

After a long pause, Roux sighed. "I don't like singing in public."

Ludovic looked around the room. "We're hardly in public."

Roux set her coffee down and made a flapping gesture with her free hand. The other still held her towel in place.

"That's not the point," she said.

He waited, but she didn't offer anything else.

"Are you going to tell me what the point is? I feel like I've offended you, but I'm not sure how."

Roux sighed again. "It's not your fault, okay? I just . . . I'm not always comfortable singing in front of other people, especially when I don't know they're there."

She picked up the coffee again and took a long sip.

Ludovic stared at her. Roux had always seemed so wonderfully confident in her own skin, so open and free, and he wanted to know why her incredible voice made her feel uncomfortable. The set of her face and the stiff line of her shoulders suggested she didn't want to talk about this, and since she'd always respected his boundaries, he owed her the same. But the look in her eyes wrenched at him. It was like her light and life had dimmed suddenly, a candle being snuffed out.

"What is this?" Roux asked, waggling the cup at him.

"A molten chocolate fracchi-something."

"Frappuccino?"

"Quite possibly. Is it nice?"

She nodded, taking another sip. "Really good. I'm surprised you went for this, though."

"I didn't know what you wanted, and I didn't understand most of the options," Ludovic admitted. "There was skinny and whip and something with syrup, and none of it made any sense. The girl behind the counter recommended this, so that's what I took."

Roux threw back her head and laughed, her earlier awkwardness apparently forgotten.

The sound of her laughter was almost as beautiful as her singing. Ludovic found himself transfixed by the shape of her throat, the droplets of water sliding down her skin like diamonds.

His blood heated. His body ached.

He was suddenly *acutely* aware that she was wearing nothing but a towel, and that towel was held in place by just one hand. If she let go, the towel would drop and then . . .

"Did you want to feed?" Roux said, misinterpreting his stare.

That barely touched the surface of what he wanted, but it was all he'd get, so he nodded, not trusting himself to speak.

"Okay, let me just throw my jammies on." Roux grabbed her pajamas and disappeared into the bathroom.

He didn't need to breathe, but Ludovic exhaled anyway.

Roux hadn't seemed to care, or even notice, that she was practically naked in front of him, but the sight of all that gorgeous bare skin had been driving Ludovic crazy.

A few minutes later, Roux emerged. She must have scrubbed a towel over her hair; the short tufts were rumpled and sticking up. Ungroomed, un-made-up, dressed in cheap, forgettable pajamas, she was a far cry from the glamorous creature she'd been in Belle Morte.

But she fired Ludovic's blood more now than she ever had back then.

Now he was seeing beneath the clothes and the makeup and the glossy beauty to the real person, and that person was turning out to be so much more than he'd imagined.

As Roux sat on the bed beside him, turning her head slightly so he had better access to her neck, he heard the thump of her heartbeat increasing. That wasn't nerves—that was excitement.

Ludovic paused, gazing at that smooth skin, then he leaned in and sank his fangs into Roux's neck. The sweet taste of blood rushed into his mouth. Roux caught her breath, her back arching slightly, but it was a noise of pleasure rather than pain.

Ludovic had drunk from a lot of women over his lifetime but he couldn't remember the last time anyone had tasted this good. Roux's skin was like silk beneath his lips, her blood like liquid sunlight flowing across his tongue. She made him *burn* with wanting.

This wasn't supposed to happen.

He and Roux were supposed to do their job as quickly and quietly as possible and then get back to Belle Morte. They were supposed to help each other, to work together. He was *not* supposed to develop feelings for her.

Abruptly he pulled back, his fangs sliding out of Roux's throat. Beads of blood welled up on her skin, but he barely noticed. If his heart could still beat, it would have been hammering.

Feelings?

He didn't have *feelings* for her.

He was deeply attracted to her, that much he'd admit, but that wasn't the same thing. He had no idea what would happen after this job was done, but it didn't involve any kind of romance between him and Roux.

It couldn't.

He licked the place he'd bitten, sealing the puncture marks. That should have been the end of it, but this close to her skin, this close to the sweet smell of her, he couldn't stop himself.

He pressed a gentle kiss to her throat, over the spot he'd bitten.

Roux tensed, and Ludovic pulled back, already regretting it. What was he doing?

"We should get some sleep," he said gruffly, climbing to his feet.

Roux blinked up at him, her eyes heavy-lidded with pleasure. "Right. Yeah," she murmured.

She flopped back onto the bed and wriggled under the covers.

Ludovic followed her a moment or two later, walking around to his side of the bed and pushing back the covers before climbing onto the mattress. The air in the room felt weighted in a way that it hadn't since they'd first arrived, and Ludovic found himself as anxious about lying in a bed with Roux as he had on that first day.

He lay as close to the edge as possible, and tried to think about anything other than the taste of Roux's blood, the memory of her almost naked in front of him, and how much he wanted to kiss her.

CHAPTER SIXTEEN

Roux

Neither of them mentioned the kiss when they woke up that afternoon, put on their disguises, and returned to stake out the Schofield house, but Roux couldn't stop thinking about it.

She'd been ready for the bite, though she hadn't expected it to feel almost as good as sex, but the kiss? That had come from out of nowhere and blindsided her.

She had no idea how to feel. Hours later, she thought her skin still tingled where Ludovic had kissed her, though it had been only a featherlight touch of his lips. Her own lips tingled with need, wanting him to kiss those too. Her head screamed that she had to stop thinking like this—*right the hell now.*

But pulling her mind away from the kiss made her think about the other thing that had happened this morning. Ludovic had heard her singing, and every time she thought of it, her cheeks blazed red and she turned her face so Ludovic couldn't see.

The way he'd complimented her voice didn't make her feel better.

There wasn't much that could embarrass Roux anymore, but singing in front of people was something she did very rarely, and always on her own terms. Ludovic overhearing her was somehow intimate, and not in a way she liked.

She peeked at him from under her lashes.

Ludovic sat with his elbow resting on the passenger door, one knuckle idly rubbing along his chin, and to anyone else he'd have looked relaxed, but Roux knew better. Beneath that casual facade, Ludovic was coiled and ready.

Her brain went back to the kiss, trying to decide why he'd done it, what it meant, and whether either of them would ever mention it.

The way Ludovic's body was angled away from her made Roux think that he didn't want to talk about it, but did that mean he regretted it?

Roux was afraid to ask, not only because she might not like the answer, but because it would mean she'd have to confront her own feelings.

Just that faint press of Ludovic's lips had sent a bolt of heat straight to her core, making her tremble. Even guys she'd *slept* with hadn't ignited that kind of reaction.

Roux gave herself a little shake. They were staking out the house where a child abductor could be hiding, and she was mooning over what could barely be called a kiss?

She swallowed the words that she didn't know how to say and pushed that kiss to the back of her mind.

But she didn't forget it.

There was no sign of Schofield that night, and when they returned to the hotel, Ludovic went straight to bed without saying anything. Even when he was asleep, the atmosphere felt charged and tense, like the room was holding its breath.

Roux stifled a sigh as she slipped under the covers.

Maybe by the time they woke up Ludovic would have got over it, and they could be normal with each other again.

Roux's hopes were dashed when afternoon rolled around, and it was time for her to apply Ludovic's disguise again. He had trouble looking at her, his eyes darting around the room, his mouth clamped shut, and Roux felt a flare of annoyance.

He had kissed *her*, not the other way around. He had no right to get pissy about it, and if he kept it up tomorrow, she'd damn well say something.

"What happens if Schofield never turns up?" she asked as they parked again in the street that led to the house, in a different spot from the previous nights. "We can't do this forever."

"He was in that house a few days ago," Ludovic said. "I know it."

"That doesn't mean he'll come back."

"Do you think he just happened to visit his mother the day before we did? That's too much of a coincidence. Even if I wasn't sure he's visiting her regularly, that neighbor was adamant that she'd seen him."

"That still doesn't mean he'll come back. What if his mum's warned him not to?" Roux said.

Ludovic didn't answer.

Resting her elbow on the door, Roux propped her cheek on her hand and resigned herself to wait.

The next thing she knew, Ludovic was shaking her awake. She straightened, swiping at her mouth in case she'd drooled in her sleep. Her arm was stiff where she'd leaned on it, and she flexed it a couple of times, getting the blood flowing again.

"Look." Ludovic pointed.

At first Roux couldn't see anything. She squinted through the windshield, blinking residual sleepiness out of her eyes. Then a shape, darker than the night, broke away from the shadows and crossed the street, heading for the Schofield house.

Roux's heartbeat seemed to triple, thumping against her ribs.

"Do you think that's him?" she whispered.

Ludovic didn't answer. His eyes narrowed as they tracked the shape.

Roux could see now that it was a man, but she couldn't get an impression of him beyond that. He was dressed all in black, blending with the shadows, and a dark woolen hat was pulled over his eyes. A thick scarf obscured the lower half of his face. That in itself wasn't unusual—it was February, after all—but there was something furtive about the man's movements. It made Roux suspicious.

The figure sloped up to the path to the house. Roux couldn't see if he knocked or not, but the door opened anyway, and Mrs. Schofield peeked out.

"That's him," Ludovic said, his voice taut with anger.

Schofield disappeared into the house and his mum shut the door.

"Gotcha," Roux muttered.

Ludovic shot her a sharp look. "You're staying here, remember."

She nodded and lifted the radio. "I'll contact Walsh."

Walsh had told them that, even though Ludovic was handling the actual capture, the arrest team would still mobilize as soon as a sighting of Schofield was confirmed, to discreetly cordon off the street so no one could come in and to reassure the neighbors.

Ludovic climbed out of the car. Roux watched him stride down the street, and tried to ignore the nerves gnawing at her stomach. Ludovic could handle this—that was why he'd volunteered. He was older and stronger and smarter than Schofield, but Roux was still worried.

However strong Ludovic was, this was still dangerous.

Ludovic

Cautiously, he approached the house. The curtains were all drawn, blocking any view inside; he couldn't tell which room his target was in. Going through the front door would cost him the element of surprise and give Schofield a chance to escape.

Ludovic had no intention of allowing that.

Bringing this sick bastard down required a little more stealth.

Silent as a shadow, he slipped around the side of the house. The garden was surrounded by a wall, but it was only chest-high—barely even a jump for an old vampire. Ludovic cleared it in a second, landing in a fluid crouch. The garden was a tangle of weeds and dilapidated wooden furniture left to rot and ruin, and Ludovic carefully picked his way around it.

He paused beneath a second-floor window. The wall in front of him was smooth, no cracks or handholds, but a thick stone sill jutted out below the window—just large enough for a sure-footed vampire.

Bending his legs, he leaped, a lithe shadow slicing through the air, and grabbed the sill with both hands. He pulled himself up without making a sound.

The window was locked, but that didn't make much difference to a vampire. Ludovic gripped it with one hand and wrenched up, breaking the lock. A faint *crack* echoed around, and he gritted his teeth, listening for any movement.

Nothing.

Easing the window up higher, he slipped into the room and paused, listening again. He was in a bedroom—Mrs. Schofield's, judging by the sensibly heeled shoes lined up along one side of the bed and the floral pajamas laid out on the pillow. The smell of too-sweet perfume lingered in the air.

The door was ajar, and Ludovic crept toward it, his feet noiseless on the carpet.

He was almost there when something made him pause. The house was too quiet—why weren't there any voices?

Ludovic's fangs slid out.

He'd come here intending to trap Schofield, but suddenly he felt like *he* was the one in a trap.

The door flew open and a figure charged in. He barreled into Ludovic, sending Ludovic staggering against the bed. Roger Schofield snarled at him, his eyes bright red and his fangs fully extended. He lashed out with both fists, catching a couple of lucky blows that might have taken down a younger vampire.

But not Ludovic.

He'd been caught off guard, and he was taken aback by the ferocity of Schofield's attack, but his surprise lasted only a second. Then he grabbed Schofield by the throat and calmly pitched him across the room. The other vampire crashed into the dressing table that stood against the wall. The mirror smashed and glass rained down around him.

Mrs. Schofield screamed from somewhere on the stairs. Ludovic ignored her.

Schofield clambered up from the wreckage of the dressing table and shook himself. Blood and glass flew across the carpet. Grabbing his throat again, Ludovic lifted Schofield off his feet and slammed him back onto the floor, with enough force to shake the furniture.

Schofield scrabbled and writhed, but he was no match for Ludovic. Ludovic started to haul him to his feet—

—and something smashed across his back.

He stumbled and dropped Schofield.

"Leave my boy alone," screamed Mrs. Schofield, brandishing an iron crowbar.

She hit Ludovic again, and pain shot up his arm. The old woman was stronger than she looked. Ludovic wrenched the crowbar out of her hand and tossed it to the floor while she screamed again, beating ineffectively at Ludovic's chest with her fists.

Schofield seized his opportunity and scrambled to his feet. Ludovic kicked him back down, and grabbed Mrs. Schofield's wrists with one hand, keeping her from hitting him. He pushed her out of the room.

"You can't take him!" she sobbed, fighting to break free of his grip.

Ludovic let her go and she reeled against the wall. "Stay out of my way," he warned.

He turned back to the bedroom, but Schofield was already charging for freedom. Going out the window would have been the quickest move, but perhaps Schofield still hadn't come to terms with what his vampire body could now withstand. He took the human escape route—the stairs.

Everything happened so fast.

Ludovic saw the crowbar in Schofield's hand and ducked to avoid it. At the same time Mrs. Schofield lunged forward and launched another futile attack on Ludovic. The crowbar missed her, too, but she stood between her son and the stairs.

Schofield could have leaped over the banister without hurting himself.

Instead, he shoved his mother out of the way.

A thin wail burst from her mouth as she toppled backward, her arms frantically wheeling. There was nothing to grab, and she fell, crashing down the stairs and coming to rest in a huddled heap at the bottom.

Schofield didn't even pause as he jumped over his mother's still form and smashed through the front door. Ludovic tore down the stairs after him. He leaped through the wreckage of the front door but Schofield was faster than Ludovic had given him credit for—already he'd disappeared among the houses, the gardens, and the little knots of trees in between.

Dimly, Ludovic registered Walsh yelling at him, but he tuned out the angry man and scanned the street, searching for any sign of movement. He spotted Roux in the car, her mouth open, and his stomach went cold. She was supposed to be out of sight. What if Schofield went after her?

Red flared in Ludovic's eyes and his hands curled into fists. If Schofield touched Roux then Ludovic would kill him.

He started across the road.

The sound of an engine cut through the night, and tires squealed as a car shot down the street; Ludovic just had time to see Schofield behind the wheel, his face twisted with rage.

Then the car slammed into him.

CHAPTER SEVENTEEN

Roux

She saw it coming but she couldn't react fast enough. A car screeched down the road and mowed Ludovic down like he was nothing.

Time seemed to stand still as he flew through the air and crashed onto the road, rolling over a couple of times.

Roux shrieked and launched herself out of the car.

Whoever had hit Ludovic didn't slow down for a second.

"Ludovic!" she screamed.

He was only a short distance away, but it seemed to take forever to reach him. Her heart crashed against her ribs the whole way. Vampires could survive a lot of things, but they could still be hurt, they could still bleed. They could still die.

Somewhere in the background, Walsh was barking orders, but she couldn't hear what he was saying. Everything was a roar of white noise in her head.

Ludovic sat up as she reached him, and her thundering heart almost leaped out of her throat. Blood ran down the side of his face, but the red fire in his eyes was anger rather than pain.

"Oh my god, are you okay?" Roux cried, falling to her knees beside him.

He nodded. "I wasn't expecting the car."

"No shit!"

Roux pressed her palms against the surface of the road, breathing deeply to control the panic that threatened to erupt inside her. For one agonizing, awful moment, when Ludovic had been crumpled in the road, she was sure that Schofield had killed him, and it was like the bottom had dropped out of the world.

Sliding an arm around his waist, she helped him to his feet, and he hissed, pressing a hand to his side.

"You're hurt. You're not okay," Roux said, her heart starting to thump again.

Ludovic closed his eyes. "I believe I may have cracked some ribs."

He said it so calmly that Roux gawped at him.

"Oh, nothing to worry about then," she said, sarcastically.

"Not particularly."

"Are you serious?"

"I'm a vampire. They'll heal."

"Humans heal from broken ribs too. That doesn't mean they're not a problem."

"I'll be all right, Roux."

Walsh stormed up to him, his face puce with rage. "What the fuck was that? You let him get away."

"I'm sorry, is Ludovic getting *hit by a car* an inconvenience to you?" Roux snapped.

Walsh glared at her.

She glared back.

"We almost had him. He'll never come back now," Walsh said.

"That's not Ludovic's fault."

Someone called Walsh's name, and he stalked back to the house.

Roux and Ludovic exchanged a glance, and Roux sighed. "We should probably see what's going on."

Walsh was waiting at the house, his hands on his hips. Several members of his team were gathered around him, and Roux peered past them, through the open door and into the hallway. Mrs. Schofield lay at the foot of the stairs, pale and still, skin and bones in a floral dress. She looked like a sad, fallen bird.

"She broke her neck when she fell," Walsh told them. "She's dead."

Roux didn't know how to feel about that.

The best parents in the world could still produce monsters, and Roux wouldn't judge them for that, but Mrs. Schofield had harbored her son, even knowing what he'd done. She'd kept quiet when all those kids had disappeared.

Yet Roux couldn't help a spark of pity for the old woman. She'd done all this for the son she loved, and he'd still killed her to save himself.

Walsh gave Ludovic a once-over. "Are you okay?"

Ludovic fixed him with a cool look. "Are you asking because you genuinely care or because you want to know if I'll still be able to go after Schofield tonight?"

Walsh shoved his hand into his pocket and yanked out his pack of cigarettes.

"How do we know he didn't let Schofield escape?" muttered another officer, eyeing Ludovic with barely disguised disgust.

"Are you kidding me?" Roux demanded.

"Why not? They're both vampires."

"Why should that matter?" Red flickered in the depths of Ludovic's eyes.

The officer shrugged.

A starburst of rage went off in Roux's chest. "You should be ashamed of yourself," she said, her voice low and hard. "Ludovic didn't create this mess but he's still risking his own life to stop it, to protect innocent people, and all you can do is insult him. What's wrong with you?"

The woman's mouth opened and shut a few times, but she couldn't seem to find words.

Ludovic raised a hand. His fingertips were speckled with blood. "If anyone's interested, I got the car's license plate."

Walsh gave him a look that was somewhere between skeptical and impressed. "You managed to memorize the plate while you were flying through the air?"

Ludovic smiled thinly. "Vampires have very good eyesight."

Walsh immediately put out an APB on the car, but there was every chance that Schofield had ditched it and continued on foot. Good luck to any human trying to track down a vampire in the dark. Schofield was proving to be stronger and faster than anyone had expected. They'd underestimated him.

It was, Roux thought as her eyes strayed to the blood drying on Ludovic's face, not a mistake they'd make twice.

She wondered if Schofield even knew that he'd killed his mum tonight.

For now, there was little more that she and Ludovic could do, but perhaps that was for the best, even if Roux felt guilty thinking it. If Ludovic knew where Schofield was, he'd go straight after him, but he needed blood before anything else. He'd brushed off his broken ribs like they were nothing, but Roux could see the pain etched across his face.

"We need to get back to the hotel," she said.

Ludovic stared down the road where Schofield had made his escape. His eyes were dark. "How far can he really have got?" he said.

"Far enough, and you're in no condition to chase anyone else tonight," Roux told him.

Ludovic's face had stopped bleeding, but all that blood was still smeared over his skin, and it made Roux's heart clench every time she looked at it.

"I told you, I'm fine," Ludovic said.

"Yeah, and I'm calling bullshit on that. You need blood and time to heal. Schofield caught you off guard tonight, and the last thing you want is for that to happen again while you're injured."

Ludovic slowly nodded. "I suppose you're right."

Roux slid her arm through his, and for once he didn't stiffen with surprise. "I usually am," she said.

The second they were inside their room, Roux propelled Ludovic to the bed.

"I know you're a big macho vampire, but humor me, okay?" she said.

He obediently sat.

Roux fetched a cloth from the bathroom and gently cleaned the blood from Ludovic's face. She could see the wound now, a ragged gash just below his hairline, and though it hadn't properly closed, it wasn't bleeding anymore.

When his face was clean, Ludovic started to get up, but Roux pointed a stern finger at him.

"Sit back down. We're not finished."

He sat, without a word of protest.

Carefully, Roux undid the buttons on his shirt. Ludovic didn't stop her but he didn't help her either. He just stared at her with those unfathomable blue eyes, as deep as the ocean.

Halfway down, Roux's fingers started to tremble. She was hardly unfamiliar with half-naked men, but this wasn't just any man. This was *Ludovic*, and as each button revealed another inch of hard, pale chest, her breath felt like it was being sucked out of her lungs.

She was checking his injuries, that was all, and she reminded herself of that with every button. But it did nothing to quell the rising wave of heat inside her.

"Oh." She let out a little cry as Ludovic's shirt finally fell open.

Bruises and scrapes, some still leaking blood, mottled his right side, shockingly bright against the paleness of his skin.

The image of the car plowing into him ran through her mind over and over again, until tears blurred her vision.

"Roux?" Ludovic sounded alarmed.

"Sorry." She swiped at her eyes.

She dabbed at the bloody scrapes but no damp cloth would fix Ludovic's broken ribs. Shoving her wig over her shoulder, she tilted her head, baring her neck. "You need to feed."

"Bagged blood will be fine."

"You're hurt. You need fresh blood."

"It's not good for you to feed me too often. I'd rather wait until I really need it."

"But this is why I'm here—"

"I've already fed from you today. Once is enough," he said firmly.

He started to get up, but Roux beat him to it. She hurried over to the freezer and fetched several bags of blood. "Stay," she ordered, pointing at the bed.

He stayed, but a small smile played about his lips. "Have you always been this bossy?"

"I think it's a new development."

Roux pushed the bags of blood into Ludovic's hands, and he ripped the first one open. He hesitated, looking at her under his eyelashes; if Roux didn't know better she'd have thought he was embarrassed. But she'd seen him drink bagged blood before and it hadn't been a problem, so why was it now? Maybe it was because she was hovering over him like a mother hen.

She stepped back, giving him space. Feeding was a very intimate experience—when a vampire bit a human, they both enjoyed it. Drinking from a bag wasn't the same; without the sensual element, Roux could only watch, and maybe Ludovic wasn't comfortable with that.

While Ludovic drank, Roux called the mansion to let them know what had happened, and by the time she was off the phone, Ludovic had finished three bags and the lines of pain had faded from his face.

Roux crouched in front of him, checking his injuries. The bruising and scrapes were gone, but she'd bet the broken bones hadn't fully healed yet.

"You should have another bag," she said.

"I only have a limited supply," he reminded her.

"We can ask Belle Morte for more."

"I know how my body heals, Roux. I'll be fine by tomorrow, trust me."

"I do trust you, but I can't help worrying," Roux said.

She looked up at him, at the hint of red burning in his eyes. Her hand was resting on his knee and she hadn't even realized.

"Sorry, I . . ."

Her whole body was starting to throb, a deep, desperate ache. She wanted to move her hand but her limbs weren't listening. Instead she found herself leaning in, until Ludovic's hair brushed her own.

"When that car hit you, I thought . . ." Roux closed her eyes, fighting a wave of emotion. When she opened them again, Ludovic's face was close to her own. "I thought he'd killed you."

Ludovic gave her a soft smile. "It would take more than that."

She laughed, and his eyes flared at the sound.

"Roux," he whispered, his voice ragged.

Electricity surged between them, scorching and relentless. Roux felt like she was teetering on the edge of a cliff, and if she fell, she didn't know what would happen. She should pull back and pretend that this had never happened. She should pretend that she didn't feel anything for him, and ignore the sizzle of desire that said otherwise.

But she couldn't. She was caught in his orbit, and she couldn't break free; she didn't even *want* to, no matter how much she knew she should.

Roux closed her eyes and stepped off the cliff.

She kissed him.

Ludovic made a startled noise, and then he was kissing her back, his lips soft and insistent, a contrast to the sharp points of his fangs. His hands slid through her wig, pulling her against him.

Roux wasn't sure how she ended up on the bed—one second she was crouching in front of Ludovic, and the next she was stretched out beneath him, the delicious weight of his body pressing down on her. His hands were everywhere, roaming eagerly over her thighs, hips, breasts, turning her to fire. She arched her hips against his, her entire body pulsing with need.

She couldn't think about the fact that neither of them were supposed to have crossed this line. She couldn't think about anything other than the perfect way Ludovic's body fit against hers, the insistent hunger of his mouth, the touch of his hands as they set her alight.

She needed more. She needed to feel his bare skin on hers—

A loud noise cut through the fog of passion clouding her head, and she broke the kiss, gasping for breath. Ludovic was still braced over her, settled between her legs. Red sparked in his eyes.

"What's that—oh," Roux said. The phone, lying on the edge of the bed, was ringing.

Ludovic moved away and Roux sat up, trying to get her breathing and heartbeat under control. Her face felt flushed and her wig was askew, and her body still tingled with the echo of Ludovic's hands.

She fumbled for the phone, silently thanking whoever was calling, because if they hadn't, she wouldn't have stopped. She'd have ripped off her clothes, then Ludovic's, and never given a single second's consideration to the fact that sleeping with him was probably a very bad idea.

"Hello?" she said.

"We found Schofield," said Walsh.

The red winked out of Ludovic's eyes.

Roux sat up straighter, the fog falling from her mind. "Where?"

"We've cornered him in a building site just off Southgate Street." Walsh sighed and it sounded like a growl. "Can Ludovic come?"

Roux glanced at Ludovic, at his rumpled clothes and mussed hair. The second his lips had touched hers, she'd forgotten about his broken ribs and the pain he might have been in. Then again, he hadn't paid much attention to it either.

Ludovic climbed off the bed and smoothed his clothes.

"We'll be there in a few," Roux said, and ended the call. "Are you sure you're up for this?" She looked pointedly at Ludovic's ribs.

"It doesn't hurt anymore," he said.

Roux wasn't sure she believed that, but they didn't have time to argue.

"Okay, then," she said, rearranging her wig. "Let's go catch a monster."

Ludovic

"Took you long enough," Walsh growled as soon as they arrived at Southgate Street.

Roux rolled her eyes, but neither she nor Ludovic bothered to respond.

Ludovic studied the site. It was a single building, the concrete walls pocked with age, crisscrossed with scaffolding. Part of the roof was missing, though he couldn't tell if it had collapsed or been removed. The place smelled old, damp, abandoned—sharp with the urine of wild animals.

Somewhere in those two stories, Roger Schofield skulked like a spider.

He wouldn't come out again unless Ludovic was dragging him.

That suited Ludovic.

He surveyed the surrounding buildings. Walsh hadn't come alone: police officers were positioned on the rooftops and in the windows around the site. A human probably wouldn't have spotted the slight glint of moonlight on metal—the officers were armed.

"Are you sure about this?" Roux asked, touching his arm.

Ludovic gazed down at her, and for a split second, the taste of her lips, the softness of her skin, blazed through his brain. If Walsh hadn't called . . .

"I can handle it," he told her.

Roux nodded but fear still shadowed her eyes. She pushed a pair of silver cuffs into his pocket, and he didn't tell her that he wouldn't need them.

Now that he was here, anger burned in his veins like fire. Schofield hadn't killed anyone like Etienne and Jemima had, but he'd taken children from their parents, with no regard for the damage he'd caused them. To Ludovic, that made him a worse kind of monster.

Schofield had killed his own mother tonight, and even if he didn't *know* she was dead, he hadn't stopped to check. Everything she'd done, however awful it was, had been because she'd loved her son. And her son had hurled that love down the stairs, leaving it broken, and hadn't bothered to look back.

At this point, the prospect of beating Schofield into submission was a lot more appealing than using the cuffs.

"Are you going to get on with this or stand here all night?" Walsh said.

Roux aimed a cold look at him, then refocused on Ludovic.

"Just be careful," she said.

Ludovic turned again to face the building, his eyes roving over the scaffolding, the windows, and the one door that he could see, directly ahead. He had no idea what this place had been used for or what it was being turned into, so he didn't entirely know what he was walking into.

He didn't care.

He felt no fear, only a steady, hot rage that sparked red in his eyes and made his fangs strain against his gums.

Schofield had done terrible things long before he'd become a vampire, but that ended tonight. He was about to find out what it truly felt like to go up against Ludovic de Vauban.

Inside, the building was a ruin. Plaster crumbled away in chunks from the walls, and thick weeds pushed through cracks and window frames. Rubble and other bits of debris turned the floor into an obstacle course, but Ludovic moved with the sure-footed grace of a cat. Nothing crunched underfoot. He kept his ears pricked for even a whisper of sound as he moved through the building.

It was common for newly turned vampires to forget they weren't human anymore, which meant it was common for them to make human errors, like breathing too loudly, though they no longer needed to breathe. Ludovic himself had made plenty of similar mistakes when he'd first been turned. So he listened for any hint of noise, the shifting of a body, the hitch of breath anywhere in the building, any clue to where Schofield was hiding.

For a long moment there was nothing, and then—

The faint scrape of feet moving.

A human probably wouldn't have heard it.

Ludovic looked at the ceiling. Schofield was on the second floor.

Swiftly and silently, Ludovic made his way to the staircase at the end of the room. The steps were cement blocks, with an iron bar acting as a handhold on the left side. Ludovic stepped over the cigarette butts and other bits of trash strewn about, and made his way up the stairs, quiet as a ghost.

At the top, he found himself in a wide hallway, and he paused.

A muttered curse reached his ears, and he smiled, his fangs grazing his lower lip. Schofield was almost dead ahead, in a room that branched off the hallway. There were no doors, and few of the windows still had glass; a chill wind flowed through the empty frames and whisked up more scattered human trash. Tendrils of ivy, curling through concrete, looked almost black in the darkness.

Right now, Ludovic truly was a creature of the night.

Any other time, that knowledge would come with the painful baggage that had weighed him down for so many years, but as he honed in on Schofield's position, there was nothing but grim satisfaction.

Tonight, being a vampire was a fucking good thing.

Ludovic strode into Schofield's hiding place.

The other vampire cowered in a corner; he leaped up as soon as he saw Ludovic and let out an animal snarl.

It was almost amusing—a kitten squaring up to fight a lion.

Either Schofield was too panicked to recognize the superior predator in the room, or he was too desperate to realize the danger he was in. He charged at Ludovic.

Ludovic calmly stood his ground, then, as Schofield reached him, intending to knock him out of the way, he grabbed Schofield by the throat, hoisted him off his feet, and slammed him against the wall with enough force to make the room shake.

Plaster and dust rained down.

Schofield tried to struggle away, and Ludovic swung him into another wall. Schofield swiped at Ludovic's face, and Ludovic smashed him against the wall again. Schofield's head struck concrete, and he lolled in Ludovic's grip, making desperate mewling noises.

Ludovic punched him, then hurled him to the floor. When Schofield hit, the sound of snapping bone echoed through the room.

No, Ludovic thought, he really wouldn't need those cuffs.

He strode across the floor, grabbed Schofield by the back of the neck, and hauled him to his feet. Schofield's eyes were dazed and glassy, and blood dripped onto his collar from where Ludovic had hit his head against the wall.

For the briefest moment, it was Maurice looking back at him, not Schofield, and Ludovic curled his hand as if he could still feel the weight of that iron poker. Fresh rage blasted through him, the memories from hundreds of years ago feeling like a physical weight. He'd never found Clemmie, and he hadn't saved Marie, but he would find the children Schofield had taken.

He dragged Schofield to the doorway, and when Schofield briefly resisted, Ludovic delivered a punch to his stomach that made the other man buckle over.

If Schofield had been human, he'd be dead already.

There were many times in his life when Ludovic had been frightened and ashamed of his vampire strength, but this time, he was glad to have it.

Ludovic hit him again, feeling Schofield's nose turn to pulp beneath his knuckles, and Schofield crumpled into a senseless heap. It took a lot to knock a vampire unconscious, and Ludovic hadn't held back.

He grabbed Schofield's collar and dragged him to the stairs.

Roux

Roux had assumed that they'd take Schofield back to Belle Morte, the same as Stephen and Delia, but the second that Ludovic emerged from the building, Walsh puffed himself up like an angry bulldog and declared that Schofield was his prisoner and would be interrogated back at the police station.

"Are you crazy? He's a vampire. He needs to be kept in a vampire cell," Roux protested.

Schofield didn't look like much of a threat now, bloodied and unconscious, but that could change in the blink of an eye.

"He's the only link to those kids, and he needs to be questioned properly."

"What happens if he breaks free?" Ludovic said.

"This is my job," Walsh said. "I've dealt with more bastards like this than you can possibly imagine, and I know how to handle this."

"How many of those bastards were vampires?" Roux said.

Walsh's mouth tightened. "Whether it's human or vampire we're dealing with, I know how to do this. You don't."

"Why are you fighting us on this? We want the same thing."

"Because I still have to operate within the law," Walsh snapped.

"Okay, I'm getting a bit confused about when we have to do that and when we don't," Roux said. "This seems like exactly the time when the rules need to be bent again."

Walsh glanced around, then lowered his voice. "Do you really want to go down the route of vampires being denied legal rights just because they're vampires? I can't see that ending well for your friends."

Roux's mouth snapped shut. She didn't much like the man, but he had a point.

"At least let us cuff him. We can't put anyone at risk," she said.

Walsh nodded.

Ludovic dumped Schofield's prone form onto the hood of the nearest car. He'd obviously opted for beating Schofield to holy hell rather than cuffing him, and Roux couldn't blame him.

She slipped her hand into Ludovic's pocket and retrieved the cuffs before he could. "Saves you putting on gloves," she said.

She snapped the cuffs onto Schofield's wrists as tightly as she could, then squatted so she could fit a second pair around his ankles.

"You done?" Walsh asked.

"Yeah."

"We're coming with you to the station," Ludovic said.

"Fine. Whatever." Walsh yanked out a cigarette and shoved it between his lips so hard he almost broke it.

They followed Walsh's car to the station, but when they arrived Walsh insisted on them waiting outside while he whisked Schofield into an interview room.

Roux pulled out her phone. "I'd better check in with Belle Morte."

Ludovic didn't respond, just stared at the closed door in front of them, his face like thunder.

It wasn't Ysanne who answered but Renie, who'd apparently taken charge of the phone for now. Roux relayed everything that had happened.

"Wow, okay," Renie said. "Ysanne's busy at the moment, but I'll let her know as soon as possible."

"Thanks."

There was a pause.

"Are you okay?" Renie asked. "Is there anything else you need to talk about?"

Roux's eyes automatically slid to Ludovic. "What makes you think that?"

"Just something in your voice."

Even over the phone, Renie knew her too well. If circumstances had been different, Roux would have been champing at the bit to tell her friend what had happened with Ludovic. That she couldn't wasn't just because Ludovic was standing there—it was also because she had no idea how to address that kiss.

If only it had *just* been a kiss.

The memory of Ludovic's body on hers, the scorching path his hands had forged, made her face heat and her pulse race. She could've chalked it up to a brief lapse of judgment or a moment of weakness, but it hadn't been just one moment. Even now, glancing at Ludovic from the corner of her eye, she was acutely aware of how his lips had felt, how the sweep of his tongue had filled her with electricity.

Now that she'd had a taste, it would be harder than ever not to go back.

"I'll talk to you later, okay?" she said, and hung up before Renie could say anything else.

Doing her best to arrange her face into neutral lines, she turned to look at Ludovic. He was glaring at the front of the station.

"I could make Schofield talk," he said, and there was no mistaking the menace in his voice.

A shiver rolled over Roux. "Are you saying you'd torture him?"

Ludovic looked at her, his eyes blazing. "To find those children? Absolutely."

"Things aren't that simple. You can't break into an interview room, snatch a prisoner from the police, and take him somewhere to torture him."

"I *could*. I'm not going to, but I could."

Roux swallowed, trying to decide if that scared the living hell out of her or not.

"Maybe Ysanne will have some ideas when she gets back to us," she said.

"And in the meantime we don't know where those children are or what might be happening to them," Ludovic snapped.

Roux scuffed her heel along the ground as her stomach gave a little lurch. "We have to consider that they may already be dead."

Ludovic's eyes burned red. He'd been different since he'd come out of that building site, more full of barely banked rage.

"Do you think I don't know that?" he said in a low voice.

"I'm not sure what to think. You've been acting weirdly since you caught Schofield, and I don't get why—"

"You don't know me, Roux," Ludovic interrupted.

She blinked, stung.

But Ludovic was right. She didn't *know* him.

She had no idea who he'd been before Belle Morte, or who he'd been when he was human.

All this was reason for her not to get more involved with him than she already was, but she had the sinking feeling that it was too late for that. She'd already stepped into the abyss and into the unknown, and she had no idea how to find her way back.

Walsh stalked out of the station. "The bastard's awake and on the phone to a public defender."

"What does that mean for us?" Ludovic asked.

"A public defender won't come out at this time, so until tomorrow, when he comes to the station to receive case disclosure, there's nothing more any of us can do," Walsh said, scrubbing a hand along his jaw.

"Have you told Schofield about his mum?" Roux asked.

"No, I'm hoping I can trip him up with that later," Walsh replied.

Roux turned to Ludovic. "We'd better get back to the hotel then. You still need time and rest for your ribs to heal."

Ludovic made a noncommittal noise.

"I'll call you if anything changes," Walsh said.

"Thanks," Roux said.

Ludovic was silent the whole journey back, staring out the passenger window, but his anger felt like a physical force, boiling the air around them.

"If he hadn't taken Schofield to the station, we wouldn't be stuck like this," Ludovic said as soon as they were back in their room.

"Maybe not, but we can't change what's happened," Roux said.

She tossed her wig onto the chair. Her head felt itchy after having been trapped for so long and she ran her fingers through her hair, lifting the flattened tufts.

Ludovic stood in the middle of the room, his arms at his sides, his eyes still gleaming red. Roux wanted to tell him that even if they were too late to save the kids, they'd make sure Schofield was punished, but it felt hollow. The worst punishment in the world wouldn't undo what Schofield had done.

She pulled back the covers and patted the mattress. "We'll think more clearly when we've had some sleep."

Ludovic stared at her. His face was a blank mask, completely closed off, every wall back in place, too high for her to climb over.

"Do you really think that's a good idea?" he said.

"Sleeping?"

"Sharing a bed anymore." Ludovic's eyes left Roux's face and traveled up, settling on a spot on the wall over her head.

Roux rolled her eyes. "Your virtue is safe with me, Ludovic. I won't ravish you in your sleep."

However much she may want to.

"What happened between us was a mistake," Ludovic said.

"I hardly thought that one kiss was a declaration of undying love." Roux was starting to get annoyed.

"All the same, I think it would be best if we—"

"If we what?" Roux said. "We've slept in this bed plenty of times without screwing each other; I think we can continue to manage. I'm not sure what you think, Ludovic, but I'm not a slave to my hormones."

"I didn't say you were."

"The implication was there."

Angry tears pricked Roux's eyes, and she looked away before Ludovic could see them. He regretted the kiss? Fine. She'd get over it. He didn't need to make a big deal about it.

"I just don't want you to get the wrong idea," Ludovic said quietly.

Suddenly, actual anger pounded through Roux's veins. She might have started the kiss but he'd given as good as he'd got, and now he was making her feel like an idiot.

"I don't know what's got into you, but if you want some distance, that's exactly what you'll get," Roux said. "I'm going to get some air."

"It's the middle of the night."

"Thank you, I had noticed," Roux snapped.

She slung on her coat. All Ludovic had to do was ask her to stay and she would. They could put this all behind them.

But he didn't ask.

Ludovic

Roux didn't slam the door when she left, but something about the quiet way she closed it felt even more reproachful.

What had just happened?

Why had he said all that?

The words had come out of his mouth, but it was almost as if they'd been disconnected from his brain, as if someone else had put them there.

Kissing Roux had been the kind of bliss he'd almost forgotten existed. The image of her pliant and writhing beneath him was scorched into his memory, and that scared him.

No, it *terrified* him.

He'd never expected to develop feelings for Roux, so the sheer force of them took him even more by surprise.

Seeing the look on her face, the hurt written across every feature, had felt like being kicked in the chest.

Why couldn't he have kept his mouth shut?

Roux hadn't given any indication that the kiss meant anything to her, but he'd done everything he could to push her away anyway, to try to kill anything that she might feel for him.

And for what?

Because he was scared?

Because he didn't deserve her?

Because he was too much of a coward to embrace a truly good thing that had come into his life?

Or because he knew he couldn't keep her. Because he knew that, whatever this was between them, it couldn't last.

Either way, it wasn't fair.

He couldn't welcome her affections one moment then push her away the next. She didn't deserve that. He didn't know what scared him more—that he was starting to feel something for Roux or that feeling something might mean opening up about who he really was.

He never had to look too hard to see the demons that haunted him. It was hard enough dealing with them, but the thought of someone else seeing them made him feel ill.

The thought of *Roux* seeing them, seeing *him*, bloody hands and all, was more than he could bear.

But pushing her away hurt just as much.

Roux was a good person—far too good for Ludovic—and like a

beacon of light, she chased away the shadows in his head. But what would happen if he got too close to her and his shadows snuffed out her light?

Could even she light up his darkest places?

Ludovic scrubbed his hands across his face, a human gesture he hadn't done in a very long time.

Whatever else happened, he couldn't leave it like this. He had to go after her.

CHAPTER EIGHTEEN

Roux

She wanted to stay angry. She didn't want stupid, pointless tears to sting her eyes as she stalked away from the hotel, but they came anyway.

One kiss, she told herself, wrapping her arms around her waist. *It was just one kiss.*

So why had it felt like so much more?

She'd noticed Ludovic from the moment she'd arrived in Belle Morte, but she'd also noticed Edmond, Gideon, Etienne, and every other hot vampire. The surface attraction she'd felt toward Ludovic had only started becoming something deeper and more meaningful during the few days she'd spent with him, and now she didn't know what to think.

Ludovic had propelled her to the edge of that emotional cliff, and then, at the last minute, he'd backed off, leaving her to fall alone.

Roux didn't want to fall alone. She wanted Ludovic to catch her. She wanted them to jump together. She wanted him to brave the unknown with her instead of running from it.

But she couldn't make him do something he clearly didn't want to do.

"Hey!"

The angry shout came from behind her but Roux kept walking,

staring down at the pavement while she tried to sort through the turmoil in her head.

Maybe all she and Ludovic needed was time to cool off. They were both adults, they could cope with—

"I said, *hey*." A hand grabbed her arm and yanked her around so hard she almost lost her footing.

Roux's sharp retort died on her lips.

Iain Johnson glared down at her, his eyes hard and cold as flint. He hadn't let go of her arm, and his fingers felt like steel.

"I know you," he said. "You're one of those fucking donors."

Roux recoiled. "What?"

Then she realized that she'd left the hotel without her wig.

Iain didn't recognize her as the Belle Morte representative with the long hair and the thick, blunt fringe. He recognized her for who she really was.

Fear curled up her spine.

"Take your hands off me," she said, trying to sound as authoritative as possible.

Iain tightened his grip until it felt like the bones in Roux's arm were grinding together. She bit back a squeak of pain.

"Boys." Iain raised his voice. "I got one."

Too late, Roux realized she didn't know where she was. She'd had her head down as she walked, paying no attention to her surroundings, and only now did she see she was standing at the end of a small street, with shops and businesses on all sides.

Shops and businesses that were all closed for the night.

There were no pubs here, no nightlife, and it was too late for people to be otherwise out and about. Roux was completely alone.

Except for Iain and his friends.

They emerged from the shadows, dressed in black with hoods covering their heads, and spread out to surround her, a tight circle of angry faces and glinting eyes.

Roux's mouth turned to sawdust, dry and sour with the taste of panic. "Let go of me," she said, hating how her voice broke. She tried and failed to twist away from him.

"Not a chance, cupcake." Real menace underlined Iain's words.

Roux looked at the men around her, silently begging them, but there was no mercy here, no reason.

"You like vampires?" asked one of them, leering. "You like shagging dead guys?"

"Fucking freak," said Iain.

Pushing the fear down, Roux lifted her chin and fixed Iain with her most withering glare. "Fuck you," she said, loudly and clearly.

A vicious grin split Iain's face. "At least she's got a backbone."

He ran a hand down her back and chuckles skittered around the group.

Iain's eyes went even colder. "Not that that'll make any difference," he said.

He punched her.

Pain exploded through Roux's cheek, and the world lurched sideways. Something cold and hard pressed against her face, and she realized she was lying on the pavement at Iain's feet. He stooped over her, puffing up his chest so he looked even bigger.

She hadn't expected him to actually hit her. Yell at her, threaten her, intimidate her, yes, but hit her?

Iain grinned at his gang as if he'd just done something heroic. A couple of them applauded.

Roux pushed herself into a kneeling position, wincing as pain shot up her hand. She'd scraped a layer of skin off her palm.

Someone planted a foot on her back and shoved, sending her sprawling.

Humiliation scalded her cheeks. "Did that make you feel like a big man?" she said, turning to face the thugs behind her.

"Screw you, bitch," one of them sneered.

Roux turned back to Iain and found him standing right in front of her, crowding her with his body. She tried to shuffle back but he grabbed her throat and hauled her to her feet.

Tears stung her eyes.

She'd seen violence before, thanks to Jemima and Etienne, but this was different. It was so casual, so unthinking, and so completely aimed at *her*.

She tried to remember Ludovic's self-defense lessons, but fear splintered the memory and everything he'd said slipped from her mind like water.

Iain slapped her. It was a light slap, but a sob still broke from her lips. He knew she couldn't fight back, and he was mocking her.

"You're a fucking vampire-loving *bitch*," he snarled, thrusting his face close to hers. She smelled beer on his breath. "You deserve everything you get."

He pushed her away so suddenly that she stumbled and almost fell again. Someone else seized her elbow, and Roux threw back her head and screamed.

Someone had to hear her. Someone had to help.

A fist plowed into her stomach and she doubled over, gasping.

Another pair of hands pushed her, this time hard enough to knock her back to the ground.

Roux tried to scream again but she couldn't breathe past the pain in her stomach. She had to get away. She had to run, to hide, but there were too many legs surrounding her, too many angry men—

And then a roar of pure fury split the night, and a dark shape smashed into her attackers.

Ludovic

He hadn't waited long before going after her, but Roux had a long stride and her head start had put a fair bit of distance between them. He didn't have a clue which way she'd gone, but he'd search the streets all night if he had to.

Then he heard her scream.

Ludovic went stock-still.

Roux's scream abruptly cut off, and something dark and primal broke free inside Ludovic, turning his vision red.

Roux was hurt. Someone had *hurt* her.

Fury burning his blood, he charged in the direction of the scream.

When he found Roux, huddled on the ground, surrounded by Iain Johnson and his cronies, he let out a roar that was more animal than human.

He seized the nearest thug and hurled him into the road. The man landed with a strangled scream. Iain ran at him and Ludovic spun, ramming his elbow into Iain's nose. There was a loud *crunch*.

When he'd fought these men before, he'd held back, maintaining the charade of being human. He didn't hold back now.

The smell of Roux's blood tainted the air. The sight of her, bleeding and terrified and helpless, ignited a killing rage in Ludovic, the likes of which he hadn't felt in a very long time.

He planted both hands on Iain's chest and pushed, sending him flying into the nearest wall.

A knife flickered through the air, but it might as well have moved in slow motion. Ludovic shifted his weight and the blade sailed harmlessly past his face. He grabbed the wrist that held it and gave a sharp twist, snapping bone.

His would-be attacker shrieked.

Without missing a beat, Ludovic slammed the heel of his hand into another man's face. An eye socket caved.

Four down, three to go.

He grabbed two more and bashed their heads together, letting them drop in senseless heaps on the ground. That left only one.

Ludovic rounded on the man, a growl trickling between his fangs.

He'd fought against Jemima and Etienne's minions. He'd killed in those battles, killed until he'd been drenched in blood, but even then he hadn't felt rage like this. He hadn't felt like the beast inside him had truly awoken and was clawing against the veneer of his humanity.

The man staggered back, holding up both hands. "Please . . . don't hurt me," he whimpered.

Had Roux said the same thing? Had she begged them? It hadn't stopped them and it wouldn't stop him.

Ludovic advanced, his eyes burning, his fangs hungering for blood.

"Ludovic, don't." Roux's voice cut through the haze of red rage in his head, and he hesitated, fighting the instincts that wanted to rip these cowards limb from limb.

A gentle hand touched his shoulder, and he stiffened. His fighting blood was up, anger and violence throbbing in his veins, but Roux wasn't scared.

She trusted him.

Slowly, the rage ebbed away. The red faded from his eyes.

He turned to look at her.

Roux's eyes glittered with tears. A bruise was blossoming on her cheek and blood stippled her left hand, but she held her head high.

"Leave them," she said.

Ludovic marveled at this girl. Iain and his gang could have killed her without losing a single second's sleep over it. Yet here she was, saving their lives.

They didn't deserve it.

Anger sparked anew, but he forced it down. No one was dying tonight.

"Are you all right?" he asked.

Roux's lower lip trembled, and she clenched her jaw, fighting back tears. "Can we go back to the hotel?"

Ludovic nodded, not sure what else to say.

Roux turned and walked down the street. Her posture was ramrod straight, but her arms were wrapped tightly around herself, betraying her fragility.

Ludovic wanted to sweep her into his arms and shield her from the ugliness of the world, but that clearly wasn't what she wanted.

So he followed her, stepping over the groaning men scattered around the street.

When Roux wasn't looking, he gave Iain Johnson one final kick.

—

When they got back to the hotel, Roux went straight into the bathroom and locked the door. Running water started almost immediately.

Ludovic stayed in the bedroom, angry and frustrated that he hadn't got there in time, and that he'd acted like such a bastard in the first place. She'd only been out there because of him.

He didn't know what to do now.

Roux wasn't crying—he'd have heard it, even over the water—but he'd seen the raw look in her eyes. She was hurting, and he didn't know how to comfort her.

His eyes went to the phone that Roux had left on the edge of the bed. At other times he'd turned to Edmond if he needed advice. He could do that again now—all he had to do was call the mansion.

Ludovic picked up the phone, studying the glass screen. Roux had talked him through it—he could do this.

But he hesitated.

Roux had told him that he relied on Edmond too much, and maybe she was right. Ludovic had caused this mess and it was up to him to fix it, without having to ask Edmond what to do and what to say.

He put down the phone.

Roux

For the longest time she stared at her reflection in the bathroom mirror. Her face was white, making the bruise on her cheek stand out even more. Her eyes were huge dark pools.

She still couldn't believe what had just happened.

She'd known that Iain and his friends were capable of violence but she'd never imagined that people she didn't know could hate her enough to attack her in the street.

Lifting a trembling hand, she touched her cheek. No one had ever hit her like that, not even in the final battle for Belle Morte.

Roux closed her eyes, trying to stem the welling tears.

Iain and his friends weren't here now, they couldn't hurt her anymore, but that did little to ease the pit of fear in her stomach.

She breathed out a long sigh and gripped the basin with both hands. "They can knock you down, but they cannot *keep* you down. No one will ever keep you down again," she told her reflection. She splashed some water on her face and squared her shoulders.

Tonight would not break her.

She'd never forget it, but she wouldn't let those bastards win in any way.

Ludovic was sitting on the edge of the bed when she opened the door, but he jumped to his feet as she came out. Roux's heart softened. He looked so anxious and awkward, like he wanted to say everything in the world but didn't have a clue where to start.

He approached her and gently tilted her head to one side so he could see her bruise. Red flickered in his eyes.

"This shouldn't have happened," he said.

Roux uttered a short laugh. "You don't need to tell me that. Thank you for saving me."

"It's my fault you were out there in the first place."

"Don't give me that crap. The only ones to blame are those bastards."

"I could have killed them," Ludovic admitted.

"But you didn't."

"Only because you asked me not to."

"You still didn't. I don't care why."

"Maybe you should," Ludovic said.

"I've never been afraid of you, if that's what you're getting at," Roux said.

"That's because you don't really know what I'm capable of."

Roux sat on the bed and patted the mattress. "Sit."

He did.

"What happened between us tonight? Why did you back off like that?"

Ludovic gave her a sideward look. "Is this really what you want to talk about now?"

"Yes."

His gaze drifted to her bruised cheek.

"I don't want to talk about *that*, before you ask," Roux said. "Maybe I will later, but not now." She nudged him with her shoulder. "But I do want to know why you reacted like that earlier."

Ludovic was silent for a moment, but Roux didn't push. Eventually he spoke.

"I was afraid," he said, his voice almost a whisper.

"Of what?"

Another long pause.

"There are so many things you don't know about me, Roux."

"Okay. So tell me."

He shifted his weight on the bed, but he didn't run from her and his walls didn't go up. Not all the way, anyway. But he didn't say anything either.

"Let's start small. Tell me why you broke Edmond's nose that time," Roux said.

"I didn't mean to, but I—" Ludovic clenched his jaw. "I didn't cope very well after the war. I'm not sure what it's called these days, but back then it became known as shell shock."

"PTSD," Roux murmured, her heart squeezing. "You were having a flashback?"

"Something like that." Ludovic stared intently at the floor.

"And Edmond was trying to help you?"

"Throughout the war, Edmond and I depended on each other completely, and when I broke down afterward, Edmond was the one who took care of me. But I pushed him away. I'd seen too much pain and darkness, and for decades I cut myself off from the world and lived as a hermit. Eventually Edmond found me—even after all that time, he hadn't given up on me. I love him like a brother, and for so long, he's been the only person I can depend on."

"You don't *let* yourself depend on anyone else," Roux pointed out. "I'm right here—you can depend on me, but you won't."

"I don't know how, and I . . ." Ludovic hung his head, blond hair hiding his face. "I'm afraid to."

"Afraid to depend on me or afraid to get close to me?" Roux said, her voice soft.

"Both."

"But why?"

When Ludovic spoke again, his voice was so quiet that Roux almost couldn't hear it. "Because I hurt people."

She sat up straighter, indignant. "You're not talking about Iain and his gang, are you, because—"

"No. I hurt people who don't deserve it."

His voice was wretched now, and it made Roux's chest ache worse than her bruised face.

"Tell me," she said, when Ludovic didn't speak.

Maybe she didn't want to hear it, but he needed to say it. The weight of whatever he was carrying around showed in the drawn lines of his face, the tense set of his shoulders. He had to let some of it out.

"I was still human the first time I killed anyone," Ludovic said, staring at the wall.

Roux slowly absorbed that. "Who was it?"

He shot her a startled look, as if he'd expected her to react differently.

"I'm not going to leap up and judge you when I don't know what happened," she said.

"I was no more than seven when my father died. It was 1709, and France was in near collapse. My father joined the army, fighting a war that, I later discovered, Edmond also fought in."

"Did Edmond and your dad know each other?"

"Edmond says not, but it still feels like something linked us long before we ever met. My father never returned from that war, and my mother soon married again." Ludovic's eyes shadowed. "Maurice was a cruel bastard who enjoyed beating his wife and stepchildren. We lived under his fists for years, but one night, my youngest sister, Clemmie"—Ludovic's throat constricted—"she disappeared. Maurice told us she'd run away, like my eldest sister had a year before. But I didn't believe him. I was sure that he'd killed her."

"I'm so sorry," Roux said.

"When he turned on my younger brothers, I was afraid he'd kill them too. So I stopped him."

"You killed him."

Ludovic raised his eyes. "I took the iron poker from the fireplace and I smashed in his skull."

"You were protecting your family."

"And then I abandoned them. I was so afraid of what would happen to me that I ran and never looked back. I never saw my family again."

"How old were you?"

"Seventeen or eighteen. Old enough to have faced what I'd done."

"You were a teenager, and you were *scared*," Roux said.

Ludovic said nothing.

"This is what you've been beating yourself up over all this time?"

Ludovic gave her a sad, broken smile. "That was only the beginning. Trust me, you don't want to hear the rest."

"Let me decide that."

Ludovic jumped up, his movements jerky and agitated. "Damn it, Roux, you don't know what you're asking."

"Yes, I do—"

"I killed my *wife*," Ludovic shouted.

His words plunged the room into silence.

Ludovic's chest rose and fell with breaths that he didn't need. His blue eyes burned with emotion.

"I killed my wife," he repeated, quieter this time.

Roux's heart raced but she didn't move. She'd seen Ludovic at his most lethal, and she hadn't been afraid of him then. She wasn't afraid of him now.

"How are you still sitting there?" Ludovic asked.

"Did you think I'd run?"

Ludovic opened his mouth but no words came out.

"You like to tell me that I don't know much about you, but I do know that you're not a cruel man, so I'm not judging you until I know what happened."

"Her name was Elise," Ludovic said. "She didn't care that I was a vampire, and when she eloped with me, I thought she was my redemption for the monster I'd become. But I was also afraid she'd want the children I couldn't give her, afraid of outliving her or losing her to some human sickness. That fear made me selfish."

Ludovic closed his eyes.

"I made her see only the positives of being a vampire, and hid all the dark, ugly parts. I deceived her until she willingly gave up her human life and let me turn her."

"If she truly loved you, she might have been willing to become a vampire even if you'd been honest with her," Roux said.

He offered a sad smile. "You're very good at making excuses for me."

"And you're very good at destroying yourself over mistakes you made centuries ago. Yeah, you were selfish, but I can't condemn you when I've never been in that situation."

Ludovic was silent for a moment.

"What happened to Elise? Didn't she survive the turn?" Roux asked.

"She liked being a vampire more than I ever had, and as years passed, she became drunk on her own physical power. She was happy to kill the humans she fed from, and angry that I wouldn't do the same. We drifted apart and I met someone else." Grief flashed through Ludovic's eyes. "When Elise found out that I was planning to leave her for Claudine, she did what she'd come to do best. She murdered Claudine. And *I* did what *I'd* come to do best—I fled. Once again, I was selfish. Once again, I was a coward. Elise was a monster of my own making, and I should have stopped her."

Ludovic sank back onto the bed, his shoulders slumped.

"Years later, I discovered that she was killing rural villagers, and this time I had to deal with her. By the time I reached her, she was mad with bloodlust, nearly rabid. I had no choice but to kill her."

Roux's eyes felt wet, and she slid her hand over Ludovic's. His fingers twitched, as if he wanted to curl them around her hand but couldn't bring himself to do it.

"You said it yourself, you had no choice," she said.

"That doesn't make it better."

"It doesn't make you a monster."

"Doesn't it? The first time I lost control of my vampire strength I almost killed a gang of thieves who'd come after me. I was so terrified of what I was capable of that I swore to avoid humans entirely, and I was still so young that drinking from animals didn't occur to me—I had no one to help or guide me. I was near starving by the time I stumbled upon a rural monastery."

His voice was heavy with regret, and Roux squeezed his hand, letting him know she was still there.

"A monk was feeding chickens in the courtyard. He tried to help me."

Dread crawled across Roux's skin; she could guess where this was going.

"Without even realizing what I was doing, I fell on that monk and drained him dry. He tried to help me and I killed him for it," Ludovic said.

"You didn't do it on purpose."

"Do you think that made a difference to the monk?"

"Well, no," Roux admitted, "but it wasn't your fault, and it wouldn't have happened if someone had taught you how to survive once you were turned. It was a horrible tragedy, and that monk didn't deserve it, but you didn't mean to kill him, and you've spent the last few hundred years beating yourself up over it. Enough is enough."

Ludovic stared at the floor. "The next time I killed, I *did* mean it. It wasn't an accident."

"Why?"

The pressure on Roux's hand increased. She wasn't sure Ludovic realized he was holding it.

"In 1917, a bomb struck our area of the trenches, killing several men and seriously wounding Edmond."

Roux's heart twisted. Renie had never told her this part.

"He was dying. Human blood was the only way to save him." Ludovic closed his eyes and a shudder rippled through him. "A soldier we knew had been injured earlier in the day. He was in the bed next to Edmond's at the casualty clearing station."

Ludovic squeezed her hand again. "I killed him. I killed a fellow soldier, someone I'd fought shoulder to shoulder with, and I fed his blood to Edmond. I saved Edmond's life but I took someone else's to do it. That wasn't a mistake. It was a calculated choice. That soldier had a family back home. He had parents and siblings and a girl who sent him letters. He might have married her one day, started his own family. I took all that away because I was afraid to lose the only friend I'd had in so long. I murdered him."

He looked at Roux, his eyes blazing with remorse.

"So please tell me, what excuse can possibly justify that?"

She was quiet for a long moment.

"If you hadn't done it, Edmond wouldn't be alive today," she said.

"It wasn't my decision to make."

"Maybe not, but . . ." Roux swallowed. "I can't say I wouldn't have done the same thing if it had been one of my parents, or Renie, or Jason. If it had been my kid or my husband, I'd have killed to save them. I'm not saying it's right, but people do terrible things for the ones they love. Because of you, someone died that night. And because of you, someone else lived."

"What about that soldier's family? What about the girl he might have married?"

"What about Renie, the girl Edmond might marry? Ludovic, you're looking at this in black and white, and it isn't. No matter what you did, someone was going to die that night, and maybe you didn't have the right to decide who, but it's what you did, and it's what a lot of people would have done in the same position."

Roux cupped Ludovic's cheek with her free hand.

"You're not the monster you think you are. You've been carrying this for so long, but you don't have to. You don't have to forget your mistakes but you don't have to let them rule your life either."

"There's blood on my hands," he raggedly whispered.

"These hands?" Roux took them, turned them over, and kissed each palm. "I don't see any blood. I think it washed away a long time ago. You're the only one who still sees it."

Ludovic stared down at his hands, and something warmed in his eyes, like the sun breaking over the morning sea.

"I haven't talked about this in such a long time, even to Edmond," he said.

"Thank you for trusting me."

Ludovic lifted his gaze to hers again, his eyes roving over her face. "Will you share something with me?"

"Like what?"

"Why don't you like people to hear you sing?"

Roux shook her head. "It's silly."

"Not to you it isn't."

Her throat closed up, and her initial instinct was to refuse, but Ludovic had confided so much in her. "At school, my voice was the one thing I thought the other kids couldn't bully me about, but I was wrong."

She swallowed around the prickly edges of the memory.

"When I was fourteen, I was determined to go onstage and sing at the school's end-of-year talent show, but I was so nervous before my audition that I went to an empty classroom to practice at lunchtime. I didn't realize my bullies were listening outside. They burst into the room and started doing horrible, exaggerated impressions of me. I knew I didn't sound like that, but they made me doubt myself. I still landed a place in the show, but when the day came, I couldn't do it. I was waiting in the wings, in my best outfit, ready to prove that I was worth something, but those kids were in the front row, and they were already laughing, ready to rip me to shreds. I wanted so badly to sing on that stage, but when I saw how much they were looking forward to tearing me down, I couldn't do it. I just left."

She shook her head, feeling embarrassed. "It's so petty compared to everything you've gone through, but singing was the one good thing in my life, the one thing that truly let me feel like myself. And they couldn't let me have it. They took away the only thing that made me feel better after each crappy day, and it sliced me open deeper than anything they'd ever done before. I couldn't ever bring myself to sing in public again."

"Then you're still letting them win. They took something special from you but you can take it back. Hiding your voice is still giving them power over you, and my Roux doesn't let *anyone* treat her like that."

My Roux . . .

Roux's heart stuttered. Did Ludovic even realize he'd said that?

"Your voice is the most beautiful thing I've ever heard," Ludovic continued. "Those bullies silenced it when you were a child but you can't let them silence it now."

Emotion stung her eyes as Ludovic's words sank in.

Roux had pulled herself out of the ashes in so many ways, but the thought of singing in public made her face burn and her stomach twist into knots, like she still expected those kids to pop up the second she opened her mouth, laughing and pointing, crushing every bit of her confidence.

But they weren't there. Roux had told Ludovic that he needed to let go of the past, and she hadn't realized she needed to take her own advice.

She took a deep breath. Her voice was good, she knew that, and most importantly, she *loved* to sing. She'd been silent for too long.

It felt like forever ago that she'd sung Phil Collins's rendition of

"True Colors" to a drunken Renie and Jason. Ludovic had just shown her his true colors, and they weren't dark enough to scare her away.

Roux opened her mouth and sang.

Ludovic

He closed his eyes.

Roux's voice was like sunshine. It quieted everything inside him, lit up the shadows, chased away the darkness.

He couldn't believe she was still here after everything he'd told her or that she hadn't judged or condemned him. Instead, she'd understood in a way he'd thought only another vampire could.

More than that—it felt as though a weight had lifted from his shoulders, as if Roux had freed him from the burden that had dragged him down for so long, as if dawn was finally breaking over the far horizon, and that dawn looked like Roux.

He opened his eyes, wanting to see her face as she sang.

She was so beautiful, and he knew that he couldn't stop himself from kissing her. His hands slid up her arms and along the line of her shoulders. Her voice faltered as he stroked her neck, and her heart beat faster.

This wasn't the right time. Roux had just been *attacked*; there probably wasn't a less appropriate time to kiss her, but he physically couldn't stop. Her skin was satin beneath his fingertips, her pulse a tempting beat that he wanted to lick. Her breath was warm on his face.

A little tremble ran through her when he touched his lips to hers.

She tasted soft and sweet. Ludovic meant to take things slow but Roux grabbed his collar and pulled him onto the bed with her, her tongue settling into an urgent rhythm with his. One hand raked through his hair, clutching him; the other trailed down his chest before slipping between their bodies to touch him where he ached the most for her.

Ludovic broke the kiss and reared back slightly, trying to read her face. Roux's breath came in short bursts. Her face was flushed, her lips swollen from his kisses, and desire made her eyes hazy and heavy-lidded. She was so lovely that it made his chest throb.

Ludovic couldn't remember the last time he'd kissed a woman, let alone made love to one. Up until now he hadn't even missed it. But he *burned* for Roux.

"Roux," he whispered, and even her name tasted sweet on his tongue. "We don't have to do this. If you want to stop, we can."

She gazed up at him. He could hear desire in every frantic thump of her heart.

"Don't stop," she whispered.

CHAPTER NINETEEN

Roux

No way in hell could they stop.

She ground her hips against his, delicious friction tingling through her. Ludovic's mouth was hard, demanding, and full of raw, masculine passion. Her tongue brushed the points of his fangs.

His hand moved down, gliding up her inner thigh to cup her, and even through her jeans the pressure of his palm felt incredible. But she needed more. Ludovic flicked open the button of her jeans and pulled the zipper down. She let out a little gasp as his hand found her, gentle but insistent.

But he still couldn't get the access he needed, and with a growl of frustration, he yanked her jeans down. Cool air hit her bared skin, and shivers rolled through her.

Abruptly, she sat up, pulling at Ludovic's clothes. She needed to see more of him, *all* of him. He helped her, tugging his shirt over his head and tossing it to the floor.

The sight of his chest, pale skin stretched tight over sculpted muscles, made Roux's breath catch. He was a Michelangelo sculpture come to life, perfection in vampire form. Impatient to see all of him, Roux pulled off her own top and reached eagerly for Ludovic's zipper. A flicker of hesitation crossed his face and Roux could guess why.

This was the point of no return. She was already naked in front of him, but they could still stop. They didn't have to cross that final line.

But Roux *wanted* to, and judging by the way Ludovic was straining against his jeans, he did too.

Roux tugged Ludovic's jeans down his thighs, and her breath caught in her throat at the sight of him, fully bared to her at last. Every inch of him was hard male beauty.

"Roux, I think you've forgotten how to breathe," he said, and for the first time since she'd met him, Roux heard a distinctly mischievous note in his voice. It suited him.

But there was nervousness, too, the vague unease of someone who hadn't been in this position for a very long time. It amazed Roux that, despite Ludovic being hundreds of years older than her, she was the one with the most recent sexual experience.

She was more than happy to put his nerves to rest.

Roux clasped both hands around Ludovic's neck and pulled him down for a long, drugging kiss. There was something exquisite about his weight on top of her, the largeness of his body as he fit between her thighs. Roux ran her hands over his shoulders and down his back, relishing the flex of hard muscle beneath all that smooth skin.

"I need you," she whispered, biting his earlobe.

Vampires couldn't get humans pregnant, and they were immune to sexual diseases, so there was no need for protection, no need to pause for anything.

Ludovic captured her mouth in another kiss, sliding his arm under her hips and shifting her into position.

Then he paused, his jaw clenching. "You know it's been a very long time for me," he said.

"I don't care," Roux said.

Ludovic kissed her bottom lip. "I might disappoint you."

"Impossible."

Roux didn't believe that people had to be in love to have sex. She'd slept with plenty of people she wasn't in love with, and she was about to do it again. She didn't love Ludovic.

But as his eyes locked with hers, flaring red as he slowly pushed inside, her chest felt full of something that she'd never felt before. It *couldn't* be love, it was too soon, but it was a storm of emotion that she didn't know how to name.

It was something new, full of hope and possibility, but also uncertainty, because it was foreign to her. It was the wind in her face as she stepped again off that cliff edge and plunged into the beauty of the unknown.

A shudder ran through Ludovic as their bodies joined, and he held himself still for a moment, burying his face in her neck.

Roux gently ran her nails down his back, sparking him to life.

At first he moved tentatively, carefully, as if he was afraid she'd break. But as she whispered his name, nipping at his earlobe again, he settled into a harder rhythm.

White lights crowded Roux's vision, her breath coming in ragged pants as she clung to Ludovic's back. Delicious pressure spread through her body, a wave building and building and building, pulling her to impossible heights of bliss.

And then the wave broke and she screamed, clutching Ludovic, her body shaking and trembling and pulsing and drowning in sweet fire. The world faded to background noise.

It felt *right* in a way she'd never experienced, and even after the wave had receded and the world came back into focus, and she was lying in Ludovic's arms, her heartbeat returning to normal, her chest still felt like it was full of light, like she was still falling into that abyss.

When she'd first offered to work with Ludovic, this was the last thing she'd seen coming, but she didn't regret it. It felt like she'd stumbled upon something she hadn't even known she'd been looking for.

But could she keep it?

She and Ludovic had shared a bed and a bathroom since they arrived at the hotel, but today it felt different. Roux was more aware of everything Ludovic did, more aware of *him*, his presence, his movements, his voice.

They snatched a few hours of sleep, and though neither of them had kissed or touched again yet, there was still something intimate about sharing the same space now. They'd gone from colleagues who shared a room out of necessity to something more, something Roux couldn't yet define.

They didn't talk much as they took it in turns to shower, and skirted around each other to get dressed, but instead of feeling awkward, Roux had never felt so comfortable.

Roux's phone rang. "It's Walsh," she said, and answered the call.

"We need Ludovic at the station *now*," Walsh barked. "Schofield's taken his solicitor hostage."

The temperature in the room plummeted and Roux squeezed her eyes shut, because Walsh hadn't really said that, had he?

"How the hell did *that* happen?" Ludovic growled.

"Just get over here!" Walsh ended the call.

"Fuck," Roux whispered. "Fuck, fuck, *fuck*."

Ludovic tossed her the car keys. "Let's go."

Roux violated every speed limit in the city and got them to the station in record time. Ludovic was too polite to say anything about her driving, but she saw him wince every time they took a corner too fast.

"It's daylight. How far does he think he's going to get?" Roux said as she parked.

"He won't burst into flames the second he steps outside," Ludovic said.

"Then if he gets out of the station, he can disappear into the city."

Red flashed in Ludovic's eyes. "I won't let that happen."

When they were a few feet from the station, Ludovic put out a hand to stop Roux. The police station had undergone a recent refurbishment, and the glass-paneled facade offered a clear view of the scene inside.

Schofield was in the reception area, his hand wrapped around the neck of a small man in a gray suit, holding him like a shield. Silver cuffs dangled from Schofield's wrist, and the skin around the bracelet was mottled and weeping.

Uniformed officers fanned out in front of him, but none of them would be fast enough to stop Schofield from breaking his hostage's neck.

Ysanne had talked often about having to maintain a careful balance between vampires and humans, and this was why, Roux realized. The Council had such strict rules and harsh punishments because only vampires could control and contain other vampires. Human police weren't equipped for it, and that was dangerous.

"How do we handle this?" Roux whispered.

"*We* don't. You stay here."

"That's not what I meant. How are you going to get to Schofield before he kills his lawyer?"

Ludovic studied the building and the scene inside. "I don't know that I can. I can't open that door without Schofield hearing."

"What if *I* opened it? He's never seen me before, so he won't view me as any kind of threat."

"Not a chance," Ludovic growled.

"He won't go after me when he already has a hostage."

"It's too risky."

Roux put her hands on her hips. "Do you have a better suggestion? If Schofield gets away, we lose our only hope of finding those kids."

Ludovic's jaw tightened.

"We don't have time to argue about this," Roux said.

"Fine."

Roux kissed him on the cheek, and Ludovic gave her a startled look.

"I'll be okay," she said.

But unease twisted in her stomach as she approached the station. She couldn't see Walsh among the assembled officers, and strangely, she wished she could. A familiar face might have made her feel better, even if it was one she didn't much like.

Sucking in a bolstering breath, Roux pulled open the door.

Schofield half turned, dragging his human shield with him, and Roux froze, her eyes widening, her mouth dropping open. As far as Schofield knew, she was just some girl wandering in from the street.

"What's going on?" she asked, letting her voice tremble.

Schofield's eyes were wild and red, his fangs fully extended. "Get the door," he snarled.

Roux made a show of fumbling for the door, before pushing it open. There was no sign of Ludovic, but she trusted him.

Schofield backed toward the door, dragging his lawyer with him. The small man's eyes bulged from the pressure of Schofield's hand on his throat.

The atmosphere was like glass—sharp and hard, ready to shatter at any moment.

Schofield hesitated in the doorway, his eyes darting over the street, probably planning where he could run to escape from the sun.

Roux hid a cold smile.

Schofield suddenly shoved his hostage at the officers still spread out in the reception area and made a run for it.

He was fast.

Ludovic was faster.

Like a bolt loosed from a crossbow, he came out of nowhere and punched Schofield three times in a blur of movement. Blood sprayed, and as Schofield's hands shot automatically to his face, Ludovic rammed both fists into the other vampire's stomach. Schofield folded like a broken doll, and Ludovic smacked his head against the pavement, hard enough that he'd have killed him if Schofield had been human.

Schofield went limp.

Roux let out the breath that had been lodged in her lungs since she'd walked into the station.

Walsh jogged out to join them. "Thank fuck," he said. He moved toward Schofield, and Ludovic held out a hand to stop him.

"He's not your prisoner anymore," he said, his voice granite-hard.

"Excuse me?"

"You almost let him escape, and we're not making that mistake again. Schofield belongs to us now."

"He needs to remain in custody—"

"I don't care," Ludovic said, and Roux caught a flash of fang.

"Who undid the cuffs anyway?" Roux asked.

Walsh stabbed his thumb at Schofield's lawyer, who was wiping tears and snot off his face. "Genius over there."

"Interrogating him while he was handcuffed was a violation of PACE and you know it. He still has rights," the man said. Red marks tinged his neck.

"Fuck that," Walsh snarled. "Those cuffs were the only thing keeping him down."

"What's PACE?" Roux asked.

"Police and Criminal Evidence Act," Walsh said impatiently. He swung back to Ludovic.

"Don't," Ludovic said, before Walsh could speak. "You had your chance and you failed."

Grabbing Schofield's collar, he threw the unconscious vampire over his shoulder. "Let's go," he said to Roux.

"You can't do this," Walsh cried.

"Watch us."

They took Schofield back to the hotel, pausing at a hardware store so Roux could buy a thick coil of chain. She wasn't taking any chances.

When they were safely inside their room, Ludovic dragged

Schofield to the bathroom, cuffed his wrists and ankles with silver, then chained him head to foot to the pedestal basin.

"Are you sure that's secure enough?" Roux said.

"Yes," Ludovic replied. "He's injured, he's been without blood, he's cuffed with silver, and he can't move enough to break out of the chains. He's not going anywhere."

"What happens now?"

"When he wakes up, I'll question him," Ludovic said, and his voice was so cold that it made Roux pause.

"Question him how?"

Ludovic met her eyes. "Whichever way gets him to talk."

"You mean torture." Roux's stomach went hollow.

"I'm willing to do whatever it takes to find those children. We can debate the moral high ground if you want, but it won't change my mind."

Roux thought of the sister Ludovic had lost. The hundreds of years that had passed since then obviously hadn't eased the pain of her loss or the guilt that he hadn't been able to protect her, and maybe he saw finding these kids as some sort of absolution.

"Do what you need to," she said.

Ludovic put his hand on her shoulder, and even that gentle touch made her pulse with awareness.

"There's one problem, though," Roux said, eyeing Schofield's slumped form. "He doesn't look like he's coming round any time soon."

"I may have hit him harder than I realized." Ludovic didn't sound remotely sorry.

"How long do you think he'll be out?"

"It's hard to say."

Ludovic shifted his weight, suddenly awkward. "I'm not entirely happy about doing this. Maybe Schofield deserves whatever he gets, but—"

"Don't say it."

A faint smile touched Ludovic's lips. "You don't know what I was going to say."

"You were going to worry that doing this means giving in to the parts of yourself that you fear."

Ludovic blinked.

"Am I right?" Roux said.

"Well, yes."

Roux stood on tiptoes to kiss him. "You're a good man, and nothing will change that."

Ludovic gazed down at her, his eyes soft and filled with what almost looked like awe. "Every time I think the darkness is coming back, you pull me into the light. I've never met anyone like you."

Roux grinned. "Well, that makes two of us."

Ludovic's expression heated. "You're amazing. Do you know that?"

"Obviously, but feel free to keep telling me. I can never hear it enough."

He lowered his head and pressed a kiss to the side of her mouth. "You're amazing," he whispered, and a shudder rolled through her. He kissed the other side of her mouth. "You're amazing." His hands slid up her hips, harder than his kisses. "You're amazing."

"Ludovic," Roux murmured. His name was so delicious, something she could roll around her tongue.

The hard length of him pressed into her hip, and Roux rubbed against him, suddenly desperate for more.

This really wasn't the time.

But neither of them could stop.

Lifting Roux off her feet, Ludovic pressed her against the wall, and she writhed against him, urgent, aching with need. She reached between them, fumbling impatiently for her zipper.

Ludovic tugged Roux's jeans down. Her legs were still locked around his waist so he could only get them as far as her knees. He lowered her, and she kicked off her boots, one at a time, then helped Ludovic pull off her jeans. He slid an arm under her thighs and hoisted her back into position against the wall. She locked her ankles around his hips, pulling him against her.

"Roux," he whispered. "I can't . . ."

She looked down. Her legs were gripping him so tightly that he couldn't undo his own jeans.

"Sorry."

Roux relaxed her grip and Ludovic flicked open his fly. Roux closed her eyes as his fingers found her, caressing, almost reverent.

"You're so beautiful," he whispered, nipping the edge of her jaw.

Roux shuddered as the clever rhythm of Ludovic's fingers stoked the blaze inside her.

Ludovic pressed his face to her neck, deeply inhaling the smell of her skin. His tongue flicked out and brushed along her pulse, and she let out a small moan.

"I want to bite you," he whispered.

Roux managed a dazed nod.

Ludovic shifted his hips, pushing inside her. Roux caught her breath, her toes curling, and then Ludovic's mouth closed over her neck, gently sucking. She was unprepared for his fangs when he bit down and she arched her back at the rush of bliss, almost pushing off the wall.

Ludovic's arm clamped around her waist, holding her in place as he thrust, slowly at first, matching the pull of his mouth on her vein. Roux shoved her fingers through his hair, clutching him, as sensation stormed her body.

"Ludovic," she groaned, the muscles in her thighs tensing as a wave of pleasure built higher and higher. The rhythm of his hips between her legs sped up, his mouth sucked hard at her neck, and it was almost more than she could handle.

She came with a hoarse cry, white lights flashing behind her eyes. Ludovic's mouth found hers. The metallic tang of her own blood was on his tongue, and she didn't care because he hadn't stopped moving, and now the pressure was building again, tighter and hotter and more exquisite than anything she'd ever felt before.

When she came again, she screamed his name, convulsing against him. A moment later he stiffened with a harsh groan.

Roux slumped in his arms, her breaths coming in short gasps. She felt like she was floating, like that last spectacular orgasm had pushed her right out of her own skin and she had no idea how to come back down to earth.

Before Ludovic, she'd thought she'd known what good sex was. But he'd blasted away any memory of guys before, and in some ways that scared her.

How would anyone else ever match up?

She slid her arms around Ludovic's neck, and let her head rest on the wall behind her. Whatever else happened, she'd enjoy this while it lasted.

Ludovic

Roux felt like heaven.

Listening to her sing brought him the kind of peace he hadn't felt in a long time, but it was nothing compared to the feeling of sinking deep inside her lean, lithe body, hearing her crying out his name.

How was it possible that he'd only really known her for a few days?

Roux relaxed her legs and slid to the floor. "That was incredible," she said.

Ludovic couldn't agree more. How could he have forgotten how good sex was? How had he gone so long without it and never even missed it?

Because it had never been as good as it was with Roux.

The thought sneaked in before he could stop it, and it made him pause. Was it true? The memories of his past lovers had faded over the centuries, but he genuinely couldn't recall ever feeling the way he did when he was with Roux. She took him to a place that felt new and special on a level he couldn't quite describe.

He needed to be careful. Whatever this was between them, he couldn't afford to get in too deep.

Roux pulled on her jeans, her movements languid, sated. "You've surprised me, you know," she said.

"Why?"

"No offense, but you can be so stiff and awkward, and I thought you'd be the same in bed, a missionary-only kind of guy."

Roux had fantasized about sex with him before they'd had it? Ludovic liked that.

"There are things about me that you still don't know," he said, and there was a teasing edge to his voice that made Roux lift an eyebrow.

Ludovic didn't normally tease, but he felt so relaxed around her, so comfortable, like he was rediscovering parts of himself that he'd thought long forgotten.

"Ludovic de Vauban, are you flirting with me?" Roux clasped her hands to her chest. "Next thing you'll be telling me all the naughty bits of your past, the wild sex and the threesomes."

Ludovic's smile grew wider; he couldn't help it.

"Wait, are you serious?" Roux said.

"Does that shock you?"

Roux snorted. "Please. Startled? Maybe. Shocked? Never." She sprawled on the end of the bed, resting her weight on her elbows. "Intrigued? Definitely. Tell me more."

Ludovic got dressed and joined her on the bed. "During the French Revolution, I rescued two noblewomen, Lucille and Régine, from the guillotine. They believed I was an angel, come to deliver them to safety."

"I can believe that," Roux said, reaching up and toying with a strand of his blond hair.

Her casual, gentle touches made his old heart ache.

"We escaped the bloodshed, found a quiet house in the country, and lived very happily, first as friends, then as lovers."

He'd suppressed the memories for years, and now they rose up: Lucille's laughter ringing through the house; Régine, quieter, softer, with eyes the color of the sky. How had he clung so tightly to the dark parts of his past and refused to remember the good parts?

Then Marie's sunshine smile filled his head, and Ludovic's mood soured.

Roux had helped him face so much of his past, but some things would never stop hurting.

Her hand touched his face, soft and warm. "Where did you just go?" she asked.

"Somewhere I don't want to talk about."

A groan drifted out from the bathroom, the clank of chains heralding Schofield's return to consciousness.

Ludovic stood up. "Turn on the television. I don't want you to hear this."

Roux pressed a kiss to his lips. "I'll be right outside this door, okay?"

"Thank you," he whispered, tucking a strand of Roux's wig behind her ears.

Then he went into the bathroom and shut the door.

CHAPTER TWENTY

Roux

Roux had no idea what Ludovic was doing to Schofield, and maybe he deserved it, but the moans coming from the bathroom still made her stomach twist.

She turned up the volume on the TV.

Finally, the bathroom door opened again, and Ludovic stepped out. Blood spotted his clothes, and his jaw was set.

"The children are at a derelict pub called the White Stag, two and a half miles outside the city. Schofield used to work there before his arrest."

Roux let out a shuddering gasp of relief. Suddenly, the TV was too loud and annoying, and she turned it off.

"Are you okay?" she asked.

Ludovic gave a short nod. "I did what I had to, and I don't regret that."

"You will," came Schofield's voice from behind them.

Roux peeked over Ludovic's shoulder. The bathroom door had drifted open, revealing Schofield slumped on the bathroom floor, his face a bloody mess.

His swollen eyes widened as he saw her. "You're the girl from the police station. The fuck are you doing here?" he said.

Roux opened her mouth but she couldn't find words.

Red crept into Schofield's stare. "You set me up. You knew that bastard was waiting for me outside."

Roux shrugged, but it was stiff and jerky. The way Schofield looked at her made her blood run cold.

"You fucking *bitch*," Schofield snarled, and blood dripped down his chin. Even though he was chained, Roux couldn't help recoiling from the viciousness in his expression.

Ludovic's eyes blazed. "Call her that again and you'll regret it," he growled.

Schofield's gaze narrowed, something cold and calculating slithering across his face. It made Roux shudder.

She marched forward and slammed the bathroom door shut.

"I'd never let him hurt you," Ludovic told her.

"Do we call Walsh now, or take Schofield to Belle Morte first?"

"We're not calling Walsh."

"Why not?"

"Schofield insists he hasn't hurt the children, so if he's telling the truth and I find them safe and sound, then I can contact the proper authorities to collect them while we hand Schofield over to the mansion. But if he's lying, then I'm coming straight back here to question him again, and I'm not giving Walsh any opening to take back charge of him," Ludovic said.

"I'll have to stay with him while you go to the pub."

Ludovic's eyes flashed red. "I'm not leaving you alone with that man, chained up or not."

"We can't leave him with no one to watch him."

"He's not in any position to break those chains."

"What if you're wrong?" Roux said.

Ludovic cupped her face with one hand. "I'd never suggest leaving him here if I wasn't absolutely confident he couldn't escape."

"Knock him out again. Just to be sure," Roux said.

"That won't be a problem."

The sun slipped behind the clouds as they drove to the White Stag, and the sky was gray and sullen. Roux's heart thumped in her chest the whole way, nerves knotting up her stomach.

Schofield might have lied about keeping the kids there.

He might have lied when he said he hadn't hurt them.

The pub came into view, perched at the top of a shallow slope of land. Roux parked nearby and climbed out of the car. The view around them was beautiful—varicolored fields split by hedges and clusters of woodland—but she was interested only in the White Stag.

It loomed over them, a sad husk of whitewashed walls topped with a shabby slate roof. Climbing plants had run wild, digging stubbornly into the brickwork, and one remaining flower basket was overflowing with weeds. There was no parking lot, just a fenced-off area of land, and the door and bay windows were boarded up. A couple of old beer bottles still lay in the weeds.

"Do you really think they're here?" Roux said, shivering as the wind sliced through her.

"There's only one way to find out. Stay here until I know it's safe." Ludovic approached the pub.

"Everything's boarded up," Roux noted. "If Schofield's telling the truth, how did he get in or out?"

Ludovic paused, surveying the pub with a critical eye. "There must be a back entrance somewhere. Not that we need it."

He strode up to the front door, grabbed the boards nailed across it, and tore them away as if they were paper.

"You keep flexing those muscles and I'm going to come over all girly," Roux said.

Maybe this wasn't the time, but cracking jokes kept her from buckling under the fear that Schofield had lied to them.

Behind the boards the door was locked, but that was no problem for Ludovic. A sharp jerk of his wrist broke the lock, and the door swung open.

Roux's breath caught, and her whole body involuntarily tensed in case it *was* a trap. Ludovic stepped into the doorway and stood there, listening.

"Well?" said Roux, after a moment or two.

"I can't hear anything."

Wrapping her arms around herself, Roux followed Ludovic into the pub.

The interior was split by an open doorway; the right side must have been a dining area, judging by the scattered tables and chairs and the dull gleam of a dropped fork among the debris on the floor, while the left side was the bar. The shelves had been stripped bare but for a dusty bag of peanuts.

"It doesn't look like anyone's been here in years," Roux said.

"There are footprints," Ludovic said, pointing to areas of disturbed dirt on the floor. He paused, lifted his head, and inhaled. "And I can smell blood." His eyes darkened. "It's fresh."

Roux's stomach plunged.

Ludovic turned in a half circle, scanning the room with eagle eyes. The boarded-up windows cast shadows in the corners, cut only by the gray winter light drifting through the front door.

"Did you hear that?" he said.

"No, but I have crappy human hearing."

Ludovic turned again, cocking his head.

"What can you hear?" Roux asked, her heart climbing into her throat.

"I'm not sure. Shuffling feet, maybe?"

Ludovic suddenly crouched, and pressed his hand to the floor. "It's coming from down here," he said.

"The cellar," Roux said. "There must be a hatch somewhere."

She hurried to the bar; Ludovic quickly overtook her.

"This way," he said, veering left. He stopped, his eyes narrowing. "It's here."

"How can you tell?" Roux asked.

The floor was almost invisible beneath a carpet of dead leaves, litter, and other unidentifiable debris.

"This has been moved recently," Ludovic replied.

He crouched and swept the debris aside to reveal a wooden floor, the varnish scraped away by countless pairs of feet. At first there was no sign of a cellar, but as Ludovic cleared more space, a large, pad-locked hatch came into view.

Ludovic grasped the padlock in one hand and pulled, exerting his incredible vampire strength. The lock snapped with a loud *clang*. He tossed it away and lifted the hatch. A set of wooden steps descended into darkness, and now even Roux could hear the shuffle of moving feet.

Her eyes prickled. They'd only known about these kids for a few days, but it felt like they'd been looking for them for much longer. Now they were finally at the end of that journey.

But Ludovic's eyes were bleak and heavy. "Stay here," he said.

"What? Why?"

Ludovic rested a hand on her shoulder. It seemed like he was going to say something, then he shook his head and straightened up. His face was still bleak and it made Roux's stomach cramp with anxiety.

She watched Ludovic head down the steps, as smooth and noiseless as a cat. The cellar was so dark that the shadows appeared solid, and seeing Ludovic disappear into them made her feel horribly alone.

The wind whistled, making her skin prickle.

She needed to know what was going on. Her pulse spiking, she clambered down the steps.

"Roux, don't. Go back upstairs," Ludovic said, his voice strange.

But she'd already stepped off the last step and onto the uneven concrete floor. She blinked as her eyes adjusted, things taking shape around her. Ludovic moved in front of her, trying to block her view, but Roux stepped around him.

And stopped dead.

"No," she whispered, something in her chest cracking.

Schofield had said he hadn't hurt them, and maybe in his twisted mind he really believed that, but the glowing red eyes that stared back at her told a different story.

Schofield had turned the kids into vampires.

CHAPTER TWENTY-ONE

Roux

Tears blurred her vision and she stumbled back, reaching for something, anything, to steady herself.

Why had Schofield done this?

A muffled growl trickled through the darkness and all those pairs of eyes glowed a brighter red. A shape lunged, snarling and snapping around a filthy gag, and even though something was restraining it, Ludovic still pulled Roux back, and placed himself between her and the young vampire.

The others started to snarl and thrash, too, and tears spilled down Roux's cheeks.

"Oh god, they're rabid," she cried.

Schofield had turned these kids into monsters, and now their families would never get them back.

Ludovic's eyes gleamed in the darkness, a hint of red creeping in. "No, they're not."

"What are you talking about? *Look* at them."

Had they ever had a chance of saving the kids, or had Schofield turned them as soon as he'd got his evil hands on them?

Ludovic clasped Roux's face with both hands. "I know better than anyone what rabid is, and trust me, they're not it." He looked back at them, his expression caught between fury and pity. "They're starving, and you being human is triggering all their predatory instincts."

Roux felt a spark of hope. "Really?"

"Once they've had blood and time to recover, they should be fine." Despite his words, Ludovic's expression was heavy with anger and regret.

"What do we do?" Roux asked.

"You need to get out of the cellar. You're driving them mad."

Roux made her way back up the steps to the square of gray light that was the hatch. Her heart felt like a lump of cement.

Had they saved the kids or not? They were still alive in that they could walk and talk and think and feel, but they were forever stuck as teenagers. Their old lives were over, and Roux had no idea how they'd fit into the world now.

After a few minutes, Ludovic joined her, sitting on an abandoned stool in front of the bar.

"Would it help if I fed them?" Roux asked.

"In that state, they'd tear out your veins," Ludovic said.

His expression flickered, not quite a flinch but close, and Roux wondered if he was thinking of the monk.

"It's too dangerous to move them. Someone from Belle Morte will have to bring a supply of blood out here."

Roux nodded. "I'll call now."

The second Ysanne was on the phone, Roux spilled everything that had happened.

There was a long silence.

"I see," said Ysanne.

"I'm sorry," Roux said.

Ysanne made a noise that could have been a sigh. "It's not your fault."

"What do we do?"

"We'll have to bring the children to Belle Morte so they can be taken care of by experienced vampires."

There was another pause, then Roux blurted, "This is going to make things worse for everyone, isn't it?"

Ysanne ignored the question. "Seamus and a team will be with you as soon as they can."

"Okay."

Ysanne ended the call.

"When it comes to fixing things with the human world, this could be the straw that breaks the camel's back," Ludovic said, staring down at his hands. "Schofield may have destroyed us all."

The defeat in his voice wrenched at Roux's chest. "Don't talk like that."

Ludovic pulled off his beanie and ran his hands through his hair. It would be strange when he ditched the human disguise and went back to his usual ponytail.

"What will we do if the system does fall apart?" Ludovic said, suddenly sounding very lost.

Roux's heart squeezed.

Anyone else would look at Ludovic and see an immortal creature who'd lived for hundreds of years. They'd see his composed facade, his vampire mask, maybe even his dark side, the predator that lurked beneath his skin.

But they wouldn't see the *man* that he was in that moment—uncertain, even scared.

Roux knew how strong and capable Ludovic was in so many ways, and it hurt to see him like this.

"Okay, let's think about the logistics of this," she said, sliding onto a stool next to him. "The kids will be vulnerable to sunlight for a long time, so they can't go home. But I can't see teenage vampires wanting to spend their whole lives inside Belle Morte. It wasn't designed for them."

Ludovic didn't respond. Maybe this was hitting closer to home for him because of what had happened to his sister.

"Does anyone at Belle Morte have experience with vampire kids?" Roux said.

"As far as I'm aware, there have never *been* any," Ludovic said curtly.

"Never?"

Ludovic's hands were fists on the bar top, his whole body rigid. "Vampires have always had an unspoken rule about not turning children, and for very good reason."

"No parent ever thought about turning their kids?"

Ludovic flinched, a full-body jerk like he'd been electrocuted. "This is no life for a child, and any parent should know that."

His voice sounded like broken glass, jagged with grief, and it was so personal that Roux's heart thumped.

Something was slowly dawning on her, and she couldn't believe she'd never thought of it before. "I thought that this brought back memories of Clemmie, but it's not that, is it?" she said.

Ludovic closed his eyes.

"Did you—" Roux's throat hitched. "Did you have kids once?"

When Ludovic opened his eyes, they shone red. "Yes," he whispered. "I had a daughter."

Roux sucked in a shuddering breath, blinking back the threat of tears.

"Her name was Marie." Ludovic's voice softened, and it tugged at Roux's heartstrings.

"You had her with Elise?"

"No. She wasn't . . ." Ludovic paused, gathering himself. "She was Régine's baby, conceived after a violent rape. Régine died giving birth to her."

"Jesus," Roux whispered.

"Marie wasn't mine biologically, but I raised and loved her as my own." Ludovic gripped the edge of the bar until the wood creaked. "She fell ill and died two months after her second birthday."

"And you thought about turning her to save her," Roux guessed. That wasn't just grief in Ludovic's voice—that was guilt too.

"I couldn't condemn her to eternity as a toddler, but after I put her tiny body in the ground, I hated myself for letting her die when I could have saved her."

"But like you said, vampires have that rule for a reason. You couldn't have forced this on Marie, and no matter what decision you'd made, you'd have blamed and hated yourself for it."

Ludovic stared at her, a thousand emotions churning in his eyes.

"And now Schofield's violated that rule in the worst way. If people turn on us, we'll be hunted, like the old days," he said.

Ludovic was head and shoulders taller than Roux, and stronger than she could ever hope to be, but Roux was overcome by a fierce wave of protectiveness.

"Whatever happens, I'll be here for you," she said.

"Roux, if vampires are forced back into the shadows, you can't come with us."

"I'll find a way. Besides, we don't know what'll happen."

"Even so, you can't stay in Belle Morte forever. You've got your own life to live."

"And I'll decide how I live it."

"You can't waste it on me. This thing between us—we both know it's not going anywhere, don't we?"

"We've never told each other anything different." Roux's voice was steady, but her heart was starting to thump, whether from pain or anger she wasn't sure.

"There's a reason that relationships between humans and vampires don't work. You have no idea how it feels to fall for someone whose life is the blink of an eye compared to your own."

"Well, that's not a problem because we're not *in* a relationship. It's just sex." The words hurt to say, but they were true, nonetheless.

Ludovic slowly nodded, but he said nothing, and his silence annoyed Roux. It felt wounded, as if she'd said something he didn't want to hear, but he was the one who'd brought it up, so why was she the bad guy for agreeing?

Roux turned away so Ludovic couldn't see the hurt on her face. She hadn't slept with him because she thought they'd fall in love and be together forever, but he'd got under her skin long before the sex, and now he occupied a little place in her heart, whether either of them wanted him to or not.

But he was still right.

She cared about Ludovic and the sex was beyond incredible, but Roux couldn't live at Belle Morte forever.

Maybe there was just no happy ending for this story.

Ludovic

It's just sex.

Those words went round and round in his head, raw and stinging. It was better if Roux thought that, too, but it still hurt to think that what they'd shared might not mean much to her.

Ludovic was afraid—of what he felt for Roux, how deep it went, and how quickly it had bloomed. He hadn't felt this way about anyone for so long, but rather than fill him with hope, it made him think about all the people he'd failed in his life. Roux had helped him face his past, but he couldn't shake the fear that he'd fail her too.

He was afraid of losing her—and he *would* lose her.

It wasn't *just sex* for him.

Roux had pulled him out of the darkness. He'd thought his hands were stained with blood, but she'd kissed them anyway. She'd heard every secret, every shame of his past, and she hadn't judged him. She was more than he'd ever deserved, and he didn't know what to do now that he'd found her.

He knew what it meant to fall for humans, how it felt to see someone he loved growing old and gray while he stayed the same. It hurt, so very, very much.

It would've been better if he and Roux had never crossed that line, but they couldn't undo it now.

Hesitantly he put a hand on her shoulder. "I'm sorry," he said.

"For what? Assuming that sleeping with you means I'll automatically fall in love with you?"

Ludovic winced. "Yes."

"Let's get something clear. I'm very capable of enjoying no-strings sex and I'm not imagining commitment where there isn't any," Roux said, but her expression softened.

"We shouldn't keep doing this," Ludovic said. "But I don't want to stop."

Roux swallowed, and Ludovic's gaze fastened on the shape of her throat.

"Neither do I," she said.

Seamus's team seemed to take forever to arrive. When they finally heard the sound of an approaching engine, Roux jumped off her stool and ran to the door.

Seamus stood in front of a black Belle Morte van with Hugh and Benjamin, two vampires from Belle Morte, his face somber.

"Is this really happening?" he asked, anger thickening his Irish brogue.

"I'm afraid so," Ludovic replied. "Do you have the blood?"

Seamus handed him a bag filled with sealed pouches.

"I won't be long," Ludovic said.

In the cellar, he set the bag on the floor, took out two pouches, and ripped the top off one. The rich, coppery smell of blood filled the air, and the young vampires went into a frenzy, their eyes blazing red and bulging out of their heads.

Ludovic wasn't afraid of them, but children pushed close to rabid was a terrible thing to witness. Marie briefly lit up his mind, her sunshine laugh and tiny dimples etched as clearly into his brain as if it had been only yesterday that he'd last seen her.

He'd have killed anyone who hurt her.

He wanted to kill Schofield for hurting these children.

Ludovic approached the nearest girl, a tiny waif with a cloud of red hair, and pulled the gag from her mouth. She was calmer than the others, but she still snapped at him, and Ludovic pulled her head back so he could pour the blood into her mouth. When the pouch was empty, he tossed it to the floor and tore open another.

By the time the girl had swallowed every drop, the haze had faded from her eyes.

Ludovic let go of her. "How do you feel?" he said.

"I—I don't . . ." Her eyes, huge and terrified, flitted around the darkened cellar. She shrank back at the sight of the other vampires, their eyes glowing red in the shadows. "I don't understand," she whispered. "What's going on?"

"What's your name?" Ludovic asked.

"Chloe," she whispered.

The last child Schofield had kidnapped.

"You're safe now," Ludovic told her.

"Where's my mum?"

Ludovic couldn't answer that.

He focused on Chloe's bloody arms and legs. Schofield had used silver wire to restrain his victims, twisting it around their limbs before looping it around thick metal bars that were bolted to the wall. The deadly metal had sunk into the children's flesh, slickening their skin with blood.

He'd foolishly forgotten his gloves, but he ignored the burning in his fingers as he wrenched the wires from the support bars then carefully unwound them from the trembling young vampire.

When Chloe's legs were freed, she sank to the floor, rocking and whimpering.

Fresh rage boiled in Ludovic's heart.

Red tears spilled down Chloe's cheeks as Ludovic peeled the wire away from her ravaged arms.

"You're all right now," he murmured, slinging the bloodied bits of metal into the corner.

She looked up at him, as timid as a kicked dog. She had no idea who he was and little reason to trust him except that he'd helped her. Ludovic hoped that was enough.

"I'm going to get you out of here," he said, and she gave a tearful nod.

Mindful of her injuries, Ludovic scooped her into his arms. She huddled against him, her hands tightly clutching his clothes, as he carried her out of the cellar.

Roux

When Ludovic emerged from the boarded-up pub carrying a red-haired slip of a girl, Roux breathed a sigh of relief.

The girl was dwarfed by Ludovic's larger frame, and she gazed up at him with such total trust that Roux's throat tightened. She'd seen Ludovic wield a sword with lethal precision, seen him splattered in the blood of his enemies, seen him take out Iain's gang like they were insects he was batting aside. She knew exactly how strong and savage he could be, but he shielded the frightened young vampire with the utmost gentleness, and she clung to him like he was her whole world.

"These are my friends," Ludovic told her as he reached the van. "They're going to take care of you."

He set the girl down and she sidled out of his arms and let Seamus gently help her into the van.

"Eight more to go," Ludovic said, gazing after Chloe with anger and pity in his eyes. She was a shadow in the back of her van, her hair a bright shock around her pale face.

"Eight?" Roux repeated, her stomach sinking.

Ludovic took a moment to answer. "Do you recall Leonard Mitchell and Curtis Bell, the two runaway children we believed weren't connected to Schofield? They're down there too. Schofield must have snatched them from the streets at some point and no one knew. Iain Johnson was right."

Tears stung Roux's eyes. Every time she thought things couldn't get worse, they did. "Who's the ninth kid?"

"I don't know." Ludovic rested his hand on Roux's shoulder and gently squeezed. "We'll find out once we get them all safely back to the mansion."

He headed back to the pub, and Roux gazed after him, her heart twisting and turning.

It wasn't just sex. Ludovic could be awkward and frustrating and closed off, but he was also a man who'd gladly walk into danger if it meant protecting someone else. He was kinder and gentler than even he realized, and that was the man Roux had come to know over the last few days, the man Ludovic had kept hidden and locked away for so many years.

That was the man who was slowly capturing her heart.

Over the span of an hour Ludovic brought up each of the kids, all exhausted and wrung out. Some of them were angry. Some were in shock. Some sobbed as they climbed into the van.

With each one, Ludovic's eyes grew darker, angrier. By the end, Roux was starting to think Schofield would be glad to go to the Belle Morte cells because at least then he'd be safe from Ludovic.

She recognized each kid but one, and her throat felt like she'd swallowed something sharp. Iain Johnson was a vicious, violent bastard, but he'd been right about this.

The one kid Roux didn't recognize was a dark-haired girl with hollow eyes, who seemed more resigned to this than any of the others.

When the kids were safe in the van, Seamus approached Roux. "Once they're at the mansion we'll come back for Schofield. You two look like you could use a break."

Ludovic clenched his fists at the name.

"Thank you," Roux said.

Seamus patted her shoulder and hurried back to the van.

Roux looked up at the pub, at the boarded windows and grimy facade where Schofield had brought his particular brand of evil, and nausea curdled her stomach.

"Let's get out of here," she said, holding out her hand to Ludovic.

His eyes were dark and swimming with rage, but he took her hand.

Neither of them spoke on the journey back to the hotel, each lost in their own thoughts.

The morning had left Roux exhausted and heartsick.

Ludovic was the one who'd freed the kids and fed them and got them out of the cellar. He'd seen Schofield's evil up close and personal, but Roux felt just as tainted by it, like it was a physical cloud she'd walked into.

Outside the hotel, Roux killed the engine, then rested her head on the wheel and squeezed her eyes shut. Ludovic rested his hand on her back. He didn't speak, but even that touch was comforting.

"We should get inside," Roux mumbled.

She wanted to burrow under the covers and pretend the world didn't exist.

She prized her hands off the wheel and sat up. Ludovic's hand fell away, and immediately she missed it.

Ludovic climbed out of the car, and Roux slowly followed. She felt sluggish and worn out, and it wasn't over yet. They still didn't know *why* Schofield had done this.

Just before she went into the hotel, the sensation of being watched prickled along her skin. She looked back, scanning the street, but there was no one there. Ludovic had already disappeared inside.

"I'm getting paranoid," she muttered, and rolled her shoulders, trying to shake off the feeling.

Schofield still lay tightly chained on the bathroom floor but he'd regained consciousness, and he shot them a vicious glare.

White-hot rage blazed through Roux. She stalked into the bathroom and stood over him. "We've got the kids," she said, her voice trembling. "You will *never* touch them again. You're going to the cells at Belle Morte, and I hope you fucking rot there."

Schofield gave her a smile like a razor. "Not before you."

Roux slammed the door in his face.

Exhausted, she stripped off her coat and tossed it onto the bed. The anger had drained away, leaving her hollow.

"Are you all right?" Ludovic said.

"No," she whispered. "This is totally fucked."

There was so much she could handle, but Schofield had pushed her over the edge. Once the tears started, they wouldn't stop.

Ludovic

He couldn't stand seeing her cry.

The way her beautiful face crumpled—it tore at him.

He didn't think; he hugged her automatically, and she melted against his chest, her body shaking. He'd tried so hard to keep her out of danger but he couldn't protect her from everything, and he hated that. He hated that she was hurting and he couldn't make it better.

Eventually her sobs turned to snuffles, and she stopped trembling. She leaned against him as if she'd collapse if he let her go.

He had no intention of letting her go.

When Roux was in his arms like this, he couldn't think clearly, couldn't understand *why* they couldn't make this work. He couldn't imagine a world in which he wasn't holding her.

Finally, Roux pulled away, wiping her eyes. Her skin was blotchy and her nose red, but she was still beautiful to him.

"Sorry," she mumbled.

Strands of her wig stuck to her wet cheeks and, making an irritated face, she tossed it onto the bed next to her coat.

"That's better," she said, shoving her fingers through her own hair to loosen it up.

"Turn around," Ludovic said.

Roux arched a curious eyebrow, but she did as he said. Ludovic couldn't take away all her hurt, but he could try to make her feel that little bit better. He placed both hands on her shoulders, where the muscles were tense and knotted.

"What are you doing?" Roux asked.

Ludovic gently massaged her shoulders, rolling his thumbs over the knots to loosen them, and Roux stiffened at first, maybe taken by surprise, then she relaxed against him with a small sigh.

This close to her, Ludovic couldn't help bending his head to breathe in the smell of her hair.

"Hold on," said Roux, her voice husky. She pulled off her shirt and climbed onto the bed.

Ludovic watched, his eyes roving over her lean body as she settled on the mattress. Propping herself on one elbow, she looked back at him.

"You can carry on now," she said.

Ludovic sat astride Roux's hips. She wriggled, getting comfortable, then Ludovic's hands settled back on her shoulders, falling into the same rhythm he had before. Her skin felt like satin against his palms, interrupted only by the straps of her bra.

As if she'd read his mind, Roux pushed up onto one elbow again, and reached back to fumble with her bra clasp. She pulled the garment off, flung it to the floor, and flopped back onto the bed.

Ludovic had only meant to work out the knots in her shoulders, but now that so much of her gorgeous skin was bared to him, he couldn't keep himself from gliding his hands down her spine, smoothing them around the narrow shape of her hips. His fingertips traced the tattoo on her left shoulder, a curving pattern of thorns and roses.

He'd seen it before but this was the first time he'd really appreciated it. It was a piece of art inked onto her skin: the gently unfurling red petals looked like velvet, the darker thorns sharp enough to draw blood.

"This is beautiful," he murmured.

She rolled over and winked at him. "The canvas isn't bad either."

"Does the tattoo mean anything?"

She shrugged. "Roses are beautiful but thorns are strong? I'm both a rose and a thorn, lovely yet sharp? There's more to me than the soft petals you see on the surface?"

She smiled, and the look in her eyes did things to him that he didn't think anyone else ever had.

Something cracked open in his chest, and he realized, to his absolute disbelief, that he might be *falling* for this girl. It should be impossible—they'd only known each other for a few *days*—but he couldn't pretend that he didn't feel it.

"Hold me?" Roux said softly.

Ludovic lay next to her, sliding one arm under her back and the other across her waist. He held her like that until she fell asleep, and then he carefully took her hand, entwining their fingers and listening to the gentle pulse of her heart, which, at that moment, seemed like the most beautiful sound in the world.

CHAPTER TWENTY-TWO

Roux

The sound of smashing glass jerked Roux awake.

Ludovic leaped off the bed, as tense and coiled as a jungle cat.

A brick lay on the floor, surrounded by glittering shards of glass. A chill winter wind blew through the broken window and set the curtains flapping.

"What the hell?" Roux said.

Everything else happened horribly fast.

Several flaming bottles flew through the window, smashing on the floor and against the walls. The reek of gasoline filled the air and blazing flames leaped up.

"Oh my *god*," Roux cried, flattening herself against the headboard.

Molotov cocktails. Someone had *bombed their room*.

The flames licked across the carpet between them and the window, where their attackers must have climbed up the fire escape. The door was closer—

Ludovic threw Roux's shirt at her and she yanked it over her head.

More bombs sailed through the window, shattering everywhere. The roar of flames filled the room, spreading with horrible speed.

They'd have to make a run for it, before the fire formed a barrier they couldn't get through.

"Wait! What about Schofield?" Roux cried.

"Leave him."

"We can't," Roux said, hating the words. "If he survives the fire we won't know about it, and he'll hurt more kids."

Ludovic didn't argue.

He kicked open the bathroom door. Schofield cowered on the floor; he didn't resist as Ludovic freed him from the basin, leaving his arms and legs cuffed, and slung him over his shoulder.

Another bottle came through the window, shattering on the headboard of the bed, and Roux screamed as flames formed a thick wall of heat, barrier to the door.

"The window," Roux choked, pressing her sleeve against her mouth.

Ludovic didn't hesitate.

He threw Schofield. The other vampire sailed over the rising fire, bound and helpless, and crashed into the far wall. Flames latched onto his clothes and he rolled, making frantic noises. Ludovic gathered Roux up, shielding her as much as he could.

She knew there was no way in hell he'd drop her, but panic still surged as Ludovic launched himself through the fire and landed in the one small area in front of the window that the trajectory of the bombs had missed.

He set Roux down, and she squeaked; Ludovic's sleeve had caught fire. He slapped a hand over the flames, muffling them.

Using her sleeve to protect her palm, Roux grabbed a shard of glass jutting from the window frame. If their attackers were on the fire escape, she wouldn't face them unarmed.

She clambered through the window. The fire escape was empty, and she scrambled down it, Ludovic close behind.

"Roux," he shouted, and she ducked as something sailed over her head.

A large body closed in, and Roux lashed out with the piece of glass, hitting nothing but air. Her attacker neatly sidestepped, his eyes glittering with violence. Recognition stirred. He'd been with Iain that night. He was one of the men Ludovic had saved her from.

The guy adjusted his grip on what she now realized was a baseball bat, and took another swing for her. Ludovic blurred in front of her, taking the blow on his arm. He grunted and dropped Schofield.

Ludovic snatched the bat from their attacker and snapped it across his knee like it was a piece of kindling. The guy paled and stumbled back.

Instinct shivered through Roux and she whirled around as another attacker came at her from behind. He grabbed her and Roux stamped on his foot, as hard as she could. He yowled and jumped back, and Roux followed through with a hard swing of her wrist. Her makeshift weapon sliced open the man's arm.

But more of them were coming, carrying bats and knives and crowbars. Roux's blood turned to ice, and then blazed red-hot with rage.

It was bad enough that these bastards wouldn't leave them alone—now they'd endangered everyone else in the hotel.

Iain appeared behind his friends, and his face was so twisted with hatred that he looked almost inhuman.

"Get them," he snarled.

His friends charged.

Ludovic pushed Roux behind him and kicked Schofield out of the way, but probably to keep from tripping over him rather than trying to protect him.

There was a blur of fists and weapons and shouting, and it was all so fast that Roux couldn't see what was happening, couldn't see whose blood was flying through the air or whose teeth scattered on the pavement.

She heard someone screaming, heard the word *police*. Above them, smoke and flames poured out of their hotel room.

A guy barely older than herself got past Ludovic's defenses. He clutched a cricket bat, but there was hesitation in his face. Maybe he wasn't a complete fanatic, maybe he didn't believe in hurting humans rather than vampires, but Roux was past caring. She drove her shard of glass into the guy's shoulder. He shrieked and dropped the bat, and Roux immediately scooped it up. Hefting it in both hands, she swung it into the guy's stomach. He folded with a gasp, and Roux hit him across the back, sending him sprawling to the ground.

Another man ducked past Ludovic, and Roux swung for his head. He dodged, and the bat clanged against the fire escape. Roux's hands went numb. The bat slipped from her fingers.

The guy reached for her but Ludovic seized the guy's arm and twisted it sharply up. Something cracked, and the guy screamed.

Someone slashed at Ludovic's unprotected back with a knife, and he let out a raw snarl of pain.

Roux snatched her bat and whacked it onto the arm of Ludovic's attacker. He staggered back and his knife clattered on the ground.

There were so many of them, and Roux quickly realized that although Ludovic *could* handle them, he was hampered with trying to keep her safe. They needed to get away.

The car was parked down the street, only a few feet away. They just had to get to it.

Taking a deep breath, Roux pulled up all her fear and anger, letting it surge through her like the fire that had devoured their room.

These people had attacked her twice, and she was fucking *sick* of it.

With a scream of defiance, she charged, swinging the bat.

The nearest guy froze, perhaps not expecting her to go on the offensive. Roux smashed the bat onto his shoulder, and he howled, collapsing to his knees. Roux darted past him, and when the next guy threw his weight back to avoid a hit to the chest, she dropped low and hit his kneecap instead. He folded like a broken puppet.

Roux leaped over him, transferring the bat to one hand while she fumbled in her pocket for the car keys with the other. For a sickening moment she thought she'd left them upstairs, but then her fingers closed around cold metal.

Footsteps sounded behind her and she whipped around, swinging her bat. It smashed across the face of a woman wielding a crowbar, and she crumpled, clutching her crooked jaw and shrieking.

Roux jammed the keys into the lock and turned them.

"Ludovic!" she screamed.

He burst through their attackers with a roar, blood splattering his face and clothes, and snatched Schofield from his prone position on the ground. One of Iain's thugs tried to stab Ludovic, but he swung Schofield around and used him as a shield. Schofield wailed as the knife sank into his arm.

Roux slung herself into the driver's seat just as Ludovic reached the car. Iain and his friends were already coming after them. Ludovic wrenched open the back door, shoved Schofield inside, and threw himself into the passenger seat.

Roux slammed her foot down and the car shot down the road. Something thudded off the rear windshield and the glass spider-webbed. Roux jumped, making the car swerve crazily across the road.

"Shit," she cried.

She veered around a corner, tires screeching, and Ludovic was jolted against her, while Schofield slid around in the back seat. She was shaking, she realized, her hands clutching the wheel so tightly that her knuckles turned white. The bat rested against her knee.

"Are you hurt?" Ludovic asked.

"I don't think so," she said.

Adrenaline rushed through her veins like a drug.

"I'm not hurt," Schofield piped up.

"No one gives a shit," Roux snapped.

She cut a look at Ludovic, and the car swerved again as her hands gave an involuntary jerk. Blood was spreading along the side of his shirt, and his jaw was clenched.

"Oh my god, *you're* hurt," she cried.

"I'll be all right," Ludovic said, but his voice was tense.

"You don't look all right."

"I—"

The van came from out of nowhere and smashed into the side of the car.

Roux's seat belt scored a painful line across her chest, and her head *thunk*ed against the steering wheel.

Blackness rushed in.

Ludovic

Groggily, he lifted his head from the dashboard.

The sound of a car horn blaring made his skull feel like it would crack apart, and when he touched his forehead, his fingers came away wet with blood.

The van had hit the car on his side, and bits of glass from the shattered window were sunk into his face, neck, and arms, but he was only vaguely aware of the sting.

His focus was Roux.

She was slumped over the steering wheel, her body limp. A trickle of blood ran steadily from her nose, dripping onto her knees.

Terror almost split him in two.

He could still hear her heart beating, but humans were so breakable compared to vampires. She could have internal injuries, brain damage. She could be dying.

He needed to get her out of the car.

That was easier said than done. The impact on his side had completely caved in the door, pinning his left leg. The smell of his own blood was thick in the air.

Ludovic was reaching for Roux's seat belt when the doors of the van flew open and two men in black balaclavas jumped out. They strode around to Roux's side and fury erupted in Ludovic's chest. If they *touched* her, he'd rip them apart.

The two men threw open the back door and seized Schofield's ankles. He groaned, dazed, fresh blood pouring down his face.

Ludovic strained an arm between the seats, trying to grab Schofield, but he couldn't reach, and when he tried to wrench himself free, pain shot through his trapped leg.

One of the men glanced at him, red sparking in his eyes—they were vampires, he realized with a jolt of shock.

They dragged Schofield out and carried him to the van, then one of them returned, a blade glinting in his gloved hand.

A lethal growl rumbled in Ludovic's chest.

The masked vampire hesitated. His friend grabbed his arm and shook his head.

Another car pulled up alongside them, shocked human faces pressed against the windows. A woman jumped out, phone in hand.

The two vampires scrambled back into their van and, with a screeching grind of metal, pulled away from the wrecked car. The van sped down the street and vanished around the corner.

Roux still hadn't moved, and Ludovic's heart felt like it was being crushed into a ball. Gritting his teeth, he set his arm against the bulging mass of metal that had been his door and *pushed*.

Spectators were gathering around the car and through the babble of voices, Ludovic heard words like *police* and *ambulance* and multiple iterations of "Are you okay?"

He ignored them all.

Finally, though it made stars of pain explode behind his eyes, he wrenched his leg free. Going through the windshield would be quicker than forcing open the crushed door; Ludovic used his good leg to kick the cracked glass until it peeled away from the frame, then braced both hands on the dashboard and hauled himself out of the car.

He slithered down the crumpled hood, ignoring the hands that reached for him, and the voices asking if he was all right, and rushed to Roux's door. A small knot of people had gathered around it, and he shoved them aside.

Roux's side of the car was mostly intact, and the door opened easily. She was still slumped over the wheel, so fragile, so still, and Ludovic focused on the sound of her heartbeat, the reassuring thump that let him know she was still alive.

He unbuckled her seat belt and carefully lifted her, cradling her against his chest. Blood ran from her arm and onto his shoes. Someone told him not to move her, that he should wait for the ambulance. Someone else told him he needed to take it easy because he was bleeding all over the place. Their words were distant echoes.

Several cars—some police, some unmarked—reached the scene, and Walsh jumped out of one.

"Jesus, fuck, are you okay?" he called, jogging toward Ludovic.

"Roux needs an ambulance," Ludovic said.

"It's on the way." Walsh's gaze traveled to the wrecked car. "What the hell happened? I heard reports of an arson attack on your hotel."

"Someone ran us off the road," he told Walsh, and the man's lips thinned.

"Schofield?" he asked.

"They took him."

"For fuck's . . ." Walsh deeply exhaled and scrunched his eyes shut.

Behind him, uniformed officers were keeping spectators back from the scene—maybe the people would be useful after all. One of them might have seen, filmed, or photographed something that Walsh could use to track that van down.

"You shouldn't have moved her," Walsh told Ludovic, looking at Roux.

She felt so fragile in Ludovic's arms, like she'd break if he let her go.

"Did you get a look at the car that hit you?" Walsh asked.

"I'm not talking about this now," Ludovic growled, his arms tightening around Roux.

Unexpected sympathy flickered across Walsh's face. "If you want us to catch whoever did this, you need to help me."

Ludovic struggled to collect his thoughts. He told Walsh everything he remembered and by the time he finished, the ambulance had arrived.

Roux stirred in his arms. "What happened?" she mumbled, opening her eyes and immediately closing them again. "Ow." She put a hand to the angry purple knot on her forehead.

"You were in an accident," Walsh said, before Ludovic could.

Paramedics jumped out of the ambulance, and suddenly they were taking Roux away, and the crowd was growing, the buzz of their voices filling the air.

A paramedic tried to lead Ludovic to the ambulance, but he shrugged her off.

His head hurt where he'd cracked it against the dashboard, the slash on his back still freely bled, and he had no idea how bad his leg was except that he couldn't put his full weight on it. He didn't care. All that mattered was Roux.

"He's a vampire, he'll be fine. Just get the girl to the hospital," Walsh said, too low for anyone but the paramedics to hear.

Too late, it occurred to Ludovic that the ambulance might have bagged blood, but by then it was already peeling away from the accident, and he wouldn't stop it for anything.

"Shit," Walsh said, catching a glimpse of Ludovic's back. "I didn't realize it was that fucking bad. You should have let them help you!"

"I'll be fine," Ludovic muttered. Also too late, he realized that he should have gone with the ambulance to keep up the facade of being human.

Roux wouldn't have made a mistake like that.

His heart clenched.

"Come on. I'll drive you to the hospital," Walsh said.

"Why are you helping me?" After his past experiences with Walsh, Ludovic couldn't help being suspicious.

"Because you need it. I don't think you have any idea how messed up you look right now."

The journey passed in a blur—before Ludovic knew it, they were pulling up outside the hospital.

"I don't know how this is done. Vampires have never been taken to hospitals before, have they?" Walsh said.

"Not that I know of."

Vampires' incredible healing abilities meant there was little that human medicine could offer, but Ludovic was exhausted, injured, hadn't fed much lately, and his skin was starting to itch. The sun was weak, but it was still sun, and he'd been exposed to a lot of it recently.

"You need blood, right?" Walsh sounded deeply uncomfortable about that.

"Yes."

Walsh breathed out a long sigh. "Right. Let me see what I can do."

Inside the hospital, Ludovic froze. Everything around him was bright and white and sterile, a completely alien environment, but beneath the chemical smells was the tang of blood. His nostrils flared and his fangs slid out.

He could ignore the pain of his injuries, but not his body's *need* for blood. He swallowed, tamping down the urge rising inside, and looked around for Walsh, but he'd already disappeared somewhere.

Ludovic had grown used to having Roux with him, helping him navigate the modern world, and now he felt a flutter of panic.

Walsh reappeared, accompanied by a young nurse. "Let's get you away from the sun," she said.

Ludovic hesitated, unable to help his guard going up around someone he didn't know.

"She's here to help," Walsh said.

Vampires were trying to kill him, and Walsh was trying to help him? Had the whole world turned upside down?

"Come on," said the nurse, beckoning.

Ludovic didn't move. "What's happening to Roux?"

"She's been taken to the ER, and I don't know more than that yet, but I'll find out. Get yourself sorted out first—you're no use to anyone in this state," Walsh said.

The nurse led Ludovic to an unoccupied private room, and pulled the shutters down. "All you need is blood and you can heal yourself, right?" she said.

Ludovic nodded.

"Wait here."

She left the room. Ludovic braced his hands on the wall and shut his eyes, pain and weariness rippling over him. He was missing something obvious, but he couldn't think straight. He stretched a hand to touch the gash on his back, wincing as his fingertips probed the ragged edges of flesh. The knife had cut deep; if he was human, he'd have been in real trouble.

Was Roux in trouble?

His heart twisted. She'd been conscious when they put her in the back of the ambulance, but that didn't mean her injuries weren't serious.

Ludovic curled his hands into fists, leaning his weight on them, pushing against the wall. Roux was in the best place she could be. All he could do was wait.

The nurse returned, carrying several bags of blood. "I don't know how this works," she said. "Do you need a certain type? Should it be heated?"

"It's fine as it is, thank you," Ludovic said.

The nurse handed him the bags. "We've never had a vampire here before."

"I've never been to a hospital before," he muttered.

Please, he thought, *don't let her be a Vladdict*. He couldn't handle that now.

"Is there anything else you need?" she asked.

"No, but please don't tell anyone I'm here."

She bit her lip. "Your friend already had to tell a couple of people. I can't just help myself to blood, you know."

Hopefully her colleagues or superiors would have more important things to do than spread gossip about the vampire in the hospital.

"Do you need anything else?" the nurse asked.

"No, thank you."

As soon as she left, Ludovic tore open the bags and gulped the blood down, closing his eyes in bliss. Cold, dead blood was nothing compared to drinking from the vein, but to his battered, exhausted body, it was like ambrosia.

The more he drank, the more the pain faded. The wound on his back knitted together, his leg stopped throbbing, and his head cleared, thoughts sharpening and coming back into focus.

Slowly, methodically, he processed the situation. He had no idea how bad the fire damage at the hotel was, but it was safe to assume that their belongings were gone, along with his supply of blood.

The car was useless.

Schofield was gone.

Roux was in hospital.

In his head, he ran back over what had happened. The van had hit the car. The driver and his companion were both vampires. They'd rescued Schofield.

Who'd want to rescue a dangerous, rogue vampire?

The answer sliced into his head like a lightning bolt.

Morris and Patel.

But would they help a man like Roger Schofield? Did they know what he'd done to those kids?

Then Ludovic realized: Morris and Patel weren't helping Roger Schofield because they didn't know who he really was. They thought they were helping Jeffrey Smith, the alias Schofield had assumed when he returned to Winchester.

He didn't know how they'd tracked him and Roux down, but it didn't matter now.

Something dark and violent stirred in Ludovic's chest.

His job had been to bring in the Five, but this wasn't just a job anymore.

He could handle his enemies coming after him, and whatever physical punishment they dished out, but by hurting Roux they'd crossed a line they couldn't come back from.

Alone in that room, Ludovic made himself a silent vow. Morris, Patel, and Schofield could run as far and as fast as they wanted, but it would never be enough. Ludovic would hunt them into the ground.

CHAPTER TWENTY-THREE

Roux

Six hours later, Roux had eight stitches in her arm, but an MRI had revealed nothing serious. Her head ached like someone had taken a hammer to it, and she had to stay in the hospital overnight in case of concussion, but things could have been so much worse.

She was more worried about Ludovic. There'd been no sign of him since she'd arrived, and that made everything inside her feel cold.

Vampires were made of stern stuff, but he'd still been hurt a lot worse than her.

Walsh abruptly pulled back the curtain around Roux's bed.

"What are you doing here?" she said, too tired and sore to be polite.

"I brought Ludovic to the hospital."

"Is he okay? Where is he?"

"He's been taken care of. He's fine." Walsh's voice softened. "Are *you* okay?"

"I'll live."

"Every available officer is looking for that van, and Iain Johnson's gang." Walsh's expression turned stormy. "That fire they started at the Old Royal . . ." He shook his head. "A woman staying on your floor never made it out."

It took a moment for his words to sink in. "Someone died?"

Walsh nodded, his mouth a grim line. "Smoke inhalation."

"Will that count as a murder charge?"

"If I have anything to do with it, hell, yes."

"Can I borrow your phone?" Roux asked. "I need to let the mansion know what's happened."

"I've already taken care of it."

"Thank you. Can you take me to Ludovic?"

"I can bring him to you."

Roux swung her legs over the side of the bed. "I can walk."

"No, no, you stay here." Walsh held out his hands like Roux would collapse if she got up.

He pulled the curtain back around Roux's bed.

Roux ran a hand through her hair. It felt gritty and smelled of smoke, and she pulled her hand away, memories of the fire roaring through her head. Her wig had burned along with all their clothes—she and Ludovic couldn't disguise themselves anymore.

It probably didn't matter now.

Even if no one in the hospital recognized her, the footage of that fight was probably already online, and any self-respecting Vladdict would recognize Ludovic. They couldn't keep this contained anymore.

Iain had screwed things up for everyone.

Roux touched the swollen knot on her head and tears filled her eyes. If that van had hit her side of the car, she wouldn't have survived. Roux prided herself on weathering whatever life threw at her, but suddenly she felt fragile, scared, vulnerable.

She wanted her friends, her family, her home.

She wanted Ludovic.

And then he was there, pushing aside the curtain, as if he'd heard her thoughts. She didn't have time to speak before she was in his arms, crushed against his chest, and she clung to him like he was the most important thing in her world.

A sob worked up her throat, but she swallowed it. She wouldn't fall apart now.

Ludovic broke the hug and cupped her face with both hands. He'd cleaned his face, washing away any blood from the accident, but also all traces of his human disguise. Someone—probably Walsh— had given him a hat that partly shielded his face, so hopefully he'd managed to keep his identity hidden from anyone they would have passed on the way to Roux's cubicle. "Are you all right?" he said.

She managed a shaky nod. "Yeah. I think you took the worst of it."

"Good," he said, and hugged her again.

Someone cleared their throat and Roux realized Walsh was standing behind them, looking awkward.

"You're staying here overnight?" he said to Roux.

"They'll move me to the main part of the hospital as soon as a bed's free, but yeah, they want me here until tomorrow," she said.

"Why?" Ludovic said, scanning her for injuries.

"To make sure I don't have a concussion."

"I'm staying, too, then."

"Not alone you're not," Walsh cut in.

Ludovic turned angry eyes on the detective. "What are you talking about?"

"Johnson and his friends already burned down a hotel to get to you. I'm not letting them target a hospital next."

"They don't know we're here," Ludovic argued.

"They weren't supposed to know we were at the hotel either," Roux pointed out.

"Exactly," Walsh said, snapping his fingers. "It wasn't easy getting you through this hospital without everyone recognizing you, and you were disguised then. Now you're not, except for that hat, and that's not enough. It would only take one stupid social media post for the whole fucking world to know, including Iain Johnson."

A chill rolled down Roux's spine and she wrapped her arms around herself. Ludovic put an arm around her shoulders.

"I'm arranging an armed guard to protect you, and I'm personally staying here until you two leave," Walsh said.

"Little below your pay grade, isn't it?" Roux said.

"I just want to make sure those little shits don't hurt anyone else. I'm also going to make sure that every single member of staff you've been in contact with keeps their damned mouths shut."

Roux didn't ask how he'd manage that. Walsh was nothing if not stubborn, and if he said he could keep everyone quiet, then she believed him.

There were no more threats or attempts on their lives that night, but it was hardly peaceful. Every hour or so a nurse came by to shine a light in Roux's eyes, and when she tried to sleep she saw the hotel room burning around them, the rage-twisted faces of Iain's gang, the ruin of their car.

Knowing that two armed police officers stood guard outside her room, along with four more spread throughout the hospital, and even *more* keeping watch outside the building, should have made

Roux feel completely secure, but her greatest comfort came from Ludovic spending the night in a chair by her bed. Walsh had wanted him to return to the side room he'd been in before, but Ludovic had flatly refused to leave Roux's side.

By the time she was discharged the following afternoon, her eyes felt like they'd been rubbed with sandpaper. Her headache had gone but a new host of aches and pains had sprung up over her body, and a red welt ran diagonally across her chest, courtesy of her seat belt.

True to his word, Walsh had stayed overnight, and by the time he came to see Roux, he was unshaven and hollow-eyed, his clothing rumpled, and smelling of coffee.

"Some of Iain's friends have been arrested, and we'll get them all sooner or later, but the van that hit you was found abandoned this morning. If Ludovic's right, and it was Morris and Patel, then they're smart enough not to stay in the same vehicle," he said.

"Crap," Roux muttered.

"Yeah. My job's much easier when I'm dealing with complete idiots."

Roux managed a wan smile.

Ludovic rose to his feet. Someone had found a clean shirt for him, but his jeans were still tattered and bloodstained. "What happens now?" he asked.

"I guess we go back to Belle Morte." Roux's heart sank. They had no choice, but it felt like failure.

"Schofield, Patel, and Morris are still out there," Walsh said, shoving his hands into his pockets.

"And we can't hunt them like this. We need to regroup and rethink."

"Maybe get some backup too," Walsh muttered. "I know you were supposed to be incognito, but too many people filmed that brawl yesterday. Even if I've managed to keep a lid on things here, I can't keep the world from knowing there's some shady vampire shit going on."

"Which means catching the rest of the Five is suddenly even more imperative. If people know that they're loose in the city, it could start a panic, which is the very thing we've been trying to avoid all this time," Ludovic said.

"We should call the mansion and let them know we're coming back. Can we borrow your phone?" Roux said to Walsh.

"I memorized all the numbers, if that helps," Ludovic said.

Roux brushed his arm with her fingertips. "That's great, but Walsh already has the number in his own phone."

"Oh."

Walsh handed Roux his phone.

"I'll call in the car. Can you give us a lift?" she said.

Walsh nodded.

Ludovic

"How the hell did Morris and Patel find us anyway?" Roux asked as they piled into an elevator, headed for the hospital's ground floor.

"They must have been tracking him somehow," Ludovic replied.

"But if they knew where he was, why not rescue him when we left him chained up in the bathroom?"

The elevator doors pinged open and they stepped into a corridor.

"Maybe they wanted us both out of the way too," Ludovic said, thinking of the blade that either Morris or Patel had wielded.

"There were witnesses filming from the moment you two escaped the fire with Schofield. If Morris or Patel saw that footage, they'd have known exactly where to go," Walsh said.

"And now we have no idea where they've gone," Roux said.

They were almost at the hospital entrance when Ludovic stopped, his ears pricked. "Walsh, are you sure no one knows we're here?"

Walsh shifted his weight. "I did the best I could, but I can't guarantee it. Why?"

Ludovic took another couple of steps forward, listening to the clamor of voices outside the hospital. "The media are here."

Walsh swore.

"I guess Morris and Patel aren't the only ones who saw that footage and put two and two together," Ludovic said.

Roux flinched, then her jaw hardened with determination.

If Ludovic had had a heartbeat, it would've spiked then. Even tired and battered and worn down, she was the most beautiful thing he'd ever seen.

"How many?" Roux asked.

"I can't tell."

Walsh looked up and down the corridor. "There'll be another way out of this place. I'll find someone to ask."

Roux lifted her chin. "Or we suck it up and go through them."

"I don't think that's a good idea."

"The cat's largely out of the bag now, and there's no point wasting time looking for a more discreet exit. Let's just push through them and get to the car."

"If you're sure."

Ludovic's gaze lingered on Roux's bruises, the dark rows of stitches in her arm, the exhausted shadows under her eyes. "What if I go out first and draw them away?" he said.

"No," said Roux, but Walsh looked thoughtful.

"I'm parked in the lot across the street. If you can give us some breathing space, I can get Roux to my car without the vultures seeing. I can get one of the armed escorts outside to come with us too," Walsh said.

"Hello, do I get a say in this?" Roux asked.

"No," Walsh replied.

Roux glared at him.

"I'm trying to do what's best for you," Ludovic told her, and her expression mellowed.

"But how will you get back to us?" she said.

"I'm faster than any human. I can easily outpace them, then double back to find you."

"Good, because we're not leaving without you."

"Wait a couple of minutes before leaving," Ludovic told Walsh.

As Ludovic strode to the entryway, it occurred to him that this would once have been a nightmare scenario for him. While some vampires embraced their celebrity status, Ludovic had always shied away from it, and walking into a crowd of vampire-chasing paparazzi would have made him recoil in horror. Now he barely spared it a second thought.

The armed guards that Walsh had stationed outside prevented the crowd from coming into the hospital itself, but the moment Ludovic stepped into view, the crowd surged.

". . . Ludovic . . ."

"What are you doing here?"

". . . the rumors are true?"

". . . Belle Morte lost control . . ."

Ludovic ignored every shouted question and camera flash. He marched through the doors, between the policemen, and into the braying mob. Once, the sight of those lethal guns would have brought memories of the war rushing back, but he had no time to feel anxious. Microphones were thrust in his face and the assault of voices was almost overwhelming, but he couldn't help a small smile, because it was working—the press were following him away from the hospital, leaving the way clear for Roux and Walsh.

He turned left, striding out of the handicapped parking area in front of the hospital, then crossed the road and continued up the street, and the press followed like lemmings.

Two minutes had almost passed—Roux and Walsh would be sneaking away now. It was time for him to join them.

Ludovic turned, so abruptly that several of his pursuers almost tripped, and pushed through them, heading back to the hospital. Despite everything that had happened, his step felt lighter than it had in as long as he could remember.

Almost losing Roux in that crash had made things very clear to him. He'd had relationships with humans before, and they'd never lasted because they *couldn't* last. A human's lifespan was so fleeting. But did that mean those relationships hadn't been worth it?

Despite how tragically Ludovic's time with Lucille, Régine, and Marie had ended, would he have changed the time he'd had with them?

No.

A relationship with Roux might not be easy, and part of Ludovic still wondered if it would be better for her to be with someone she could grow old with, but he couldn't make that choice for her, and he wouldn't insult her by pushing her away under the misguided belief that it was for her own good.

Roux had made him feel things he'd thought were long lost to him. If they both wanted it enough, maybe they could make it work, and that realization was a shining light at the end of a long, dark tunnel. However hard it was, Roux was worth fighting for.

A screech of tires drew Ludovic's gaze to a car peeling out of the parking lot opposite the hospital. He'd never seen the car before, so there was no reason for that sudden feeling of dread, but Ludovic still felt like he'd been plunged into icy water. Every instinct he possessed screamed that that car was a threat.

"Roux," he whispered, and ran.

He wanted to be wrong.

He wanted that wrenching feeling in his chest to be nothing more than paranoia, but when he reached the parking lot, his heart fell out. Walsh sat on the ground amid a small group of people trying to help, his hand pressed against a bloody scrape on his head. The armed escort who'd come with them from the hospital lay nearby, his gun slack in his hand, his eyes closed. Several people were crouched over him, one of them talking rapidly into a phone.

"Where's Roux?" Ludovic cried, shoving through the humans.

Walsh looked up at him with heavy eyes, his mouth a flat line. "They took her," he said. "I'm so sorry."

Ludovic spun around, scanning the parking lot, but the car was gone.

Roux was gone.

CHAPTER TWENTY-FOUR

Ludovic

Ludovic clutched his head, a roar of desperate fury building in his throat.

This had been his stupid idea. He'd left Roux alone when she'd needed him most.

"Who was it?" he growled.

Walsh dragged himself to his feet, wincing. "I don't know for sure, but based on the balaclavas, I can guess."

Why would Morris, Patel, and Schofield have come back for Roux?

"I'm sorry," Walsh said again. "They came at us from behind. Took my phone too."

He crouched next to the fallen officer and pressed two fingers to the man's neck. "He's still alive," he reported, his voice heavy with relief.

"Don't try to move him," said someone behind Ludovic. "Help is on the way."

"We have to find Roux," Ludovic said to Walsh. The injured officer mattered, too, but the hospital was *right there*. He wasn't in danger—Roux was.

Walsh straightened. "I didn't see the car—"

"I got a photo of it," interrupted a young woman, lifting her phone like a wand. Her whole face glowed as she looked at Ludovic, and a tiny fang pendant dangled from her neck.

She handed him the phone.

"Right," Walsh said, looking over Ludovic's shoulder. "Let's go."

"I need to take this," Ludovic said to the woman.

She giggled, and even though she was helping them, Ludovic felt a rush of irritation. Didn't she understand how serious this was?

"It's yours," she said. "Maybe we could—"

Ludovic was already hurrying after Walsh.

Walsh and Roux had almost made it to the car when the attack happened; it took seconds for Ludovic and Walsh to reach it.

"*Fuck,*" Walsh yelled, and kicked an empty soda can.

Fresh rage surged through Ludovic. Two of Walsh's tires had been slashed, and the car listed to one side, undrivable. Schofield and his friends hadn't taken any chances this time.

He spun around, and he had no idea what his face looked like, but the nearby humans fell back a few steps. Ludovic looked past them to the road that separated the hospital from the parking lot, and started running again.

Walsh called after him, but Ludovic didn't stop.

A taxi appeared at the end of the road, and Ludovic charged in front of it, forcing it to stop. The driver made an angry flapping gesture with both hands.

Ludovic pulled open the door and climbed into the back seat.

"Dude," the driver said, gaping at him. "You could have flagged me down; you didn't have to walk out in the middle of the road."

"I need you to find a car," Ludovic said.

Behind him another driver honked loudly.

The driver twisted in his seat and peered at Ludovic through the plastic partition that separated them. "Huh?"

"It's a black car. The license plate is AV65 PHX."

The driver shot him an incredulous look. "That's not how this works, mate. I'm a *taxi*."

Ludovic curled his fingers under a slot in the partition and wrenched the whole thing off the framework of the car.

"Jesus Christ!" The driver almost jumped out of his skin. He fumbled for his door handle but Ludovic was faster. He grabbed the man's shoulder and slammed him back in the seat.

Behind him, cars continued to honk. Someone was shouting.

"Listen very closely," Ludovic said, curling his lips to show off his fangs.

The driver let out a whimper and cowered.

"You're going to help me track down that car, without complaining or questioning. If you don't, I'm going to hurt you."

Ludovic hated the words coming out of his mouth, but something had taken him over, something primal and dangerous and angry. He couldn't tell if he was bluffing or if he'd follow through on his threat, and he hoped he wouldn't find out.

The door opened again and Walsh climbed into the seat next to Ludovic, breathing heavily.

"Don't leave me behind. I can help," he said.

The taxi driver swallowed hard as he looked between them, debating his options.

"Please," said Ludovic. Every second wasted was a second that Roux was getting farther away from him.

The man looked at the twisted piece of plastic lying on the seat next to Ludovic. He looked at Ludovic's hand still gripping his shoulder, at Ludovic's red eyes and protruding fangs.

He swiveled in his seat and started the engine.

Walsh took the young Vladdict's phone from Ludovic, entered a number, and barked orders into it.

"I've put out an APB on that car," he told Ludovic. "They won't get far."

Ludovic nodded, though he didn't understand what that meant.

"I've also put in a request to the NPAS," Walsh said.

"The what?"

"National Police Air Service. If they can get a helicopter out, they can track down that car from above. I should warn you, though, the chances of them getting one to us on such short notice are very low."

As they turned corner after corner, driving up and down street after street, tension built in Ludovic's chest. The sun was setting, turning the clouds to fire and stealing one of the advantages Ludovic had over the Five.

Anger bristled beneath his skin like a living thing, shifting and turning.

The phone rang, and Walsh spoke into it, but Ludovic didn't hear what he said. There was a dull roaring noise in his ears.

Walsh snapped his fingers in Ludovic's face, and Ludovic blinked. "The car was seen turning off Edgar Road a few minutes ago. There's a demolition site that way."

"Is that close?" Ludovic asked.

"About five minutes away."

The driver abruptly pulled to the curb and braked. "I'm done."

"Drive," Ludovic snarled, fangs out.

"No fucking way. I'm not getting involved with whatever vampire shit you're mixed up in."

Ludovic could force him. But he'd thought himself a monster for so many years, and it was Roux who'd helped him realize that he wasn't. If he hurt this man, he'd be the thing he'd always feared, the monster that Roux had always believed he wasn't.

"We'll go the rest of the way on foot," Walsh said, throwing open the door.

Swallowing a growl of frustration, Ludovic climbed out of the taxi. It sped away the second he closed the door.

"Straight down the road and turn left," Walsh told Ludovic.

Ludovic broke into a run, too fast for Walsh to keep up.

When he reached the demolition site, there was no sign of the Five's car. The site spread out in front of him, two large buildings of concrete and glass surrounded by temporary security fencing. Beyond the fencing, huddled around the building were huge machines, the last of the sunlight glinting dully off silent metal cranes.

The street dead-ended here; there were no other roads the Five could have taken, which meant they were here somewhere.

Roux was here.

And he would find her.

Ludovic prowled through the site. There were tire tracks in the dust; they'd been trampled as though someone had tried to scuff away the evidence with their feet—but it wasn't enough. He followed the tracks until he reached a paved area of ground, and then he crouched, studying the pattern of dirt on the concrete. It looked as though the car had started to turn right but had abruptly turned left instead.

Ludovic looked up. A section of security fencing caught his eye. It was out of line with the others, and there were fresh drag marks on the ground. Someone had moved it, very recently. The tire tracks indicated the car had gone in the opposite direction, but there were footprints in the dirt.

Some of them would have been from workers earlier in the day. Some of them had to be from the Five. Ludovic studied them. Most were a jumble of booted feet crossing over each other, but he picked out two distinct sets heading from the fence toward the farthest building. Between them, the ground was scuffed, as if something had been dragged.

Or as if someone had fought her captors.

Despite the fear and anger tearing him up inside, Ludovic felt a spark of pride: Roux hadn't made this easy for the bastards.

Ludovic pulled the section of fencing aside, just wide enough for him to slip through, and then paused, ears pricked.

Nothing stirred.

The sky was darkening, reds and pinks turning to blues and grays, the sunset fading behind the blocky shapes of the buildings. The harsh call of a crow echoed around the space.

As Ludovic moved forward, he spotted a gleam of metal on the other side of the fence. The car that had fled the hospital was parked behind one of the demolition machines. It was empty now.

Ludovic looked up at the two towering buildings—ten stories each of thick concrete walls and sturdy glass windows.

Roux had to be inside one of them.

Parts of the nearest building had already been demolished; Ludovic picked his way around heaps of rubble and twisted bits of metal. The stench of dust was heavy in the air.

The footprints became more jumbled until Ludovic could no

longer separate them, but they all led in the same direction: the second building.

Ludovic would tear it apart piece by piece if he had to.

Air stirred behind him, and he ducked. Something whipped past his head, and he struck out with a clenched fist, not turning to see who'd attacked him.

There was an *oof* and the thud of a body hitting the ground. Ludovic pivoted to face his attacker, his eyes burning red and his fangs extended.

The man lying at his feet was human, his heartbeat juddering with fear and blood streaming from his mouth where Ludovic had hit him. The smell of it called to the predator under Ludovic's skin.

"Who are you?" Ludovic demanded.

The man staggered to his feet, brandishing a broken piece of metal pipe. He aimed a clumsy swing at Ludovic's head, which Ludovic easily avoided.

Ludovic batted the weapon out of the man's hand. Another punch broke his nose. As he staggered back, Ludovic flowed behind him with vampire speed and latched a hand around his throat.

"Who are you?" he repeated.

"Please . . . don't hurt me," the man stuttered, his throat convulsing under Ludovic's palm.

"Why did you attack me?"

"Some guy paid me to take a crack at anyone who came in."

Ludovic's nostrils flared. Beneath the fresh blood spilling from the man's mouth, Ludovic smelled older, staler blood. His gaze traveled down the man's arms, noting the bruised injection marks in the crook of his elbow. There was a glassy, unfocused look in his eyes.

Why had the Five paid a drug addict to guard this place for them rather than guard it themselves?

"Are they all here?" Ludovic asked.

"What are you talking about?"

Ludovic shook him, and the sharp smell of urine stung the air as the man wet himself.

"The men who paid you," Ludovic said.

If this was a trap, he needed to be careful.

Huffing breath behind him heralded Walsh's arrival. He bent double as he reached Ludovic, bracing his hands on his knees as he sucked in air.

"Not as fit as I used to be," he gasped.

"There was only one guy. People come here at night to fuck or shoot up, and he wanted me to make sure that didn't happen tonight," the man babbled.

That didn't make sense. If Morris and Patel had rescued Schofield, why was one of them now acting solo? It had to be Schofield—the others had no reason to come after Roux.

Ludovic flung the sobbing addict to the ground. "Watch him," he told Walsh.

He raced into the building and up the first staircase he found. Ten stories and he didn't know which one Roux was on.

The first floor was empty, but as he neared the second, the smell of blood wafted into his nostrils. *Roux's* blood.

For a moment he felt so weak it was like he was human again.

A door lay directly ahead and he pulled it open, his hands shaking. The smell of blood came from inside; Roux was on this floor—somewhere.

Behind the door was a vast room, supported at regular intervals by large pillars. Most of the windows still had glass, but the light fittings had been torn from the ceiling, leaving dangling wires and patches of cracked concrete. Wires, cables, pipes, and bits of metal and rubble were strewn across the floor.

Ludovic sidestepped the biggest obstacles as he made his way through the room, listening for any sounds.

He could not be too late.

Ludovic rounded another pillar, and his world fell apart.

Roux lay in a corner, a tiny huddled shape among the ruin of the room. Her face was deathly pale and splashed with blood. There was no heartbeat, no lift and fall of her chest as she breathed.

And there never would be again.

Because Schofield had killed her.

Roux was dead.

CHAPTER TWENTY-FIVE

Ludovic

His chest felt like it was full of shattered glass.

How could he have left her? How *could* he?

Ludovic crumpled to his knees.

Roux was supposed to go back to her family, her friends, and live the rest of her life safe and happy, chasing every dream she wanted. Instead, her body lay in an abandoned building, discarded like trash.

Grief tore him open, and he bent double, pressing his head to the dusty floor. "Roux," he whispered.

The back of his neck prickled—a warning.

Ludovic threw himself to one side, rolling over and coming up in a crouch.

Schofield was frozen behind him, his arm raised, one hand clutching a knife, obviously hoping to kill Ludovic before Ludovic knew he was there.

He'd failed.

Looking at the man who'd killed Roux, Ludovic's vision turned red, and an animal roar tore from his lungs.

He lunged.

Everything faded to a blur. He was aware of throwing punches, his fists crashing into something, bone cracking and the smell of blood filling the air, but he couldn't focus, couldn't think straight.

There was only rage, grief, and utter, utter hatred.

A noise reached him, and he wasn't sure what it was, but it pulled him back from the brink, the world reordering around him.

Schofield lay on the floor beneath him, his face a bloody ruin. Ludovic knelt astride him, pinning him down, and his knuckles were skinned and raw, slashed by Schofield's fangs. He hadn't felt it.

Then there was that noise again—a soft moan.

Ludovic's ears roared and he fell away from Schofield. Something sparked through the agony, a flicker of hope that he couldn't bear to acknowledge but didn't dare ignore.

Slowly, he turned.

Roux lay where Schofield had dumped her, and there was still no heartbeat, still no breath, but as Ludovic stared at her, the world tilting around him again, she moved.

Her head shifted to one side.

Her hand twitched.

Her lips parted and a small whimper escaped.

Finally, Ludovic understood what Schofield had done.

He'd turned Roux into a vampire.

Everything inside him went very still. For a beat of time, he could only kneel there, staring at her.

Roux struggled to sit up, and Ludovic's chest felt like it was splitting open. Her eyes shimmered red, and the hints of new fangs appeared when she tried to speak.

Schofield had blamed Roux for his capture, and probably blamed her for the rescue of the children too. She was the one who'd confronted him about it. Had he turned her so he could punish her? So that, no matter what he did to her, she'd heal and then he could hurt her all over again?

Feet scuffed on the floor as Schofield staggered upright. Ludovic tore his gaze away from Roux, looking back at the man who'd killed her.

Schofield's nose and cheekbone were shattered to pulp, one eye swollen shut, his lips smashed. But he was still standing. With enough fresh blood, he'd heal.

Ludovic climbed to his feet, his blood boiling. Schofield was a dead man—and this time he *wouldn't* come back.

But then Roux moaned again, debris moving around her as she shifted. Ludovic automatically turned to her, taking his eyes off Schofield.

Something hard smashed against the side of his head, and he reeled. A second blow followed, rattling his skull, and wet warmth streamed down his face.

A brick thudded onto the floor next to him, smeared red with his own blood, and he heard Schofield's footsteps bolting for the door.

Ludovic lurched upright, swiping blood from his eyes.

Roux whispered his name, and every thought went out of Ludovic's head.

He crouched beside her, laying a hand on her cheek. Her face was white, her skin like ice, her eyes fluttering closed as unconsciousness sucked her under again. Her bumps and bruises from the crash were gone. The wound on her arm had healed. She seemed so small, so impossibly fragile that Ludovic was almost afraid to touch her.

Carefully, he lifted her limp body.

She'd died because of his carelessness. Ludovic squeezed his eyes shut, and clenched his jaw until it hurt, but that changed nothing. When he opened them again, Roux was still slumped against his chest.

She was still a vampire.

Rage and self-loathing threatened to drown him, but Ludovic couldn't fall apart now. He had to help Roux.

He carried her down the stairs.

Outside, Schofield's would-be human guard was cringing at Walsh's feet. The smell of cigarette smoke hung in the air.

"Ah, fuck, is she okay?" Walsh asked, his face falling.

"No," said Ludovic shortly.

"Was that Schofield coming out of here with his face smashed up?"

"He's living on borrowed time," Ludovic said.

Schofield could never run far or fast enough to get away from Ludovic for good.

Schofield's guard made a sudden run for it, but a well-aimed kick in the small of his back sent him sprawling. Ludovic gently propped Roux against the wall, then he approached the man, grabbed the scruff of his neck, and hauled him to his knees.

"Did you know about this?" he snarled, pointing at Roux.

"What?" The man's eyes slid to her. "No!"

His heartbeat doubled—that was a lie.

Ludovic growled, his fangs sliding out, and the man started sobbing.

"Okay, okay, I knew, but he told me not to ask questions. I don't know who she is."

Ludovic released his grip and the man fell on all fours.

"Please," he begged, clutching Ludovic's ankle. "Please, don't kill me."

Ludovic could do it, so easily. He *wanted* to. Every predatory instinct he possessed told him to butcher this sniveling coward, but he still needed him.

He dragged the man closer to Roux.

Before he'd left Belle Morte, Edmond had told Ludovic that Roux wasn't made of china, but that was exactly what she looked like now. Her skin was like porcelain.

"What are you doing?" Walsh asked.

Ludovic ignored him.

The guard continued to plead for his life, until Ludovic backhanded him. Blood flew from the man's mouth, and Ludovic's fangs reacted at the sight of it.

"Shut up," he snarled, bringing his face close to the guard's. "You didn't worry about *her* life, did you? Why should I show you mercy when you showed her none?"

"Ludovic," Walsh said, his voice a warning.

Ludovic wrenched the addict's wrist to his mouth, and bit down. The man let out a pitiful squeal. Ludovic pulled back, grimacing at the bitter, tainted blood, and cupped Roux's pale cheek.

"Roux," he said. "I need you to wake up. Come on, sweetheart, wake up."

Her eyelids fluttered.

The guard tried to squirm away and Ludovic yanked him back. "Cooperate and you won't get hurt. Try to run and I'll break your legs."

Ludovic stroked his thumb along Roux's cheekbone and was rewarded by her eyes cracking open.

"Ludovic?" she whispered.

"I'm here."

A shudder ran through her and she clutched her stomach. "What's happening?" She gasped.

Ludovic lifted the guard's bloody wrist to her mouth. "Drink," he said.

Roux automatically recoiled, but her back was against the wall.

"You have to do this," Ludovic told her. "Trust me."

She tilted back her head to look at him, and he saw in her eyes that she *did* trust him. It should have elated him but all he could think was how that trust would fade once she realized how much he'd let her down.

"Oh, fucking hell, is she a vampire now?" Walsh said, belatedly catching up.

Ludovic offered the man's wrist to Roux again, knowing the scent of fresh blood would call to the predator that now lived inside her. Eventually, that would overrule her human qualms.

Roux's new vampire instincts quickly took over and she latched onto the offered wrist. Ludovic stroked her hair while she drank, but his heart was a rock.

He'd promised that he'd never let Schofield hurt her, and he'd failed, in the most miserable way.

A feeble moan drew his attention back to the guard. His wrist was still clamped in Roux's mouth, and his eyes were rolling up in his head, the color draining from his face. Roux needed the blood and it was no more than the bastard deserved, but Roux wouldn't want to kill him.

"That's enough," Ludovic said, gently prizing her off the man's arm.

She bared her fangs, but it was half-hearted. The fresh blood would help her body through the turn, but it wasn't enough. Already she was slipping back into the dark.

The process of becoming a vampire differed from person to person. Some woke up straightaway, already fully established in their new skins. Others suffered through days of the turn, drifting in and out of consciousness. It was impossible to tell how long it would take until Roux woke up for good.

She needed to be at Belle Morte, where she'd be safe.

"Phone," he said, holding out his hand to Walsh.

Walsh handed it over.

Ludovic still found these bits of plastic strange, but he'd face all the technology in the world if it meant helping Roux.

He entered the mansion's number and lifted the phone to his ear.

"Roux?" Renie's voice was heavy with relief when she answered. "Thank god! I've been so worried about you."

"It's Ludovic," he said.

"Oh. Okay. Are you still at the hospital? Where's Roux—" Renie broke off, and Ludovic could practically feel her growing trepidation.

"Where's Roux?" she said again, and this time her voice was low and heavy with dread. "Ludovic, where is she?"

He'd never know how she'd known there was something wrong. Maybe it was pure instinct, or maybe she'd heard it in his voice, the pain and anger in the two words that he'd spoken.

"I'm sorry," he said.

There was dead silence on the other end of the phone.

Then he heard a rustle, a muted sob, and finally a familiar voice that made his knees buckle with relief.

"Ludovic?" said Edmond. "What's going on?"

Ludovic told Edmond everything, forcing out the words like they were broken glass in his mouth.

"I need to get her back to the mansion," he finished.

"We'll pick you up. Where are you?"

"A demolition site just off Edgar Road."

"Stay there. We'll be as quick as we can." Edmond hung up.

Schofield's would-be guard continued to cry, hugging himself on the ground. "Are you going to kill me?" he whispered.

"No," Ludovic muttered. "But you stay until I say you can go."

Walsh lit another cigarette. "This is really fucked-up," he said around a mouthful of smoke.

Stuffing the phone into his pocket, Ludovic slid down next to Roux. She didn't move as he eased her into his lap. She was feather-light, like her bones were made of glass, even though as a vampire she was stronger than ever before.

Tears burned his eyes.

This hadn't been Roux's choice.

Like the children, Schofield had ripped away her human life and forced a new one on her—one she hadn't asked for and probably didn't want. Ludovic knew exactly how that felt, and he hadn't saved her from it.

Closing his eyes, he rested his forehead against Roux's.

It wasn't long until he heard car doors slamming and voices calling his name.

He blinked, bringing the world back into focus.

Edmond and Renie had just jumped out of a black car parked on the other side of the security fencing. Edmond flung a panel out of the way with one hand, and it crashed noisily to the ground. Then Jason pushed through them and raced toward the building where Ludovic waited.

He skidded to a halt, his chest heaving, his face flushed. His hands were balled into fists.

"How the fuck did this happen?" he yelled. He started to say something else, and whatever it was, Ludovic could have taken it, he *deserved* it, but Edmond put a hand on the younger man's arm.

"Not now," he said.

With a visible effort, Jason swallowed his words. But furious emotion still churned in his eyes.

Ludovic tried to climb to his feet, but his legs felt heavy, uncooperative, like they were made of cement. Briskly, Edmond scooped Roux up, turned, and hurried back to the car. Ludovic managed to push himself upright, and when he swayed on the spot, Renie caught his arm.

"Come on," she said softly. "You need help too."

Ludovic had almost forgotten about Schofield's attack with the brick. He touched his head and found his hair matted with blood.

"Is there anything I can do?" Walsh said.

Ludovic shook his head. "But thank you."

They'd never have been in time to stop Schofield from turning

Roux, but she hadn't been alone with him long enough for him to hurt her in any other way, and that was down to Walsh.

Walsh nodded, and flicked his cigarette butt away. "Will you let me know how she is?"

"We will," Renie said.

Once they were in the car, everything faded out again. Ludovic was aware of Edmond reassuring him that Roux would get the help she needed. He was aware of Jason driving them back to the mansion as fast as he could, gripping the steering wheel so tightly it was a wonder he didn't pull it off. He was aware of every twitch of Roux's hands, every time she moved at all, but he couldn't seem to move himself.

As they passed through the gates onto the grounds of Belle Morte, he was aware that the protestors were mostly gone, and the stragglers were little more than background noise.

Seamus and Ysanne were waiting outside the front door. Ysanne's face was as expressionless as ever, but Seamus looked wretched.

When the car pulled to a stop, Ludovic still felt frozen in place. It wasn't until Edmond lifted Roux out and carried her into the mansion, Jason and Renie hurrying behind, that Ludovic found the strength to move again. He dragged himself out of the car.

Ysanne and Seamus both spoke to him as he passed but he couldn't hear what they said. Someone touched his shoulder but he didn't know who and he didn't look back.

Edmond carried Roux upstairs and into a spare room in the north wing.

Somewhere along the way, Renie disappeared, then returned with her arms full of bagged blood.

"If she needs fresh, she can take it from me," Jason said, pulling back the covers so Edmond could lay Roux down.

Renie unloaded the blood onto the foot of the bed, and patted Jason's shoulder. "Hopefully it won't come to that."

Ludovic had meant to stay by Roux's side the whole time, but now he felt helpless, useless. He could only watch as Edmond took charge, briskly propping Roux against the pillows and tearing open a blood pouch.

He, more than anyone else, would understand what Ludovic was feeling right now, because he'd gone through this just a few days ago when Renie went through the turn.

Ludovic found himself backing away, toward the door. Edmond and Renie would help Roux through the turn better than he could, and they wouldn't let her down the way he had.

Running away now was weak and cowardly, yet he couldn't stop himself.

He left the room, loathing himself with every step.

Slumping against the wall in the corridor, Ludovic closed his eyes. Everything was spinning out of control, and he was powerless to stop it.

After a while he heard the bedroom door open and close, and soft footfalls crossed the carpet toward him. The footsteps stopped, but the sound of a heart beating continued.

Jason, then.

He was the only one left among them who still had a heartbeat.

Ludovic opened his eyes.

Jason's features were granite-hard, and anger kicked his heart into a steady *thump thump thump*, but whatever he had to say couldn't be worse than what Ludovic already thought about himself.

"You were supposed to take care of her," Jason accused, tears glittering in his eyes.

"I know, and I'll never forgive myself for not protecting her. I'd *die* rather than see her hurt. If I could go back in time . . ."

Jason's mouth fell open but no sound came out.

Ludovic realized what he'd just said—and realized that he'd meant every word.

Finally he had a name for the feeling he got every time he looked at Roux, like he was flying and falling at the same time—the light and warmth that filled his heart whenever he saw her smile.

Love.

Somewhere along the way she'd taken his heart, and he didn't know how or when, only that she held it and it was hers for as long as she wanted it.

It seemed ridiculous, *impossible*. They hadn't known each other long enough. But he couldn't choose how he felt, or stop those feelings once they'd taken root.

He loved her, and he couldn't change that.

He needed to say it out loud.

"I love her," he said, meeting Jason's eyes.

Jason let out a shuddering breath, his shoulders slumping. "Shit," he muttered. "What happens now?"

"Nothing else matters but getting her through the turn." Ludovic could barely think beyond that.

Jason's expression hardened and he took a step forward. "I have no idea what's going on with you two, but don't you dare hurt her," he said.

"That's the last thing I ever want to do," Ludovic said.

But it was too late for that, wasn't it? He'd let this happen to her, and if he'd ever deserved her, he certainly didn't now.

Ludovic stumbled away from Jason and headed out of the north wing. He made his way outside, where it was fully dark now, frost already glittering on the grass. When he heard the whisper of footsteps behind him, he turned, thinking Jason had followed him.

Edmond stood a short distance away, his face impassive. "What are you doing out here?" he said.

Ludovic had no idea how to answer. Everything that had just happened, including the realization that he was in love with Roux, had left him raw and reeling, struggling to put himself back together.

"It wasn't your fault," Edmond said, moving closer.

"Yes, it was. I'm the one who suggested splitting up. I'm the one who left her alone." Ludovic turned away and kicked a tussock of grass.

Edmond grabbed his shoulders, and spun Ludovic back around. "You couldn't have known that Schofield would come after you there, let alone so soon. You can't tear yourself apart over a mistake."

"I can when it's a mistake that cost Roux her life," Ludovic argued.

"You thought you were doing the right thing."

"And I was wrong."

Edmond started to say something, and Ludovic cut him off.

"She *died*, Edmond. She died and there wasn't a damn thing I could do to stop it."

Edmond was silent for a moment, understanding dawning in his eyes. "You're in love with her, aren't you?"

Ludovic gave a shaky nod.

Neither of them spoke for a while.

"If you love her, then stop hating yourself for something you couldn't have prevented, and can't change. When Roux wakes up, she'll need the support of all the people who care about her, and that includes you," Edmond said.

Ludovic stared at his friend. Edmond knew him inside and out, better than anyone, and his words were like a punch to the heart. Ludovic was prioritizing his own self-loathing above everything, even Roux.

"Do you know how she feels about you?" Edmond asked.

Ludovic spread his hands.

Roux had come back every time he'd pushed her away. She'd always forgiven him, never judged him, and would she have done all that if it really was just sex to her?

Or was he fooling himself because he wanted her to feel the same as he did?

"You should go and be with her," Edmond said.

"What if she doesn't want to see me?"

His friend offered a shrug. "It's better that you're there and she turns you away than if she wants to see you and you don't come."

"But how can I face her?"

"Because you have to. This is about her, not you, and that means you must be strong enough to support her when she needs it, and strong enough to face her rejection if she gives it." Edmond's voice softened. "I know exactly how hard it is to let someone in after so long, but it is worth it."

He put his hand on Ludovic's shoulder and squeezed.

"If you truly love Roux, then no matter how scared this makes you, or how difficult it is, fight for her."

Roux was exactly where Ludovic had left her, lying pale and still, nestled among wine-red sheets. The bed frame dwarfed her, making her look tiny. Renie sat next to her, stroking Roux's forehead.

She glanced up as Ludovic came in, and he braced himself, expecting the same anger that he'd got from Jason.

But Renie just looked tired.

Tired and sad.

"How is she?" Ludovic asked.

"She's doing okay. As well as can be expected, anyway."

Ludovic edged closer to the bed. "I'd give anything to change this."

"I know," Renie said, giving him a brief smile.

Ludovic plucked up the courage to sit on the edge of the bed. "I almost thought you'd blame me."

"Talk about a role reversal."

"What do you mean?"

"Do you remember when Edmond turned me?"

Ludovic would never forget it; after all, he was the one who'd told Edmond to do it.

"And you remember what happened to Edmond afterward?" Renie continued.

He'd never forget that either. Vampires were forbidden to turn humans without express permission from the Council, and because Edmond had broken that rule, he'd been chained with silver and imprisoned in the cells.

"I thought you might blame me for that," Renie said.

When she woke up as a vampire, she hadn't remembered that Ludovic had told him to turn her. She'd been afraid that Ludovic would see her as the source of all Edmond's trouble, and would hate her accordingly. Ludovic had been quick to correct her.

Now here they were, having a similar conversation, only this time Ludovic was on the other side of the fence.

"When I first woke up as a vampire, I blamed Edmond for turning me," Renie said. "I projected my fear and anger and confusion onto him, but I didn't mean a single word, and I'm not making the same mistake now. I don't blame you for any of this, and I don't think Roux will either."

"I'm more worried about what'll happen to her now."

"Good. I'd hate to think you're only worrying about yourself," Renie said.

It was so similar to what Edmond had said that Ludovic almost smiled. They really were perfect for each other.

"Roux didn't choose this life," he said, staring at her still form. "I know you didn't have much of a choice, either, but it was still more than Roux had. How is she supposed to adjust?"

What if it was as hard for her as it had been for him?

"Roux's one of the strongest people I know," Renie said.

"That's not an answer."

"I know."

Roux whimpered, turning her head on the pillow, and Renie leaned over her, murmuring in Roux's ear.

"I don't know how she'll adjust," Renie said once Roux had quieted.

"All we can do is be here for her and help her through the turn." She looked up at him. "Got any tips on that?"

Ludovic shook his head. "Edmond's the one you should ask. He had someone to help him after he was turned. I didn't."

Something touched his hand and he jumped, looking down to see Renie's fingers tangling with his.

"Roux will be okay," she said softly. "She's strong, she's resilient, and she's not the kind of person who wallows in self-pity." She made a wry shape with her mouth. "She'll handle this better than I did."

Tentatively, Ludovic squeezed Renie's hand.

The door opened and Ysanne entered the room.

"How is she?" she asked.

"She's coping," Renie replied, letting go of Ludovic's hand.

They wouldn't know anything further until Roux woke up properly, and there was no telling how long that would be.

"I need to know exactly what happened," Ysanne said to Ludovic.

He climbed off the bed and told her everything. Halfway through, Edmond came back and joined Renie on the side of the bed. He took her hand, and Ludovic's own hand suddenly felt empty.

"Do you think Morris and Patel know what Schofield's done to Roux?" Ysanne asked.

"Walsh says they helped kidnap Roux, but they definitely weren't at the demolition site. Schofield would have called them for help if they were," Ludovic said.

"That doesn't mean they don't know."

"No."

"Do you think they knew about the children?"

Ludovic shook his head. "If Schofield had any connection to Morris or Patel prior to being turned by Etienne, he wouldn't have adopted a false identity. I don't think they have a clue who he really is."

"Then why help him?" Renie asked.

"They lived together at Bushfield for a while, they wanted the same thing, so maybe they became friends. Or maybe they decided to stick together after escaping Belle Morte because there's safety in numbers," Ludovic replied.

"Is there anything else that Schofield told you about the children that you may have forgotten to tell me?" Ysanne asked.

"No. Why?"

The tiniest furrow appeared between Ysanne's pale eyebrows. "Considering that no one knows *why* Schofield abducted these children, or the victims he snatched five years ago, I thought it prudent to question them once they were lucid enough to understand."

"Walsh said he didn't physically hurt any of his previous victims, beyond neglecting them," Ludovic said.

"This time doesn't seem to be any different. According to the children, Schofield kept them restrained, and he didn't feed them as often as he should have, probably because he couldn't always sneak away from Bushfield to tend to them, but he never tried to hurt them."

"Except turning them without their permission," said Ludovic.

"Except that," Ysanne agreed.

"So we still don't know why he did it," Renie said.

"No, but apparently he refused to call any of them by their names. Instead, he referred to the boys as Liam and the girls as Eliza," Ysanne said.

"All of them?"

Ysanne nodded.

Renie wrinkled her nose. "Okay, that's weird."

"Do those names mean anything to you?" Ysanne asked Ludovic.

"Not at all."

"No one's mentioned them?"

"Not once."

"I see." Ysanne tapped her fingernail against her chin. "I'll contact DCI Walsh and see if he can shed any light on this."

"How are the children doing?" Ludovic asked.

Ysanne paused at the door. "They've been fed and taken care of, so physically they're all right. But I fear it will be a long time before any of them come to terms with what's happened."

"What do we do now?" Edmond asked.

"Hunt Schofield into the ground?" Ludovic suggested, clenching his fist.

Renie clicked her fingers. "I like it."

"You can't do this by yourself anymore," Edmond said. "We didn't keep this contained, and if the world doesn't yet fully know what's going on, they soon will. We need to catch Schofield and the others before that happens."

He glanced at Roux, curled on her side, her face buried in the pillows.

"When Roux wakes up, she'll need you here, not out in the city. I can go after Schofield tonight," Edmond continued, his eyes moving to Ludovic.

"If you're going, so am I," Renie said, climbing off the bed and folding her arms.

"It's too dangerous. We don't know how long this will take, and you're still too vulnerable to the sun."

"You can't go after these bastards alone."

Edmond showed off a hint of fang. "I'm not afraid of them."

"That's not the point. The whole reason Roux went with Ludovic is because he doesn't understand the modern world, and you don't either. That's still the one big advantage Schofield and the others have over you, and you can't do this on your own any more than Ludovic could. No offense," Renie added, glancing at Ludovic. "Besides, where would you even start?"

"I can get help and information from Walsh," Edmond said.

"And how will you stay in contact with him? You disappear every time I even mention teaching you to use a phone."

Sheepishly, Edmond looked at the floor.

If Edmond went after Schofield, Ludovic should be the one who had his back. But that would mean leaving Roux.

The last time he'd left her, she'd been kidnapped and murdered. He couldn't do it again.

"I have to go with you," Renie told Edmond. "We can't take any more chances—too much has gone wrong already."

Her gaze drifted back to Roux, and pain constricted her features.

"Ysanne? What do you think?" Edmond said.

The Lady of Belle Morte was silent for a moment.

"Schofield has destroyed any chance we had of keeping this under wraps," she said. "This would have reflected badly enough on us without Schofield abducting and turning nine innocent children."

"Who was the ninth girl?" Ludovic asked.

"Her name is Jodie Nelson. Apparently, she was taken four days ago, but her parents never reported her missing."

"What kind of shitty parents are they?" said Renie indignantly.

"The kind with serious substance abuse issues," Ysanne replied. "I fear that a storm is brewing, and it'll be far worse than the one that Etienne and Jemima started. The only chance we have of mitigating this, even a little, is to bring those three vampires to justice as soon as possible. This is no longer a job for one person."

"You still can't go. Once the prime minister hears about this, you'll have a lot of fires to put out," Renie said.

"Unfortunately, I must agree. But I still believe that a certain amount of stealth is required."

"But everyone knows that something's going on now."

"They do, and I don't wish to cause any further panic by drawing more attention to this. I need a small, discreet team to go after these vampires, and that means more than just you, Edmond," Ysanne said. "Who would you trust to work with you?"

Edmond didn't think for long. "Gideon," he said.

Ludovic felt a tug of discomfort. Edmond and Gideon were both strong and capable, but Ludovic still considered Schofield his responsibility—even more so now.

Schofield had hurt Roux. But Ludovic couldn't leave Roux here while he chased after revenge.

Someone knocked on the door.

"*Entrez*," said Ysanne in clipped tones.

Seamus poked his head around the door. "Detective Chief Inspector Walsh is outside. He wants to see you."

The faintest flicker of surprise crossed Ysanne's face. "I'll come down," she said.

"No," said Ludovic. "He should come up here. We're all involved with this."

Ysanne's lips thinned. "This is the north wing."

"I think we're a little past sticking to the rules, aren't we?" Renie said.

There was a long pause.

"Very well," Ysanne said. "Send him up. Gideon, too, if you can find him."

A few minutes later, Walsh walked into the room. For the whole time Ludovic had known him, Walsh had taken up space, through his voice and his attitude, and his habit of puffing himself up, but he looked somehow diminished here, awkward even, like he was out of his depth.

"How is she?" he asked, looking at Roux.

"She's doing well," Ludovic said, and hoped it was true.

He'd only turned one person in his life, and Roux was doing better than Elise.

His wife had spent three days and nights locked in a state of near-wild semiconsciousness, moaning and howling when she was awake, clawing at him in her unconscious state. Roux was quiet and still, shifting only occasionally.

Walsh nodded. "Good."

"Why are you here?" Ysanne asked.

"We've got a lead on Schofield." Walsh's gaze moved to Ludovic. "The NPAS came through for us and sent a helicopter out after you took Roux back here. They spotted Schofield's car leaving the city and tracked him into the countryside, where he apparently went off-road and cut across several fields before stopping in a small patch of woodland. The car's still there."

"And Schofield?" Ysanne said.

Walsh grimaced. "Not sure. Unfortunately, vampires don't show up on thermal imaging cameras. Schofield could still be in the car or he could have made a run for it. My money's on the latter."

Ludovic felt a sharp surge of frustration. "Then he could be anywhere by now."

The door opened again, and Gideon came in. He absorbed everything in the room with an unreadable look, then quietly leaned against the nearest wall.

"Maybe not," Walsh said. "Schofield was in pretty bad shape when he escaped that demolition site—"

"Good," Renie interjected.

"—and he'd have needed blood to heal, right?" Walsh continued.

"Correct," Ysanne said.

"There've been no reports of attacks on people between him fleeing the site and his car leaving the city, so I'm guessing he hasn't had time to feed. I think he's got a bolt-hole somewhere, and that's why he went off-road. He's going there to lick his wounds and regroup."

"Could he be going to Bushfield?" Ludovic asked.

"Wrong direction," Walsh said. "But a little less than three miles from where Schofield's car is currently parked, there's what's left of an old farmstead. The house was gutted during a fire about ten years ago, but as far as I know, there's still an intact barn and other outbuildings."

"Perfect place for an injured vampire to hide," Renie said.

"That's what I'm thinking," Walsh agreed.

Something niggled at Ludovic. "Why didn't he change cars?"

Walsh gave him a questioning look.

"After Morris and Patel ran us off the road, they were smart enough to quickly abandon that vehicle and find another so it would be harder for anyone to track them down. Why wouldn't Schofield do the same now?"

"Maybe it was Morris and Patel's idea, not his," Renie suggested.

"Even so, Schofield can't be so stupid as to have forgotten it. It was only yesterday," Ludovic said.

"Maybe he didn't have time? Or maybe *that's* why he went off-road?"

"He won't find a replacement car in the middle of nowhere," Walsh said.

Renie deflated. "Oh yeah. Good point."

Edmond pensively narrowed his eyes. "Schofield must have known there was a helicopter tracking him. Those things aren't exactly quiet." He turned to Ludovic. "Does Schofield know that you care for Roux?" he said.

In his periphery, Ludovic saw Ysanne give the tiniest of double takes.

"I think he can guess by now," he said, recalling the moment when he'd pummeled Schofield's face into raw meat.

"So it's become personal in a way it wasn't before," Edmond said.

"He did hit me with a car," Ludovic said.

"And I bet you're a hell of a lot angrier about what he did to Roux," Renie said.

Ludovic's fangs started to lengthen.

"Schofield already knows that you were after him, and now you're more motivated than ever. It would be in his best interests to get rid of you for good," Edmond said.

Understanding dawned. "You think this is a trap," Ludovic said.

"It's a possibility we should consider."

"How could it be a trap, though? I don't get it," Renie said.

"Maybe Schofield *wanted* to be followed," Edmond explained.

"Why, so he could lure Ludovic out to the country somewhere?" Renie said.

"Not somewhere—to that farmstead."

"Still, that's pretty vague," Renie said.

"Perhaps he thought that making it more obvious would be *too* obvious. He won't want Ludovic to *think* he's walking into a trap."

"I'm walking into it, trap or not," Ludovic said.

Edmond started to object but Ludovic cut him off with a slash of his hand.

"I'm not letting this opportunity slip through my fingers. Even if Schofield's set a trap, I won't be walking in blind."

"But it won't just be you walking into it, will it?" Renie pointed out.

"I'll gladly do this alone—"

"Enough." Ysanne's voice cracked like a whip. "I'll not have any more of my people hurt."

"We're *all* going to be hurt if we can't get this under control," said Gideon quietly.

Edmond squeezed Renie's hand. "I agree with Ludovic. Even if this is a trap, we can't miss this chance to catch Schofield. The longer he's free, the more chance he has of leaving Winchester and vanishing somewhere else in the country."

"He has done that before," Walsh said.

"And this isn't just about damage control for the vampire world. Schofield murdered nine children. If he escapes, he'll do it again," Ludovic said.

Renie bit her lip. "I hadn't thought about that."

"Neither had I," Ysanne said. "You're right, Ludovic. We must put a stop to this now."

"So you're coming with us now?" Renie asked Ludovic.

Ludovic felt that tugging feeling in his chest again. He'd told himself that he'd have to stay with Roux rather than chase after Schofield, but somewhere during the conversation he'd become determined to hunt Schofield down.

He looked back at Roux, so pale and still in bed, and a grim resolve settled on him. He didn't want to leave her, but Schofield had to be stopped.

Roux would understand.

He hoped.

"I'm coming too," Walsh announced.

"Not this time," Ludovic said.

Walsh glared at him. "Yes, this time."

"It's not safe."

"I know where that farmstead is. You don't."

"We can find it."

Walsh's expression flattened. "Look—"

"I'm trying to do what's best for you," Ludovic interrupted.

Walsh looked around the room, and unleashed a heavy sigh. "Fine, but at least let me take you to the point where Schofield went off-road. If nothing else it'll save time."

Ludovic glanced at Ysanne, who nodded.

"When do we leave?" Walsh asked.

"I'll have Seamus fetch a van. You'll leave as soon as possible," Ysanne said. She headed for the door, then paused. "One more thing. Do the names Liam and Eliza mean anything to you?"

Walsh frowned, thinking. "Yeah, but I can't place why."

"That's what Schofield was calling all the children he abducted."

"Oh shit." Walsh's expression cleared. "Those are the names of Schofield's kids."

"He has kids?" Renie said.

"His wife took them abroad years ago and never came back."

Ludovic opened his mouth to say something, then a soft noise behind him made every thought disappear.

He turned.

Roux opened her eyes.

CHAPTER TWENTY-SIX

Ludovic

Roux shifted and groaned, trying to prop herself up on her elbows. "Hey, hey, take it easy," Renie said, putting both hands on Roux's shoulders.

"Renie?" Roux blinked up at her. "What are you doing here?"

"You're back at Belle Morte," Renie said gently. She brushed a few strands of hair off Roux's forehead. "How do you feel?"

Roux frowned. "Weirdly okay."

Renie looked up at Ludovic, her eyes wide with surprise. "Does this mean . . . ?"

"She's already through the turn," Ludovic said, his heart soaring.

"That quickly?"

"It varies from person to person. Roux's turn was only slightly faster than my own."

Renie's face broke into a smile. "That's my girl."

That's my *girl*, Ludovic thought.

"I don't . . . what's going on?" Roux asked.

"Do you remember what happened?" Renie said.

Roux blinked a few more times, and then her hand shot to her mouth, feeling for the tips of her fangs.

"Schofield," she whispered, and every muscle in Ludovic's body tightened at the mention of the name.

Roux looked at him, her eyes full of questions, and his throat closed up. Where did he begin?

Renie slid off the bed. "I think you two need some time to talk things over."

She ushered everyone out of the room and closed the door.

Roux pulled her knees up to her chest and rested her cheek on them. Pain gleamed in her eyes.

Ludovic struggled for something to say. "You need to drink," he said at last.

"I'm not thirsty," Roux mumbled.

"You will be. Trust me."

Roux didn't argue.

Ludovic fetched a pouch from the foot of the bed and opened it. "Here," he said, sitting next to her.

She didn't tense up or edge away from him, but he still hesitated before getting too close. It was ridiculous. He'd seen her naked, kissed her bare skin, buried himself deep inside her. The things they'd done together should have stopped him from ever being awkward around her again, but he couldn't help himself. Roux seemed to be taking all this remarkably well, but was that real—or was it a front, because she didn't know how else to handle it?

Then Roux looked up at him, those beautiful eyes shadowed with pain and grief, and he shuffled closer and slipped an arm around her shoulders.

He offered her the bag of blood and she took it, staring down at the thick red liquid inside.

Drinking blood was something that most humans naturally recoiled from, and they couldn't turn off those instincts the moment they became vampires. He still remembered his first taste of human blood, the horror at what he was doing clashing with the newfound *need* inside him.

"This is real, isn't it?" Roux said, her voice very small and lost.

"Yes."

A shudder ran through her and she closed her eyes. She didn't need to breathe anymore, but she took several deep breaths anyway.

"Okay," she said, opening her eyes. "I'm a vampire now."

In one swift motion, she tipped her head back, the movement dislodging Ludovic's arm from her shoulders, and poured the blood down her throat.

Ludovic felt a warm spark of pride. This was the Roux he'd fallen in love with, the strong, capable, brave, and resilient girl who'd broken down his walls and captured his heart.

Roux drained the bag and wiped a trembling hand across her mouth. "Huh," she said. "It actually tastes good."

She shivered again. Ludovic took the empty pouch and placed it on the bedside table with the others.

"What happens now?" Roux said, her voice small again. "I'm a vampire, I can't . . ." Her voice broke and she pressed the back of her hand to her mouth.

Ludovic put his arm back around her shoulders, and Roux?

Roux flinched.

Ludovic froze.

She wasn't scared of *him*. She'd just been kidnapped and murdered so it was hardly surprising she didn't want to cozy up to him, but seeing her recoil like that, her eyes wide and haunted, made Ludovic's heart ache.

He'd give anything to take away her pain and make her world safe again, but he couldn't.

"I'm sorry. If I hadn't left you . . ."

She looked up at him, her eyes filled with astonishment. "You think I blame you?"

"I'd understand if you did."

"Listen to me, Ludovic de Vauban. There's no way in hell you could've known this would happen," said Roux fiercely.

"Forget about me," he said, shifting position to face her. "You're the only one who matters now. Talk to me."

She looked away, picking at the bedcovers. "I don't know what you want me to say."

"Anything you want. Or nothing at all, if that's better for you."

Roux was silent for a long while, and Ludovic sat patiently with her. It didn't matter if she stayed silent for minutes, hours, even days. It didn't matter if she stayed silent for *years*; he'd still sit with her.

"I don't know where to go from here," Roux said at last. "Do I live in Belle Morte now? Can I go home?" She shook her head. "Of course I can't."

"You don't need to think about this yet," Ludovic said.

"When else am I supposed to think about it?" Roux shoved her hands through her hair. "I can't go home," she said, and the desolation in her voice felt like a knife between Ludovic's ribs.

"You'll always have a place here," he said.

Maybe it wasn't what she wanted to hear, but she needed to know that she wasn't alone. She had her friends and she had him—if she wanted him.

"How did you feel when you first woke up a vampire?" Roux asked.

"Confused. Scared. I didn't have a choice either."

"You didn't? What happened?"

"After I ran away from home, I joined up with a band of thieves, and one night we attacked the wrong carriage. A vampire was inside, with his wife. She was rabid, and she—" Ludovic broke off as the memory of maddened red eyes and gnashing fangs raced through his head. "She slaughtered my friends and tore into my throat like a piece of meat. Her husband finally put her out of her misery, and then decided to save me by turning me, only to decide he didn't want anything more to do with me."

"You know how I feel then."

"No," Ludovic said. "I didn't have a choice, but, like Renie, it was either that or bleed to death. You weren't in that position—Schofield didn't turn you to save you. He did it to punish you. That's completely different than what happened to me."

"What happened to Schofield?" Roux asked, her voice hardening.

"He got away." Ludovic hated saying it. He wanted to tell her that he'd caught the man who'd done this to her, and made sure that he could never hurt anyone again. "It was a choice between going after him or staying with you. I chose you."

Roux rested her head on his shoulder. Encouraged, Ludovic slid an arm around her waist, and though he felt her stiffen slightly, she didn't pull away.

"When do we go after him?" Roux asked.

"We?" Ludovic repeated. "Roux, you're not coming."

This time she did pull away. Red flashed in her eyes. "The hell I'm not. That bastard made it personal, and if you think I'm not going to be there when he's finally brought down, you're so very wrong."

"You've been through enough—"

Roux stabbed a finger at him. It shook with the force of her emotion. "I'll decide how I feel and what I'm capable of. You really want to know what'll make me feel better? Catching the son of a bitch who did this to me."

Ludovic was torn. He wanted Roux to stay as far away from the bastard who'd killed her as possible, but she was as physically strong as Schofield now. He could never use her human fragility against her again.

"I just want to keep you safe," Ludovic said.

As soon as he said it, he cringed. He hadn't kept her safe when she was human; how was he arrogant enough to think he could do it now?

Roux brushed her fingers against his hand.

"This isn't just about me. I'm the latest in a long line of Schofield's victims, but I'm going to be the *last* victim. If nothing else, I can help make sure he doesn't hurt anyone ever again." Her voice was hard and angry by the time she finished.

She tilted back her head to look Ludovic in the eye. "Did you at least get in a good punch or two before he got away?"

"I nearly pulverized him," Ludovic said.

"Good."

Renie peeked into the room. "Sorry to interrupt but we're ready to head out, if you're still coming."

Roux lifted her chin and set her jaw. "I'm coming too."

"You sure?"

"I'd like to see anyone try and stop me."

Roux

She almost couldn't begin to process how much everything had changed now that she was a vampire.

When Jason came to ask if she needed any more blood, Roux could hear the *thump* of his heart, the rush of blood in his veins. It made her mouth water, and though she'd known this was what happened to vampires, it was fucking scary to experience it firsthand.

For the first time she truly understood why Ludovic had been afraid of what he could do. She was so strong now—and she hadn't even tested her strength. She could so easily hurt people, and that frightened her in more than one way.

Roux wanted to hurt Schofield.

She'd never considered herself a violent person, and even when she'd killed a vampire with a curtain rod and broken the jaw of one of Iain's friends, it had been in self-defense.

What she felt about Schofield was very different.

That was a burning, bone-deep rage, like fire in her veins. The horror and powerlessness she'd felt when he'd sunk his fangs into her neck and started to drink was scorched into her brain. The memory of his mouth on her skin made her want to throw up, but she couldn't do that anymore.

She wanted revenge.

Schofield had stolen her *life*.

Roux would never be human again.

She could barely begin to comprehend how many choices he'd taken away.

In the bathroom, Roux slowly changed her clothes. Part of her didn't want to—it felt like she was literally shedding her human skin. The other part couldn't wait to be rid of the clothes she'd been killed in.

Ludovic was waiting on the other side of the door, and Roux's heart did a little flip. She didn't know where to *begin* tackling the subject of what this change meant for their relationship, but that was a discussion for later. After they'd dealt with Schofield.

Roux opened the door.

"Are you sure you want to do this?" Ludovic said, his eyes roving over her.

Schofield's face flashed through her head, the gleam of his fangs before they pierced her skin, the gut-wrenching sensation of him sucking the life right out of her, and she gripped the door handle to keep her legs from buckling.

The thought of seeing him again terrified her, but she would not be left behind. She would not let him take anything else from her.

"I'm coming," she said.

When Roux and Ludovic came downstairs, Edmond, Renie, Ysanne, Gideon, and Walsh were already gathered in the vestibule, and Jason was hovering in a corner. It felt unspeakably strange— the last time Roux had walked down these steps she'd been human. Then, Belle Morte had still felt like a home away from home, a place she'd be forever tied to, but now it was more than that. Now it was a place she might be forever *limited* to.

"Good to see you on your feet, kid," Walsh said.

He sounded genuine, which surprised Roux. She'd expected him to be more hostile to her now that she was a vampire.

"Are you sure there's nothing I can do to help?" Jason asked. "Maybe I could come—"

"No," said Gideon, Seamus, and Roux at the same time.

Jason blinked.

"It's too dangerous," Gideon clarified, but he looked at the space around Jason rather than at him directly.

"He's right," said Roux.

"You're staying here, where it's safe," Renie added.

Jason nodded, but his eyes were unhappy. "I don't like that you're all going off to fight Schofield and I'm stuck here."

"This isn't an adventure," Roux reminded him.

He looked up, surprised. "Oh, I know. I don't want to go up against the guy, I just hate that you have to and all I can do is sit around here and wait for news. It makes me feel useless."

"You're not useless, Jason." Roux glanced back up the staircase. "There are nine new vampire kids in this house who are probably still reeling from what's happened. Maybe you can help them."

"I did offer, but Ysanne doesn't want me to," Jason said.

"She needs your help, whether she realizes it or not," said Roux, giving Ysanne a little look.

Ysanne raised an eyebrow.

"All older vampires are completely out of touch with the modern world, so how is she or anyone else in Belle Morte supposed to understand these kids?" Roux gently poked Jason's chest. "*You* can understand them. *You* can help them. Don't take no for an answer."

Roux hugged him. Jason's heart thumped between them, so strong and so fragile at the same time. Roux resisted the urge to touch her own chest, where her heart would never beat again. This whole being dead thing would take some getting used to.

"Be careful out there," Jason said.

"We will."

"I'm coming part of the way with you, same as Walsh," Seamus said. "We'll park near where Schofield abandoned his car and wait there for you to contact us to come and pick you up."

Standing in the vestibule, preparing to head out in pursuit of the Five, felt vaguely surreal, as if the last few days had never happened, and they were doing this for the first time.

But real life didn't come with do-overs.

"You'll need these too," Seamus said, holding out several sets of silver handcuffs.

Roux reached for them, but Seamus pulled his hand back, looking sadly at her. For a moment she didn't understand, and then understanding rushed in.

She couldn't handle the cuffs anymore.

It was only a small thing, nothing compared to everything else she couldn't do now—so much that she hadn't even *realized* yet—but it made her eyes prickle.

"I'll get some gloves," said Jason, and sprinted up the stairs.

Roux flexed her fingers. Her hands looked the same—maybe paler than normal—but they'd never be the same again.

Jason hurried back downstairs, clutching several pairs of gloves, which he handed out to everyone.

"I guess that's it, then," he said, looking a bit lost.

His eyes strayed in Gideon's direction, but the vampire didn't seem to notice.

"We'll get this sorted tonight, once and for all," said Renie, sounding more confident than Roux felt.

Schofield had thwarted them time and time again. He might not be as strong as Ludovic, Edmond, or Gideon, but he was cunning, and he knew exactly how to use that.

Roux wanted to believe that tonight was the night they really would put an end to this, but Schofield had slipped through their fingers too many times for her to take anything for granted.

Night pressed in around them as they left the city, but Roux's new eyes cut through the shadows with ease. It was disconcerting, and after a while she stopped looking out the window and stared at the dashboard.

She'd asked to sit up front with Walsh while he drove; being cooped up in the back reminded her too much of being shoved into the trunk of Schofield's car.

"You sure you're okay with this?" Walsh said, glancing at her.

She nodded.

A few minutes passed before he spoke again.

"I'm sorry," he said.

"For what?"

He took one hand off the wheel and vaguely gestured. "You know, what happened to you."

"You mean because I'm a vampire now."

"Yes."

"You probably think it's a bad thing," she said.

"Do you?"

"I've never thought about it because it was never an option before. Now I just have to live with it." Roux gave a bitter laugh. "Or not, as I'm not technically alive anymore."

She could feel Walsh's eyes on her, but she didn't look at him.

"You're allowed to be mad about it," he said.

Roux closed her eyes, emotion forming a thick knot in her throat. "It wasn't my choice," she whispered. "It *should* have been my choice."

"For what it's worth, I've got a lot of fucking respect for you," Walsh said.

"Thanks."

"And we will nail that bastard tonight, one way or another."

"Do any of the kids know what's going on?" Roux asked.

"Ysanne didn't say, but I'd guess not."

Roux leaned her elbow on the door and sighed. "Do you think we'll ever really know why he did this to them?"

"Ludovic didn't tell you?" Walsh said.

"Tell me what?"

"Schofield refused to call any of them by their actual names. Instead, he called them all the names of his own kids."

Pieces slid together in Roux's head, and a picture began to take shape.

"Is that what this has always been about? Is that why his previous victims said he never physically hurt them? He was using them as replacements for his own kids."

"It explains the age discrepancy. His previous victims were much younger because that's how old his kids were then. This time, he went for teenagers, because his kids are now teenagers."

Roux swallowed the thickness in her throat. "This doesn't make him any less of a monster."

"I know."

After a while, Walsh pulled off the road and drove across a dark stretch of field before finally stopping close to a small patch of woodland. He climbed out and opened the doors at the back, letting the others out.

Roux stayed in the passenger seat, steeling her nerves and staring at herself in the rearview mirror. She was as strong as Schofield now, but he still terrified her in a way that he hadn't previously.

She clenched her teeth, feeling her fangs prick her lip. Later, when they'd neutralized this threat, she could scream and cry and rage as much as she wanted. She could fall apart and it wouldn't matter, because she'd have all the time in the world—literally—to deal with it.

She didn't have that time tonight.

"You can do this," she told her reflection. "He's not going to hurt you again, and you're not going to live in fear of him."

Someone knocked on the window, and she jumped, clutching the dashboard.

"Sorry," Renie said.

Roux could hear her as clearly as if she was inside.

"It's okay," she said.

Renie stepped aside as Roux pushed open the door. Smells rushed into her nose: grass and cold air, exhaust fumes and animal droppings. It was almost overwhelming, and she braced a hand on the door.

"It can be a bit much, can't it?" Renie said.

"How did you get used to it?"

Renie gave a little laugh. "I'm not. Not yet, anyway. I'm still learning, still adjusting. Every time I think I've come to terms with everything, I remember I'll never eat brownies again and it makes me want to cry. Only I can't do that either, because vampires can hardly ever cry. Then I feel sad, which just makes me want brownies even *more*."

"So how do you deal with it?" Roux asked.

Renie gave her a wicked grin. "Sex with Edmond."

"Somehow I don't think I'll be trying *that* method."

"You and Ludovic—"

"I don't want to talk about that now," Roux interrupted.

Renie gave her a quick hug. "No one will think any less of you if you stay here with Walsh and Seamus."

"I know, but I need to do this."

Nobody would keep her down, not anymore. It didn't matter what they did, nobody would beat her. Nobody would destroy her. She was stronger than that. She would *always* be stronger than that.

Renie grinned, showing off her fangs. "Let's get on with this, then."

As they approached the knot of trees, Roux spied a gleam of metal.

"That's Schofield's car," Ludovic said, narrowing his eyes.

"Why abandon it here?" Roux looked around but there was no sign of the farmstead.

"He's probably still trying to make it look like this isn't a trap."

They approached the car. Schofield had attempted to hide it under shrubs and winter-bare branches, but that wasn't enough to keep a vampire from spotting it.

Roux stopped dead, a wave of nausea washing over her.

Could vampires throw up?

She'd always thought not, but maybe she was about to prove that wrong.

"Roux?" Ludovic was at her side in an instant.

"Sorry, it's just . . ." She swallowed.

Her head was a tangle of memories: Schofield grabbing her, slapping his hand over her mouth so she couldn't scream, dragging her to the car, throwing her into the trunk and slamming it shut, sealing her in the dark.

That terror—worse than anything she'd ever felt in her life—was still inside her, welling back up and turning her to ice.

"You don't have to do this," Ludovic said.

"Yes, I do," Roux said fiercely.

This fear might stay with her forever, but it would not own her.

Walsh pointed down the black swath of countryside ahead of them. "Just keep going straight for another three miles."

"Are you sure you don't want us to come farther with you?" Seamus asked.

Ludovic shook his head. "If Schofield hears the engine, he'll know exactly when we're coming."

"Right. Good luck then."

Three miles wasn't far to walk, but Roux was still amazed at how swiftly they covered the distance, and despite the freezing temperature, she felt like she could have gone on forever.

This was how she'd cope with everything she'd lost by becoming a vampire: by reminding herself of everything she'd gained. It was the only way to keep that flame of positivity burning inside.

Ludovic paused suddenly, looking intently at the frosty ground.

"What is it?" Roux asked.

Ludovic gestured to something she couldn't see. "Footprints."

"Schofield must have walked from the car though, right? Why are footprints surprising?" Renie said.

"There's more than one set," Ludovic replied. "Schofield's not alone."

"It must be Morris and Patel," Roux said.

Ludovic nodded.

"Still, nothing more than we can handle," Edmond said.

After another half mile, the farm came into view. It was ringed by a low stone wall, but it didn't allow for much land, which made Roux think it hadn't been used as a proper farm for a long time, even before the fire that had gutted it. The house still stood, but the roof was gone, and the exposed walls were charred and blackened. Thick creepers of ivy, bramble, and bindweed twisted in and out of the window frames; eventually they'd obscure the place altogether. A rusted car was haphazardly parked outside, the doors hanging off their hinges. A bird swooped out of a hole in the roof and vanished into the night.

"Now what?" Renie whispered, eyeing the scattered outbuildings.

Roux waited for Ludovic to tell them which way the footprints were going, but his head was lifted, his eyes focused on the wooden barn.

"Do you smell that?" he said.

Roux inhaled and caught the metallic stench of blood.

Ludovic and Edmond shared a look, wordless communication flowing between them.

A sudden moan drifted out from the barn—a high, thin noise, clearly female, and raw with pain.

"Ludovic and I are going in. You three spread out and be prepared for anything," Edmond said.

"I'm thinking *that's* the trap," Renie said.

"Most likely, but we're the oldest and strongest, so we stand the best chance of getting through it, and we can't stand here while someone's suffering."

Renie grabbed his hand. "Be careful," she said.

Edmond smiled and kissed her. "Always," he murmured.

Ludovic glanced at Roux, then looked away.

As she watched Edmond and Ludovic run toward the barn, silent as whispers on the frozen ground, Roux's heart felt like it was trying to climb into her throat—which didn't make sense because it couldn't even beat anymore.

She didn't like that Ludovic and Edmond were walking into a potential trap while the rest of them waited out here.

She *hated* that Schofield could be in that barn, watching, waiting, a toxic spider crouching at the corner of his web, waiting to trap his prey.

The moan came again, higher pitched this time, and Roux's ears picked up something else: clinking metal. It triggered something in her brain, but she was too tense to place it.

The thick smell of blood made her fangs push out of her gums, and she couldn't help touching the dagger-sharp points. She glanced at Renie and saw her doing the same thing; when their gazes met, Renie gave her a sheepish grin and a small shrug. Apparently, she wasn't completely used to her fangs yet either. Roux took some comfort in that.

Edmond and Ludovic each grasped one of the pair of doors that led into the barn and flung them open. They strode inside.

The loud creak of ropes sounded from somewhere in the roof, then a torrent of blood poured down, drenching Edmond and Ludovic.

"What the fuck?" Renie said.

That metallic clinking came again, louder this time, and suddenly Roux knew why it sounded familiar.

Chains.

Something was chained up inside that barn.

Shapes blurred through the shadows, too fast for Roux to pinpoint, and then there was one long rattle, which made her blood run cold.

It *was* a trap, just not one any of them could have anticipated.

Four haggard vampires emerged from the darkness, their red eyes fixed on Edmond and Ludovic.

"Oh my god," Roux whispered, as something fell into place. She *knew* those faces.

"What? Who are they?" Gideon said.

"Etienne's mystery four vampires," Roux said, the words bitter in her mouth.

She'd all but forgotten about them—there hadn't seemed much point worrying about them until the bigger threat of the Five had been dealt with.

Now both threats had come together.

The four vampires attacked.

CHAPTER TWENTY-SEVEN

Roux

None of those vampires could match Ludovic or Edmond for strength, but the second Roux saw a threat heading for Ludovic, she instinctively charged forward.

She wasn't fast enough to reach him before the vampires did.

One of them leaped at Ludovic like a wild dog, but Ludovic caught him midleap and neatly lifted him over his head, slamming him onto the barn floor. Ludovic's eyes flashed red and his fangs slid out. The younger vampire thrashed in his grip, snapping and snarling. A second vampire jumped onto Ludovic's back, but Roux pulled her away.

The vampire faced her, wild-eyed and slathering, and for a moment Roux froze, overcome by fear.

Ludovic's self-defense lessons rushed back into her head and this time she refused to let them slip away. Her fist plowed into her attacker's nose, sending the woman skidding across the floor.

Roux had time to feel a kind of grim delight.

Her opponent clambered to her feet and ran at her again, and Roux neatly dodged to the side. She kicked the other vampire in the back of the leg as she lurched past, and then delivered a crushing punch to her head.

Something scraped overhead, and Roux looked up, her vampire

vision cutting through the dim light. Someone was up there, hiding in the rafters like a grotesque spider.

Schofield?

Rage and hatred boiled through her veins.

Everything else faded away.

She didn't know if Renie and Gideon had joined the fight, or how the fight was even going.

She couldn't hear anything but a dull roar in her ears.

Her fangs pricked her lower lip and she tasted blood. It fed the fury inside her.

Schofield wasn't getting away this time.

The barn walls were reinforced with thick wooden beams, and Roux used those like a ladder, deploying her new speed and agility to climb up to the roof.

The figure hiding in the rafters shifted, moving back as Roux reached his level, and she was hit with a scorching blast of disappointment.

Morris, not Schofield, stared back at her, his eyes widening, and she wondered what she looked like in that moment—if he could see the fire that fueled her.

"What the hell? Isn't that the Belle Morte girl?" said a voice.

Roux turned her head.

Patel was crouched in the rafters farther along the roof, wearing an expression of shock.

"Smith *turned* her?" Patel said.

"You helped kidnap me from the hospital—what did you *think* he was going to do?" Roux said, her eyes stinging.

"He told us he was going to use you as a bargaining chip to make Belle Morte back off and leave us alone," Patel said.

"He lied," Roux spat. "And his name's not Jeffrey Smith."

Patel blinked, and when Roux glanced back at Morris, even he looked taken aback.

"What are you talking about?" he growled, shifting his weight.

"You fucking idiots," Roux said. "All this time you've been helping him and you don't even know who he is."

Morris puffed out his chest. "We have to stick together, look out for each other."

"He murdered nine *kids*," Roux shouted, the words scorching her throat.

Patel moved along the rafters. "What are you talking about?" he said.

"His real name is Roger Schofield. His alcoholism cost him his family and now he steals other people's kids as replacements. There are nine kids currently recovering at Belle Morte because he turned them into vampires against their will. Then he did the same to me," Roux said.

Disbelief dawned in Patel's eyes, and he gripped the rafters to steady himself.

"This is bullshit," Morris snarled. "That bitch would say anything."

"Why would she lie about that? And why did Smith *turn her*?" Patel said.

"Why does that surprise you? You tried to kill me and Ludovic," Roux snapped.

Patel just stared at her, as if he was only now realizing what he'd been doing. "He said you were going to kill us . . ." He trailed off and stumbled back. "It wasn't meant to be like this."

Roux had no pity for him. He'd still come after her and Ludovic.

He'd still helped Etienne and Jemima attack Belle Morte. There was still blood on his hands.

Morris snarled and launched himself at Roux. The force of his attack hurled her back against the sloping roof; the old wooden slats splintered under her weight, and then she was falling, pulling Morris with her.

They hit the ground hard, and pain jolted through Roux's body. Instinctively she tried to catch her breath, then remembered she didn't have any to catch. She shoved Morris off her, and he rolled away with a groan.

Roux scrambled to her feet.

Ice flooded her veins.

A dark figure stood outside the barn, sloshing something up and down the walls, and this time Roux *knew* it was Schofield. The acrid reek of gasoline reached her, and Roux finally understood why Schofield had lured them here. Maybe he'd hoped that the mystery four vampires could take out anyone who came after him, but if that didn't work, he planned to burn them all alive inside the barn.

Schofield pulled a lighter from his pocket and Roux raced toward him.

He heard her coming, but she still managed to smack the lighter from his hand before he could react. The flame went out before it hit the ground. Schofield's eyes widened—maybe he hadn't expected Roux to be up and about so soon.

Roux wondered if he could see that fire burning inside her. She hoped he could because he was the one who'd lit it.

Schofield suddenly lunged, wrapping his hands around Roux's throat and throwing her to the ground. He couldn't strangle her, but her instinct was still to panic when someone had her throat like that. She scrabbled at Schofield's face, trying to scratch his furious, glittering eyes, but he twisted his head to the side. Keeping a firm grip on her neck, he half lifted her and slammed her back against the ground.

Pain shot through her spine, and Roux choked down a cry. "You bastard," she snarled. "I won't let you win."

Schofield thrust his face close to hers. His eyes shone red, dancing with malice, and his fangs gleamed like daggers.

A growl trickled from his throat, then suddenly he arched his back and screamed, a horrible, raw sound. Something splashed Roux's arm, eating through skin and flesh, and she couldn't hold back a shriek of her own.

Walsh stood over them, a metal flask clutched in one hand.

As Schofield reeled back, letting Roux go, Walsh splashed him with the flask again. Schofield screamed, clawing at his face. Blood streamed from bubbling patches on his skin.

"Have a little liquid silver, you sick fuck," Walsh yelled.

The injured vampire staggered to his feet. His right cheek was a mess; the silver had blistered great patches of his skin and burned away part of his ear.

Walsh lifted his flask again, then Morris surged forward with an animal roar. He kicked Walsh in the chest, and Roux heard the crunch of ribs cracking. Walsh crumpled to the ground.

Schofield had fallen to his knees, his hands clutching his damaged face, and Morris grabbed Schofield's arm and slung it over his shoulder, hauling the other man to his feet. They scrambled over the stone wall that ringed the wall and fled.

Roux rushed to Walsh's side. He groaned and tried to sit up. Roux supported him, letting him lean against her.

"Are you okay?" she said.

"Other than feeling like I got hit by a bus? Sure." Walsh ground the words out through gritted teeth.

"He could have killed you!"

"Right back at you." Walsh groaned again, clutching his chest. "You looked like you needed help."

"You're not supposed to be here."

"Fucking sue me."

Roux eyed the flask in his hand. Her arm still hurt like crazy from where its contents had hit her, but it was nothing compared to Schofield's injuries. "Liquid silver?"

"Colloidal silver. Close enough," he said.

"That's hardly police issue."

He tried to laugh, but it turned into a stifled sound of pain. "Paid for that out of my own pocket. It seemed like it would come in handy."

Ludovic emerged from the barn, shaking blood from his hair and dragging an exhausted, cuffed vampire behind him. He dropped his prisoner when he saw Roux and Walsh, but his stare was only for Roux.

He ran to her.

"I'm okay, I'm okay," Roux said. "Is anyone hurt?"

Ludovic shook his head.

"The vampires?" Roux asked, looking past him.

Gideon, Edmond, and Renie emerged from the barn, each pulling a captured vampire with them.

"We didn't hurt them. Like the kids, they're completely out of their minds with hunger; they didn't know what they were doing," Ludovic said. "These are the mystery four, aren't they?"

"Yeah."

"Have they been here all this time?" Ludovic looked back at the barn.

"I don't know."

"Schofield?"

Roux looked at the wall that Morris and Schofield had climbed over, and suddenly she was furious with herself. She'd let him slip through her fingers.

"I couldn't leave Walsh," she said.

Ludovic surveyed the darkened countryside around them. "He can't have got far. We'll find him."

"Excuse me," said a hesitant voice behind them, and they both spun around to see Kashvi Patel walking out of the barn. He held out both hands as if expecting someone to cuff him. "I'd like to give myself up."

Roux called Seamus and asked him to bring the van. The captured vampires huddled on the ground, too weak and exhausted to resist. Roux wasn't sure they were even aware of what was happening.

"What happens to them now?" Walsh asked, one hand pressed gingerly to his ribs.

"They'll be taken back to Belle Morte. Maybe they can shed some light on what Etienne had planned for them and why they've been out here all this time," Ludovic said.

"One of us will have to stay with them until Seamus arrives," Gideon said.

"I'll do it," Renie offered.

"If you're staying, so am I," Edmond said.

"You don't need to do that."

"Yes, I do. If something goes wrong, you're not facing it alone."

"But the others need you."

"You two stay here and I'll go with Roux and Ludovic," Gideon said. "We can handle it."

"But—"

"The longer we dick around here, the more chance Schofield has of getting away. That's not happening again," Roux said.

Walsh tossed her his metal flask, and Roux caught it with reflexes she hadn't had as a human.

"There's a little left inside. You might need it," Walsh said.

Roux turned away, gazing over the shadow-wrapped swathe of countryside that surrounded them. Schofield was out there somewhere. This ended tonight.

"Let's go," she said.

Ludovic

"You can still track Schofield, right?" Roux asked.

"Every step of the way."

Roux gave him a quick, fierce grin, and the force of it hit him straight in the heart. He wanted to see that smile every day for the rest of his life. He wanted to wake up to it. He wanted to know that he was the one who'd put it on her face. He wanted to kiss it.

Later.

Telling Roux how he felt would be the dawn at the end of this long, dark night, but tackling Schofield came first.

Ludovic inspected the ground around the barn. Everything was a mess, multiple prints flattening the grass, and scuffed patches where the captured vampires had been dragged out. Farther along, among a scattering of broken boards, was the imprint of a body.

"That's where Morris pushed me," Roux said.

"He pushed you through the roof?" Fresh anger pulsed in Ludovic's veins.

Roux poked his chest. "Track now, fuss later." She moved to the stone wall. "This is where they climbed over."

Ludovic joined her, noting the splashes of fresh blood.

"How badly was Schofield hurt?" Gideon asked.

"Walsh threw liquid silver in his face, so pretty bad," Roux said.

"Good," Gideon said.

On the other side of the wall, they descended into silence, Roux and Gideon shadowing Ludovic as he tracked. Twice he lost the trail, and twice he found it again, using his nose as well as his eyes. Wounds caused by silver took longer to heal than regular injuries, which meant there was a good blood trail to follow.

Roux reacted to every breaking twig or disturbed leaf, looking at Ludovic, and every time he shook his head. He knew animal sounds when he heard them.

Until something made him pause.

He cocked his head. He couldn't say exactly what he'd heard, a mere whisper of movement, but he was an old, experienced vampire, and his instincts were well honed.

Rather than signaling for Roux and Gideon to stop, he gave them both a warning look, but didn't stop walking. Until he could pinpoint the noise, it was better to lull their enemies into a false sense of security.

After another few dozen feet, he paused and crouched, pretending to study the ground while instead studying their surroundings in his peripheral vision. That suggestion of sound came again, drawing Ludovic's eyes to an overgrown hedge on his right. The blocky shape of it stretched across the fields, and Ludovic couldn't see if anyone hid behind it, but his eyes picked out a small gap, not far ahead.

Still pretending to study tracks on the ground, Ludovic subtly veered closer.

Twigs cracked underfoot and then Schofield staggered through the gap in the hedge. His face was a patchwork of pinkish burns, his mouth and chin stained with fresh blood. When he saw them, he whimpered and fell back.

Ludovic wanted to charge over there and rip Schofield's head off, but something held him back. The twigs cracking, Schofield's sudden appearance, it was all too convenient.

Like he'd meant to give himself away.

Like he was a distraction.

Ludovic whipped around, a warning forming on his lips, but Schofield had already got the split-second distraction he needed.

Morris charged out of a cluster of trees on their left, wielding a pitchfork with both hands.

Gideon shoved Roux out of the way.

Morris plunged the pitchfork into Gideon's chest.

CHAPTER TWENTY-EIGHT

Roux

Gideon let out a choked cry and staggered back.

Morris wrenched the pitchfork free and aimed it at Gideon's head, but Ludovic was faster. A roar of pure rage exploding from his throat, he wrenched the pitchfork from Morris and threw it. Like a javelin, it soared into the night.

Roux might have kept it, but Ludovic's fists were weapon enough.

Morris tried to run, but Ludovic hauled him back.

Movement flickered in Roux's periphery, and she whirled around to see Schofield slinking away. Utter contempt made her blood boil. Morris might be a piece of shit but he'd stood by Schofield throughout everything, and now, while Morris was fighting for his life, Schofield was abandoning him to save his own skin.

Nope.

Roux threw herself in front of Schofield, blocking his path, her hands clenched tight.

"Don't make me kill you again," Schofield snarled.

"I'd like to see you try," Roux said, and punched him.

Anger made her unsteady, throwing off her aim, and her knuckles skidded along Schofield's jaw rather than breaking his nose like she'd hoped, but it was enough to let him know she meant business.

Schofield's eyes glowed red, making his burned cheek look even worse, and his fangs jutted over his lips. He started to say something, and Roux hit him again, punching the words back down his throat. Schofield stumbled and lost his footing.

If Roux had had that pitchfork, she'd have run him through with it.

A terrible howl split the night as Ludovic shattered Morris's leg.

Morris rolled onto his back, glaring up at Ludovic. "Fuck you," he snarled.

Ludovic smiled and it was like ice.

Then he tore out Morris's throat.

Schofield made a choking noise.

At first Roux thought it was rage. Then she realized it was fear.

All this time, Schofield had relied on his cunning and cruelty, and his deluded friends to have his back, and now his last ally lay dead at Ludovic's feet.

Roux wasn't surprised when he fled.

At heart, he was a coward.

He was unsteady on his feet; he wouldn't get far.

Ludovic started to go after him then stopped, crouching beside Gideon.

"How bad is it?" Roux cried.

The pitchfork had caught Gideon on the right side of the chest. It had missed his heart, otherwise he'd already be dead, but if it had punctured a lung—

Roux caught herself. Gideon was a vampire. A punctured lung wouldn't kill him.

Ludovic pulled open Gideon's shirt, and the other vampire growled in pain. The pitchfork had gouged across his chest, rather than plunging into it as Roux had feared, and Roux couldn't stop her fangs from reacting at the sight of so much blood. Embarrassed, she closed her mouth.

"I'll live," Gideon muttered, bracing his hand on Ludovic's knee so he could pull himself into a sitting position. His voice was tight with pain. "It'll take more than a goddamn pitchfork to kill me."

Schofield was a small shape slowly disappearing at the end of the field. If he were at full strength, he'd have run faster, but injuries and a lack of human blood were clearly taking their toll.

Ludovic rose to his feet. "I'll get him."

"No," said Roux, a strange sense of calm filling her. "He's mine."

"Roux—"

"No." She faced Ludovic. "He killed me."

"I know—"

"If I don't do this, I'll always be afraid of him."

Ludovic gazed back at her, torn.

Roux cupped his face with both hands and kissed him. "It's not your decision to make," she whispered against his mouth. "I can take him. I need this."

All he could do was nod.

Ludovic

Watching Roux go was agony, but if he tried to stop her, she'd never forgive him. Roux wasn't stupid and she wasn't reckless. She wouldn't go after Schofield unless she was sure she could beat him.

He stood and watched the woman he loved go after the man who'd killed her, even though every instinct told him to go after her.

"She can't do this," Gideon rasped.

"She has to," Ludovic said.

"He could *kill* her."

Schofield had already done that, but Roux was a vampire now. Her strength was equal to Schofield's, and she had something that Schofield never would: a flame of pure steel burning at her core.

It was passion and determination and love combined, all qualities that Schofield couldn't hope to have.

"Roux can beat him," Ludovic said, fierce pride sparking in his chest.

This was his woman, his light, his love.

She wouldn't shrink away from the man who'd done this to her.

She wouldn't give him any more power.

She'd take it all back from him.

Gideon shifted slightly and hissed with pain, fresh blood spurting from his wounds. "I can't believe I let him sneak up on me like that."

"It wasn't your fault," Ludovic said.

"But a pitchfork? What century are we in?"

Ludovic flared his nostrils, drawing in the scents of the night, picking up a distinct foxy musk. But he couldn't go hunting while Roux was after Schofield.

"Can you hold on a little longer?" he asked Gideon.

Gideon gritted his teeth and nodded. "Neither of us is going any-where until Schofield is dead."

Roux

As she ran, she swore she could still hear her heart thumping in her ears. It was nothing but a phantom echo, but it spurred her on.

Schofield bobbed in her vision, getting steadily closer and closer as her feet flew over the frosty ground. For the first time, Roux felt like Schofield was afraid of her, and that knowledge buoyed her, fueling her rage.

She launched herself at him and knocked him to the ground. He jabbed an elbow into her ribs, loosening her grip, and then threw her off.

They scrambled to their feet at the same time, glaring at each other.

"You don't want to do this," Schofield said, but his eyes darted left to right, betraying his anxiety.

Roux wasn't threatened by him anymore.

"Yeah," she said, "I really do."

She threw a punch and this time her aim was steady. Her knuckles crunched into Schofield's nose. He reeled back, snarling. Roux hit him again, just below the ribs.

"*Bitch*," he spat, and was rewarded with another punch.

He lunged, grabbed a fistful of her hair, and slung her around. Roux's scalp sang with pain, but her hair was too short for Schofield to keep his grip, and as soon as he let go, she kicked him in the knee-cap, putting as much force behind it as she could. If she'd known how to deliver a really good kick, she could have broken bone. Unfortunately, he just stumbled.

"Your boyfriend's not coming to help," he said.

"I don't need him to," Roux said, making fists the way Ludovic had taught her.

"What kind of man lets his girlfriend fight his battles?"

"The kind who knows his girlfriend is capable of it. What kind of man kills his own mum?" she said.

Schofield froze. "What?"

"Don't you remember knocking her down the stairs?"

"I . . ." Schofield frowned, his eyes swiveling back and forth.

"You knocked her down the stairs to save yourself, and then you never bothered contacting her to see if she was okay." Disgust laced Roux's voice.

Schofield was silent, his jaw clenched.

"You really are a piece of shit," Roux said. "All your mum ever did was protect you, and you didn't spare a single thought for her safety. She's been dead for *days*, and you didn't know because you didn't bother to find out."

"Shut up," Schofield said, his voice quiet and deadly.

Maybe there was some part of him that *did* care about his mum, some tiny remnant of the little boy he must once have been, but he was still the one who'd killed her.

"Why? Is the truth too much for you?"

Schofield snapped and lunged at her. Roux threw up an arm to protect her face as they hit the ground, while driving her knee into his stomach. Schofield grunted, but his weight still bore down on her, pushing her against the frosty grass.

Roux sank her fangs into his shoulder, tearing at him. Schofield shrieked and rolled away from her—clearly he hadn't considered using his fangs as weapons. Roux was surprised that more vampires *didn't* use them that way. They were very effective.

She spat out a mouthful of Schofield's blood.

He crouched a few feet away, glaring at her with burning eyes. His hand clutched his shoulder, blood pulsing between his fingers.

"I'm going to kill you," Roux told him, and there was no emotion, no anger in her voice, just cold, simple fact.

Fear flickered across his face, and Roux felt a surge of dark satisfaction.

Schofield ran—not at her, but *away* from her.

He didn't get far.

Roux tackled him. Grabbing his shoulders, she flipped him over, ignoring the punches he landed on her chest and torso. Walsh's flask was a cold weight in her pocket, and she pulled it out, using her thumb to flip open the cap.

Silver seared her skin, but the pain was nothing compared to her determination. Pinning Schofield down, she emptied the rest of the silver onto him. She'd aimed for his throat, hoping it would burn through his neck, but he wriggled like a fish, and the silver poured directly into his snapping mouth.

Schofield let out a terrible scream, bucking and writhing with such force that he knocked Roux to one side. He rolled onto all fours, gasping and gagging, spitting out blood and thicker things.

Roux looked around.

A fallen branch lay beneath a knot of nearby trees.

Roux stepped over Schofield, still thrashing and howling in the grass, and picked up the branch. She broke it across her knee and tossed one piece to the ground while keeping a firm grip on the other—the piece with the sharp end.

It almost seemed ridiculous to use a wooden stake on a modern vampire—who the hell was she, Buffy?—but at the same time it was oddly fitting.

As she approached him, Schofield suddenly exploded to life and threw himself at her. Roux lost her footing and slipped, Schofield landing on top. He snarled, spraying blood in her face, and she shoved a hand against his mouth, forcing it away from her. His fangs sliced open her fingers. The silver had corroded his mouth, and bits of his lips stuck to her palm.

Frantically, he tried to bite her, and Roux swung her makeshift stake up, slamming it through his cheek. Schofield screamed, gobbets of his tongue dribbling from his ruined mouth.

Roux wrenched the stake out of Schofield's face, and shoved him. He fell back, and Roux pounced on him, using her knees to pin down his arms.

She didn't waste time savoring the moment or relishing the look of terror in his eyes. She simply plunged the branch into his chest, smashing through his ribs and impaling his heart.

Schofield shuddered and writhed, and then at last, went still. The red faded from his eyes.

Roux climbed off him, leaving the branch stuck in his chest.

A chill winter breeze danced through the air, and she closed her eyes, lifting her head and deeply inhaling.

It was over.

Schofield was dead.

She sensed movement behind her, and turned to see Ludovic approaching. He paused a few feet away, giving her space if she needed it.

For a moment, Roux stared at him, her heart a tangle of emotions.

Now that Schofield was gone, there was a lot that she and Ludovic needed to talk about, and she didn't know where to start.

Something was rising inside her, a powerful swell of emotion that she'd never felt before, and she didn't know how to put it into words.

She ran to him and leaped into his arms, and in that moment, everything felt right with the world.

CHAPTER TWENTY-NINE

Roux

They left Schofield's body where he'd fallen, to be burned up by the sun when it rose, and made their way back to Gideon, who was propped against a tree.

"The warrior returns," he said, with a faint smile.

"Victorious," Roux said.

Now that the adrenaline was wearing off, she was becoming aware of her bruises and burns, the gashes on her fingers from Schofield's fangs. She slumped down next to Gideon.

"How are you holding up?" she asked.

"I've been worse."

Ludovic touched the other man's shoulder. "I'll get you something to eat."

Gideon shook his head. "I can wait until we get back to the mansion."

"You need blood now," Ludovic said, his tone of voice brooking no argument.

Roux gently nudged Gideon. "Listen to your elders."

He gave her an arch look. "How do you know I'm not the older one?"

She didn't know if he meant older in vampire years or human years, so she said nothing.

"I won't be long," Ludovic said, and strode off into the night.

Gideon and Roux sat in silence for a minute or two. "Are you all right?" he asked.

She thought about it. Schofield was dead, and in killing him, she felt like she'd taken back something important, something he'd stolen from her. She still hadn't come to terms with being a vampire, and there was a lot of adjustment ahead, but she had to deal with that because she had no choice.

For every negative aspect of her new life, she'd find a positive one.

"I'm getting there," she said.

"It's not always easy standing up to someone who's hurt you," Gideon said.

Roux gave him a curious look. "That sounds like you're speaking from experience."

He looked away. "You should probably call the mansion and let them know this is over."

It wasn't over—not fully.

Schofield and Morris were dead.

The rest of the Five and Etienne's mystery vampires were all in custody.

But there were questions that still needed answering, and a lot of fallout still to deal with. All the changes facing the vampire world had to be addressed.

Just for tonight, though, Roux would enjoy a victory.

Roux called Renie and told her what had happened.

"We've dropped the prisoners off at Belle Morte, so we're just taking Walsh to the hospital and then we'll come pick you up, okay?" Renie said.

"Thanks." Roux ended the call.

Ludovic returned, carrying a freshly killed fox, which he handed to Gideon. Roux climbed to her feet and moved a few paces away, giving Gideon some privacy.

Ludovic came up behind her, and Roux leaned against his chest. He slipped an arm around her waist, gently holding her.

"How do you feel?" he asked.

"Like we're finally coming to the end of a very long night."

"That's exactly how I feel," he said, and pressed the smallest kiss to the tip of her nose.

"I know other dark nights are still coming, but we got through this, so we can get through everything else."

"You always see the positive in everything," Ludovic said, his arm tightening around her. "That's why I love you."

Roux tensed.

What?

Had he . . . did he . . . ?

Ludovic must have felt her tension; he pulled back slightly, the shutters coming down over his eyes.

Roux ran her hand through her hair, then immediately wished she hadn't. Her fingers were still bleeding.

"I'm sorry," they both said at the same time.

Roux laughed, but even she could hear how stiff it was. She couldn't process this.

Ludovic said nothing, his face as still as a mask.

He'd said that he *loved* her.

"Ludovic," she said, trying to decide how to broach this.

He looked at her, and though his expression—or lack thereof—didn't change, hope flickered in his eyes.

"Did you mean that?" she asked.

Ludovic swallowed—one of the most human tics she'd ever seen on a vampire. "Yes," he said, his voice barely a whisper.

"But you can't . . . I . . . we don't *know* each other."

"Don't we? I've told you things I don't tell anyone. I've opened up to you in a way that I never thought I'd be able to again." Passion sparked in Ludovic's eyes, and Roux felt an answering tug in her chest. "You made me *feel* again," Ludovic said.

Roux's eyes prickled. She didn't know what to say. "It's too soon. We've only known each other a few *days*."

Ludovic pressed his palm to her cheek, his thumb stroking her skin. "Don't say anything."

"But—"

He kissed her, long and slow, until her legs felt like they were buckling, and she was clutching his arms to steady herself.

Ludovic broke the kiss and rested his forehead on hers. "I love you, Roux Hayes. You don't have to say anything now, you don't have to say anything *ever*, but I needed you to know. I'm not putting up walls anymore."

While Roux was racking her brain for a response, the rumble of an engine echoed through the stillness.

Ludovic smiled down at her, but it was tinged with sadness. "That'll be Seamus. I'll go and help Gideon."

He kissed her once more and then he was gone.

Roux stayed where she was, wanting to laugh and cry at the same time, but too confused to do either.

Ludovic loved her.

He *loved* her.

Everything was happening too fast.

Words crowded on Roux's tongue, but she couldn't organize them, or even work out what they were trying to say. All she could do was climb into the van beside Seamus, and wait to go home.

Renie, Edmond, Ysanne, and Jason were waiting for them when they got back. Renie and Jason both ran for Roux—Renie was faster—and Roux sagged gratefully in her friend's arms. A moment later, Jason hugged them both, squashing them against his chest.

His eyes widened when he saw Gideon pass by, covered in blood, but he didn't let go of his friends.

"When you're ready, please come to the dining hall. We have some things to discuss," Ysanne said.

The other vampires went into the mansion, leaving Roux and her friends standing outside the front door.

"You got Schofield?" Jason said.

"I did," Roux replied.

He grinned. "Never doubted my brave, beautiful girl."

"Something's still wrong," Renie said, her eyes boring into Roux.

"It's Ludovic," she said.

Jason's eyes narrowed. "What did he do?"

Changed for me.

Fought for me.

Gave his heart to me.

Took mine in return.

"He told me he loved me," she whispered.

The anger faded from Jason's face. "Okay." It wasn't a question, but his voice made it sound like one. And the way he looked at her, expectantly, made it seem like he was waiting for an answer.

"I don't know *what* to say," Roux said.

"Let's start with what you said to him when he told you," Renie said.

Roux looked at the ground. "I didn't know what to say."

Renie pursed her lips. "Okay, maybe he sprang it on you when you weren't ready, but surely you know how you feel."

It seemed so obvious when she put it like that.

Before Ludovic had dropped that bomb, Roux would have said she knew how she felt about him.

She knew that when he looked at her it felt like dawn breaking on a new day.

She knew that when he laughed she wanted to wrap herself up in that sound.

She knew that he'd given her the gift of trust, and she knew exactly how hard it had been for him to do that, and how precious a gift it was.

She knew that lying in bed with him made her happier than she'd ever been in her life.

She knew that she couldn't imagine her life without him in it.

But . . .

"You realize we've only known each other *a few days*," she said. "People don't fall in love that quickly."

Renie pursed her lips even more. "I'll have to disagree with that."

"Me too," Jason said. "My grandparents got married after knowing each other for three days, and they stayed together for fifty years. Sometimes when you know, you know."

"I . . ." The words stuck in Roux's throat.

There was nothing she couldn't tell Ludovic, and she didn't imagine there was anything he wouldn't tell her in return. That kind of trust and honesty wasn't easily given. She *did* know him—she knew his heart and soul, and all the little things that made him the man he was.

No one else made her feel the way he did, and she couldn't imagine anyone else ever making her feel that way again. He'd come to occupy a place in her heart, and that wouldn't change, even if she never saw him again.

Emotion swelled in her chest, bright and warm and beautiful, making her eyes prickle with unshed tears.

She knew.

She *knew*.

She'd thought before that being with Ludovic was like stepping off the edge of a cliff, not knowing what waited at the bottom, but the only thing waiting for her was him. And she'd gladly step off that cliff every single day of her life, knowing that he'd always be there to catch her.

Just as she'd always be there to catch him.

"There it is," Renie said, reading Roux's expression.

A small laugh burst out before Roux could stop it. The feeling in her heart was too big to contain. "I love him," she said.

"Well, duh," said Jason, with a massive grin.

Roux laughed again, pressing her hands to her face. She'd been trying to fight something she didn't need to fight. "This is the longest, strangest night of my life," she said.

She'd died, come back, killed her murderer, and realized she was in love, all in the space of a few hours.

A smile crept across her face.

She was in love with Ludovic.

He was in love with her.

She grabbed Renie's and Jason's hands and squeezed.

"Ow. Take it easy, Wonder Woman, you don't know your own strength now," said Jason, wincing.

"Sorry." But she couldn't keep the grin off her face.

"I'll let you off, since you're all soppy and in love."

Roux gave Jason's hand another squeeze, careful to be gentler this time.

"Help me find Ludovic," she said.

They found him in the dining hall, and Roux's heart sank a little as they walked in.

Edmond, Ysanne, Seamus, and Gideon were already there, sitting at the end of the long table. Gideon had obviously fed, and someone had given him a clean shirt. Ysanne's phone was propped on a book in the middle of the table, and when Roux drew closer, she saw Walsh's face on the screen.

"I heard you took down Schofield. Congrats," he said.

His voice was still tight with pain, but his eyes gleamed with satisfaction, and Roux smiled at him.

"I'm more impressed that one of these old-timer vampires managed to video call you," she joked.

Ysanne gave her a haughty look. "I'm not completely incompetent when it comes to these things."

Behind her back, Seamus shook his head and pointed to himself.

Roux stifled a laugh.

"Please sit down," Ysanne said. "We have a lot to discuss."

Roux and her friends took their seats.

"First, you should all know that the nine children Ludovic rescued from that cellar were not Schofield's only victims. Further police investigation of the surrounding area uncovered several shallow graves containing human remains. Walsh believes that these are homeless men and women Schofield kidnapped and used to practice turning humans into vampires before he went after the children. Since he successfully turned all nine children, we can safely conclude that he must also have successfully turned other adult victims. But there are no traces of them, so Schofield likely killed them after turning them, and let their bodies burn up in the sun. Tragically, we may never know how many people he really killed."

Ysanne waited a beat before continuing.

"The four vampires in the barn have been there ever since Etienne turned them. Rather than soldiers, he wished for them to be test subjects. Once he learned he could train June like a dog, he thought he could do the same with other rabids, only there weren't any others." Ysanne looked down at the table for a long moment. When she looked back up, anger and disgust warred in her eyes. "Through beatings, starving, and general cruelty, Etienne was trying to *create* rabids. He didn't fully trust Jemima—"

"Shocker," Renie muttered.

"—and if he could create and train more rabids, he'd have the kind of protection even Jemima couldn't match. By the time he realized he didn't have full control of June, it was too late."

"Also, no one can create a rabid because no one knows why it happens," Edmond said.

"No one knew those vampires were at the barn, so after Etienne died, they were trapped there. Until, by a stroke of sheer luck, Schofield stumbled upon them while he was scouting potential bolt-holes and realized he could use them as weapons against anyone who might come after him."

"How did Patel and Morris find us in the hotel?" Ludovic said.

"When Schofield realized you and Roux were after him, he contacted his friends for help. Morris and Patel tracked you to the hotel when you took Schofield there, but they couldn't launch a rescue effort without knowing what they were getting into. By a nasty twist of fate, Morris was friends with a member of Iain Johnson's gang, and he told that gang where you were staying. Because we hadn't publicized the names of the Five, Morris's friend was unaware that he'd become a vampire, and unaware that Morris was using him to draw you out," Ysanne said.

"Did he know they were going to burn down the hotel?" Roux asked.

"Patel doesn't believe so. Morris was unaware how much Iain hated vampires, or that you'd had any prior interaction with Iain."

"What happens to Patel now?"

He'd finally realized things had gone too far, but that didn't undo the damage he'd already helped cause. It didn't bring the victim of the fire back to life.

"He's in the cells too," Ysanne said.

Walsh sighed and raked a hand through his hair. "Fuck, I don't know where we go from here. I can charge him, but he's a vampire.

We can't put him in human prison, and a life sentence isn't that big a deal to someone who'll live forever."

"We'll have to discuss that with the prime minister at a later date," Ysanne said. "For now, the prisoners will remain here."

"This is fucked-up," Walsh told Ysanne.

"Yes. It is," she said.

"But we have hope now," Roux said.

Ysanne looked at her, her expression unreadable.

"We did what we set out to do. We stopped the Five and we found the mystery four, and we did it within a few days."

"But at what cost? Nine children were turned into vampires. So were you. It's another black mark against vampires, perhaps the most serious of all. We lost donors in the cross fire of our battles, and we covered up June's murder, but . . ." Ysanne shook her head. "Schofield stalked children, snatched them from their homes, forced them to become vampires, and then imprisoned them. I fear that whatever backlash we've faced so far will pale when compared to what we'll face when this is made public," Ysanne said in a heavy voice.

Silence fell again, everyone in the room contemplating the uncertain future that lay ahead.

"Maybe it'll be bad, but we stopped Schofield from hurting anyone else. That has to count for something," said Roux determinedly.

"I hope it will," said Ysanne, but she didn't sound convinced.

"When are you going to tell McGellan?" Seamus asked, resting his elbows on the table.

"Tomorrow," Ysanne said.

Walsh cleared his throat.

Ysanne glanced at him. "Assuming you agree, of course," she said, her voice slightly rigid.

"Yeah," he said. "Bringing this all out in the open will probably cause another shitstorm, and you've all earned a break."

Ysanne leaned both palms on the tabletop and surveyed the room. For once, she didn't look like a queen gazing down upon her subjects. She looked tired and earnest and almost human.

"Thanking you all for what you've done is not enough, but it's all I can do for the moment. So, thank you," she said.

"We'll all still be here tomorrow, to carry on helping," Renie said.

She didn't need to say more than that. Belle Morte was their home and, though none of them shared blood ties, they'd become family. Whatever trials still lay ahead, they'd face them together.

CHAPTER THIRTY

Roux

Ludovic was first out of the room, and Roux was too surprised to run after him.

"He's giving you space," Jason said, noticing her expression.

"I don't want space."

"He doesn't know that, does he? Vampires can't read minds."

"Sometimes I think it would be easier if they could."

Jason cleared his throat. "I'm *very* glad they can't." He looked meaningfully in Gideon's direction.

A smile crept across Roux's lips. "Ohhh, I see. Dirty dreams?"

Jason pretended to clutch his heart. "They're all I have. Don't take that away from me."

"Never."

The humor faded from Jason's face. "Seriously, though, you've got your own vampire to worry about. Go after him."

"I would if I knew where he'd gone."

"Good point." Jason scrunched up his forehead, thinking. "Ludovic's the brooding type, so I'm guessing he's gone to his room."

"I don't know where that is."

Jason brightened. "I bet Edmond does."

Roux looked over at where Edmond was talking quietly with Renie. The unguarded adoration on his face made her heart ache.

Was that how Ludovic looked at her? Was that how she looked at him?

"Go ahead, ask him." Jason gave her a little nudge.

"What about you?" Roux said.

"Ludovic's hot but I don't think he wants me to join in the fun. Besides, I've got my eye on a different blond vampire."

"You know what I mean. If everything works out between Ludovic and me, then I'll probably move into his room. Where will that leave you?"

Since neither of them had wanted to be alone after the first Belle Morte attack, Roux and Jason had started sharing a room after Renie moved in with Edmond, but if Roux moved in with Ludovic, then Jason would be on his own—and not just in the bedroom. He was the last donor left in the whole mansion.

Jason smiled. "I'll be okay."

"But—"

Jason put his hand over her mouth. "Honey, no. I'm a big boy, and I can handle being on my own. There's a hot vampire waiting for you, and you need to go get him."

Nerves twisted in Roux's stomach as she approached Edmond. She wasn't nervous about talking to *him*, but she was about to bare her heart and soul to the one person who had the power to crush both if he wanted to, and that was scary.

Edmond smiled down at her when she told him what she wanted, and there was something knowing in his gaze.

"I'll take you to his room," Edmond said.

For an awful moment Roux thought Renie and Jason would offer to come, too, and they'd all hover outside the door while she told

Ludovic she loved him, and she honestly couldn't imagine anything more cringe-inducing. Fortunately, her friends knew better than that.

As she followed Edmond to the north wing, Roux tried to rehearse what to say, but the words were all wrong.

It should have been simple—*I love you*—but that didn't feel like enough. When Ludovic had said those three precious words to her, he must have hoped she'd say them back.

She hadn't.

That had to be weighing on his mind, no matter what he'd said about giving her space to sort everything out.

All too soon they were standing outside a door, only two along from Edmond's bedroom. Roux swallowed, the writhing feeling in her stomach getting worse.

She'd never loved anyone like this. This was holding out your heart to someone and trusting that they wouldn't drop it. This was baring the most vulnerable parts of yourself to someone, even the ugly parts, and trusting that they still wanted you.

That, she realized, was what Ludovic had been doing all along.

Little by little he'd exposed himself to her, peeling away the layers he'd built up around himself until she could see the beautiful, shining core of him. He'd come to trust her in such a special way.

While she prepared herself to give him her heart with trembling hands, he'd already given her his, and she hadn't even realized it.

"Just be honest," Edmond advised.

He kissed her cheek and walked away.

Roux gazed at the door in front of her. She'd faced far scarier things, but her heart still felt like it was in her throat as she knocked on the door.

When Ludovic opened it, she froze.

He froze.

For a span of time, they both stood there, staring at each other.

Roux tried to paste on a smile, but it felt fake. "Can I come in?" she said.

Ludovic stood to one side.

It occurred to Roux that this was the first time she'd seen his bedroom. The walls were dark green, subtly patterned with gold, and the wooden floor was painted charcoal gray. The curtains matched the floor, sweeps of charcoal across the windows. The furniture was all dark wood, beautiful and elegant.

She realized Ludovic was still looking at her, and she tore her gaze away from the decor and turned to face the man she'd fallen in love with.

"So," she said, and immediately winced. That was the best she could come up with?

Roux clasped her hands in front of her, but that felt too formal so she linked them behind her back, but that wasn't any better. She let them hang loose at her sides, but that made her feel awkward.

Why was this so difficult?

Over the last few days, she'd come to be more comfortable with Ludovic than she'd ever been with anyone, and suddenly it was like they were strangers again.

"Ludovic," she said, and this time when she smiled it felt real.

He didn't smile back, but his eyes warmed, and that gave her the courage to keep going.

"I don't really know how to say this, because I've never said it before. I'm probably going to mess everything up and start rambling incoherently, so just bear with me, okay?"

Ludovic nodded, the faintest smile tugging at the corners of his mouth.

"I've never met anyone like you. You make me feel happier and more special than I ever thought anyone could. Whenever things get dark, you're there to fight away the shadows. When you look at me, it's like I'm the most important thing in the world."

"You are," Ludovic said, his voice hoarse. "To me, you're everything."

"And I realized something tonight," Roux said.

Hope flickered in Ludovic's eyes.

"You're my everything too," she said. "I can't believe I didn't realize it sooner, and I can't believe I ever thought it wasn't possible, but I love you." Her smile grew, warmth and love swelling in her heart. "I really do love you."

Ludovic hesitated. "You needed space—"

"No." Roux shook her head. "I know exactly how I feel."

"Don't you want more time—"

"Ludovic." She cut him off. "I'm in love with you. I don't need time to think about it. I don't need to come to terms with it. I love you more than I ever thought it was possible to love someone."

There was such hope on Ludovic's face, but fear, too, as if he couldn't quite believe this was happening, as if he was afraid this was all a dream.

Roux backed up a few steps until the footboard of the bed pressed against the back of her legs. Keeping her eyes locked on Ludovic, she pulled off her shirt and tossed it to the floor.

"This isn't me confusing what I feel. This isn't some trauma reaction. This is real," Roux said.

She unclasped her bra.

Ludovic's eyes flashed red.

"I have a very long life ahead of me now, and I want to spend all of it with you," Roux said, undoing the button on her jeans.

She looked him up and down, her gaze heated.

"And I want you to take your clothes off now."

"Roux," he whispered, his voice ragged as his eyes roamed over her bare skin.

"I hope you're not going to tell me you've changed your mind, because that would be *really* awkward," she said, and it felt good to tease him again. It felt *right*.

"Never," he growled. "You're the best thing that's ever happened to me."

"Then show me." Roux slid her jeans down around her thighs.

Ludovic's eyes burned, and Roux felt her blood heat in response.

"I love you," he said quietly.

"I know you do."

Roux stripped off the last of her clothes and stood in front of him, fully naked.

Ludovic's control snapped.

He lunged forward, lifted Roux off her feet, and clasped her to him. She locked her legs around his waist and raked her fingers through his hair as their mouths crashed together.

Roux would never forget the first time they'd kissed, but in some way, this felt like a first kiss all over again, because it was the first one after they'd told each other how they felt. That made it infinitely precious.

Ludovic climbed onto the bed, Roux still clinging to him.

She felt like she was going up in flames, burning hotter for him than she ever had. This was a need so primal she almost couldn't stand it. She pulled at Ludovic's clothes, forgetting about her vampire strength until she heard the sound of fabric ripping.

She'd torn his shirt in half.

"Sorry," she whispered.

"I'm not."

In the blink of an eye, Ludovic had shed the rest of his clothes.

Roux feasted her eyes on the hard planes and angles of his body, the way his marble skin pulled tight over the bulge of his muscles.

"Now, there's something I'll never get tired of seeing," she said, with a happy sigh.

Ludovic pinned her arms above her head, his weight pressing down on her. "I'm very glad to hear it," he murmured, nuzzling her neck.

He kissed his way down her body, and everywhere his lips touched, her skin seemed to sizzle. Sex had always been something Roux enjoyed, and she'd had plenty of it once she'd blossomed into the confident woman she now was, but even the best sex she'd previously had couldn't compare to sex with Ludovic.

His tongue and hands worked her to a place where she was writhing and moaning, her fingers tangled in his hair, and then he moved up her body, bracing his hand on her hip as he gently slid inside.

"I love you," he whispered, nipping her lower lip.

Roux could only manage a gasp.

At first, Ludovic was gentle, rocking his hips against hers while he whispered how much he loved her in between kisses. But when Roux dug her nails into his back, locked her ankles tighter around his hips, he responded in kind. He didn't have to worry about hurting her, didn't have to be careful about her human fragility anymore, and he increased the rhythm until the bed was smacking against the wall. Roux clung to him, sinking her teeth into his shoulder as pleasure built and built and built until she almost couldn't take it anymore. It felt like she was going to explode.

Bracing himself on his elbows, Ludovic gazed down at her, his eyes filled with something like awe.

"Ludovic," she gasped, a scream building in her throat.

He didn't take his eyes off her for a second.

Pleasure crested until it was almost painful, and then Ludovic slipped a hand between them to touch her where she was most sensitive.

The world turned white and shattered.

As waves of bliss thundered through her, wringing hoarse cries from her lips, Roux heard Ludovic cry her name as his whole body stiffened and shook. She flopped, boneless, on the bed, and Ludovic rolled off her, keeping hold of her hand.

"For a guy who lived like a monk for so long, you're very good at that," she said, when she found her voice again.

Ludovic smiled.

Something suddenly occurred to Roux, and she put a hand to her nose, feeling for the tiny hole that was her piercing.

Ludovic lifted a questioning eyebrow.

"I thought it might have closed up," she explained.

"It happened before you became a vampire. You've got it forever now," Ludovic said. "But you'll never be able to get anything else pierced."

"Dang it. There go my dreams of pierced nipples."

Ludovic's eyes widened.

"I'm kidding." Roux laughed.

Ludovic ran his hands around her breasts. "You don't need to do anything to them. They're already perfect."

"We can both agree on that."

Ludovic sat up halfway, gazing down at her with serious eyes. "Will you move in here with me?"

"As far as I'm concerned, I already have," Roux said, reaching up to tuck a strand of blond hair behind Ludovic's ear. "Although I have no idea how to introduce you to my parents."

There hadn't been time to tell them what had happened, and that made her stomach squeeze into a knot. Explaining that she'd died and come back as a vampire, fallen in love with another vampire, and was moving in with him would be a lot for her parents to take in.

Ludovic stiffened.

"You're not nervous, are you?" Roux said, giving him a mischievous smile.

"No," he said gruffly. "Maybe."

"Don't be. My parents love me and they want me to be happy. They'll understand that I'm happy with you."

"Maybe so, but you need to consider that they might blame me, in part, for what's happened—at least, at first," Ludovic said.

A little frown marred Roux's forehead.

"But whatever happens, we'll get through it," Ludovic added.

Roux gave his chest a playful poke. "Look at you, being all positive."

He captured her finger and kissed it. "I never thought I'd get another chance at love; I never felt I *deserved* it, and part of me still feels like I don't deserve you, Roux, but you still chose me, and I'm going to spend the rest of our very long lives showing you how much I love you. I know this storm isn't over yet, and things might get worse before they get better, but for the first time in as long as I can remember, I'm looking forward to the future."

Roux slid her hand around Ludovic's neck, tugging him closer. "Tonight, I just want to think about you and me, and all the fun we're going to have in this bed."

Ludovic's lips twitched, his gaze traveling down Roux's body. She shifted, throwing a leg over his hip and grinning at him.

"You're already hungry for more?"

Roux smiled wider, showing a glimpse of her fangs. "Baby, you have no idea."

Ludovic rolled over, pinning her beneath him, and Roux locked her legs around his hips, eagerly guiding him back inside. He was gentler with her this time, his strokes slow and shallow, his eyes locked on her face, his hands moving over the slopes of her body, until Roux clutched his shoulders, tensing and shattering as a raw cry broke from her lips.

She moved her hands up his back, stroking his hair while aftershocks of pleasure sparkled through her system.

"I love you," she whispered, feeling as though she'd never get tired of saying that.

Ludovic raised his head to look at her, stroking her chin with his thumb. "I love you more."

"Not possible."

The smile he gave her was so relaxed it was almost lazy, the kind of smile he so rarely gave. Roux took a certain thrill in knowing she was the only one who could make him smile like that.

And she planned on making him smile like that a lot more in the future.

ACKNOWLEDGMENTS

As always, the first thanks have to go to my amazing publishing team.

Jen and Rebecca, thank you for your endless patience and diligence, and for your reassurances when I start to doubt myself. It's always such a pleasure to work with you.

Irina, the best creator manager anyone could ask for, I don't know what I'd do without you. Thank you for always being there.

Ysabel Enverga, thank you for another absolutely amazing cover. This one may be my favorite!

Rachel and Maeve, my publicists, thank you for every fantastic opportunity you work hard to put together.

And special thank-yous to Nick Bettesworth, for your tireless assistance in making sure that the police work in this book was accurately portrayed, aside from the creative license I've taken, and Whitney Saunders, for catching all my medical mistakes. Your advice has been invaluable.

My family—I'm so lucky to have you all. We've grown by one more member since the previous book, so welcome, baby Freyja. I wonder if we will grow even more by the next book!

My readers, thank you for being you. Every comment, every message, every photo, every post is so rewarding and amazing to see. Without you, I wouldn't be here.

Finally, my cat, Sootica. Thank you for all the years you gave me, and for your absolute love, devotion, and companionship. I wish we'd had more time together, but I'll treasure every second that we shared, until we meet again at the Rainbow Bridge. Sweet dreams, my darling.

ABOUT THE AUTHOR

Bella Higgin fell in love with vampire fiction after reading an illustrated copy of *Dracula* as a kid, so it was inevitable that her debut novel would be about vampires. She is the author of the Belle Morte series, and her works on Wattpad have amassed more than twelve millions reads. Bella currently lives and writes full-time in a small English town not far from the sea. One day she hopes to have enough money to build a TARDIS in her garden.

SURRENDER YOURSELF TO THE
BELLE MORTE SERIES

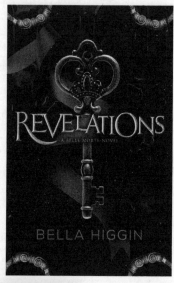

Look out for the final installment of
the Belle Morte series

CHANGES
Coming Soon